PRAISE FOR SIMON BRETT
AND THE FETHERING MYSTERIES

'A skilful and entertaining .... hich oozes
clues, re......................... hops, of
deductiv......................... e reminds
us, pa......................... hering'

'It's hard to resist a title like *Death Under the Dryer*,
especially when the author is that king of the witty
village mystery, Simon Brett . . . an enjoyable read'
Sunday Telegraph

'A feast of red herrings, broadly drawn characters and
gentle thrills and spills litter the witty plot'
Guardian

'Simon Brett writes the kind of good whodunnits
that could have been written fifty years ago . . . and
he has a sly sense of humour'
The Times

'An irresistibly old-time mystery'
Daily Mail

'This is lovely stuff, as comforting – and
as unputdownable – as a Sussex cream tea.
More please'
Brighton Evening Argus

DEATH UNDER THE DRYER

Simon Brett worked as a producer in radio and television before taking up writing full time. As well as as the much-loved Fethering series, the Mrs Pargeter novels and the Charles Paris detective series, he is the author of the radio and television series *After Henry*, the radio series *No Commitments* and *Smelling of Roses* and the bestselling *How to Be a Little Sod*. His novel *A Shock to the System* was filmed starring Michael Caine.

Married with three grown-up children, Simon lives in an Agatha Christie-style village on the South Downs.

Death Under the Dryer is the eighth novel in the Fethering Mysteries series. The ninth, *Blood at the Bookies*, is available now

SIMON BRETT

DEATH UNDER THE DRYER

A FETHERING MYSTERY

PAN BOOKS

First published 2007 by Macmillan

First published in paperback 2008 by Pan Books
an imprint of Pan Macmillan, a division of Macmillan Publishers Limited
Pan Macmillan, 20 New Wharf Road, London N1 9RR
Basingstoke and Oxford
Associated companies throughout the world
www.panmacmillan.com

ISBN 978-0-330-51961-8

1 3 5 7 9 8 6 4 2

A CIP catalogue record for this book is available from
the British Library.

Typeset by Intype Libra Ltd
Printed and bound in Great Britain by
CPI Mackays, Chatham ME5 8TD

Visit **www.panmacmillan.com** to read more about all our books
and to buy them. You will also find features, author interviews and
news of any author events, and you can sign up for e-newsletters
so that you're always first to hear about our new releases.

To Margaret and Daiva,

with thanks for all those haircuts

Chapter One

If her hairdresser had not been killed, Carole Seddon would never have become involved in the murder at Connie's Clip Joint. Though she knew the salon well – and indeed had to walk past it every time she went along the High Street to the inadequate local super-market Allinstore – Carole had never before crossed its threshold. There was something too public about actually having her hair done in Fethering. Since she had moved permanently to West Sussex some ten years previously, her reclusive instincts had favoured an anonymous salon in Worthing, where every six weeks her straight grey hair would be trimmed to helmet-like neatness by a taciturn man called Graham. The arrangement had suited her. She and Graham were polite, but showed no curiosity about each other, and their haircuts were blissfully silent.

The first time Carole knew anything about his life outside the salon was when she heard that Graham had been killed in a motor-cycle accident. This had happened when she rang to make her latest regular appointment. The emotion in the voice of the girl who relayed the sad news decided Carole that she needed to find another salon. She didn't want the perfect detachment of her relationship with Graham to be spoiled by the maudlin reminiscences of other hairdressers after his death.

So the question then was where should she go. She checked the *Yellow Pages*, but was paralysed into indecision by the sheer number of options available. Carole hated the hidebound nature that made her react like that. About everything. Why did she have to make an issue of things? She ought to have grown out of that kind of introspection by now. She was well into her fifties – about to become a grandmother, for God's sake – and yet, contrary to the appearance she gave the outside world, still vacillated about decisions like a young teenager.

Eventually, as part of her knew she would end up doing, she consulted Jude. Her next-door neighbour's bird's-nest style was probably not the best of advertisements for the art of hairdressing, but she must get it cut somewhere.

Predictably, Jude turned out to be not that bothered where she went. Her haircuts weren't conducted according to a rigid timetable. She would just wake up one morning feeling that her blonde locks were getting a bit shaggy, or be passing a salon and go in on a whim. She did, however, say that Connie, of Connie's Clip Joint on the High Street, was 'absolutely fine'. Also, Fethering rumour had it, the salon wasn't doing that well, and so booking in there would be supporting local industry.

These arguments – together with the unruly state

2

of her hair – were enough to sway Carole. She seized the phone that very day, a Wednesday, and had a telling lack of difficulty in booking the first, nine o'clock, appointment at Connie's Clip Joint for the following morning.

As she stood waiting outside on the pavement at ten past nine, she regretted her decision. Local people, lightly dressed for the soft September day, were walking past. She knew who they were; they knew who she was; some of them were even people she spoke to. And now they all knew that she was waiting to get her hair cut at Connie's Clip Joint. From when she was a child, Carole Seddon had always wanted to keep an air of secrecy about what she did; she hated having her intentions known.

She tried to look nonchalant, as if she had just stopped outside the salon to check its window display. But the beautifully coiffed women and men whose photographs gazed artfully from behind rubber plants were not objects to retain the interest for long. In spite of her pretences, Carole Seddon looked exactly what she was: a middle-aged woman locked out of the hairdresser's.

Discreetly she drew up the sleeve of her Burberry and looked down at her wristwatch. Although the only other person in sight along Fethering High Street at that moment was a pensioner deep in his own thoughts and a duffel coat, Carole moved as if she was under the scrutiny of a prison camp watchtower.

Twelve minutes past nine. Surely she hadn't got the

time wrong . . . ? Surely the girl who answered the phone hadn't said the first appointment was nine-thirty . . . ? Such doubts were quickly banished. No, she had definitely said 'nine o'clock', and Carole had planned her whole morning around that time. She had taken her Labrador Gulliver out for his walk along Fethering Beach, and after she'd had her hair cut, she was going to do her weekly food shop at Sainsbury's.

Oh, this was stupid, just standing about. Trying to give the oblivious pensioner the impression that moving away from Connie's Clip Joint after precisely seventeen minutes (being Carole, she had of course arrived early) was a long-planned intention, she set off firmly back towards her house, High Tor.

As she took the first step, a silver hatchback screeched to a halt outside the salon, and a small, harassed-looking woman in her forties jumped out. She looked as if she had dressed in a hurry and clutched to her bosom an overflowing leather bag. Her brown eyes were tight with anxiety. No make-up . . . and her red-streaked hair, untidily swept back into a scrunchy, was not a good advertisement for the business she ran.

Because of course Carole recognized her instantly. Connie Rutherford, after whom Connie's Clip Joint was named. Fethering gossip ensured that almost everyone in the village knew who everyone else was, but village protocol demanded that you still didn't speak to them until you had been introduced. So Carole continued her stately progress towards High Tor.

The hairdresser, however, showed no such inhibitions. 'Mrs Seddon!' she called out.

Which, Carole supposed, was better than using her first name. She turned graciously. 'Yes?'

'I'm sorry, you're the nine o'clock, aren't you?'

'Well, I thought I was,' came the frosty response.

'Look, I'm so sorry. That idiot girl was meant to be here to open up at quarter to nine.' The woman fumbled in her bag for keys. 'I wonder what on earth's happened to her.' Still getting no reaction from her client, she said, 'I'm Connie. Connie Rutherford. I run the place.'

'Oh.' Carole received the information as though surprised by the identification. 'I'm Carole Seddon.'

'Yes, I know. You live next door to Jude.'

Carole was slightly miffed to think that this was her claim to fame in Fethering. No one knew about her past, her career in the Home Office. Here she was just Jude's neighbour. And Jude hadn't lived in Woodside Cottage nearly as long as Carole had been in High Tor. She shouldn't have been surprised, though. Jude was outgoing. Jude was easy with people. Everyone knew Jude.

Having opened the salon door, Connie Rutherford ushered her client in and went across to switch on the lights, chattering the while. 'This is really bad. Kids these days, they have no sense of time-keeping. You give them a job – and are they grateful? They don't even understand the basics of turning up when they say they will. God, if I ever have any children, I won't let them behave the way most of the youngsters do these days.'

Judging from Connie's age, Carole decided that, if

5

she was going to have any children, she'd better be quick about it.

But the hairdresser was off into another apology. 'I'm so sorry, Kyra should have opened up and been ready to greet you at nine. I gave her the spare set of keys – I've only got the one – I thought I could trust her. Then she was meant to wash your hair, so that it'd be ready for me to cut when I came in. Oh well, don't worry, I'll wash it. May I take your coat, Mrs Seddon? Now, I can call you "Carole", can't I?'

'Yes,' her client conceded.

'Well, you just take a seat here, and I'll put on some music. You'd like some music, wouldn't you?'

'No, I'm quite happy not to—'

But Connie was already away, fiddling with a CD player. 'I think Abba, don't you?'

'Erm, no, I—'

'Nothing like Abba for clearing away the cobwebs in the morning, is there?' As she spoke, the sounds of 'Dancing Queen' filled the room. 'Now would you like . . . ?' Connie stopped, apparently thinking better of the suggestion.

'Would I like what?'

'Nothing.'

'What I would like, if you don't mind, is for you to do my hair . . . since I already am a bit behind schedule.' Carole hoped that made it sound as if she had a more impressive destination later in the morning than the pasta aisle in Sainsbury's.

'Very well.' Connie turned on a tap above the sink.

'Just give the water a moment to heat up. It's cold first thing in the morning. And let's get this robe on.'

While the water warmed, Carole took a look around the salon. The pine boarding on the walls and the large cheese plants in the windows gave it a slightly dated feel, which was not dispelled by the Greek holiday posters and photos of models with exotic hairstyles. The basic decor probably hadn't changed for a good ten years, and endorsed Jude's suggestion that Connie's Clip Joint was not doing great business.

The stylist flicked her hand under the pouring water. 'Nearly warm enough.' Then she caught an unwelcome glimpse of herself in the mirror. 'Haven't had time to put a face on yet. Oh dear, if Kyra had been here when she was supposed to . . .'

But she decided that going on about the short-comings of her staff was probably not the best way of recommending her salon to a new client. Instead, she stood behind the chair, rather closer than Carole might have wished, so that their two faces stood one on top of the other in the mirror. Connie ran her hands gently over her client's hair.

'So . . . how would you like it, Carole?'

She got the same reply all hairdressers had got for the past fifteen years – a gruff 'Same shape, but shorter'.

'You haven't thought of giving it a bit of colour?' suggested Connie.

'I have thought of it, but decided against the idea.'

'Not even highlights?'

'No, thank you.'

Connie Rutherford was far too practised in her profession to argue with a new client. 'I think you're right, Carole. This style really suits a strong face like yours.' Another test of the water, and a towel was fixed neatly in place around the neck. 'Now may I take your glasses off?'

'I'll do it,' replied Carole, aware of how graceless she sounded. She removed the rectangular rimless spectacles and placed them next to the sink. Her pale blue eyes looked naked, even threatened.

Expertly Connie swivelled the chair round and lowered the back, so that her client's neck slotted neatly into the groove at the front of the basin. Every time she underwent this manoeuvre, Carole could not quite erase the mental image of a guillotine. Even through the protective towel, she could feel the coldness of her ceramic yoke.

By now the temperature of the water was just right and Connie, though long since graduated beyond such menial tasks, had not forgotten the skills of hairwashing. Her strong fingers probed down into the scalp, working in a way that was both sensual and invigorating. Carole began to relax.

And the flow of Connie's talk matched the flow of the water, soothing, rippling away the tensions of her client. She had quickly caught on to Carole's private nature and knew better than to ask for personal information. Instead she kept up a light prattle about the concerns of Fethering: the fact that there had been more visitors than expected that summer; the possibility that English seaside holidays were coming back into fashion; the difficulty of parking in the High Street.

Only at one point was a detail of Carole's personal history mentioned. Connie, who wore no ring on her wedding finger, mentioned in passing that she was divorced, and added, 'Just like you.'

Immediately realizing that she had to cover this lapse, she explained, 'Jude mentioned that when she was in here once.'

Oh yes? And how much else, Carole wondered, has my neighbour been telling all and sundry about me? But she couldn't really make herself cross about it. Jude was by nature discreet, and in a hotbed of gossip like Fethering everyone's marital status was fair game.

'So is Seddon your married name?'

'Yes.' Though Carole wasn't sure what business of the hairdresser that was.

'Yes, I got stuck with mine too. By the time I thought about reverting to my maiden name, the other one was on so many legal documents and what-have-you . . . Of course, the divorce was particularly difficult for me, because Martin was involved in the business too. Yes, we started Connie's Clip Joint together. We'd met when we were both working in a salon in Worthing and . . .' she shrugged ruefully as she looked around, 'I suppose this was our dream. Like most dreams, it fell apart when it came up against reality.'

Recognizing that this was too downbeat a note for her performance as your friendly local hairdresser, she picked herself out of the potential trough. 'Anyway, let me tell you, any divorce is a nightmare, but one where you're also trying to divide up business assets . . . well, I hope yours didn't involve that . . !

The cue was there to volunteer information about the end of her marriage, had Carole wished to pick it up. Unsurprisingly, she didn't. Connie moved quickly on. 'Still, mustn't grumble. Got a very nice little business here. Having a High Street position . . . well, of course that helps. As they always say, "Location, location, location". All going very well.'

Remembering Jude's words about the precarious state of Connie's Clip Joint, Carole took this assertion with a pinch of salt, and ventured a question of her own. 'And your ex-husband . . . is he still involved in the hairdressing business?'

Connie Rutherford's lips tightened. 'You could say that. Yes, he runs one of the biggest chains of salons along the South Coast.'

There was clearly a lot more information available and Carole felt she had only to issue the smallest prompt to release an avalanche of resentment. She refrained from doing so and fortunately, before Connie could self-start into her diatribe, the salon door opened to admit a slender man in black leather jacket and trousers. A gold chain showed against tanned flesh in the open neck of his shirt. His neat tobacco-coloured hair was highlighted in blonde and his teeth were veneered to a perfect smile. Over brown eyes as dark as coffee beans, he wore tinted glasses with small gold stars at the corners. From a distance he might have passed for twenty-five; close to, he was well into his forties.

'Morning, Theo.'

'Morning, Connie love.' His voice was light, self-consciously camp.

'This is my nine o'clock. Carole Seddon. First time she's been here.'

'Really? I'm Theo.' He gave a little wave; she couldn't have shaken his hand from under the robe, anyway. 'But you do look awfully familiar, Carole.'

'I live right here in Fethering. Just along the High Street.'

'Oh, then I must have seen you around.' A hand flew up to his mouth in mock-amazement. 'With a dog! Yes, I've seen you with a dog. Lovely big Labby.'

'He's called Gulliver.'

'Ooh, I'm such a dog person. I've got a little Westie called Priscilla.'

'Ah.'

'Connie's into cats, aren't you, love. I can never see the point of cats. Nasty, self-obsessed, spiteful little beasts.'

'Takes one to know one,' riposted Connie.

'Ooh, you bitch!'

Their badinage was a well-practised routine, insults batted back and forth without a vestige of malice. Carole Seddon got the feeling that for regulars it was as much a part of the Connie's Clip Joint ambience as the Abba soundtrack.

Theo looked around the salon. 'Where's the human pincushion?'

'Late. She'd got the spare set of keys and was meant to open up at eight forty-five. No sign of her.'

'Probably stayed in bed for naughties with that young boyfriend of hers. And actually . . .' he raised an eyebrow towards his boss's mirror image '. . . you look as if you might have been doing something similar.'

His insinuation prompted a rather sharper response. 'Don't be ridiculous!' Embarrassed by her own outburst, Connie looked at her watch. 'I don't know what she's doing, but when she does finally deign to arrive, I may have a thing or two to say to Miss Kyra Bartos.'

Theo slapped his hands to his face in a parody of Munch's *Scream*. 'Oh no! I'll have to wash my nine-thirty's hair myself!'

'Just as I've had to do with my nine o'clock.'

'Yes.' Theo grinned in the mirror at Carole. 'I hope you're appreciative of the quality of service you're getting.' And he flounced off to hang up his leather jacket.

Carole caught Connie's eye and mouthed, 'What did he mean about "the human pincushion"?'

'Ah. Young Kyra's taste for body piercing. It seems to be her ambition to get more perforations than a tea bag.' Another peeved look at her watch. 'Where is the bloody girl? I'll ring her when I've finished with you. Now do you want the cut slightly layered?'

'No,' Carole countered doggedly. 'I want it the same shape, but shorter.'

'Right.' Whatever reservations Connie might have had to this conservative approach, she kept them to herself, and started cutting.

At that moment Theo's nine-thirty skulked into the salon. In spite of the mild September day, she wore a raincoat with the collar turned up, a headscarf and dark glasses.

'Sheeeeeena!' Theo emoted. 'Sheena, my love, how gorgeous to see you.'

'Not gorgeous at all, Theo darling,' his client drawled. 'That's why I'm here. Morning, Connie,' she said as Theo removed her coat.

'Morning, Sheena. This is Carole.'

'Hi. I tell you, Theo, I just need the most total makeover since records began. When I looked at myself in the mirror this morning . . . well, it took great strength of will not to top myself on the spot.'

'Oh, come on,' Theo wheedled, 'we'll soon have you looking your beautiful self again. Now let's take off that scarf and those glasses.'

'No, no. I'm just not fit to be seen!'

'You're amongst friends here, Sheena darling. Nobody'll breathe a word about what you looked like *before* . . . Will you, Carole?'

Though rather unwilling to pander to the woman's vanity, Carole agreed that she wouldn't.

'And when we get to *after*, Sheena . . . *after* I've worked my magic . . . you'll look so gorgeous, men in the street will be falling over each other to get at you.'

'Oh, Theo, you're so full of nonsense.' But it was clearly nonsense his client liked.

After further dramatic delays, Sheena was finally settled into the chair, and there followed the great ceremony of removing her scarf and glasses. Carole, squinting at an angle into the adjacent mirror, wondered what horrors were about to be unveiled. What

13

optical disfigurement lay behind the glasses? What tri-chological disaster beneath the scarf?

After the build-up, the revelation was a bit of a dis-appointment. Sheena was a perfectly attractive woman in her late forties – and, what's more, one whose blonded hair appeared to have been cut quite recently.

But she had set up her scenario, and was not going to be deterred from playing it out. 'There, Theo. Now that's going to be a challenge, even for you, isn't it?'

Her stylist, who must have been through the same scene many times before, knew his lines. 'Don't worry, darling. Remember, Theo is a miracle worker. So what are we going to do?'

'We are going to make me so attractive, Theo, that I become a positive man-magnet.'

'Too easy. You're a man-magnet already.'

'I wish. I don't understand.' Sheena let out a long sigh. 'There just don't seem to be any men in Feth-ering.'

'Ooh, I wouldn't say that,' he said coyly.

'Are you saying you've taken them all, Theo? I bet you never have any problem finding men.'

The stylist let out an enigmatic, silvery laugh.

Throughout Carole's haircut, this archness contin-ued. Connie, who had tried commendably hard to keep conversation going with her client, eventually gave up and joined in the false brightness of Sheena and Theo. Carole found it quite wearing. A little too lively for her taste. She wasn't sure whether Connie's Clip Joint was going to be a long-term replacement for Graham and the anonymous salon in Worthing.

On the other hand, Connie did cut hair very well. Though keeping within Carole's minimal guidelines, she had somehow managed to give a freshness to her client's traditional style. With glasses restored, Carole couldn't help admiring the result she saw in the mirror.

'Excuse me for a moment,' said Connie, 'I must just ring Kyra and find out what on earth's happened to her. Now, I've got her mobile number somewhere.' She crossed to the cash register table and started shuffling through papers.

Carole felt awkward about the business of paying. When booking the appointment, she hadn't asked how much it would cost and now she was worried it might have been very expensive. Prices varied so much. And then there was the big challenge of tipping. Should she tip and, if so, how much? She'd never tipped Graham – that had been an accepted feature of their austere relationship – but she was in a new salon now and she wasn't sure of the protocol.

Connie listened impatiently to the phone. 'Well, she's not answering.'

She was poised to end the call, when suddenly they were all aware of a new noise, cutting through the harmonies of Abba. The insistent jangle of a phone ringing.

Carole and Connie exchanged looks. The hairdresser huffed in exasperation, 'Oh, don't say the bloody girl's left her mobile here.'

As Connie moved towards the source of the sound, Carole, curiosity overcoming her natural reticence, found herself following.

A door led through to the back area, storeroom, kitchenette and lavatory. As Connie opened it, there was a smell of stale alcohol and cigarette smoke. Beer cans and a vodka bottle on its side lay on a low table. On the work surface beside the sink stood a vase containing twelve red roses.

But it wasn't those that prompted the involuntary scream from Connie's lips. It was what she could see – and Carole could see over her shoulder – slumped in a chair over which loomed the dome of a spare dryer.

The girl's clothes were torn. There were scratches on her metal-studded face.

And, tight as a garrotte, around the neck of her slumped body was the lead from the unplugged dryer.

Chapter Two

'Drink this.' Jude placed a large glass of Chilean Chardonnay on the table in front of her neighbour. 'You look as though you need it.'

The extent of Carole's trauma could be judged from the fact that she didn't look at her watch and ask, 'Isn't it a bit early in the day . . . ?' It was in fact only two-thirty in the afternoon, but a lifetime seemed to have elapsed since she had entered Connie's Clip Joint that morning. She hadn't felt it proper to leave until the police had arrived and, once they were there, she couldn't leave until she had submitted to some polite, though persistent, questioning. Her training in the Home Office told her that they were only doing their job, and she knew that they were starting from an empty knowledge base, but she did feel frustrated by the depth of information they seemed to require. Though she kept reiterating that it was the first time she had ever entered the salon, the police still wanted her to fill in far more of her personal background than she thought entirely necessary. What business of theirs was it that she was divorced? Surely, rather than following up such fruitless blind alleys, they ought to have been out there finding the murderer. Again she reminded herself of the huge mosaic of facts from which a successful conviction was built up, and managed to endure the questioning with the appearance of co-operation. But she hadn't enjoyed the experience.

And it had all been made considerably worse by the presence of Sheena. Theo's client had taken the discovery of the girl's body as a cue for a full operatic mix of posturing and hysterics. 'Something like this was bound to happen!' she had wailed. 'I knew when I got up, this was an inauspicious day. I shouldn't have left the house. I should have stayed in bed. It's horrible! Though the poor girl may have deserved something, she didn't deserve this!' But through the woman's tears and screams, Carole could detect a real relish for the drama of the situation. Kyra's murder was the most exciting thing that had happened in Sheena's life for a long time.

Eventually Carole had managed to escape. While the Scene of Crime Officers embarked on their painstaking scrutiny of the premises, the detectives told her they were from the Major Crime Branch, and would be working from the Major Crime Unit in Littlehampton police station. They gave her a list of contact numbers, and urged her to get in touch if she thought of or heard anything which might have relevance to the investigation.

'I've done a bacon and avocado salad,' said Jude, and went off to the kitchen to fetch it. That was quick, thought Carole. But then perhaps more time had elapsed from the moment when she had knocked on her neighbour's door at the end of the interrogation and the moment she had come back to Woodside Cottage. Her recollection was a bit hazy. She had gone to High Tor and taken Gulliver out to do his business on the rough ground behind the house. And she had stood for a moment of abstraction, from which his barking had roused her. Maybe it had been a longer moment than she thought. Maybe that too was a measure of the shock she had suffered.

'So . . .' said Jude, finally nestled into one of the shapeless armchairs in her untidy front room, 'tell me exactly what happened.'

And Carole did. Unaware of the speed at which she was sinking the Chilean Chardonnay, or the readiness with which Jude was replenishing her glass, she told everything. Dealing with unpleasant subject matter during her Home Office days had taught her the value of drily marshalling facts and investing a report with the objective anonymity that made its horror containable.

At the end of the narrative Jude let out a long sigh and sat for a moment with her round face cupped in her chubby hands. As ever, she was swathed in many layers of floaty fabric, which blurred the substantial outlines of her welcoming body. Her blonde hair, which had been innocent of the attentions of a hairdresser for some time, was twisted up into an unlikely topknot, held in place by what looked like a pair of knitting needles.

'So you didn't get any insight into who might have killed the girl?'

'For heaven's sake, Jude. This morning was the first time I've even stepped inside that place. I don't know anything about any of the people involved.'

'I wasn't meaning that. I thought perhaps the police might've let something slip about the direction in which their suspicions are moving.'

'So far as I could tell, they're clueless. When they arrived, they had as little information as I had. Besides, you may recall from past experience that even when the police do start having theories about the identity of a murderer, people like us are the last they're going to share them with.'

Jude nodded ruefully. 'True.'

'In fact, you're probably a more useful source than I am.'

'How do you mean?'

'Well, you actually know all the people involved. You're a regular at Connie's Clip Joint.'

'Hardly a regular, but I suppose you're right.'

'And,' Carole went on, unable to keep out of her voice the note of envy that such thoughts usually prompted, 'people always confide in you, so probably you actually know a great deal about Connie Rutherford and her set-up.'

'A certain amount, yes.'

'She isn't one of your *patients*, is she?' This word too had a special recurrent intonation for Carole. Jude worked as a healer, which to Carole still meant that she operated in the world of mumbo-jumbo. And the people who believed that such ministrations could do them any good were, to Carole's mind, gullible neurotics.

'You know I prefer to use the word "client",' Jude responded calmly. It wasn't in her nature to take issue about such matters. She knew that healing worked. Some people shared her opinion; some were violently opposed to it. Jude was prepared to have her case made by successful results rather than verbal argument. And she knew that depriving Carole of her scepticism about healing would take away one of the pillars of bluster that supported her prickly, fragile personality. 'But no,' she went on, 'I haven't treated Connie. I just know her from chatting while I've been having my hair done.'

'Well, she volunteered to me that she was divorced – and that the divorce hadn't taken place under the happiest of circumstances . . .'

'What divorce does?'

Carole did not pick up on this. Though some ten years old, her own divorce from David was still an area as sensitive as an infected tooth. And lurking at the back of her mind was a new anxiety. Her son Stephen's wife Gaby was soon to give birth. Grandparenthood might mean that Carole was forced into even more contact with David. Resolutely dispelling such ugly thoughts from her mind, she went on, 'And I gather that she and . . . what was her husband's name? . . . Martin, that's right . . . used to own Connie's Clip Joint together, but now he's got a rather more successful set-up . . .'

'That's an understatement. He owns Martin & Martina. You must have seen their salons.'

'Oh, yes, I have. I'd never particularly paid attention to them, but they've got that big swirly silver logo, haven't they? There's one in Worthing.'

'Worthing, Brighton, Chichester, Horsham, Midhurst, Newhaven, Eastbourne, Hastings. Martin Rutherford seems to have the whole of the South Coast sewn up.'

'So every time Connie sees one of his salons, it must rather rub salt in the wound of the divorce.'

'Yes, Carole. Particularly since the name of the woman he left her for was Martina.'

'Ah. Not so much rubbing salt as rubbing her nose in it.' Carole tapped her chin reflectively. She was relaxing. The Chardonnay and Jude's calming presence were distancing her from the horrors of the morning. 'And has Connie found her equivalent of Martina? Has she got someone else?'

'No one permanent, as far as I know. I think she has had a few tentative encounters, but from what she said, most of them had a lot in common with car crashes. I don't think Connie's a great picker when it comes to men.'

'Pity. Because she seems to have a pleasant personality . . . You know, under the professional hairdresser banter . . .'

'Yes, she's a lovely girl. And very pretty. Always beautifully groomed.'

'Well, she wasn't this morning. No make-up, hair scrunched up any-old-how.'

'Really?' Jude looked thoughtful. 'That's most unlike her. I wonder why . . .'

'No idea. She implied she would have done her make-up in the salon . . . you know if Kyra hadn't been late . .'

'Unfortunate choice of words in the circumstances, isn't it?'

'Yes, I suppose it is.' The thought brought Carole up short. The screen of her mind was once again filled by the contorted, immobile face, and she felt the reality of what had happened. Someone had deliberately cut short a young girl's life.

'Did you know her? Kyra?'

'She washed my hair last time I was in the salon. Didn't say much. Rather shy, I thought. Or maybe she was concentrating on learning the basics of practical hairdressing before she moved on to the refinements of inane client chatter. So, no, I can't really say I knew her.'

'Theo mentioned there was a boyfriend. Did Kyra say anything about anyone special in her life?'

Jude shook her head. 'Poor boy. I should think the police would be getting very heavy with him.'

'Yes. He'd be the obvious first port of call. And from the look of the back room of the salon, Kyra had been entertaining someone there. Empty bottles, beer cans, you know . .'

'Adolescent passions are very confusing . . . they can so easily get out of hand,' said Jude, with sympathy.

'Yes,' Carole agreed, without any.

'Hm.' Jude refilled their glasses. Still Carole made no demur. 'So we're back in our usual position when faced with a murder . . . total lack of information.'

'And not much likelihood of getting any,' Carole agreed gloomily.

'Oh, there may be ways . . .'

'Like . . . ?'

'Well, obviously Connie's Clip Joint is going to be closed for a few days. It is a Scene of Crime, after all. But, assuming it does reopen . . . I think I should have a haircut.' Jude shook her precarious topknot; it threatened to unravel, but the knitting needles just managed to keep it in place. 'I could certainly do with one.'

Chapter Three

'So what's the word on the street?'

'How should I know?' Ted Crisp replied gruffly. 'I never go out on the street if I can help it.'

'All right,' said Jude patiently. 'What's the word in the Crown and Anchor?'

'Ah, that's a different matter entirely.' Irregular teeth showed through the thicket of his beard in a broad grin. 'What happens in the pub I *do* know about. In fact, not a lot goes on in here that I don't know about. And there's not a lot said in here that I don't hear either.'

'Well then,' said Carole with less patience than her neighbour, 'what is being said in here about the strangling in Connie's Clip Joint?'

Deliberately delaying his reply, the landlord took a long swallow from his beer mug. It was near closing time, the only part of the day when he allowed himself any alcohol. He'd watched too many landlords drink away their health and profits to start any earlier. 'There is a general consensus,' Ted began slowly, 'that the girl's boyfriend dunnit.'

'And is that based on anything more substantial than speculation?'

'Well, Carole, speculation is obviously the biggest part of what people are thinking, but there are a few other details that might point in the same direction.'

'Like what?' asked Jude. 'We know nothing about the boyfriend, not even his name.'

'That I can supply. Nathan Locke. Sixteen . . . seventeen. Still at college, somewhere in Chichester. Parents live here in Fethering. I've seen him in the pub.'

'With Kyra?'

'Really can't remember. Those students tend to come in mob-handed, hard to tell which one's which or who belongs to who. And I'm so busy watching out for which ones of them are underage that I'm not concentrating on much else. The photo of the girl they showed on the television news looked vaguely familiar, but whether I'd seen her with anyone particular, I couldn't say. Certainly not as part of a regular couple.'

'She looked rather different from the photo on the news. She'd had some piercing done on her lips and eyebrows,' said Carole, for whom the image was uncomfortably recent. There was always something poignant about photographs of young murder victims – particularly girls – when they appeared in the media. Frequently they were out of date, posed school pictures of children who didn't look old enough to inspire adult passions. Which only seemed to make their fate more painful.

'What was her surname?' asked Ted. 'I must've

heard it on the news, but it was in one ear, out the other.'

'Bartos,' Jude supplied.

'Oh yes, I knew it was something foreign. "Bartos" . . . now where do you reckon that would come from? Spain perhaps . . . ? South America . . . ?'

'Originally maybe, but there's such a variety of surnames in this country, it doesn't necessarily mean she's "foreign".'

Ted took Jude's reproof on board. 'Yeah, OK, but it is an unusual name.'

'So's Crisp.'

'Nonsense. There's Crisps everywhere. Behind this bar here I've got salt and vinegar, cheese and onion, barbecue, smoky bacon—'

The two women groaned as one, both aware of the huge blessing the world had received when Ted Crisp gave up being a stand-up comedian.

Carole was quick to put such frivolity in its proper place. 'Bartos still sounds a foreign name to me.'

'Everything sounds foreign to you, Carole.' It was an uncharacteristically sharp response from Jude. Usually she let her neighbour's prejudices pass without comment.

'Well, it's true. Bartos doesn't sound English.'

Jude couldn't resist the tease. 'And does Seddon?'

And Carole couldn't resist the affronted knee-jerk reaction. 'Seddon is very definitely an old English name. It's been around since at least the fourteenth century. And it's common in Lancashire.'

'I thought you thought everything in Lancashire was common.'

'Jude! If you—'

Ted Crisp was forced into the unusual role of peacemaker. 'Don't know what's got into you two tonight. Can we just leave it that "Bartos" is a slightly unusual surname and could possibly be of foreign origin?'

'Very well,' said Carole huffily.

Jude just smiled.

'Anyway, Ted . . .' Carole reasserted her position as a serious investigator. 'You said you knew something about the boyfriend . . . ? Nathan Locke.'

'Only, as I say, that he did come in here sometimes.'

'He must have been quite a regular for you to know his name,' Jude observed.

'No, but one of my regulars does know him fairly well. Lives down the street from his family.'

'Who is the regular?'

Ted Crisp gestured over towards one of the pub's booths, in which an old man mournfully faced the last few centimetres of his beer. 'Les Constantine. Holds the Crown and Anchor All-Comers Record for the longest time making a pint last.'

'Could you introduce him?' asked Jude.

'He may not want to talk to us,' said Carole, her natural distrust of strangers asserting itself.

'You buy him a pint and he'll want to talk to you all right. Buy him a pint and he'll tell you anything you want.'

'Haven't you called "Time", though, Ted? You can't serve him, can you?'

'Listen, Carole, I'm landlord of the Crown and Anchor. I can do what I like.' He lumbered across towards the booth. 'Oy, Les, couple of ladies want to buy you a drink.'

The old man looked up lugubriously. 'They're probably only after my body.'

'Do you find that's what it usually is with women?'

'Oh yes.'

He moved daintily towards them. He was quite short and his long-lasting pints of beer hadn't put any flesh on his thin bones. He wore a dark grey suit which shone here and there from too much ironing, and a broad sixties flowered tie in a neat Windsor knot under a frayed collar. But though the clothes had seen better days, everything was spotlessly clean.

Ted made the introductions and set a full pint in Les's hand. Carole waited for a grateful mouthful to be downed before asking, 'So you actually know Nathan Locke?'

The old man looked disappointed. 'Oh, so you mean it wasn't my body you were after?'

'Just a few questions first, then we'll get on to the sex. What do you fancy – a threesome with the two of us?'

Carole was appalled by the suggestion, but once again was forced to admire Jude's uncanny skill of hitting the right note with people. That kind of outrageous badinage was the response Les Constantine wanted; she had instantly tuned in to his wavelength.

'All right,' he wheezed. 'We'll sort out the fine-tuning later . . . you know, "Your place or mine?" How's that?'

'Sounds perfect.'

'Sounds perfect to me too, Jude.' He relished the taste of her name on his lips. 'So what can I do you for? Presumably you're interested in the boy because of what happened down the hairdresser's?'

'Well, yes.'

'You and everyone else in Fethering. Yes, suddenly – just thanks to a geographical accident, living down the road from the boy – I'm very popular.' He took another swig of beer. 'Not the first free pint I've got this evening for my . . . inside knowledge, is it, Ted?'

The landlord guffawed agreement, and for a moment Carole wondered whether they had been seduced into a handy little scam between publican and customer. Then, with a wink, Ted Crisp wandered off to collect up glasses from the slowly emptying tables.

'I live in Marine Villas,' Les went on. 'You know where I mean?'

'Parallel to Beach Road, running down to the Fether.'

'That's it. I been there nearly forty years now. With the wife Iris I was, till she passed away . . . 1999 that was.' The recollection still caused him a pang. 'Anyway, the Lockes moved in about a year after that. Nathan was, I don't know, ten, maybe younger. Nice kid, not one of these that's always causing trouble and nicking your dustbins and throwing McDonald wrappers in your front garden and that. More interested in books and schoolwork, I gather. Whole family's a bit arty-farty, from what I hear.'

'So do you actually know Nathan?'

'Just to say hello to. Not bosom pals, but in a street

like Marine Villas . . . well, you hear a bit about everyone's business. Like, I suppose, most of them know
about everything I get up to . . . that is, except for the
Torture Chamber in the cellar and the Dominatrix,
obviously.'

'Oh, I'd heard rumours about her,' said Jude, again
finding exactly the right level.

'Blimey O'Reilly! You can't keep anything secret in
a place like this, can you?' He shook his head at the
prurience of Fethering residents.

'Anyway,' Carole pressed on, 'do you know anything
about Nathan Locke's relationship with Kyra Bartos?'

'She's the dead girl, isn't she?'

'Yes.'

This time the headshake was more measured and
regretful. 'Heartbreaking, isn't it? Kid like that. Got
everything ahead of her . . . you know, could have been
a mum, had lots of kiddies . . . and this, it kind of all
stops it, doesn't it? I saw that photo of her they had on
the telly . . . just a little girl. Reminded me a bit of my
Iris when I first met her . . . We used to do our courting
in Brighton . . . nice dance hall there was there then . . .'
With a more resolute shake of his head, he jolted himself out of maudlin reminiscence. 'Anyway, what was
the question? Did I know anything about Nathan's
"relationship" with the dead girl? Not really. Just heard
along the old Marine Villas bush telegraph that he'd got
this girlfriend who worked up the hairdresser's . . .
General feeling was that it was good news, because
he'd always had a reputation of being a bit bookish,
you know, coming from an arty-farty family, apparently

hoping to go to university and that . . . and I think everyone thought he deserved a bit of fun, like. "All work and no play" . . . you know what they say.'

'Do you know what he's hoping to read at university?' asked Carole.

'Read? I've no idea. I told you I didn't know him that well, so I don't know what books he reads.'

'Carole meant: what does he want to study at university?' Jude explained.

'Ah. Right. I don't know . . . language or something like that. Not anything useful.'

'What do you mean by "useful"?'

'Well, it's not something that might've, like, taught him a trade. Just all to do with books. That's all any of them seem to learn these days. I mean, when I was young, boys of that age done an apprenticeship. You know, learned something that might be useful in later life.'

'Is that what you did?' asked Jude gently.

'Too right. Couldn't wait to get out of school. My dad worked in boat-building . . . pleasure boats, yachts, you know. Got me an apprenticeship at the yard where he worked in Littlehampton, Collier & Brompton. I loved the work. My dad thought it'd last for ever.'

'You imply that it didn't?'

'No, but at least my old man never knew that. When he passed away, I was . . . what, early twenties? Just met Iris, we was courting, but me old dad never saw us married. Never saw what happened to the leisure boat-building industry either.'

'What did happen?'

'Fibreglass, that's what happened. Started in the fifties, then more and more in the sixties. And suddenly the skills I had . . . you know, woodworking skills, suddenly there's not so much demand from them down the boatyards. Oh, a few keep going with the old methods, some adapt. Collier & Brompton, yard I worked in, they did. They ask me if I want to retrain, but putting fibreglass in moulds, that wasn't my idea of boat-building. And I was in my forties by then . . . old dogs and new tricks, you know. So I give up the boats.'

'And haven't you worked since?'

'Oh, blimey, yes. Got a job putting in fitted kitchens. Bit overqualified I reckoned I was – a trained shipwright trimming edges off MDF shelf units, but . . . well, can't be too choosy when you haven't got no income. Did that till I was sixty-five, but by then the old hands were getting a bit shaky and I wasn't finding it so easy to lug all them units around, so . . . heigh-ho for a happy retirement. Which it was . . . till . . !' He didn't need to complete the sentence.

Carole broke the ensuing silence. 'So you can't tell us any more about Nathan Locke . . . ?'

'Well, no. Except that everyone in Fethering reckons he topped that poor kid.'

'And have they any reason for saying that?' asked Jude.

'He was definitely due to meet up with her the evening before she was found dead.'

'Do you know where they were due to meet?'

'Certainly not her place, I'll tell you that for free. Apparently her old man didn't approve of Nathan . . .

or any other young man who come sniffing round his daughter. No, the Fethering view is that, since Kyra had got the keys to the salon – you know, because she was due to open up the next morning – she entertained her boyfriend there.'

'Ah.' Carole nodded. The theory fitted in with the empty bottles she had seen in the back room of Connie's Clip Joint. And perhaps the red roses. 'Well, presumably, as we speak, the police are questioning Nathan Locke about just that.'

'I'm sure they would be,' said the old man, 'but they can't.'

'Why's that?'

'Because nothing has been seen of the boy since he left his home in Marine Villas at seven o'clock that evening.'

'Oh.'

'Which is another reason why all of Fethering have got him down for the job of murderer.' Wistfully, Les Constantine drained the last dregs of his pint. 'Oh well, I'd better be off.' He lowered his thin limbs gingerly down from his bar stool.

'Aren't we coming with you?' asked Jude, with a look of innocent sultriness.

'What for?'

Carole found herself blushing as her neighbour replied, 'For that threesome.'

'Ooh yes,' said the old man. 'Yes, I'd really like to do that. Trouble is,' he added with an apologetic smile, 'today I've got a bit of a cold.'

Chapter Four

Jude didn't make an appointment. From what she'd heard about the commercial health of Connie's Clip Joint, she didn't think it'd be necessary – even with the added attraction for Fethering people of having their hair cut at a murder scene.

The salon had reopened on the Friday, eight days after the discovery of Kyra Bartos's body. Jude reckoned the first few days would have mopped up the locals booking out of prurient curiosity, and it was the following Tuesday morning when she wandered in.

By then very little more had been heard from the police about their investigations. There had been some televised press conferences in the first few days, at which the detective chief inspector in charge of the case had demonstrated a caginess which could have meant he was within minutes of cracking the case wide open, or alternatively that he hadn't a clue what the hell was going on. Fethering opinion, lavishly expressed in the Crown and Anchor and at church, as well as in Allinstore and the rest of the local shops, continued to cast Nathan Locke as the murderer. There had still been no sign of the boy, and some local

Jeremiahs reckoned it was only a matter of time before he turned up as a 'Fethering Floater'. People who drowned from the seashore or, more frequently, in the fast-running waters of the Fether estuary, tended to be washed up on the beach before too long. But if a remorseful Nathan Locke had committed suicide by jumping into the river on the night of the murder, the sea was slow to return his body. 'Fethering Floaters' usually came back within twenty-four – or at the most forty-eight – hours. Jude felt pretty confident that, somewhere, Nathan Locke was still alive.

When she walked into Connie's Clip Joint, she received a cheery greeting from the owner and a polite nod from Theo. That Tuesday the owner's hair and make-up were immaculately in place. Both stylists were actually occupied, but Connie said she'd be through in ten minutes, so if Jude would like to wait . . . ?

This suited her purposes very well. Her vision enlarged by the description Carole had given her of the tragic scene in the back room, Jude just wanted a few moments to absorb the atmosphere of the salon. Murder, she had found, left a psychic signature on a setting that was at least as informative as a fingerprint or a bloodstain.

That morning there was no music playing, which again was helpful to her. The less distractions, the better. She disguised her intense concentration on the feeling of the place by flicking idly through the pages of a magazine. Hairdressers always offered a wide selection of reading, though – as was appropriate in Fethering – the magazines in Connie's Clip Joint favoured a more mature clientele. Apart from the predictable gossip-mongering of *OK!* and *Hello!*, also present were *Marie Claire*, *Vogue* and even *Country Life*.

Jude chose a *Vogue* and, while the surface of her mind was amused by the void between the stage-managed images on its pages and the reality of living women's looks, at a deeper level she tuned in to the aura of the salon.

There was discord there certainly, and it dated from long before the recent crime. Perhaps the conflict which had soured the atmosphere had been Connie and Martin's deteriorating relationship, its pressures increased by the necessity of maintaining a front of harmony while they worked together.

It certainly had nothing to do with Theo. Jude could detect an almost tangible warmth between the two stylists. They enjoyed working together; there was no discord there. And yet within each of them she could sense depths of personal conflict, directed at people outside the hermetic world of Connie's Clip Joint.

Jude hadn't got far, but she had extracted a sense of the place, a platform on which she could build future conjecture. Since she knew she wasn't going to get any further that morning in the psychic direction, she concentrated instead on the behaviour of the two clients having their hair done. Which, as things turned out, was a cabaret in itself.

Theo was dealing with the woman's hair, Connie with the man's. Theo must have been at work longer, because his client had clearly already gone through a colouring and washing process. Now both had reached the same stage, as though there were a prearranged plan to make the two haircuts finish at the same time.

Theo's client was a small, sharp-featured elderly woman, whose heavy make-up didn't quite coincide with the contours of her features. Her hair was newly red, though not a red that featured anywhere in the natural world. It was the defiant red of a burning oil-spill, and Theo was cutting it into the kind of 'Dutch bob' favoured by the silent-film star Louise Brooks. From the way he was working, this was clearly not a new style, but one he had been assiduously re-creating for some years.

The male client had broad amiable features gathered round a large squashed-in nose. Thinning a little on the crown, his remaining hair was thick and steel grey, with a corrugated effect, as though its natural curl had been subdued by a lifetime of brushing back.

Jude was very soon left in no doubt that the pair were married. The woman seemed much more interested in what was happening to her husband's hair than her own.

'No, shorter over the ears, Connie. You like it shorter over the ears, don't you, Wally?'

Wally, who appeared to have lived a life of listening to rhetorical questions from his wife, did not bother to reply.

'We don't want him walking round Fethering like some beatnik, do we, Theo?'

Theo agreed that that wouldn't be the thing at all.

'Do you know,' the woman went on, 'I can't believe the behaviour of young people these days, the sort of things they're always doing.' She almost dropped the final 'g' from the last word, a little giveaway that perhaps her origins weren't quite as refined as the voice she now used. 'I went into Allinstore only last week, just to buy some kippers . . . because you like a kipper, don't you, Wally?' Again her husband did not feel he had to confirm this self-evident truth. 'And of course it came from the freezer. I'd rather buy kippers, you know, like, fresh, but where'm I to do that since the fishmonger closed? I ask you, we've still got fishermen working out of Fethering, but if you want to buy fresh fish, you got to go all the way to Worthing . . . Not of course that a kipper is strictly fresh, because it's been kippered, but one from the fishmonger does look better than something out of the freezer that comes sealed in a bag with a little flower-shaped dab of butter on it. You say you can tell the difference in the taste, don't you, Wally?' With no pretence at waiting for a response, she went on, 'Anyway, I take the kipper up to the checkout and the girl behind takes it, and I give her the money, and she doesn't say a word. Not one word. It was like I was putting my money in a slot machine. So, as she gives me my change, I say to her, "Aren't you girls taught to say 'Thank you' any more?" And she says, "No, it's printed on the till receipt." Ooh, I was so angry when I got home. I was that angry, wasn't I, Wally? Yes, I was.'

She paused for breath, and her husband ventured,

'Similar thing happened to me as happened to Mim when I went to Tesco's in—'

'Don't talk while she's cutting your hair, Wally.'

He was obediently silent again. But in the few words he had spoken Jude was aware of a long-buried accent. The 'w' of 'went' had contained undertones of a 'v'.

'I don't know what young people are coming to today,' Mim went on. 'Makes me glad Wally and I was never blessed with children . . . well, though I don't think "blessed" is probably the right word. "Cursed" with children might be a better word, the way some of them behave these days. Because, of course, you had that terrible business here, didn't you, Connie?'

'Yes.'

If Mim was surprised by someone actually responding to one of her rhetorical appeals, she didn't show it. 'Drugs at the back of it,' she announced knowingly. 'Drugs at the back of most of this stuff, you know.'

'I don't actually think Kyra ever had anything to do with drugs, Mim,' said Connie.

'No, her old man wouldn't let her do anything like that,' Wally agreed. 'Was very angry when she had her ears and nose pierced. He always had standards, Joe.'

Mim looked a little miffed, as though allowing her husband space to inject three sentences into the conversation was somehow a failing on her part, and quickly resumed her monologue. 'Yes, more parents should have standards, and they don't. What are kids brought up on these days? Fast food, discotheques and video games . . . that's what they're brought up on, aren't they, Wally?'

Her husband, still basking in the glow of his recent conversational triumph, didn't feel the need to respond.

'I think bringing back National Service would do them all a lot of good. Your time in the Army didn't do you any harm, did it, Wally? Then these kids wouldn't go round smoking stuff and sticking needles in themselves and stuffing substances up their noses. Me and Wally worked in the music industry, where there was supposed to be lots of drugs going round, and we never saw any of them, did we, Wally? No . . . whereas these days the kids can buy drugs as easy as ice lollies – and they don't think no more of taking them than they would of eating an ice lolly. No wonder it all ends up with violence and murder.'

'But as I said,' Connie repeated patiently, 'Kyra didn't have anything to do with drugs.'

'I'm not saying she did. But the boy . . . the boy must've done. People don't go round strangling people for no reason. The boy must've been on drugs.'

'We have no means of knowing that,' said Connie, trying to bring a little rationality into the conversation. 'And nor, indeed, do we know that Kyra's boyfriend is the guilty party.'

But Mim's prejudices weren't so easily shifted. 'Oh, come on, if he didn't do it, why's he disappeared? If he's innocent, if he's got an alibi, why doesn't he come forward and tell the police about it? No, I'm sure he was on drugs.'

'Now let's blow it into shape, shall we?' said Theo, and started fluttering around Mim with the hairdryer.

'On drugs,' said Wally, taking advantage of the diversion to continue dramatically, 'or in the grip of a passion that he could not control.'

Mim once again seemed to regret the lapse that had allowed her husband to get a word in. 'Don't talk, Wally. You always move your head when you talk, and that makes it very difficult for Connie to cut your hair. Doesn't it, Connie? You come out of here with a cut on your ear, Wally, and it'll be your fault, not Connie's. Won't it, Connie? Incidentally, Connie, did you know the boy . . . you know, this Nathan, the one who killed the girl?'

Jude, who'd been taking in everything, listened with even greater attention.

'Yes, I had met him,' the hairdresser replied, 'and you really must stop saying that he killed her.'

'That's what everyone else in Fethering is saying.'

'I know, Mim, but in this country everyone is innocent until they're proven guilty.'

'That's nonsense. Was Hitler innocent? He never went to trial, he was never proved guilty, but are you telling me he wasn't?'

'No, I'm not. But that wasn't in this country and—'

'I think it's rubbish, that business about people being innocent until proven guilty. There's some people who should be locked away from birth. Paedophiles, and some of those illegal immigrants.'

Realizing that she wasn't participating in the most rational of arguments, Connie contented herself with saying, 'Well, as I told you, I did meet Nathan a few times. He'd sometimes pick Kyra up after work, and to me he seemed a very nice boy. Shy, not very sure of himself – only sixteen, I think – but I wouldn't have said he had a violent bone in his body.'

'It's the quiet ones you have to watch.' Mim pronounced the words as if they were an incontrovertible truth that clinched her argument.

'There,' said Theo, showing off his handiwork to his client in the mirror. 'That's how we like it, isn't it?'

She responded admiringly. 'Back to my natural look, yes.'

'Just a little whoosh of spray to fix it, and we can unleash you onto the streets of Fethering to break all the men's hearts, eh?'

'Yes.' Mim preened in the mirror. 'I could do with a few compliments. Never get any compliments from you, do I, Wally?'

'There – you're done too.' Connie stood back from her client, the co-ordinated timing of the haircuts having worked to perfection. 'Look all right, does it?'

The question had, inevitably, been put to Mim rather than Wally. She looked appraisingly at her husband's hair. 'Little more off the back. Don't want it trailing over his collar like some errand boy.'

While Theo made a big production of the final primping of his client, Connie duly did as she was told to hers. The couple were pampered into their coats. They paid their money, with Mim duly tipping both stylists. (Jude wondered whether Wally was allowed to carry any money of his own.) Then Connie crossed to the appointments book. 'Usual five weeks, shall we say? The Tuesday again. Same time?'

'Oh yes.'

'So that'll be nine-thirty for you, and the ten forty-five slot for the gentleman.'

'Doesn't matter. We'll come at the same time, and you'll sit and wait, won't you, Wally?'

Once again long experience told her husband that no response was required.

'Grenston's their surname,' said Connie. 'Wally and Mim Grenston. He was quite a successful musician – had his own band and did a lot of arranging, I believe. And she was a singer – also a very good career, but she gave it up when they got married . . . as women often did in those days.'

'But she said they didn't have children.'

'Maybe she didn't need them, the way she treats Wally. They're absolutely devoted to each other, you know.'

'I could see that,' said Jude thoughtfully. 'And Wally implied that he knew Kyra's father . . .'

Chapter Five

Like Carole, Jude had the privilege of having her hair washed by the salon's owner. 'I must get another junior soon,' Connie had said, 'but it seems, I don't know . . . so recent after what happened to Kyra.'

'Yes. Will it be hard to find someone?'

'God, no. Hundreds of girls still want to be hairdressers . . . in spite of the rotten pay. I get a dozen letters a week from kids asking to be a junior here, some with a bit of training, some not even left school yet. But the problem is getting the right one, one who's going to take the job seriously and actually be of some use to me.'

'Was Kyra one of those?'

'I think she could have become quite good. I mean, she was only seventeen. Like most girls of her age, she was easily distracted, mind often away somewhere else, not concentrating on the job in hand. But she was interested in the hairdressing business, and she definitely wanted to make something of herself. Get a bit of independence . . . her home life wasn't that easy.'

'As Wally implied.'

'Yes. Her father's very old. Kyra was the product of

his second marriage, but then her mother died a few years back. If she didn't get something of her own going, Kyra could see the prospect of being stuck here in Fethering as a carer for her old dad.'

'He must have taken it hard . . . you know, what happened to her.'

'I assume so. I don't know. Although he lives only in the next street to me, I've never actually spoken to him. I don't think he goes out much.'

Jude's hair was now towel-dry. Connie appraised it in the mirror. 'You're lucky, you know, not to need colouring . . .'

'At my age.'

'I didn't say that.'

'No, but you thought it. You're right, though. I am lucky. I think I've got the kind of hair where I won't suddenly start finding grey ones. I think it'll just get paler and paler until one day I look at it in the mirror, and it's all white.'

'Maybe.' Connie grinned. 'Now, is today going to be the day?'

'The day I look at it in the mirror and—?'

'No, no.'

'The day for what then?' Jude asked innocently.

'You know perfectly well. The day you decide to do something different with your hair.'

'Are you about to use the dreaded "short" word, Connie?'

'Look, it's lovely hair. It should be shown to advantage. It's funny, Jude, I don't think of you as someone who's afraid to take risks.'

'I'm not. And let me tell you, my hair has probably been through more metamorphoses than Madonna's. Back when I was modelling . . . God, it was a new style every couple of days. Which is why I really feel I've done my experimenting. I'm happy with it the way it is.'

'But you could look so much smarter. With it like this you look like . . . I don't know . . .'

Perhaps delicacy prevented Connie from continuing, but Jude provided a suggestion. 'A superannuated hippy?'

'You said it. Come on, Jude, make today the day.'

Firmly, the client shook her head. 'Nope. Don't feel like it. One day I will feel like it, and I promise you, when that happens, I will have the transformation done at Connie's Clip Joint. But today is not the day.'

'Huh.' Connie picked up her scissors without enthusiasm. 'So today it's just like your neighbour's, is it?'

'What do you mean?'

'"Same shape, but shorter."'

The impression wasn't perfect, but it did capture something of Carole's manner, and Jude chuckled. 'That's right.'

Connie started cutting, and her client relaxed into the experience. Theo didn't have an appointment for a while and sat reading a motor-racing magazine, a choice that seemed butchly at odds with his public demeanour. Jude was once again amazed at how people in certain jobs coped with the waiting. Shop assistants, restaurant staff and hairdressers had an ability to slip into a half-life, go inert and yet come immediately to energetic life when a customer entered. That was another part of the job, she reflected, that a salon junior like Kyra might have found hard to cope with.

'Ooh, Jude, something I was going to ask you . . .'

'Yes?'

'You're into alternative therapies and that, aren't you?'

'Well, to some extent,' Jude replied cautiously.

'I'd really like to talk about that at some point.'

'Why? Have you got some problem that you need help with?'

'No, no, it's not for that, not for me. It's just increasingly salons are offering other services, apart from the straight hairdressing. Manicure, ear-piercing, massage, all that stuff. Lot of modern salons are getting more like beauty spas. Sunbeds, detox wraps, you name it. That's certainly the way Martin & Martina are going.' She couldn't keep the resentment out of her voice when she mentioned her ex-husband's business. 'I just wondered if you were into any of that stuff, Jude . . . ?'

'Not really. What I do is therapeutic . . . you know, helping people feel better.'

Connie grinned. 'So you're just like a hairdresser. I tell you, we're very definitely therapists – for all the listening we do, apart from anything else.'

'Yes, I'm sure you are.'

'Well, if there were some service, you know, that I could refer my clients to you for . . . we'd make it a business deal. Look, take one of my cards. That's got my mobile number on it too. And give me a call if you can think of a way we can make it work.'

'I will.' Jude couldn't envisage anything coming of it. She didn't want her healing services to become part of anyone's pampering regime, but discussion of the project might be another way of keeping in touch with the hairdresser and maybe, eventually, finding out more about what had happened at Connie's Clip Joint. In the meantime, the best way of eliciting information remained the direct question.

'Have you had any more contact from the police, Connie, you know, since you reopened?'

'No, thank God. The amount of questioning I had to go through in the first couple of days . . . it was pretty wearing. They wanted to know all kinds of things that I wouldn't have thought could be relevant in a million years . . . asking about my marriage and a whole lot of other private stuff.'

'Did they talk to your ex-husband as well?'

'Yes, I gather Martin went through quite a grilling. But after the first couple of days, they seemed to decide there was nothing more I could tell them.'

'Did they lay off him too?'

She seemed about to make a different answer, but then said brusquely, 'That I wouldn't know. Anyway, the good thing was that quite suddenly they seemed to lose interest in me. Maybe that was when they got more news about Nathan Locke disappearing . . . I don't know. The detectives in charge told me to stay in touch, but – thank God – since then they've left me alone. Oh, they've given me lots of numbers to ring if I remember anything else, or if anything happens that might have a bearing on the crime. But then I can't imagine that anything is going to happen that has a bearing on the crime.'

'Unless Nathan Locke suddenly turned up on your doorstep one day . . . ?'

'I can't think that's very likely.'

'Do you mean you share the general Fethering view that he's committed suicide?'

'It'd be an explanation, wouldn't it?'

'Mmm.' There was a silence, disturbed only by the snipping of Connie's scissors. Eventually Jude broke it. 'You said you hadn't met Kyra's father?'

'That's right.'

'But Wally Grenston knows him. Talked about him as Joe, didn't he?'

'Yes. When Wally was last in he said hello to Kyra like he'd met her somewhere before. Probably seen her round her old man's place. From what he says, he's one of the privileged few who's allowed in there. The Bartos place backs on to my garden, but I've never had so much as a "How do you do?" from the old boy.'

'Mmm.' Jude looked thoughtful. 'Do you still live in the house you did when you were married?'

'Yes. Part of my settlement. That and this place . . .' she smiled ruefully '. . . while Martin went on to greater things.'

After a few moments' silence, Jude said, 'You know, I'd like to talk to Wally Grenston . . .'

She had no inhibitions about saying this. You could tell everything to a hairdresser. Whatever you said, they'd always heard worse. And generally speaking, they were discreet about keeping things to themselves.

'He's in the phone book.'

'Right.'

'Mind you, Jude, if you're going to call him, I'd recommend you do it on a Thursday morning.'

'Oh. Why?'

'That's when Mim goes out to her flower arranging club.'

Chapter Six

'Is that Mrs Seddon?' The voice on the telephone was male, cultured, even slightly academic.

'Yes.'

'You don't know me. My name is Rowley Locke. I am the uncle of Nathan Locke.'

'Ah.'

'And I'm sure I don't need to tell you that my nephew is currently the subject of a lot of local gossip.'

'No. It's hard to escape it.'

'The fact is that, without any evidence, without any trial, Nathan is being spoken of as the murderer of that poor girl in the hairdresser's.'

'I had heard that suggestion, yes.'

'Well, I apologize for troubling you, Mrs Seddon . . .' He was extremely polite in his approach '. . . but, from the perspective of our family, this is very distressing . . .'

'I'm sure it is.'

'And . . . I hesitate to ask you this, but I understand you were at the hairdresser's when the murder victim was discovered . . . ?'

Carole confirmed that she had been.

'Look, you may think this is an awful cheek . . .
and I will fully understand if that is your view . . . but
I wondered if we could talk to you about what you
saw . . . ?' Carole wondered who the 'we' was. 'The fact
is, Mrs Seddon, that, apart from constantly questioning
us about Nathan's whereabouts, the police are giving us
nothing in the way of information about what happened . . . which makes it very difficult for us to build
up a defence for the poor boy . . . when he finally does
turn up again.'

'You are confident that he will turn up again?'

'Yes, of course.'

He sounded bewildered that the question should
have been asked, so, without spelling out the other
local rumour that the boy had topped himself, Carole
moved quickly on. 'I don't quite understand, Mr Locke.
What is it you want me to do for you?'

'Just talk to us about what you saw in the hairdresser's that morning. I realize that you may think this
is a police matter and that you shouldn't discuss it with
anyone else . . .'

The priorities of her Home Office past made Carole
think exactly that, but on the other hand she was being
offered the opportunity to garner more information
about people involved in what she and Jude were
increasingly thinking of as *their* next investigation . . .

'I have telephoned the two hairdressers who were
there that morning, and they have both taken the
view that they shouldn't talk to us . . . which, as I say,
is entirely their prerogative . . . but I was just wondering, Mrs Seddon, whether you felt the same . . . ?'

'I can see their point of view completely,' Carole began. 'On the other hand, I'm also feeling slightly frustrated by the lack of information I'm receiving from the police, so if we were to pool our knowledge, I think it might be mutually beneficial.'

'I am so glad to hear you say that.'

'So what do you want to ask me?'

'Well, if it's not inconvenient, I would rather the conversation were conducted face to face than on the phone.'

'That's fine by me.'

'I don't know how committed your time is . . .' His phrasing was again scrupulously polite.

'I'm retired, so I'm . . .' Carole overstated the truth '. . . relatively free.'

'Good. Because, seeing from the phone book where you live, I was wondering whether it might be possible for us to meet up at the house of my brother and sister-in-law . . . Nathan's parents . . . ?'

Better and better, thought Carole.

As soon as she arrived at Marine Villas that same afternoon, it was clear that, though Arnold Locke owned the house, Rowley was the dominant brother. There was a strong family likeness between them. Both were tall and spare, with thinning straw-coloured hair and large surprised blue eyes, which made them look unworldly almost to the point of vulnerability.

The front room into which Carole was ushered deliberately showed the Lockes to be an artistic family.

At the end away from the window stood an upright piano, and beside it a Victorian wooden music stand, which suggested at least one other instrument was played in the house. Nearby shelves held neatly upright books of sheet music. The same tidiness had been brought to bear on the extensive collection of CDs in parallel racks. Carole felt pretty certain they'd all be of classical music. Some tasteful framed prints on the walls and rigidly marshalled bookshelves re-emphasized the Lockes' rather intense interest in culture.

Also present in the room were Arnold's wife Eithne, and Rowley's daughter Dorcas. The former was a dumpy woman whose ample figure strained against the buttons that ran all the way down her flower-printed cotton dress. She wore her dark grey hair in a generous bun low at the back of her neck. Carole couldn't help being reminded of the figure from a childhood pack of 'Happy Families', Mrs Bun the Baker's Wife.

Dorcas, on the other hand, with honey-coloured eyes, long spun-gold corkscrew curls and a tall slender body, was the kind of girl who would have been earnestly pursued as a model by the Pre-Raphaelites. The clothes she affected, long eau-de-nil top over ankle-length pale green skirt, encouraged the impression. Her speech showed the same academic earnestness as the other Lockes', but with a slight lisp. It made her sound more childish than her age, which Carole estimated at about twenty.

'My wife Bridget would have liked to be here too,' Rowley apologized, 'but sadly she has to work. She's a teacher in Chichester.' Maybe at the college where Nathan was a pupil?

Carole was struck by how relatively calm Arnold and Eithne Locke seemed. If her son Stephen had disappeared under suspicion of having committed a murder, she didn't think she would be behaving with such equanimity. But Nathan's parents appeared to think that everything was in hand and, from the way they looked at him, that Rowley was the one who had it in hand.

'I hope you don't mind meeting us all together, Mrs Seddon.'

'That's no problem. Please call me Carole.'

'Thank you. And I'm Rowley. But this is obviously a family thing we're talking about. And it's quite serious.'

'Particularly because it involves Fimby,' added Dorcas.

In response to Carole's look of puzzlement, Rowley explained, 'Sorry, Fimby's a nickname we have for Nathan.'

'Everyone in the family has a nickname,' said Dorcas.

Carole hoped she wasn't about to be told what they all were, and fortunately Rowley continued, 'I must tell you, Carole, that our starting point is that Nathan did not kill Kyra Bartos.'

'Do you have any evidence to support that?'

'The evidence we have is our knowledge of the boy's personality. We've all watched him grow up. He's only sixteen, and he does not have a violent nature.'

'People's nature can change . . . under provocation.'

'Maybe, but I can't see Nathan's nature changing that much. He's a gentle boy. His main interest is English literature.'

'Rowley . . .' Carole didn't find that the name tripped easily off her tongue, '. . . I'm playing devil's advocate here, but it is quite possible that someone whose main interest is English literature, who is what one could call "bookish", might have great difficulty in adjusting to the realities of the real world and, you know, particularly in an emotional relationship . . .' She left them to fill in the rest of the sentence.

Rowley nodded in acknowledgement of her argument, noting it down as a good debating point. 'I agree that is a possible scenario, but not in the case of Nathan.'

'No, we really can't imagine him doing anything like what he's being publicly accused of,' Arnold contributed, and the 'we' he used seemed to encompass not just himself and his wife but the whole family.

'But you don't have anything handy like an alibi for him at the time when he was supposed to have been with Kyra?'

'No.' After his brother's brief intervention, Rowley once again took up the reins of the conversation. 'And, indeed . . . I'm telling you this, Carole, because I respect the fact that you've agreed to come and talk to us this afternoon, and because I trust you not to spread the information around . . . we are pretty certain that Nathan did actually see Kyra Bartos the evening before she died.'

'You haven't heard that from Nathan himself?'

'We've heard nothing from Nathan himself.'

'And you don't think he's just run off, for reasons which have nothing to do with the murder?'

Rowley was puzzled by the question. 'Why on earth would he do that?'

'Young people do it all the time. You know, if they're unhappy at home . . .'

'Nathan was not unhappy at home,' said Rowley firmly. 'We are a very strong family, and he always enjoyed being part of it.'

This was spoken so much like an article of faith that Carole found herself wondering what it must have been like for any family member who questioned the party line. She knew she'd find such a set-up impossibly claustrophobic. Maybe Nathan did too . . .

Eithne Locke, perhaps because she feared being thought unmaternal, interjected at this point. 'Of course he wouldn't want to run off. Listen, we haven't seen Nathan since he left here early that evening, round seven. Arnold and I are obviously worried sick.' But she didn't sound worried sick. Still, Carole knew that that meant nothing. The woman's surface calm might well be a coping mechanism for her anxiety.

'We are sure he will come home eventually,' the boy's mother went on, 'but he must be aware that he's a suspect and I'm sure he's terrified of the police getting hold of him.'

'Our fine boys in blue,' said Rowley Locke, clearly speaking from a long-held agenda, 'do not have the best reputation in the world for the way they deal with suspects. Human rights tend to cover only what can be seen; they frequently cease at the door of the interrogation room. We don't want Nathan to have to go through that.'

Carole, whose experiences in the Home Office had given her a less cynical attitude to the British police, did not think that this was the moment to take issue. Nor did she think it was the moment to raise the question of suicide with the boy's parents. It seemed to have entered their thoughts no more than it had Rowley's, and Carole was not about to create new anxieties for them.

'Have you any idea how the police's search for Nathan is going?'

Rowley Locke shrugged. 'As I say, we're not very high up the distribution list for police information.' Join the club, thought Carole. 'They've asked us about where he might be, obviously.'

'They even had the nerve,' said Eithne, 'to search this house to see if he was hiding somewhere.'

'Though they did ask our permission first,' her husband pointed out.

'Yes, but only because they would have had to get a search warrant otherwise,' Eithne added.

'And they looked for him in our house as well,' said Rowley. 'We too gave permission. We have nothing to hide. They even searched Treboddick.'

'Treboddick?'

'Oh, sorry, Carole. It's a place we have in Cornwall. They thought Nathan might have hidden himself away down there.'

'Well, I suppose that's a reasonable suspicion, isn't it? If it's a family place?'

'Huh.' Rowley Locke was not temperamentally inclined to listen to any arguments in favour of 'our fine boys in blue'. 'Anyway,' he went on, 'the reason for wanting to talk to you, as I said on the phone, is because the police are telling us nothing. And it's very difficult for us to get a handle on what Nathan might or might not have done, when we don't know exactly what it is he's been accused of.'

'He hasn't been accused of anything yet.'

'All right. What he's suspected of having done. And I just thought . . . because you were actually on the scene when the body was discovered, you might know something . . . well, more than we do, anyway.'

Carole nodded thoughtfully and looked around the room. She felt justified in taking her time. What the Lockes were asking could be considered as a major intrusion into her privacy. They weren't to know she was at least as desperate to find out everything about them as they were about her.

The framed photographs on the mantelpiece and walls corrected an image of the family that she had received. Dorcas's prissiness had suggested to Carole that she was an only child, but the evidence negated that impression. All the pictures showed lots of children, and both sets of parents, in a variety of relaxed holiday settings. Both Nathan and Dorcas had siblings, one of hers being an identical twin. Carole got the strong impression that the Locke cousins did everything together. And no doubt, she thought with a mental cringe, they all had nicknames like Fimby.

'I see you're looking at the photographs,' said Rowley. 'That's Nathan.'

The boy he pointed out had darker hair, but the same susceptible pale blue eyes. He was good-looking, probably about thirteen when the photograph had been taken. The massed children were on a boat in a creek that looked Cornish, the Helford River maybe. Presumably the setting was somewhere near Treboddick. The other children were taking up nautical poses for the camera, like something out of *Swallows and Amazons* (a book which Carole suddenly felt certain the Lockes would have read with enormous relish). But Nathan looked detached, almost embarrassed by the play-acting around him. Maybe it had only been a phase, an adolescent grumpiness which had afflicted him that one particular day, but Carole got the impression of the boy as an unwilling outsider in the claustrophobic world of the Locke family.

'Thank you. I haven't met him obviously,' she said. 'And I'm afraid I don't know much about the background or the history at Connie's Clip Joint. That morning was the first time I had been in the salon.'

'It must have been a terrible shock for you. But do you mind telling us what you actually saw?'

'No, not at all.'

'And is it all right if I take notes?'

Carole shrugged permission. Rowley Locke took a small plain leatherbound notebook out of his jacket pocket, and then unscrewed a large fountain pen. He opened a page on which she could see neat italic writing in brown ink. She had a feeling that everything Rowley Locke did in his life would be balanced on that fine line between individuality and pretension.

Her description of what she had seen in the back room at Connie's Clip Joint was delivered as impassively as she could make it. When she had finished, Rowley Locke completed his last note with a neat full stop.

'Thank you so much, Carole. There were quite a lot of details there we didn't know about.'

'Oh?'

'Well, we knew how the girl had been strangled, and what had been used to do the deed, but we didn't know anything about the vodka bottle and beer cans. Or the red roses.'

'Those all seem to suggest that Kyra had been entertaining someone in the salon that evening. She had the keys, you see, so that she could open up the following morning.' Carole remembered something Les Constantine had told her, and could see no harm in passing it on. 'I gather that Kyra's father was very protective of her, wouldn't have liked the idea of her having boyfriends around at home. So I suppose, if the girl wanted to be alone with Nathan, Connie's Clip Joint was the obvious place for them to go.'

Eithne Locke, interpreting this as some obscure slight on her as a parent, insisted that Nathan had always been welcome to bring Kyra to Marine Villas. 'We made that very clear to him. Arnold and I have very liberal attitudes to that kind of thing. Diggo had one girlfriend virtually living here just before he went to university.'

Carole assumed this was another of the ghastly Locke nicknames, probably for Nathan's older brother, but she didn't ask for an explanation. Instead she went on, 'I haven't heard it as a fact from the police, but I had assumed that the vodka bottle and beer cans might have given them a direct link to Nathan. You know, through his DNA or fingerprints.'

'Yes, except that they don't have his DNA or fingerprints on file – and we refused to let them take any samples from the house. We know our rights.' Rowley Locke was mounting another of his human rights hobby horses. 'I am aware that this government would like to have everyone's details on file from birth, but at the moment they can only keep such records for people who have actually been found guilty of a crime. And I am glad to say that my nephew has never fitted into that category.'

'But you're not denying,' asked Carole, 'that it does look likely that Nathan spent some time with Kyra in the salon the evening before she was found dead?'

'No, none of us is denying that. We think it very likely that he did spend time with her. What happened while they were together . . .' For the first time he looked embarrassed. 'Carole, you didn't gather from the police whether there had been any sign of . . . sexual activity . . . on the girl's body?'

'They're no more likely to have told me that than they are you.'

'No, I suppose not. I wasn't suggesting rape or . . . I was thinking of consensual sex.'

'Do you know whether Nathan and Kyra were sleeping together?'

Instinctively Rowley looked to the boy's mother to answer this question. 'I can't actually be sure,' said Eithne Locke, 'but I would have thought it likely. According to everything one reads in the newspapers, young people seem to be sexually active from about the age of fourteen these days. And certainly Nathan would have encountered no disapproval of such behaviour in this house, would he Arnold?'

Her husband concurred. 'No, we're not prudish at all.' But he contrived to sound prudish as he said it.

'Had you actually met Kyra?'

Arnold looked to his wife for consent before saying, 'Not really. Well, that is to say, Nathan never brought her back here to introduce us, did he, Eithne?'

'No. Which one might have thought was rather odd.'

Carole didn't find it at all odd. 'You said "Not really", Arnold . . .'

'Yes. Well, Eithne did once meet them together in Fethering High Street, didn't you?'

'Yes. And it was a situation where Nathan couldn't avoid introducing the girl to me. Though he didn't do it with very good grace . . . almost as though he were ashamed of her.'

Much more likely that he was ashamed of you, Carole thought. 'And neither of you ever met Kyra's father?'

'Oh no,' said Arnold.

'Right!' Carole turned back to the dominant – not to say controlling – brother. 'So, Rowley, your view would be that Nathan did spend some time with Kyra in the salon that evening, then, after he'd left, someone else came along and murdered her?'

'That seems to me to be the most likely scenario, yes.'

'Well, it looks as though all such speculations are going to be no more than speculations until the boy reappears and gives an account of himself.'

Rowley Locke agreed.

'And presumably . . . I'm sorry to ask you this, but I feel I have to . . . none of you have any idea where Nathan might have gone?'

They all confirmed that they hadn't. So, with assurances on both sides that they'd get in touch to share any further information that might come up, Carole left the house in Marine Villas and walked back the short way to High Tor – with an uncomfortable feeling that she had just been interrogated.

Chapter Seven

Jude had borne Connie Rutherford's advice in mind, and waited till the Thursday morning to contact Wally Grenston. She had been through various possible excuses for her call, but, not being by nature a devious person, had opted finally for the truth. 'I was in Connie's Clip Joint on Tuesday morning when you and your wife were having your hair done . . .'

'Oh yes. You were waiting. Blonde lady, am I right?'

'You are. Plumpish.'

'Well covered, I would have said.'

'You're a gentleman, Wally.'

'So I like to think.'

'Look, I'm going to be honest with you. I've got rather interested in what happened to Kyra Bartos . . . how she came to be killed . .'

'You and the rest of Fethering.'

'Yes, and you said something about the girl's father . . . you know, as if you knew him . . .'

'Right.' For the first time there was a note of caution in Wally Grenston's voice.

'I just wanted to follow up on that . . . find out more . . . ask a few questions . . .'

'Are you some kind of journalist, Jude?'

'No, I'm just . . . as I said . . . interested,' she finished lamely.

'Interested in protecting the boy who's supposed to have murdered her . . . or interested in finding out who really did it?'

'Both. But why did you ask that question?'

'I have my reasons. Tell you what – you want to talk, you can come round here. Straight away, though. And you have to be gone by quarter to twelve.'

'Sounds good to me,' said Jude.

'Hello?'

Carole was taken aback. 'Oh, sorry. I wasn't expecting anyone to be there. I was just going to leave a message.' Then, aware of her daughter-in-law's condition, she asked anxiously, 'Are you all right, Gaby?'

'Yes, of course. I'm not ill, I'm just pregnant.'

'I know. But you being home in the middle of the day . . .'

'Just taking a couple of days off to try and get the baby's room sorted. Steve keeps saying he's "going to do it at the weekend", but his weekends seem to be as busy as his weeks at the moment.'

'Yes.' Not for the first time, Carole wished she understood more about her son's high-powered and extremely lucrative job. It was to do with money, and computers came into it too, but whenever Stephen tried to provide more detail on the subject, she found her mind glazing over. 'And how long are you going to keep on working?'

'Plan is to go till the end of the month. That'll give me four weeks till the ETA.'

'Sorry?'

'Estimated Time of Arrival.'

'Oh yes, of course. Twenty-eighth of October.' The date was engraved on Carole's memory.

'That's assuming I can still reach across the desk to pick up my phone, and deal with all those penny-pinching producers.' Gaby worked as a theatrical agent. 'I'm getting absolutely massive. Well, I was no sylph to start with.'

The image of Gaby's chubby body came into her mother-in-law's mind. She hadn't been showing much when they last met. Carole realized that that had been more than two months before. 'It'd be lovely to meet up,' she said, rather guiltily.

'Yes. We were saying that only last night.'

'You and Stephen?'

'Well, and David. He'd come round for supper.'

'Ah.' Carole felt a pang of something that included jealousy. She had always worried about the post-divorce David being closer to Stephen than she was . . . or now being closer to Stephen and Gaby . . . soon perhaps to be the favoured grandparent to the forthcoming baby.

'He was actually saying it was daft we hadn't invited you last night as well. Sorry, we didn't think, but it would have been a great idea.'

No, it wouldn't, was Carole's immediate, but unspoken, reaction.

'I mean, you both managed so well at the wedding.

David was saying how great it was that the two of you could at last be together again without any strain.'

Clearly, thought Carole, his recollection of the wedding was very different from hers. All that the prolonged exposure to her ex-husband had made her think was what a good idea the divorce had been. If she'd had her way, she would have liked a written guarantee that she'd never have to see David again for as long as she lived. But she knew Gaby – and particularly Stephen – were very keen on a rapprochement between the estranged parents. She could see their point of view. With the baby coming, it would be so much nicer to have family harmony, both grandparents coming together every time they visited the new arrival. But if that was Stephen and Gaby's ambition, Carole was afraid they were going to be disappointed.

'Well, it would be nice to meet up,' she said.

'Yes.'

Was she being hypersensitive to detect a lack of enthusiasm in Gaby's tone? Was she regarded as a 'difficult' mother-in-law? In private, did Stephen and his wife giggle about her? Did Gaby groan every time he said that they really ought to see his mother?

'That'd be great,' the girl went on, still with not quite enough enthusiasm for her mother-in-law's taste. 'I'll check with Steve. His diary's always so much busier than mine. And then we'll get back to you and sort out a date.'

'That sounds fine.'

After the phone call had finished, Carole felt restless. Though she had always loved Stephen, she still felt guilt for not being as maternal as she should have been. And now there was the challenge of forming a relationship with the next generation. She didn't feel she'd been a great success with her own child. Would it be different if the baby was a girl? (Though Stephen and Gaby had had the opportunity at various scans to know the gender, they'd chosen not to.) For the millionth time in her life, Carole Seddon wished she could have a personality transplant.

Wally Grenston's old face creased into a grin as he handed Jude the coffee. It was in a bone china cup with a delicate design of shrimp-pink and gold. On the saucer lay a small silver spoon whose thin handle ended in a wooden bead like a coffee bean. The sugar bowl and tongs were similarly decorated.

The grin stayed as he sat back in his chair. 'Let me enjoy this moment.'

'What do you mean?'

'Mim – that's my wife . . .'

'I saw her at the hairdresser's.'

'Yes. Well, she's gone through her life imagining that, the minute her back's turned, I am immediately entertaining some attractive woman . . .'

'Ah.'

'. . . and let me tell you, this is the first time it's happened.'

'Right.'

He leaned forward a little. 'Could you tell me something, Jude? Are you wearing lipstick?'

'No. I very rarely wear any make-up.'

'Oh, dash it,' he said, with mild regret.

'What's the problem?'

'Just, if Mim came back, and she found a second coffee cup here, *with lipstick on it* . . . well, that really would set the cat among her pigeons.'

'Do you want to upset her?'

He was affronted by the suggestion. 'Of course not. I adore the old bat. But it doesn't do her any harm to be kept on her toes.'

This seemed to him disproportionately amusing and, while he chuckled, Jude took in the room around her. The most striking thing was the number of awards it contained. In purpose-built chestnut-framed display cases stood cups, figurines, engraved glassware, abstract sculptures and calligraphed citations, all naming 'Walter Grenston' as their winner. Jude didn't recognize any of the awards, but all their artwork seemed to imply success in the field of music, and this impression was confirmed by the white grand piano at the back of the room. The rest of the decor was busy and fussy; lots of little objects – photographs in elaborate silver frames, statuettes, vases and animals made of swirling coloured glass – were everywhere. Though her own sitting room at Woodside Cottage was equally cluttered, the impression could not have been more different. Every object in the Grenstons' house looked as though it was dusted and had its alignment checked every hour on the hour.

They lived in Shorelands, a large estate on the west side of Fethering, whose denizens had to comply with a daunting number of local regulations, policed by a committee of residents. People had to be extremely rich to live there, so clearly during his musical career Wally Grenston had collected money as well as awards. The house was on one of the Shorelands Estate's prime sites, and its picture windows showed a perfectly maintained garden leading down to the sea. In fact, the openness of the English Channel seemed at odds with the claustrophobia of the overcrowded room, which might have been more suitably set in the depths of a middle-European forest.

Having indulged his laughter to the full, Wally moved on to business. 'So you wanted to know about Joe Bartos?'

'Yes.'

'And just to confirm again . . . you have no professional axe to grind here? This is out of pure curiosity?'

'Murder makes everyone curious, doesn't it?'

'Maybe.' The idea brought a new seriousness to his manner. 'Though for many, murder has been a signal to stop curiosity. Don't ask any questions. Play safe. Do not put your head above the parapet.'

'Are you talking about during the war?'

'A lot of things that were true during the war are still true now. People do not change . . . enough . . . sadly.'

'You weren't born in this country, were you?'

He shook his head, unoffended by the question. As ever, Jude's directness worked its magic.

'No, I came here early in 1939, just before it all happened, but when it was already pretty clear what was going to happen. I was nineteen . . . one of the ones who got away.'

'One of the lucky ones?'

He smiled sadly. 'I didn't say that, did I? But, as things turned out, lucky, yes. I would rather have gone back to the world in which I grew up, but that world very soon ceased to exist, so there was nowhere to go back to.'

'Are you talking about Germany?'

'It was true of Germany as well, but that was not my country. My country – though some would say that a Jew does not really have his own country – is Czechoslovakia. Have you been there?'

Jude nodded. 'A couple of times. Before the . . . what did they call it? . . . "Velvet Revolution"?'

'They always have a new name for changes in my country. And they always have new changes. Once somebody renamed my country "The Protectorate of Bohemia/Moravia". I tell you, Czechoslovakia has had more invasions and occupations than you have had hot dinners.' He chuckled, trying to shift himself out of an encroaching gloom. 'You wanted to know about Joe Bartos . . . So, if you see yourself as an amateur sleuth . . .'

'I didn't say that I did.'

'Then why else are you so interested in this murder?'

'Well . . .'

'Anyway, if you *do* see yourself as an amateur sleuth . . . you will no doubt have worked out how I know Joe Bartos . . . ?'

Jude shook her head. 'I'm sorry. I'm clearly not a very good amateur sleuth.'

'No, you are not. Do you not know where the name "Bartos" comes from?'

'Spain, maybe . . . or . . . ?'

Wally Grenston shook his head and clicked his teeth in exasperation. 'No, no. You think that because everyone here pronounces the name wrong. With an "s" sound at the end. No, it's pronounced "Bartosh". The name is Czech.'

'Ah. So you knew Kyra's father back in Czechoslovakia?'

'No, I met him in England. And not that long ago. In Brighton there is a club for people who originated in my country. I have met Jiri there once or twice.'

'Jiri?'

'His real name. When he comes to England, no one can pronounce it or spell it, so he settles for "Joe". Makes life easier.'

'Ah. And did you meet Kyra at the club too?'

He shook his head. 'Not at the club. I've met her in Connie's salon, and then once or twice when I went to her father's house. But I did not go there very often. Mim did not like me going to Jiri's house.'

Jude's quizzical eyebrow was greeted by a huge laugh. 'Mim does not like me going anywhere without her, remember? Does not like me out of her sight. She is afraid that, if she is not watching me, I am off serenading beautiful women.' With surprising ease for someone his age, he levered himself out of the armchair and crossed to the piano stool. His fingers instantly found the keys and started to play a wistful ballad. In a voice that was not really a singing voice, but which could still find the right weight and value of each word, he sang:

'*There is no one I have ever wanted by my side.*
Just to have you with me is a source of pride,
Knowing you're the one in whom I can confide,
Whenever I want to . . .
Whenever I want you.

There is nothing I have ever wanted more than this.
Just to be beside you is the height of bliss,
Knowing I can lean across and take a kiss,
Whenever I want to . . .
Whenever I want you.'

The song spiralled away in a little tinkling of notes.

'Did you write that, Wally?'

'Of course. And Mim sang it. A minor hit. I don't think it would get far now on *Pop Idol*.'

'It's a beautiful tune.'

'Oh yes, of course. All my tunes are beautiful.'

'And sad.'

'All my tunes are sad.' He was silent for a moment, then firmly closed the lid of the white piano and came back to sit opposite her. 'So, what do you really want to know about Jiri Bartos?' He looked at his large old gold wristwatch. 'We must be quick. I am about to lose my . . .' he smiled, '. . . window of opportunity.'

'I really want to know about his relationship with

his daughter. Someone suggested that he was quite a difficult father.'

'Difficult . . . ? Strong . . . ?' The old man opened out his hands in a gesture of helplessness. 'Perhaps they are different words for the same thing. Jiri, like most of my generation who come from Czechoslovakia, has quite a long history. He is an old man, older even than me. He was married when he lived in Czechoslovakia, with children I think. Then the war came and I do not know what happened. He never talks about such things, but when he came to England, he was alone. His first family . . .' Wally gave an expressively hopeless shrug. 'So he was old, seventy perhaps, when he married again. To an English girl . . . well, I say "girl", but she was no chicken either . . . Young enough, though, to give him a child. A little girl, Krystina.'

'So "Kyra" was . . . ?'

'Yes. The young always want to reinvent themselves, don't they? New names, new clothes, new body-piercings . . .'

He sounded contemptuous, so Jude said, in mitigation, 'They're only trying to find their own identities.'

'Of course. And that is something that people like Jiri and me understand all too well. "Grenston" – do you think that is my real name? I think "Grünstein" might be closer to the mark. But who cares? What is a change of name if you feel happier with the result, if you fit in better because of the result? We all find our own ways of survival.' He looked thoughtful, but a glimpse at his watch brought him out of introspection. 'Anyway, "Krystina" is a good Czech name. "Kyra" . . .

76

I don't know where "Kyra" comes from. The girl only changed her name to annoy her father.'

'It was an adversarial relationship, was it then?'

'It was not an easy relationship. But for reasons that came from outside, the pressure of events. Krystina's mother died when the girl was only twelve. Breast cancer. Not an easy time for a child to lose a parent. So she was left with Jiri, who was . . . not the most natural person to look after a teenage girl.'

'Was he cruel to her?'

'Not deliberately. He did the best he could, did what was right according to his view of things. But his view of things was . . . I suppose you would say old-fashioned. Children, he felt, should always be on their best behaviour, always respectful to their parents. He didn't encourage his daughter to make friends. I don't think she ever invited anyone from school back to the house. And, of course, Jiri had no domestic skills, so after his wife died, Krystina was expected to do everything about the house. He did not want her to leave him. He could not manage without her.'

'Are you saying that in the emotional sense?'

'Jiri would deny it. He would say he only needed the girl to act as housekeeper for him. But Jiri was never one to wear his heart on his sleeve. To show his emotions costs him more than he is prepared to pay.'

'So presumably . . . a man like that . . . he would not have found it easy when his daughter started to lead a life of her own . . . when she got a job . . . when she got a boyfriend . . . ?'

Wally Grenston shrugged. 'I would not have thought

so, but I don't know for sure. Jiri Bartos is an acquaintance, not a close friend. He doesn't unburden his feelings to me. Mind you, I don't imagine he unburdens his feelings to anyone.'

'Do you think he'd agree to talk to me?'

The old musician's mouth narrowed doubtfully. 'It depends what you were offering him. Maybe, if you had some information that would tell him how his daughter came to die . . . ? I don't know. I cannot speak for him.'

'But do you have his phone number?'

'It is in the local phone book. There is no secrecy about where he lives.'

'No.'

Wally Grenston looked uneasily at his watch. Jude realized her window of opportunity was closing. She thanked him for talking to her, and said she must leave.

'Yes. I am sorry it cannot be for longer. I would like to play you some other tunes. I always like playing tunes for a beautiful lady.' But even as he spoke the words of flirtation, he looked worried. From seeing the two of them in Connie's Clip Joint, Jude had got the impression that Wally wasn't genuinely henpecked, that his subservient behaviour to Mim was part of a public double act. But his current anxiety made her question that assumption. Maybe he really was afraid of his wife.

Still he kept up his facade of roguish gallantry. 'It is a pity that you do not wear make-up, that you could not have left the tell-tale trace on the coffee cup . . .'

Jude grinned at him and, reaching down into the

bottom of her capacious African straw basket, produced a battered lipstick. She painted her lips, and then deliberately picked up her cup and pretended to drink. A very satisfactory smudge of pink appeared on the gold rim of the china.

Wally smiled, absolutely delighted. 'Oh, that is good, very good.' But his eyes could not stay long away from his watch. 'I think perhaps though, the time has come . . .'

'Of course.'

'Would you mind,' he asked nervously, 'going down the back way, through the garden? There is a gate at the end that only opens from this side. It leads directly on to the beach path.'

'No, that's fine. It's a nicer walk back.'

So that was the route by which she left, clandestinely, like a spy or a lover. When she reached the gate to the beach, Jude looked back. She could see the huge wide window of the sitting room. Next to it was a smaller one, clearly belonging to the kitchen. In front of this, Wally Grenston, unaware of her scrutiny, was carefully washing both coffee cups.

Chapter Eight

Jude looked up Jiri Bartos's number as soon as she got back to Woodside Cottage. She rang it straight away and he answered. But before she had finished saying, 'Mr Bartos, I wanted to talk to you about your daughter', he had put the phone down.

Carole and Jude had agreed to meet for lunch in the Crown and Anchor that Thursday. They both ordered Ted Crisp's recommendation of Local Pork and Leek Sausages with Mash and Onion Gravy and, while they waited for them to appear, sipped their Chilean Chardonnays and brought each other up to date on their investigations.

What Jude had found out from Wally Grenston seemed pathetically little in the retelling. 'Couldn't be more contrast between the two families,' Carole observed when her friend had finished. 'Joe Bartos is very closed in, just him and his daughter . . . though now of course just him . . . and it doesn't sound as though Kyra had many friends . . . whereas the Lockes seem to do everything as a pack.'

'Did you find out how many children there were there?'

'The way they talked there seemed to be hundreds. Nathan's certainly got at least one brother, and Dorcas has an identical twin sister. Mind you, it's doubly confusing because they've all got nicknames. And they have that quality close families often have, of assuming that everyone knows all about them, so it wasn't easy to work out who was who.'

'Did you discover whether the Lockes had actually met Kyra Bartos?'

'Eithne had, but only by accident. And, given how his parents kept going on about how liberal they are, and how they wouldn't mind him having a girlfriend in his room . . . well, that might suggest the boy deliberately kept them apart.'

'He wouldn't have been the first young man to have done that,' Jude mused. 'A new relationship being seen as a new beginning . . . particularly if it represented getting away from a family where he wasn't happy.'

'The Lockes would have denied stoutly that Nathan wasn't happy. They seemed to have this . . . I'm not quite sure how to explain it . . . pride, I suppose. Pride in themselves as a family unit . . . as if being a Locke was the highest achievement anyone could hope for. And they were at pains to give the impression Nathan subscribed to that view too.'

'And yet from something you've said, Carole . . . or something someone's said . . . I get the feeling Nathan felt differently . . . that he found all that family stuff a bit claustrophobic . . . suffocating even.'

'It's funny. I get that impression very strongly as well.'

They were interrupted by the arrival of their Local Pork and Leek Sausages with Mash and Onion Gravy, which were delicious. Ted Crisp's recommendations always were. Carole looked across to the bar where he stood, a bearded scruff in a colourless T-shirt, regaling late holidaymakers with more of his dreadful jokes. She still felt shock at the knowledge that they had for a time been lovers. But it was not a wholly unpleasant feeling.

The Local Pork and Leek Sausages kept them quiet for some time, and it was only when they were mopping up the last of the Mash and Onion Gravy that Jude returned to the subject of Nathan Locke. 'And you say they didn't seem at all worried about where he was? Or that he might have committed suicide?'

'No, that was really the strangest thing about the whole morning.'

'Well, it would suggest one of two things.'

'Which are?'

'Either they have no imagination at all . . .'

'Unlikely. I got the impression that all of the Lockes lived quite vividly in their imaginations.'

'Then it must mean that they've heard from Nathan since he disappeared. They know where he is.'

Her neighbour wouldn't have done what Jude did that afternoon on her way home from the Crown and Anchor, but Carole had had to hurry back to take

Gulliver out for a walk, so Jude was alone when she found herself passing Connie's Clip Joint. And since she could see through the window that there were no clients, she dropped in to talk to the owner.

Connie was sitting at the small desk, going through a pile of correspondence, but she seemed to welcome the distraction.

'I came in about that massage idea you talked about the other day,' said Jude, offering her hastily prepared cover story.

'Oh yes. Nice to see you.'

'Not stopping you from doing something you should be . . . ?'

'No, just going through some application letters. Like I said, I must appoint another junior soon, but somehow it seems, I don't know, with Kyra only just . . .' Connie shook herself and stood up. 'Would you like a coffee?'

'Lovely, if you're sure it's no—'

'I was just about to have one.' And Connie crossed to the machine in the back room, leaving the door open so that they could continue their conversation.

'You given Theo the afternoon off?'

'He's given himself the afternoon off. He's not an employee.'

'Oh?'

'No, he just works out of here as a freelance. Rents a chair from me. He hasn't got any appointments this afternoon, so he's off home.'

'Ah.' Theo's independent status was perhaps

another indication that business at Connie's Clip Joint was not exactly booming.

Jude wondered whether she should begin by saying something more about her therapies, but since the girl's name had just been mentioned, there did seem to be a natural cue . . . 'Must be strange for you, Connie, being here without Kyra . . .'

'It is. And sort of stranger as time goes on. You know, at the beginning there was the shock, and then I was busy with the police and everyone was talking about it, but now, as things have settled down . . . well, I'm more aware she's not here.'

'How long had she been working with you?'

'Oh, only about four months. And we hadn't always seen eye to eye. I'd had to put her right about a few things. Youngsters starting out at work have often got attitude problems, but Kyra wasn't a bad kid . . . She certainly didn't deserve what happened to her.'

'I don't think anyone would have deserved that.'

'No.' Connie was silent for a moment, then brought her mind back to the coffee. 'Milk or sugar?'

'Just black, please.'

'You know, I think my insides must be totally coffee-coloured,' the hairdresser said as she brought the cups across. 'I hate to think how many cups I get through in a day. Live on the stuff.'

'Do you have lunch?'

'No. If I'm busy, there's no time. And if I'm not busy . . . well, I forget about it.' Connie sat cosily beside Jude in one of the leather armchairs for waiting clients.

'Was here Kyra's first job?'

'No, it wasn't actually.' The hairdresser's face clouded. 'She'd started at a salon in Worthing. A Martin & Martina.'

'Ah.' Jude was fully aware of the subtext of those words.

'But it only lasted a few weeks.'

'Why?'

'She hadn't got on with the management.' Jude stayed silent, hoping she was going to get more. And she did. 'Well, not the management of the salon, the management of the chain.'

'Are you talking about your ex-husband and his new wife?'

'Yes.'

'You don't think he's got anything to do with her death, do you?'

'What?' Connie looked totally incredulous. 'Martin? But why on earth . . . ?'

'Don't know.'

'Look, he may have done me wrong, but there's no evil in him. He's basically a good man.'

'Are you defending him now?'

'No, no, I—'

'You sound a bit as if you are. Do you still see each other?'

'Only when we can't possibly avoid it,' Connie replied fervently. She looked confused for a moment. Then she seemed to reach some decision and said, 'Martin never comes over this way. The Worthing branch is his base, really. That's where he has his office.' Her bright brown eyes were thoughtful for a moment, assessing how much she should confide. Fortunately, Jude's presence worked its usual magic and Connie decided she could tell everything she wanted to. Her words came out like a prepared speech. 'The fact is, Martin has never behaved very responsibly with the junior staff. I don't think he ever did, even when we were working together. Shows how naive I was, didn't even notice how he was chatting up the girls – and touching them up too. He seemed to think, because he was their boss, it gave him some sort of right to . . . I don't know . . .'

'*Droit de seigneur* . . .' Jude suggested.

'I've never heard of that, but if it means a boss thinking he's got a God-given right to come on to any of his female staff . . .'

'That's exactly what it means.'

'Well, I must remember the expression.' Suddenly Connie felt the need to defend herself. 'Look, I'm not just saying this to badmouth Martin. It is true.'

'I believe you.'

'Well, good, 'cause I know women talking about their ex-husbands aren't always the most reliable witnesses . . . And when I first suspected what he was doing, I thought I must have got it wrong, must be making things up in my mind, but the more it went on . . . and on more than one occasion the girls would complain to me, you know, when Martin wasn't there . . .'

'You mean he used to do it when you were working together in this salon?'

'Oh yes. As I say, at first I didn't believe it, made

excuses for him. Amazing what you'll do when you're in love, isn't it?'

'Yes,' Jude agreed. She'd done some pretty stupid things in her time too. 'But I thought when you two split up, Martin remarried . . . ?'

'To Martina, yes.'

'Well, do you think she'd put up with him coming on to the staff?'

'Martina . . . how can I put this . . . ?' Connie's mouth screwed up with the effort of finding the right words. 'Martina is a businesswoman. The success of the Martin & Martina chain is all down to her. Martin's got a lot of surface charm, he's good front-of-house, but he's got no commercial sense. All that comes from Martina. I think when she took him on, from her point of view, it was purely as a business venture. I don't think there was much love involved there.'

Jude grinned knowingly. 'Now what was it you said . . . ? "Women talking about their ex-husbands aren't always the most reliable witnesses"?'

'Yes, all right. I'm probably not being fair. I certainly don't want to be bloody fair to either of them. Maybe there was some wonderful magical moment of connection between the two of them . . . one day their eyes met across a crowded salon, and in an instant Martin and Martina knew it was the real thing, they were *in lurve* . . . Maybe that's what happened. As you say, I'm probably not the best person to comment on that. From the way it seemed to me, Martina looked at Martin and saw a first-class ticket to a very nice lifestyle, thank you very much. From then on she devoted herself single-mindedly to getting hold of that ticket.'

'And succeeded.'

'Yes.' Connie sighed. Though some years had passed since then, the defeat and humiliation were still with her. She took a savage sip of her coffee.

'And what about Martin coming on to the juniors in all the salons? Are you saying that Martina doesn't know about that?'

'She can't not know about it. She's not as young and naive as I was. She's a tough, hard-bitten foreigner.'

'Oh. Where from?'

'I don't know. Hungary? One of those places like that. Martina's just a gold-digger.'

'But a hard-working gold-digger.'

'Oh yes. Even I – who have great difficulty saying anything nice about the bloody woman – cannot deny that she's a hard worker.'

'So, going back to her husband groping the staff—'

'How charmingly you put it, Jude.'

'You say she must know it goes on . . . ?'

'Must.'

'. . . but is prepared to turn a blind eye?'

'I guess so.'

'I'm surprised.'

'Why?'

'Well, because it's quite a risky thing for a man to do these days. There's so much more legislation about sexual harassment and stuff. And young girls know all about it. Martin could be putting himself at risk of a court case if he goes on behaving like that.'

'Yes.' Connie's agreement contained a degree of satisfaction.

'What? Are you saying someone has registered a complaint about him?'

'Well, yes and no.'

'Sorry?'

'Look, when Kyra approached me about getting a job here . . .'

'Yes?'

'She was very upset. She'd just been unceremoniously asked to leave the Worthing Martin & Martina.'

'Because she'd objected to Martin coming on to her?'

'Basically, yes. He'd denied it obviously, and found some other reason to have her sacked. That was always his strength, you see – will always be the strength of men with power who behave like that. "You tell anyone about what I did to you and you'll lose your job." And who's going to believe the word of a teenager against the boss's? It usually worked for Martin, anyway.'

'And was it just chatting them up, giving them the odd grope . . . or was he trying to get them to go to bed with him?'

'No. It was just the groping.' Disgust twisted Connie's face. Jude couldn't lose the feeling that the hairdresser was somehow play acting . . . or maybe just enjoying her dramatic revelations. 'I think I'd almost feel better about it if it was full sex he was after. Somehow that makes it more acceptable, just good old-fashioned lust. But no, he just liked touching them. And he even used that as a defence when I finally realized what was happening and challenged him about it. "What's your problem," he said. "I'm not being unfaithful to you. I don't go to bed with any of them." As if that somehow justified his behaviour. Yeugh, from my point of view, it seemed to make it worse.'

'Perhaps that argument works for Martina?'

'Maybe it does. I think she just closes her mind to it, concentrates on the business and the lavish lifestyle it's brought her.' Connie could not keep the naked envy out of her voice.

For a moment there was silence. Then Jude pressed on. 'You said someone was going to register a complaint about him. Are you talking about Kyra?'

'Yes. When she came to see me, she was so upset about what had happened—'

'Was that why you took her on?'

'One of the reasons, yes. And also because I thought that shouldn't be allowed to happen to a kid her age. I thought she was in a perfect position to make a complaint against Martin.'

'On the grounds of sexual harassment?'

'Yes.'

'And did Martin know that this was about to happen?'

'Oh yes.' There was no disguising the satisfaction in Connie's reply.

When she'd heard Kyra's story, she'd seen the perfect way of getting some kind of revenge on the man who'd humiliated her.

But that wasn't the dominant thought in Jude's mind. She now knew of another person for whom Kyra Bartos's continuing existence had represented a considerable threat.

Chapter Nine

Carole had just got back with Gulliver from their walk and was towelling the sand off his paws, when Jude dropped by to share what she'd heard at the salon.

At the end, Carole asked, 'Do you think Connie's likely to have told the police about the threat to Martin . . . you know, over the sexual harassment charge?'

'I didn't actually ask, but she must have done, mustn't she?'

'Yes, from what you say about their relationship, she would have volunteered it at the first opportunity. Putting the police on to him as a murder suspect might be a very good form of revenge on an ex-husband.'

'Maybe.'

'Still, even if Connie didn't tell them, the police might have got the information from another source. You don't know whether Kyra had got as far as consulting a solicitor about what happened?'

Jude shook her head, and Carole sighed with exasperation. 'It is frustrating, isn't it, not having a clue what's happening in the official investigation?'

'Not an unusual position for us, though, Carole.'

'You're right. Do we have any means of contacting Martin Rutherford?'

'Well, Connie said the Worthing branch is his head-quarters.' Jude ran her fingers through the knot of her recently trimmed tresses. 'But I guess there's a limit to the number of times one can book in for a haircut. And, also, I doubt whether Martin himself does much of the actual cutting these days. Mind you, it might be worth trying. Get a bit of background . . .'

'Maybe.' Carole wasn't really listening any more; she was tense and restless. 'I do wish there was some-thing else we could do. Somewhere else where we could get more relevant information.'

'Apart from Martin Rutherford, the other person we really need to talk to is Joe Bartos.'

'Who, from what you say, clearly doesn't want to talk to anyone.'

'No.' Jude tapped her teeth thoughtfully. 'I wonder if we can approach him through some different route. I might have another word with Wally Grenston. And maybe you can follow up with the Lockes.'

'How?'

'Come on, Carole. I thought Rowley Locke asked you to keep him up to date with any new informa-tion you got on the case . . .'

'Yes.'

'Well, would you say that Kyra Bartos's threat to bring a charge of sexual harassment against Martin Rutherford constituted new information?'

'Yes. Yes, I suppose I would.'

*

93

The Lockes liked working on their home ground. In some families that might have been from a sense of insecurity, but in their case it was the opposite impulse, a desire to impress visitors with their united-front solidity. That was the impression Carole got as Dorcas Locke led her into her parents' house in Chichester on the Saturday morning. The day before Rowley had said on the phone that meeting at their house would be simplest, 'if you're likely to be in the Chichester area'. Carole had immediately remembered the half-truth that she needed to buy some dog food in bulk for Gulliver, and replied that by chance she did have some shopping to do in the city's Sainsbury's the following morning. Though making no claims to aura-detecting antennae like Jude's, Carole still recognized the value of the information that an environment could impart.

The Lockes' lack of insecurity was emphasized by the fact that Rowley and his wife were not at home when Carole arrived at the agreed hour of eleven-thirty on the Saturday morning. The house was a substantial one – probably five bedrooms – out in Summersdale, beyond the Festival Theatre to the north of the city. It was one of the most sought-after suburbs of Chichester, with house prices to match, so there was money some-where in the Locke family. Or at least there had been money at one time. The weeds poking up through the gravel of the drive, the blistered paint on the fascia boards and sagging window frames suggested that no routine maintenance had been done for some years. Or

maybe the priorities of an artistic family like the
Lockes lay elsewhere.

'Mummy and Daddy won't be long,' said Dorcas.
She was dressed in a long skirt and top of pale coral
cotton, which again emphasized the red-gold of her
outward-spiralling hair. Although she recognized Carole,
her manner was distant, her patent lack of interest just
the right side of bad manners. 'Come through.'

The room into which Carole was led was larger and
less cluttered than Arnold and Eithne Lockes', but its
bookshelves, piano and artlessly abandoned guitar put
across the same message: 'You are in the home of cultured people.' Like the exterior of the house, the decor
could have done with a bit of attention, and the sofa
and armchairs were worn and frayed. Here too the
walls were adorned with photographs of the massed
Locke family, siblings and cousins mixed together in a
variety of settings. Fancy dress featured a lot, and there
was more *Swallows and Amazons*-style posturing in
boats. Again the background scenery looked Cornish.
Mementos of more family holidays at Treboddick.

By a low table on the floor sat two girls, probably
about fourteen and twelve. They had the same hair as
Dorcas and their clothes, in pale tones of respectively
raspberry and blue-grey, made them look as though
they had been cloned from her. Had they not been so
thin, the three diminishing sizes of sisters could have
emerged from the same Russian doll.

The younger girls hardly looked up at the visitor's
arrival. They were engrossed with some game laid out on
the table. But it was not a commercially manufactured

game. The map, which acted as a board, was hand-drawn and painted in coloured inks. The manikins were two-dimensional, cardboard cut-outs on cardboard stands: knights, heraldic beasts, dwarves and goblins. Open exercise books beside the map were covered with densely handwritten text, which swirled around embedded hand-drawn illustrations.

But everything was worn and faded. The map was criss-crossed with parallel lines from much folding. The paint on the figures was smudged and dull, and it was impossible to tell the original colour of the now-beige exercise book covers. On the map the words 'Kingdom of Verendia' and 'Forest of Black Fangdar' could be read. Oh no, thought Carole, we're not into Tolkien country, are we? (Such things did not appeal to her. She was of the view that coping with a single universe was quite enough of a challenge, without creating any parallel ones.)

Indicating an armchair for Carole, Dorcas had made no attempt to introduce her sisters, but instead joined them on the floor and continued with the game, as if there was no one else in the room. When they spoke, the younger girls had a lisp just like hers. Carole wondered idly whether it was caused by a genetic physical abnormality, or had been learned. Maybe the as-yet-unmet Bridget Locke would turn out to have the mother of all lisps, which had been passed down to her daughters . . . ?

Though incomprehensible to an outsider, the rules of the game the girls were playing made sense to them and there was a high level of excitement in their playing. For a few minutes Carole tried to follow what was happening, but soon gave up. After a time she almost got used to cries from the floor of 'I challenge thee to the Ordeal of Furminal, vile Tritchbacker', 'Your Eagrant magic has not power in the Vales of Aspinglad' or 'Let not the valiant offspring of Leomon cross swords with one of the blood of Merkerin.'

She was just sneaking a look at her watch to discover that the Locke parents were nearly a quarter of an hour late, when Dorcas clapped her hands and said, 'One last sortie, girls. Then you must do your music practice.'

Though deeply engrossed in the game, her sisters did not complain. They each had a 'sortie', which so far as Carole could tell was like a roll of the dice in any other game. But there was nothing looking like a dice in evidence and she had no idea what force dictated where on the map one of the figures should move next. When their 'sortie' was finished, both girls obediently rose to their feet. 'Will you leave it out, so's we can have another Grail-search tonight?' asked the younger one.

'No, sorry, Tarnil. Daddy says it must always be put away, so that each Grail-search starts anew.'

'Tarnil!' thought Carole. It must be another of those wretched nicknames, like Fimby and Diggo. But then again, parents who called their eldest daughter 'Dorcas' were quite capable of having another one actually christened 'Tarnil'.

The two smaller girls made no further argument, but left the room. Carole heard their footsteps clumping up the stairs and, later, the sounds of distant music wafting from their bedrooms. One appeared to be learning the oboe, the other the clarinet.

As she gathered up the pieces of the game and placed them, in long-remembered sequence, into an old flat biscuit tin, Dorcas felt no need to apologize for her parents' lateness – or indeed to say anything else.

Carole, inept as ever at making small talk, asked what the girls' names were.

'Their real names are Chloë and Sylvia, but they're called Zebba and Tarnil.'

The assertiveness of Dorcas's tone put Carole off asking the obvious question: Why? Instead she observed that the girls had been playing what looked like an interesting game. Dorcas did not think the comment worthy of response.

'Is it something you're going to develop commercially?'

'What?' The girl stopped packing the game away and for the first time looked directly at her visitor. The eyes, which Carole had previously noted as 'honey-coloured', were, close to, more complex than that, a very pale hazel flecked with black.

'Well,' Carole explained, 'you keep reading in the papers of people who've made huge fortunes from devising computer and—'

'This is not a computer game!' Dorcas snapped. 'It's a board game. Daddy wouldn't have a computer game in the house.'

'No, but hearing you playing it, it sounds very similar to a computer game.'

'It is nothing like a computer game!' The girl's pale face was now red with anger.

'All I'm saying is that that kind of game can be very lucrative. If it's a good idea you've got there, you could—'

'Nobody wants to make money out of the Wheel Quest.'

'But just think about it. You know, when all that fantasy stuff is being so successful . . . *Lord of the Rings*, *Narnia*, *Harry Potter*, there could be quite a demand for—'

Dorcas Locke was deeply affronted by the suggestion. 'We don't want to have other people playing it.'

Her indignation was so strong that she might have said a lot more, had she not heard the sound of a car scrunching to a halt on the weedy gravel outside. Carole turned to the window to see a beat-up Volvo estate, out of which Rowley Locke and his wife were emerging.

Bridget Locke was a good-looking woman, nearly as tall as her husband. Her hair was shoulder-length ash-blonde, with a well-cut fringe. The dark trouser suit gave her an aura of efficiency, separating her from the feyness of her daughters. Indeed, they didn't appear to have inherited any of her genetic make-up. She unloaded Waitrose carrier bags from the back of the estate, while her husband came straight through into the sitting room to greet Carole.

'Good of you to come,' he said, with no apology for his lateness. 'Has Dorcas offered you coffee?'

The girl gave her father a look which implied that was the last thing she'd have done.

'No, but it's fine. I don't want anything, thank you.'

Dorcas put the biscuit tin containing the Wheel Quest in its regular place on the shelf and announced, 'I'm going to read.'

'All right, Doone,' said her father. Oh God, another nickname, thought Carole.

Bridget Locke had by now come in through the front door and was presumably taking her shopping to the kitchen.

'How old is Dorcas?' asked Carole.

'She's twenty-one, just finished at uni.' It was a surprise to hear the abbreviation from a man of Rowley's age.

'Has she got a job lined up?'

He shook his head. 'No, she needs a bit of time to chill out. She's worked hard the last three years.'

'What was she studying?'

'English with drama.' That figures, thought Carole. 'At Reading.'

'So you just have the three girls?'

'No, there's a fourth. Doone – Dorcas – has a twin. Mopsa. She's, erm, working in Cornwall at the moment, arranging holiday lets.'

'Ah.' Mopsa! You wouldn't need a silly nickname if you were called that. Though in the Locke family, Carole would have put money on the fact that Mopsa had one. 'Is that near your own place?'

'Sorry?'

'When we met before, you said you had a family place in Cornwall, called Treboddick.'

'Well remembered, Carole.' His tone was patronizing, the omniscient teacher to the aspiring student. 'Yes, the cottages are in Treboddick. Mopsa's staying down there for the duration.'

'So you have four girls.'

'Yes,' said Rowley with pride. 'I do girls. Arnold and Eithne do boys.'

'How many have they got, apart from Nathan?' She thought it might be intrusive to call him 'Fimby'. And she couldn't have brought herself to do so, anyway.

'Just the one. His older brother Julian.'

Diggo, thought Carole. I'm getting the hang of this.

'Arnold never had my sticking power.' It was delivered as a joke, but Carole got the feeling that there was some truth behind it as well. Seeing the two brothers together, she had been left in no doubt that Rowley was the dominant one. And he, rather than the boy's father, was very definitely leading the family investigation into Nathan's disappearance.

Further revelations of sibling rivalry were prevented by the arrival of Bridget Locke from the kitchen. Carole was immediately impressed by how sensible she seemed, a beacon of sanity in the midst of her flaky family. Maybe, to allow the family to be as flaky as they appeared, someone had to be in touch with the real world.

'I'm sorry I wasn't able to meet you the other day in Fethering,' Bridget apologized. 'One of us has to work, I'm afraid.'

The words weren't spoken viciously, but there was no doubt they represented a dig at her husband. Carole wondered what Rowley Locke did for a living. Not a lot, was the answer implicit in his wife's remark.

'Don't worry. I did seem to meet quite a lot of the family.'

'That's always the case when you mix with the Lockes.' Rowley Locke spoke as if Carole were the recipient of a privilege, but his wife's 'Yes' again suggested less than full-bodied support for his view.

'Have you come here because you know something about Nathan's whereabouts?' Carole realized that this was the first time she had heard anxiety about the boy's fate from any member of the family. Bridget Locke was not the sort to give in to panic, but she was obviously deeply worried about Nathan.

'No, sadly, I don't know anything about that.'

'Don't worry about it, Bridget. The boy's just lying low for a while,' Rowley said.

'And where does a boy of sixteen lie low for more than a fortnight? What does he live on? Eithne says he hasn't drawn any money out of his account.'

Carole felt this gave her an opportunity to mention the unmentionable. 'The gossip around Fethering is that the boy might have committed suicide.'

'Well, that's nonsense!' said Rowley forcibly. 'Like all gossip it's totally unsubstantiated.' His wife was not so sure. 'Oh, come on, Bridget, you've known Nathan for ten years. He's not the kind to harm himself.'

'Not under normal circumstances, no. But who

knows how any of us would react to being the prime suspect in a murder investigation?'

'We'd do what Nathan has done. Go underground until it all blows over.'

'You make it sound so easy, Rowley. You can't just disappear in a country like this. And also the idea that a police investigation is just going to "blow over" is, I would say, at the very least naive.'

Carole did not get the impression that the Lockes normally argued like this. Maybe her presence in connection with Nathan's disappearance was the catalyst that enabled Bridget to unburden herself of what she was really feeling.

'And I wonder whether what Carole calls "Fethering gossip" may not have some truth in it. Particularly if . . .'

'Particularly if what?' asked her husband sharply.

Bridget Locke took a deep breath. She knew he wasn't going to like what she was about to say. 'Look, Nathan's at a difficult age and he was in the throes of his first big love affair. That's confusing enough for anyone. Particularly for someone who's never really engaged with the real world.'

'That's a very unfair description of him.'

'No, it's not. It's accurate. So there's Nathan, facing the conflicting pressures of love and lust and the girl's demands and his parents' disapproval and—'

'Now that's unfair, Bridget. Arnold and Eithne are the most tolerant parents in the world. They wouldn't mind Nathan bringing a girl home and going to bed with her. They didn't mind when Diggo had—'

'No, they wouldn't disapprove of Nathan having sex, but they would disapprove of the girl he was having sex with.'

'They never really met Kyra.'

'I'm not talking about Kyra. They'd disapprove of anyone who Nathan fancied. No girl would be good enough for the Lockes.'

'Now you're just being silly.'

'No, I'm . . .' But she didn't continue. It was an old argument, not worth reviving in the presence of a stranger. 'All I'm saying is that we should at least entertain the possibility that Nathan might have . . . harmed himself.' As her husband snorted disagreement, Bridget Locke chose her next words very carefully. 'Particularly if he was actually responsible for the girl's death.'

Rowley was appalled. 'You can't say that! You're talking about your nephew. You can't say he's a murderer.'

'Until it has been proved otherwise, you must at least acknowledge why the police see him as a major suspect.'

'No. The police have got it wrong,' he insisted, before appealing to Carole. 'Come on, you've got something new to tell us. You said on the phone there was someone else who had a motive to kill Kyra Bartos.'

Carole quickly recapped what Jude had heard from Connie Rutherford about her ex-husband. Rowley Locke seized on the information avidly. 'Well, there you are, you see! This Martin Rutherford, he wanted to stop Kyra Bartos shopping him about the sexual harassment. He must have killed her. It was nothing to do with Nathan.'

Bridget looked at Carole. 'Do the police know about this? Did Connie tell them?'

'I didn't actually ask her, but I think we can safely assume she did.'

'Hmm.'

'If we don't know for certain that they have been told, then we must see to it that they are,' Rowley announced.

'How?' asked his wife.

'I'll tell them.'

'I don't think that's a very good idea.'

'No,' Carole agreed. 'Going round scattering murder accusations at people can get you into serious trouble.'

'I'm not suggesting that I'll tell the police in person. I'll just see that they get the information.'

'What will it be, Rowley? An anonymous letter? A call from a phone box with you holding a handkerchief over the receiver?'

Rowley Locke didn't enjoy his wife sending him up like this. With a rather petulant cry of 'I've got to sort out some stuff,' he left the room, and Carole heard his footsteps stomping upstairs.

'I'm sorry.' Bridget Locke sighed. 'He can be very childish at times.'

'I'm sure you're all under a lot of stress at the moment.'

She nodded agreement, as Carole went on, 'You really think Nathan might have killed the girl?'

'Without further information, what else is there to think?'

'And that he might have killed himself too?'

Bridget Locke sighed. 'Again, there is a logic to the idea. He's certainly disappeared off the face of the earth. If he had somehow killed the girl, I hate to think of the kind of state he'd have been in.'

'But you think he'd be capable of killing himself?'

'Yes. I've got to know Nathan quite well. He has dark moods, and sixteen isn't the easiest age for a boy. He could have done it . . . done both perhaps, I mean. The murder and the suicide.' Carole had a mental image of the photograph she'd seen at his parents' house, of the brooding figure amongst all the extrovert children on the boat.

She nodded, then said, 'You're not Rowley's first wife, are you?'

'No. Sorry. Should have made that clear. His first wife, who was called Joan . . . went off with someone.'

'So the girls . . . ?'

'Are hers. All of them. Not that she's ever in touch. Rowley used to teach at a local girls' school. I met him when I got a job there.'

'But I gather he's no longer teaching . . . ?'

'No.' Bridget Locke chose her words with delicacy. 'Rowley's always had a problem with authority. He's one of those teachers who'd rather make a lasting impression on his students than guide them through the required curriculum.' Her mouth set in a rueful expression. 'Just coming up for our tenth wedding anniversary.' She looked pleadingly at Carole. 'I'm sorry, he doesn't often behave like he did this morning. There's much more to him than he sometimes shows to strangers.'

There would need to be, thought Carole.

'Do you think he will go to the police about what I told him? Because I'm not sure that that would be wise.'

'I'll see to it that he doesn't.' Bridget Locke spoke with assurance. Her husband might never encounter any opposition from the other members of the family, but when necessary his wife could stand up to him. 'The way he's behaving at the moment is because he's really worried about Nathan. It's his way of showing it. Quite exhausting though.' Bridget Locke wrinkled up her nose in wry amusement. 'Being part of the Locke Family Roadshow can sometimes be very wearing.'

Chapter Ten

Jude had been lucky to get an appointment at the Worthing Martin & Martina. When she rang the day before they'd just had a cancellation. Saturday was the busiest day of the week in any provincial hairdresser's, and Jude seemed to be in the town's most popular one. The decor was in marked contrast to that of Connie's Clip Joint. Everything looked gleaming new. There was a lot of black glass with trim in brushed aluminium. And the silver 'Martin & Martina' logo was omnipresent. Looking round the salon, Jude saw a scene of almost manic activity. With all the chairs full, twelve stylists were snipping away, while clients sat under dryers or sipped coffee in the waiting area. There was a buzz about the place, an air of deliberately orchestrated chaos.

Jude introduced herself to the woman at the reception desk and was told that her stylist Kelly-Jane was just finishing with another client and would be ready for her very soon. Would she like a cup of coffee? Jude accepted and took the only free seat in the waiting area, which was adjacent to the reception desk. The woman sent off a junior to get the coffee. She didn't do menial tasks like coffee-making. There was an air of authority about her, and the speed at which the junior moved showed that it didn't do to cross her.

The woman was so smartly dressed and made up that she looked as though she'd just been taken out of her packaging. A slate-grey business suit with a froth of white blouse at the neck. Light brown hair cut immaculately short (maybe similar to the style Connie had had in mind for Jude). Blue eyes above Slavic cheekbones, and full red lips. But the eyes were cold, and the line of the mouth was hard.

Jude flashed a grin at her, and was rewarded by a professional smile in return. 'I am Martina,' the woman said. Her English was immaculate, but still flavoured with an accent from somewhere in central Europe.

'Martina of Martin & Martina?'

'Yes, Martina Rutherford. My husband and I run the chain.'

'Congratulations. It seems to be doing very well.'

'Yes, we have put a lot of work into the business and I am glad to say it is now paying off. We are opening a new salon in Folkestone soon.'

'Moving all the way along the South Coast.'

'We hope in time to go north to some of the big towns nearer London.'

'And then throughout the whole country?'

She took the question at face value. 'Why not? Our standards are higher than most of the opposition. We are very successful.'

'It certainly looks that way.' Jude knew she must take advantage of the situation into which she had so serendipitously arrived. She had come hoping to find out more about Martin & Martina, and here she was being offered one half of the partnership on a plate. 'This is my first time in one of your salons,' she began cautiously.

'I know. I have not seen you before.'

'Do you remember all the clients in all the branches?'

'Pretty well. I move around a lot, but we have our main office here.'

'Previously I've had my hair done at Connie's Clip Joint in Fethering.'

'Ah.' Clearly Martina knew the name, but she responded without a flicker of any other intonation.

'Presumably you heard about the dreadful thing that happened there?'

'Of course.' The phone interrupted them. Martina answered with practised charm, booking someone in for highlights the following Wednesday. When she'd ended the call, she looked across at the row of stylists. 'Kelly-Jane has nearly finished. She will be able to look after you soon.'

'Thank you. So, the death at Connie's Clip Joint . . .'

'Yes.' Martina was too much of a professional to change the subject when a client was talking, but she seemed to have little interest in what had happened at the Fethering salon. No doubt, being so close, the event had already been the subject of a lot of gossip amongst her clients, and she was sick of it.

'I gather that the girl who died had worked here . . .'

'Yes. Very briefly.'

'Oh?' It was the lightest of interrogatives, but it asked for an explanation.

Martina shrugged. 'Not everyone is suited to this business. It takes a special kind of personality to be a hairdresser, a special attitude. A lot of young girls start without having really thought about what the job entails.'

'But in the case of Kyra Bartos—'

'Ah, here is Kelly-Jane.' A lanky girl in her late twenties, with jet black hair rising in little spikes over her head, came across with a welcoming smile. 'This is your client. Jude, is that right?'

'Yes.'

'Nice to see you, Jude. Come with me. We'll get your hair washed first.'

As she moved across to the chair, Jude was aware of the shrewd scrutiny of Martina's blue eyes following her. She wondered if there was anything sinister in the interest, or was it just another manifestation of the woman's control-freak personality?

Jude might have known there would be no problem having another haircut so soon. There is nothing stylists like better than running fingers disdainfully through someone's hair and asking, 'Who on earth did this?' And after she'd had her hair washed by a junior, that was exactly what Kelly-Jane did.

'Oh dear,' she said. 'Bit of a salvage job, is it? I can tell it's only been cut a couple of days ago. Normally I wouldn't mention how badly someone's hair's been cut,' the girl lied, 'but since you've come in here so quickly after, I'm not telling you anything you don't know already.' The stylist trailed despairing fingers through the blonde tresses. 'Dear, oh dear. Now do tell me where this was done.'

'No, I'm sorry, I can't.' Although she'd already mentioned the salon to Martina, Jude had too much loyalty to betray Connie to Kelly-Jane. Besides, she knew that there had been nothing wrong with the haircut she'd got in Fethering. But it was a point of honour amongst all stylists to disparage everything that had been done to a client before she had the good fortune to find them.

'Oh well.' Kelly-Jane didn't pursue the matter. She perhaps thought it better for the perpetrator of the previous haircut to remain anonymous. She didn't want to intrude on private grief. Lifting Jude's hair out to the sides and letting it drop, she said, 'So . . . what are we going to do with it? You know, you'd look smashing with it really short.'

Why is it everyone wants me to have short hair? Jude wondered. Could it be that stylists, like everyone else, like to see a positive effect for their efforts? Yes, there must be some kind of satisfaction in making a total transformation, completely changing the appearance of your client. But Jude, having rejected the 'short' option with Connie, wasn't about to grant the honour to Kelly-Jane. Besides, she thought mischievously, since having my hair cut seems to be my main means of investigation in this case, I'd better proceed slowly, an inch at a time.

'No, thanks,' she said easily. 'I'd just like it tidied up, you know, maybe about an inch shorter all round.'

Kelly-Jane gave a token sigh – she was clearly used

to clients not knowing what was best for them – but didn't press the point. Instead, she started combing Jude's hair preparatory to the cutting. 'Haven't seen you here before. Your first time at a Martin & Martina?'

'Yes.'

'Oh well, now you've found us, you'll never change. It sounds like boasting, but it's not boasting if something's true. Martin & Martinas are by a long way the best salons on the South Coast. You'll never want to go anywhere else.'

Jude wasn't convinced. Guilty for the badmouthing Connie's skills had just received, she felt defensive. A new sense of loyalty developed within her. In future she'd regard Connie's Clip Joint as her regular hairdresser's.

'It's all down to the training, you see. All the staff at Martin & Martina salons are intensively trained. Martin – he's the boss – is very hands-on.'

So I've heard, thought Jude wryly. But now his name had come up, she wasn't going to waste the cue. 'So he's a good person to work for?'

'Oh yes. None of the staff ever want to leave, and if that's not the measure of a good boss, I'd like to know what is.'

Kyra Bartos had wanted to leave. For a moment Jude wondered whether Connie's account of the circumstances of that departure had been entirely accurate, or had it been embroidered by the venom of a spurned wife?

'And do you actually see a lot of Martin?'

'Oh yes. As I said, he's very hands-on. Goes round

all the branches, but his office is here, so we probably get to see more of him than the others.'

'Is he in today?'

'Always here on a Saturday, yes. I'm surprised he hasn't put in an appearance yet.'

Good, thought Jude. And I've already met Martina. So my investment in a second haircut won't be completely wasted. At the very least I should get to know what Martin Rutherford looks like.

She pretended ignorance for her next question. 'And are he and Martina actually married? Or are they just partners whose names give a nice unisex feeling to the salons?'

'Oh no, they're married. Very much so. I don't think Martin ever does anything Martina doesn't know about.' The warmth with which Kelly-Jane had spoken of Martin Rutherford did not extend to his second wife.

Given that kind of monitoring, thought Jude, Martin must be very discreet in his approaches to the salon's juniors. Maybe Connie had overdone her description of his behaviour, making out her husband was worse than he actually was. Now she thought about it, there had been something false and prepared about what she'd said.

'Yes, I was just talking to Martina.' What she said next didn't reflect her true feelings, but she thought it might prompt some more confidences. 'She seems very nice.'

Kelly-Jane, however, was not about to be drawn into indiscretion. She just said, 'Oh yes. Mind you, I'm surprised she's here today.'

'Why?'

'Last weekend of the month she usually flies over to Prague. Her mother's out there and not very well. Oh well, maybe she's not going this weekend, or catching a later flight or something.'

'Does Martina actually cut hair?'

'No. Used to be a stylist, but doesn't do any now.'

'And what about Martin? Does he still do any hairdressing?'

'For a few favoured clients. He'll do a bride's hair for her wedding, something like that. Not very often, though. He's too busy schmoozing.'

Jude took another look at Martina Rutherford. She was very beautiful, but her strength of will was written in every feature. Connie's good-natured fluffiness would not have stood a chance against the force of that personality. And, though she hadn't met Martin Rutherford yet, what Kelly-Jane had hinted at reinforced the feeling that he too would crumble to his wife's every wish.

Nothing was said for a few moments while the haircut began. Then suddenly Kelly-Jane asked, 'Do you want to know a way of making money?'

'What?' Jude was wary; she had expectations of being lured into some pyramid selling operation.

'It's to do with hairdressing.'

'I haven't got any skills as a hairdresser.'

'You don't need any.' Kelly-Jane stopped cutting and put her hands behind her back. 'All you have to do is bet people that they can't tell you which fingers hairdressers use to hold their scissors.'

'Well, it's obvious, isn't it?' Jude looked down at her right hand and found that she was instinctively miming cutting with the two fingers next to the thumb. But that couldn't be right. Fine for a visual shorthand, but you couldn't get enough grip and you couldn't move the scissors like that. 'No, not those.'

'Right, not those,' said Kelly-Jane, biding her time with the confidence of someone who had played the game many times before.

'So let me think . . . Oh, this is daft. Goodness knows how many times in my life I've had my hair cut . . . Do all hairdressers use the same fingers?'

'All,' the girl assured her. 'All over the world.'

'Right, let's be logical here. I think the thumb must be involved . . . Yes, because that would give you a bit of leverage . . .' Jude was fishing for some kind of clue, but the stylist's face in the mirror remained impassive. 'OK, there aren't many options. It can't be the little finger, because that's not strong enough . . .' She looked down at her hands in frustration. 'It must be . . . It must be . . .' She made her decision. Pressing the top of her middle finger against her thumb, she announced, 'It must be those two.'

With gleeful triumph, Kelly-Jane brought her hands round from behind her back. 'Wrong!' She raised her right hand, and showed Jude the unexpected combination of digits that hairdressers have always used for the purpose of holding their scissors.

'Gosh, you're right,' said Jude. 'Yes, I think you could win a few bets that way.' Something to tell Ted Crisp. Another way for him to amuse his customers at the Crown and Anchor. And certainly better than his jokes.

Kelly-Jane grinned as she resumed cutting. She'd done the little party trick she tried out on all her new clients. And once again it had worked. Back to more conventional chat. 'Do you live in Worthing?'

Jude had hardly got out a 'Fethering' before they were interrupted by a whirlwind of bonhomie. 'Good morning, and how are you, Kelly-Jane? Looking lovely, as ever. And a new client – how exciting! What a pleasure to see you in Martin & Martina. I am one half of the salon's name – Martin. And you . . . ?'

'I'm called Jude.'

The first impression was of an attractive man in his early forties, though closer inspection revealed him to be a well-preserved man in his early fifties. Perhaps as much as ten years older than Connie. Jude wondered how they had met. In some salon where she'd been another junior he'd come on to . . . ? He was of average height, and kept himself in shape. He wore a charcoal linen suit over a slate grey shirt, and the blackness of his short hair looked as if it might have been assisted. His teeth too were unnaturally white and even; some expensive veneer work had been done there. But his brown eyes were shrewd.

'And where are you from, Jude?'

'Fethering.'

'Oh, so close. So why haven't you been into a Martin & Martina salon before, you naughty girl?'

She'd actually got him there. She wouldn't get a better chance of raising the subject of Kyra Bartos's murder. So Jude finessed the truth and said, 'I normally have my hair done at Connie's Clip Joint.'

'Ah.' He had been taken by surprise, but was far too cool an operator to let it show. 'And how is dear Connie?'

'Pretty good.' Jude couldn't see any other way of proceeding than the crassly direct. 'I gather she's your ex-wife.'

'Yes. Pity it didn't work out. Lovely girl. But, you know, we were young and . . .'

She may have been young, you weren't that young, Jude thought. 'Have you managed to stay friends?'

'I'm sure we'd be perfectly pleasant to each other if we ever met, but we haven't seen each other for ages.' He was keen to move on. 'So, anyway, Kelly-Jane, what are you going to do to Jude's hair to make sure she never strays from the path of Martin & Martina again?'

'Well, I—'

Jude interrupted. It wasn't her usual style, but they were meeting her for the first time and weren't to know that she wasn't by nature a woman of galumphing tact-lessness. 'Of course, you heard about the dreadful thing that happened at Connie's Clip Joint? You know, that girl who was strangled?'

'Yes, of course. It was all over the television news. You couldn't miss it. Apart from the fact that none of the clients in the salon talked about anything else. Horrible for poor Connie. I was going to ring her to offer my sympathy, but, you know, there never seems to be any time for—'

Having taken on the persona of a diplomatic

rhinoceros, Jude stuck with it. 'Connie said that Kyra Bartos used to work for you . . .'

'Yes, yes. She was in this salon briefly.' But he didn't want to be drawn on the subject. 'I really must be checking other clients and—'

Finding new extremes of crassness, Jude announced, 'Connie mentioned that there was something funny about Kyra's dismissal from here . . . that the girl had been consulting a solicitor about the rights and wrongs of it.'

This time there was no mistaking the shock in Martin Rutherford's face, even though he managed quickly to cover it up. 'Well, it's been such a pleasure talking to you, Jude. Welcome once again to Martin & Martina. Now excuse me . . .' And he swanned over to another client. 'Darling, you're looking just too fabulous. Is it for a special occasion or just your natural beauty shining through . . . ?'

Jude was afraid that Kelly-Jane might have thought her conversation with Martin odd, but she needn't have worried. The stylist had gleaned one piece of information though, and that was all she wanted.

'So it was Connie who did your previous haircut, was it?'

Jude felt terribly disloyal.

'I don't know why I behaved like that. It's not my usual style.'

'But did it work?'

'Not really. I didn't get any information out of him.

I've probably just forfeited his goodwill and made him very suspicious of me. If any further investigative approaches need to be made to Martin Rutherford, I think you'd better take them on, Carole.'

'Right.' She fingered the steel-grey helmet of her hair. 'I can't really pretend this needs doing again.'

'No, and I think we must find a different sleuthing modus operandi. Having constant haircuts is very expensive, apart from anything else. Martin & Martina was nearly double the price of Connie's Clip Joint.'

'Hmm.' There was a silence. Both sipped their Chilean Chardonnays. They'd agreed to meet in the Crown and Anchor when they returned from their respective Saturday morning expeditions. Just for a drink, they'd said, but Ted Crisp's recommendation of the Cheesy-Topped Fisherman's Pie had proved too tempting.

Carole idly flicked through the Martin & Martina promotional brochure that Jude had brought back from the salon. Expensively produced, it featured news from the branches, ideas for hairstyles, a photograph of the Stylist of the Month, and so on. The publication gloried in the company's achievements. Again Carole was aware of the contrast with the small-scale operation that was Connie's Clip Joint. At the back of the brochure, portraits of the owners framed a message of welcome to their customers. A good-looking couple, glowing in their shared success.

'I think I behaved as I did,' Jude said thoughtfully, 'because I feel we're getting nowhere on this case. We're surrounded by blind alleys. We can't get anywhere on the Locke side of the case until Nathan is found. Getting in touch with Joe Bartos seems to be impossible.'

'Did you talk to Wally Grenston again?'

'I did – gave him a call to thank him for my coffee. He didn't have any ideas. I think he got rather protective of his friend Joe. The old man's mourning the death of his daughter. Wally implied that if he doesn't want to speak to us, that's his right, and his wishes should be respected.'

'Which is of course true.'

'Yes. So I suppose I just wanted to shake things up. I thought maybe being rude to Martin Rutherford, possibly even frightening him with reference to Kyra's proposed legal action might . . . I don't know . . . make something happen.'

'Rather a risky strategy,' said Carole primly.

'Yes.' Jude looked contrite and uncharacteristically down.

Then their attention was drawn by a raucous shout from the bar. 'You owe me a fiver!' roared Ted Crisp. Jude giggled.

'What is it?'

'Before you arrived, I was talking to Ted. I told him this way of making money by betting which fingers hairdressers use to hold their scissors.'

'Really?' Carole looked down at her hand and moved the digits around. 'So which fingers are they?'

'Ah,' said Jude. 'That'd be telling.'

Chapter Eleven

There were a lot of dog owners in Fethering, but Carole Seddon prided herself on usually being on the beach with Gulliver before any of them. Waking early was a habit dinned into her all her life, to be ready for her daily train journey to school, and then her commute to the Home Office. During the relatively brief period she took off work after Stephen's birth, the baby's imperatives had also ensured early rising and, though in retirement the demands on her time were less, the habit was engrained. For Carole, rising late would have been an unacceptable indulgence, on a par with watching breakfast television. And getting up early on a Sunday, when most of the world was having a lie-in, gave her an even greater sense of being on the moral high ground.

Besides, Carole liked to be active as soon as she woke up. Lying in bed, being immobile even for a moment, was dangerous. It was at such moments that she could be ambushed by unwelcome thoughts. Her mind was a pressure cooker, whose lid needed to be firmly tightened down.

Gulliver didn't care when she got him up, so long as

there was a walk involved. He still became puppyishly exuberant at the prospect of being taken out, particularly to Fethering Beach, where the melange of sharp smells and the range of flotsam and jetsam represented a canine nirvana.

That Sunday dog and owner were on the beach before six o'clock. The early morning air was a cold breath of impending winter. It was hardly light when she had left High Tor and, as September gave way to October, she knew she would have to start her walks later, unless she wanted to set off in total darkness. There'd be a brief respite when Summer Time ended, and then winter would once again inexorably put its squeeze on the early mornings.

End of October the clocks changed. Carole always remembered details like that. In retirement she needed more than ever to have her year delineated, to have fixed points in the potentially unstructured void of her life. And also by the end of October, she remembered suddenly, Stephen and Gaby's baby will probably have arrived. I will be a grandmother. The thought filled her with an uneasy mixture of excitement and apprehension.

Gulliver had the personality of all Labradors, which meant that at times he could be exceptionally soppy. But on Fethering Beach he became a hero. Beleaguered on all sides by potential attacks from waves, stones, swathes of bladderwrack, ends of rope, water-smoothed spars and broken plastic bottles, he triumphed over them all, scampering off in sudden sallies, only to return breathless to his mistress's side with the gleam of victory in his eye. King Arthur never had a more gallant knight errant than Gulliver on Fethering Beach.

Carole didn't always take him on the same route. Like all creatures of habit, she hated to be thought of as a creature of habit. Where the road met the beach, she would sometimes turn left towards the Yacht Club and the mouth of the Fether; other times she would go right, where the dunes stretched as far as the eye could see. Coming back, too, there were alternative routes possible. They could either take the High Street directly to High Tor, or they could walk along the bank of the river and cut back along one of the little roads parallel to the sea. Or then again, if she felt like it, having curtailed Gulliver's freedom by putting his lead back on, Carole could take him along the little service road which ran behind the High Street shops.

For no very good reason, this was the route she chose that morning. Though busy with deliveries during the week, the road was virtually unused at weekends because there were no houses there. On one side was an area of scrubland, its surface a mixture of sand and earth, from which the local residents discouraged summer picnickers. And on the other were the backyards of the shops: some double-gated parking bays for major delivery vehicles, others like the ends of gardens, wooden-fenced with small doors. The back of Connie's Clip Joint was of the second kind, and as Carole led Gulliver along the road that Sunday morning, she saw a man come through the door and hurry to a gleaming new Mini. Something about his movement was furtive. Just before he got into the driver's seat, he gave a quick look around, and Carole recognized a face whose photograph she'd seen only the day before.

It was Martin Rutherford.

Chapter Twelve

'Well, what does that suggest? Why was he there, do you think?'

Jude pinched her upper lip between thumb and forefinger for a moment, then said, 'It suggests he's still got keys to the place.'

'Connie's Clip Joint?'

'Yes.'

'But Connie said the only spare keys were the ones she gave to Kyra.'

Jude shrugged. 'Maybe Martin copied a set before he handed them back to her . . . ? Maybe he handed over the keys to the front, but hung on to the one for the back door . . . ?'

'So what would he have been doing there this morning?'

'I don't know, but, given the state of armed conflict between Connie and him, I can't think he was paying a social visit.' A thoughtful smile came over Jude's features. 'Maybe my clumsy approach had some effect . . .'

'How do you mean?'

'Remember I mentioned to him that Kyra had been planning legal action about her dismissal from Martin

& Martina in Worthing. Maybe he was checking out Connie's Clip Joint to see if any incriminating evidence had been left there?'

'Pretty unlikely that there would have been. And if there were, you'd have thought the police would have found it, and then surely they'd have been on to Martin pretty sharpish to find out what had been going on . . . The police must've spoken to him since the murder, mustn't they?'

'Yes. Connie said they did . . . you know when I went to have my haircut before last. She said the police questioned her and Martin quite extensively for the first couple of days, and then seemed to lose interest in them . . . well, in her, anyway.'

'Right.' Carole sipped at her coffee. It was nearly cold. They'd been chatting too much since she arrived at Woodside Cottage. She'd taken Gulliver back to High Tor after his walk and then gone straight next door. It was early, but the news she had to impart couldn't wait. 'Of course,' she went on, 'if Martin Rutherford does have keys to Connie's Clip Joint . . .'

'Yes?'

'. . . then he could have got in there the night Kyra Bartos died, couldn't he?'

'He could.'

'Because there was no sign of forced entry, was there? So far we've been assuming that's because Kyra invited her killer in to the salon, but if Martin had keys . . .'

'Yes.' Jude looked at her watch and picked up the

card the hairdresser had given her. 'As soon as it's a reasonable hour, I'm going to ring Connie.'

The hairdresser did not seem particularly surprised when she answered the call just after ten. But she did sound sleepy, and Jude felt guilty that the phone had probably woken her.

'I'm sorry to be calling so early.'

'Don't worry. I should be up. I overslept.' Connie sounded snugly drowsy. 'It's just I . . . you know, always wiped out at the end of the week.'

'Well, as I say, I'm sorry.'

'It's fine.'

'But I thought I ought to ring you, because something's happened that might have a bearing on the case.'

'Case?'

'Kyra's murder.'

'Oh yes. Of course.'

'My friend Carole – you remember her?'

'Certainly. "Same shape, but shorter". Again the impersonation was spot on.

'Yes, her. Anyway, she was taking her dog for a walk on the beach early this morning, and she came back via the service road . . . you know, behind the shops.'

'Mmm?' Suddenly Connie was alert, the drowsiness gone from her voice.

'And she saw your ex-husband leaving from the back gate of Connie's Clip Joint.'

'Ah.' There was a long silence. When she broke it,

Connie sounded hesitant. 'And what's she going to do about it?'

'Well, tell the police presumably.'

'Why? Is it a police matter?'

'Surely it is? If Martin had keys to the back of Connie's Clip Joint to get in there this morning, then he probably would have had them if he'd wanted to get in on the night Kyra was killed.'

'Right.' Now it made sense to Connie. 'Sorry, I was half-asleep. Yes, of course, I hadn't thought of it that way. The police must be told. But, Jude, can you think of any reason why Martin might have been round to Connie's Clip Joint?'

'Well, if one were to go to the extreme hypothesis that he was actually the murderer . . .'

'Oh, I don't think so.' Instinctive loyalty for her ex-husband prompted Connie. 'I can't imagine Martin ever doing anything like that.'

'He had a motive.'

'Did he? Sorry, I'm being very slow this morning. I'm not properly awake yet.'

'You told me about it. That Kyra was threatening to sue him for constructive dismissal over the sexual harassment business.'

'Oh yes.'

'Well, it could be argued that he therefore had a very good motive to get her out of the way.'

'I suppose so. Maybe I overstated that, anyway. Kyra wasn't *definitely* going to take him to court. It was just an idea we discussed, not entirely serious.'

Why was she backtracking on that? Jude wondered.

She'd sounded fairly definite about it when the subject last came up.

'Anyway,' Connie went on, 'I still can't see Martin killing anyone.'

'All right. Say he didn't kill her, but he still knew about the threat of legal action . . .'

'I'm not sure whether he did know about that.'

'Oh, he did.' And Jude was embarrassed to realize that she would have to own up to what she'd said to Martin Rutherford in the Worthing Martin & Martina the day before. She did so, as quickly as possible, with the minimum of apology.

Connie took the news in slowly. 'And how did he react?'

'He changed the subject and moved on.'

'Yes, I'm not surprised.'

'But what I'm saying, Connie, is that, having heard about the potential legal action against him, Martin might have let himself into Connie's Clip Joint this morning, hoping to find and destroy any evidence . . . you know, papers Kyra might have got together for her case against him.'

'Yes.' Connie seemed very relieved to have a possible explanation for her ex-husband's appearance at the salon. 'Yes, that would make very good sense.'

'But, whatever his reason for being there, I think the police should be told about it. Even if it's not criminal, it is at the very least rather odd behaviour. I mean, that is assuming that you didn't know he was going to be there . . . ?'

'Good heavens, no!' Connie responded vehemently.

'Well, I suppose Carole could talk to the police. She has got a connection with the case, after all, having been there when the body was discovered. They did give her contact numbers, but . . . there's always a danger that the police will treat her as some nosy local crank. Alternatively, you could do it . . .'

'That'd make much more sense,' said Connie firmly. 'It was my premises he was making an illegal entry into, after all. No, leave it with me, Jude. I'll speak to the police.'

And she sounded relieved that that decision had been made.

Chapter Thirteen

'The question is,' said Carole, 'do I share this information with the Lockes?'

'Ah, I hadn't thought of that.'

'Rowley asked me to pass on anything I found out that might be relevant to the case . . .'

'Yes.'

'On the other hand, to tell them I saw Martin Rutherford coming out of Connie's Clip Joint this morning would be tantamount to making an accusation against him.'

'Which I'm sure the Lockes would seize on. Anything which offered a suspect apart from their precious Nathan.'

'Hmm. Again, you know, Jude, it struck me as odd yesterday how little Rowley Locke seemed to be worried about Nathan.'

'Well, I suppose the boy's not his son. He's only his nephew.'

'Yes, but when I met the parents, they were equally unruffled about it.' Even though her own maternal skills might be open to criticism, this still seemed odd to Carole. 'Not natural.'

'People hide their emotions.'

'Of course they do. But I still have a sneaking suspicion that the reason they're so calm about it is that they know Nathan's all right. They're in contact with him. They know where he is.'

Jude grinned ruefully. 'I don't think I can help you much in following up on that. You're the one with an open invitation to the Lockes' camp. Maybe you should tell them about seeing Martin this morning. It'd at least maintain the continuity of contact.'

'Yes.' But Carole felt disinclined to pick up the phone in a hurry. A little of the Lockes, she had found, went a long way. 'I won't do it straight away. See what else develops.'

'Maybe when Connie tells the police about Martin, that'll be the breakthrough they've needed.'

'You think he did it?'

Jude shrugged. 'I've no idea. But what Connie said about Kyra and the sexual harassment thing does at least give him a motive. Though there's still something odd about the way she told me that. I still can't quite put my finger on it. The whole story came out too pat, as though she'd prepared it. I don't know . . . Anyway, Connie's and Martin's does seem to have been a very bitter divorce.' Out of sensitivity towards Carole, she restrained herself from adding 'like most divorces'. 'Maybe there's another motive out there of him trying to sabotage the business prospects of Connie's Clip Joint.'

'I'm not sure that he needed to do that. From what you were saying, the salon's not very healthy, anyway.'

'No.' Jude screwed up her face in puzzlement. 'I get the feeling we're missing something.'

'I get the feeling we're missing everything,' said Carole tartly. 'Our investigation can't really be said to be making much headway, can it?'

'But I'm sure there's someone else we should be talking to . . . someone we've forgotten about.'

'Well, there's Joe Bartos. You've tried without success to make contact there.'

Jude screwed up her eyes and shook her head. Even after two haircuts in a week, there was enough left for her topknot to wobble precariously. 'Someone else . . . Someone who had something to do with the day of the murder . . . or the day of the discovery of the murder . . .'

'Well, I can't—'

Jude's brown eyes sprang open. 'The woman! The other woman in Connie's Clip Joint when you had your hair cut. The very dramatic one.'

'Oh, her. Her name was Sheena. That's all I know about her.'

'But there was something you told me she said.'

'I can't remember. She was behaving so hysterically, she said all kinds of things.'

'No, there was one thing . . . Something about Kyra deserving her fate . . . ?'

Carole's memory cleared, and the words came back to her, exactly as she had heard them that morning. 'Yes. "Though the poor girl may have deserved something, she didn't deserve this!"'

'Well, wouldn't that suggest to you that this Sheena knew something about Kyra or her background?'

'Yes. Yes, it would.'

'In that case,' said Jude, 'I think we ought to see if we can get in touch with Sheena.'

'And how do you propose to do that?'

'I'll ring Connie back. She'll have a number.'

'Hello?'

'Hello.' The voice was so tense with emotion that at first she didn't recognize it. 'It's Stephen.'

'Stephen. What on earth's the matter?'

'It's Gaby. She's been taken into hospital.'

'What – something wrong with the baby?'

'With the baby, with her, I don't know.' He sounded totally distracted, so unlike himself, not the buttoned-up distant personality he had presented to the world ever since his mother could remember.

'Calm down, Stephen. Tell me what happened.'

'It was in the middle of the night. I don't know, one-thirty, two . . . ? Gaby woke up, feeling pain in her stomach. And, you know, we thought maybe the baby was starting, because it's due in less than four weeks and I suppose it could be premature . . .' He still didn't sound in control of his speech. 'So we rang the hospital and I suggested I should drive her round, but they said, no, they'd send an ambulance . . . and then Gaby was bleeding a bit . . . and they took her in . . . and she's on a drip and . . . I don't know. I don't know what I'd do if anything happened to Gaby.'

'Stephen . . . Is the baby moving all right?'

'What? Oh, yes, yes, apparently so.' In his anxiety about his wife, their unborn baby was an irrelevance. 'Or at least the doctor said it was OK.'

'What else did the doctor say?'

'The one I saw said Gaby'd be fine. But that they wanted to keep her in for observation.'

'Well, if that's what he said, I'm sure that's what he meant.'

'But suppose he only said it to keep me calm? I mean, she's been bleeding and I don't know what—'

'Stephen . . . That kind of thing can happen. There are very few completely straightforward pregnancies. I had a similar scare when I was expecting you.'

'Did you?' He was shocked, partly by the information itself and partly by the fact that he and his mother were talking about such a subject.

'Yes, David and I were scared witless, just as you are now. It was a couple of months before you were born. I was kept in overnight, then sent home and told to take things easy. I did just that and, as you know, everything was fine. As I'm sure it will be with Gaby.'

'Yes.' He didn't sound convinced, but he must have relaxed a bit, because he now became aware of the kind of conversation he was participating in. 'I'm sorry to worry you, Mother.' Not that relaxed, thought Carole wryly. Not relaxed enough for a 'Mum'. He went on, 'I just couldn't think of anyone else to talk to.'

Carole liked that a lot more.

'I mean, Gaby's mother . . . well, I don't think she's strong enough to cope.'

Even better. 'No, probably not. Have you talked to your father?'

Stephen seemed amazed by the suggestion. 'What would be the point of talking to him? He wouldn't know what to do. It'd just make him flap.'

He was right. Just the sort of news to send David into a tailspin of panic. Carole couldn't deny herself a little glow from the fact that she had been Stephen's first port of call in the crisis. Emboldened, she said firmly, 'Stephen, Gaby's going to be absolutely fine. So's your baby.'

What she spoke was what she felt. Though by nature perpetually prone to self-doubt and suspicion, Carole Seddon had never had any misgivings about the safe arrival of her forthcoming grandchild. She had no medical knowledge, she wasn't privy to Gaby's current state of health; she just knew the birth would be all right. The only anxieties she had were about her ability to form a bond with the imminent arrival.

'Would you mind telling her that, Mother?'

'What, telling Gaby?'

'Yes. She's so scared. I've never seen her looking so scared . . . even when, you know, she was worried that someone was trying to murder her. If you could just have a word . . . ?'

'Of course. Can I ring her?'

'No, no mobiles allowed in the hospital. I'm out in the car park talking to you now. Gaby's not allowed out of bed at the moment, but I think they bring a phone trolley round to the wards or something, so she could ring you. Are you going to be about later?'

'I'll have to take Gulliver out for another walk at some point, but basically I'm here.'

'Oh, great. I'll get Gaby to call you. I just hope she's . . .' Once again he sounded lost, like one of those rare moments when he came home from school having got into trouble for transgressing some rule he did not understand.

'Stephen, Gaby and the baby will both be fine.'

'Right. Thank you, Mum.'

He'd never know how much that last word had meant to her.

Gaby rang just before lunch. Carole was very calm and reassuring, and in fact the mother-to-be was also more relaxed. Her panic of the early hours had receded. The bleeding had stopped and she drew comfort from being surrounded by experts in pregnancy and childbirth. Gaby had sent Stephen home to catch up on some sleep, and she thought she'd probably doze through the afternoon herself. She was definitely going to be kept in overnight, but she'd know more after her consultant had done his rounds in the morning.

Carole was surprised how easily she found herself sharing her own comparable experience with Gaby. She'd never really talked about such things, except to a doctor. Carole Seddon had never been part of a group of female friends who discussed their entire gynaecological history. Finding herself talking to her daughter-in-law about these things, building on the bond of their mutual gender, was a novel experience, but a rewarding one. When she put down the phone at the end of their conversation, she felt she had really been of use to Gaby.

And she tried to keep at bay the insidious thoughts that maybe her uncharacteristic confidence was misplaced, that there really was something wrong with the pregnancy.

She contemplated steeling herself to ring David. He was secure in his little flat in Swiss Cottage; maybe he ought to be informed of the family crisis. Oh dear, that would mean talking to him, something she had pretty thoroughly avoided since they'd both put on such a good show of being civilized to each other at the wedding. It would also mean looking up his telephone number. Her photographic memory for figures blanked out that particular piece of information. Still, she supposed she should ring him.

But then she thought: why? As Stephen had said, hearing the news about Gaby's scare would just make him flap. David had always been prone to flapping. When her son needed a rock in his life, it was his mother he turned to, not his father. The knowledge gave Carole a surge of guilty pleasure.

Chapter Fourteen

Jude was a shrewd judge of character and, even though they hadn't met, Carole's description had made her certain Sheena was the kind of woman who would seize any opportunity to talk about herself. So it proved. In response to a phone call from a complete stranger who wanted to talk about what she'd seen at Connie's Clip Joint, Sheena was more than ready to fix a meeting. 'Soon as you like. Friend was going to come down and see me today, but he's cried off. Apparently has to spend the weekend with his *wife*. What a feeble excuse. Bloody men, eh?'

So a rendezvous at the Crown and Anchor when it opened at noon was easily arranged.

Sheena must have been there waiting before Ted Crisp unlocked the doors, because she was well into a large gin and tonic when Jude arrived only a couple of minutes after twelve. 'Oh, I should have got you a drink, Sheena. I set this up.'

'Don't worry, darling. You can get the next one. What're you having?'

Sheena managed to get Ted's attention away from the customer whom he was asking which fingers hairdressers use to hold their scissors, and bought a large Chilean Chardonnay for her interrogator. Jude had instantly recognized the woman from Carole's description. As when she'd made her entrance that morning at Connie's Clip Joint, Sheena was wearing dark glasses and had her hair swathed in a scarf. She was maintaining that illusion of unobtrusiveness so often affected by people who like to be the centre of attraction. Her silk top and linen suit were expensive, showing just enough fussy decoration to be designer garments.

'There you are, darling. Cheers!'

It was still warm enough to sit outside – and that might have been a justification for the dark glasses – but Sheena had selected one of the pub's shady individual booths. Again the attempt at self-effacement had the reverse effect, exacerbated by the loud husky whisper in which she insisted on talking. Any casting director looking for someone to play a spy would have rejected her as too obvious.

'Jude, I'm so glad you got in touch. Because I must confess I'm still traumatized by what I saw that morning at Connie's. I keep wanting to talk about it, but holding back. You know, a shock on that scale is not something you can talk about to just anyone.'

But evidently – and fortunately for Jude – something she could talk about to an unknown woman who'd rung her up out of the blue that morning.

'I mean, let me tell you, mine has been a life not without incident. I've had a few shocks in my time – particularly where men have been concerned – but nothing like this. Actually to have been present at a murder scene – it's the last thing in the world I would have wanted to happen to me.' Even though the opposite was clearly the case, this was spoken with great vehemence. 'And the thought that the perpetrator of this awful crime is still at large . . . well, it's too, too ghastly even to think about. I mean, when I wake up in the middle of the night, I am positively *terrified*. I am currently living on my own and I get these appalling fantasies. Suppose the murderer wants to silence all the people who were witnesses to his crime . . . ?'

She left a pause for this awful thought to sink in, thus giving Jude the opportunity to interject, 'But you weren't strictly a witness to the crime, were you?'

'I was a witness to the effects of the crime. I saw the poor girl with that flex around her neck. I tell you, the image of her face is one that I will keep with me to my dying day.'

She attempted to punctuate this line with a dramatic swallow from her gin and tonic glass, but found it to be empty. Jude went up to the bar for refills. Ted Crisp was betting another customer a fiver that he couldn't say which fingers hairdressers held their scissors in.

When she returned with the drinks, further discussion of Kyra Bartos's murder was delayed by Sheena saying, 'I see you don't wear a wedding ring, Jude. Have you had trouble with men?'

'Yes, sometimes,' came the even reply. 'I have also had more pleasure with men than with anything else in my life.'

'Oh yes, me too,' Sheena hastened to assure her.

'I have known the heights of sexual ecstasy . . . many, many times. But I have also known the hideous free-fall from that ecstasy . . . the moments of betrayal . . . the moment when one realizes one has just been too trusting . . . that one has once again listened to too many lies. It's heartbreaking, but it's the fate which we women are born to.'

This did not coincide exactly with Jude's view of relationships with men, but she didn't want to break the growing mood of complicity, so let it pass with a casual 'Mmm.'

Which Sheena, of course, took as agreement. 'Have you ever been married?'

'Yes,' Jude replied, rightly confident that she would not be asked for any more details. Very few people knew about her marriages – or indeed her divorces. Jude's soothing company drew confidences from people about their own lives rather than questions about hers. Which suited her well. And so it proved in the current situation. It was her own experiences Sheena wanted to discuss, not anyone else's.

'Oh, I was married. For twelve years. I thought we loved each other. I thought he loved me. But suddenly, after twelve years, he said he wanted it to end. Now why would he do that?'

'Emotional exhaustion' was the answer that offered itself to Jude, but she kept it to herself. Anyway, the question turned out to have been only a rhetorical flourish. 'I'll tell you why he did that. Because he had another woman. For seven of the twelve years we had been together, he had been seeing another woman.

A stupid girl at his office, hardly out of her teens. She couldn't offer any of the things I could offer him.'

Like bent ears, thought Jude.

'And he's now gone and married her – and serve him bloody well right.'

'You don't know whether they're happy together?'

Sheena let out a derisive laugh. 'I can hardly think they would be. The girl's total number of brain cells is in single figures.'

'There's no logic to who gets on with who.'

'There certainly isn't. Otherwise he'd still be with me. God, the adjustments I've had to make in my lifestyle since the divorce!'

'Were you left very hard up?'

'Well, I got a house down here, but it's not nearly as big as the house we used to live in. Where Miss Pinhead is currently doing her impression of the Lady of the Manor.'

'But have you had to work hard to make ends meet?'

'No, not work as such. But my house has only got four bedrooms, hers has got six. I'm not nearly as well off as she is.'

Jude's sympathy for the divorcee's plight was waning. From what she said – and from the clothes she was wearing – she hadn't done at all badly out of the settlement. Her feelings might not yet have healed, but in material terms she was OK.

Time to move the conversation on. 'Going back to that morning in Connie's Clip Joint—'

Fat chance of getting Sheena off her favourite subject, though. 'Since the divorce,' she went on, 'I've had many attempts to find love again, but they've all ended in disappointment. Men are such bastards, why do we love them so much?'

Jude didn't offer an opinion. She reckoned she'd have to ride out the tide of anti-men hatred before she got back to investigation.

'I mean, this man I was meant to be seeing this weekend . . . usual thing. We meet, it's all magical. The sex is just stunning. He's never met anyone like me. And then it slips out that he's married. OK, I've been there before. But his marriage is a sham, he hasn't made love to his wife for years. And everything's so wonderful with me, he never wants to see his wife again. And I say, OK, divorce is a possibility, you know. People do it. I'm living proof that people do it. And he says, yes, great, he'll talk to his wife. But time passes and he hasn't got round to talking to her. And then I discover they've got children. And, of course, he doesn't want to hurt his precious children. So I say, well, look, you've got to make some choices here, and he says yes he will, because he adores me and he's never known sex could be like that. And still he doesn't do anything. But this week he promises he's going to talk to his wife, and does he? Does he hell? No, instead the bastard rings me and says he still loves me and he can't wait to be with me, but this weekend, no, sorry he can't make it. His wife's ill and he's got to stay at home with her and look after the children. Huh!'

Jude hoped the pause for breath would be an opportunity to get back to the murder, but Sheena hadn't finished yet. 'And how does that leave me? Washed up on the shore once again, like some piece of rubbish that's past its sell-by date. He was younger than me, of course. Men of my own age just don't seem able to keep up with me. And I suppose he was immature. Didn't know when he was well off. Thought opportunities of being with a woman like me would keep cropping up for him. Huh, he'll find out. Serves him bloody well right.' Her hand moved instinctively up to the scarf covering her head. 'I'll go to Theo tomorrow. Get a completely new style. I can't stand the sight of myself in the mirror with this one.'

Jude did the sum. Another restyling so soon after the previous one. If Sheena used a visit to Connie's Clip Joint to resolve all her emotional crises, it could be an expensive business. Mind you, Jude thought, I'm a fine one to be criticizing, me with my two haircuts in five days. But mine, she reassured herself, were in the cause of investigation.

Still, Sheena had at least brought the subject back to the murder scene. Better grab hold of that before she flitted off again. 'The morning Kyra Bartos's body was found . . .' Jude began firmly.

'Yes. Oh, it was terrible! I was just sitting there having my hair done when—'

'I do know everything that happened. My friend Carole told me.'

'Carole?' What Jude had said on the phone that morning, her minimal justification for getting in touch, had already been forgotten. Sheena didn't care about the reason people wanted to talk to her, so long as they did want to talk to her.

'Yes, I've heard all the circumstances of what was actually seen, but I was interested in something you said at the time.'

'How do you know what I said. You weren't there.'

'No, but as I explained, my friend Carole was there and she told me everything that happened.'

'And she actually remembered everything I said?' Sheena was quite impressed.

'She remembered one thing in particular. You said that Kyra Bartos deserved something, but not something as bad as what had happened to her.'

'Did I? I honestly can't remember. I was in such a terrible state. I mean, I'd left home that morning feeling sort of doomy, like it was going to be a bad day, and suddenly I'm at a murder scene and I'm being interviewed by the police and . . . Oh, it's too, too ghastly,' she announced with relish.

'What you said,' Jude persisted, 'implied that you knew Kyra.'

'I'd seen her around in the salon. She'd washed my hair a few times.'

'No, that you knew more about her than that.'

'How do you mean?' Either Sheena was very stupid or she was deliberately prevaricating.

'You said "Though the poor girl may have deserved something, she didn't deserve this." Now to me that implies that you knew something about the girl's past, something about her behaviour, which meant that she deserved some kind of punishment.'

'Oh, I see. Well, I didn't know her well. As I say, she just did my hair. But, you know, you often get chatting to the girls who wash your hair . . .'

'Yes.'

'And we were talking about men . . .' I bet I know who was doing most of the talking, thought Jude. 'And she was saying that she'd got this boyfriend . . .'

'Called Nathan Locke.'

'I don't remember her saying the name at the time, but from what I've heard since that must've been who she was talking about. Anyway, she said she didn't know how serious it was and she didn't want to get involved if it was likely to go pear-shaped. And she didn't want to raise the boy's expectations if the relationship wasn't going to go the distance.'

'That sounds eminently sensible. She didn't deserve punishment for that.'

'No, I agree. But we're only talking about what she told me. You may change your mind when I tell you what I heard from another source.' She held her hands dramatically apart, asking Jude to let her pace her own narrative. 'Anyway, I said to Kyra at the time that the only real test – or at least the first test of a relationship – has to be: is the sex any good? And do you know – she was amazingly reticent about that. I mean, I thought these kids nowadays were screwing everything in sight from the first flicker of puberty, but you wouldn't have believed it from the prim way that girl Kyra talked about sex.'

'Again, nothing wrong with that.'

'Jude, will you please let me tell the story my way!'

'Yes, yes, of course.' Sheena was not a woman used to being crossed. Maybe another reason why her relationships with men hadn't worked out.

'All right, that was how Kyra talked to me, playing the little, shy, butter-wouldn't-melt-between-her-legs girl. I heard a rather different story from Theo.'

'Oh?'

'Well, she was actually out of the salon when he was doing my hair – I was trying strawberry blonde that time – and he said that young Kyra was "a right little cock-teaser".'

'Did he?'

'Yes. Which was quite strong language from Theo. He usually hasn't got a harsh word to say about anyone. But he said Kyra was leading this poor boyfriend of hers a terrible dance. You know, blowing hot and cold – ooh, unfortunate turn of phrase there perhaps. Theo said the boy was a really nice boy – yes, Nathan, he did mention the name Nathan – and that he deserved better than being messed around by "a right little cock-teaser".'

She seemed to relish repeating the phrase, and her penetrating whisper of it had prompted some uncomfortable reactions from worthy Fethering pensioners enjoying a Sunday drink at adjacent tables.

'So Theo knew Nathan?'

'Well, he'd at least talked to him. I can't think that Kyra was going to describe herself as "a right little cock-teaser".' The whisper was even louder this time. Old men cleared their throats and tried to avoid the eyes of their wives. 'No, Theo clearly felt sorry for Nathan. He said it was awful how a good-looking boy like that could be messed around by some little . . .' The old men froze in anticipation, but in fact Sheena contented herself with '. . . tart.'

'Hmm.' This did open up a new dimension. Jude was more inclined to accept Kyra's own presentation of herself, as a young girl confused by her first love affair, than the alternative description reported by Sheena. But why should Theo be so violently anti the salon junior? Unless, of course, she was monopolizing the attention of the young man who he himself had his eye on . . . ? It was a thought.

Jude didn't really think she was going to get a lot more useful information out of Sheena, and she was right. But that realization did not allow her to escape another hour of the woman's self-dramatizing moaning. And keeping pace with Sheena's drinking meant that she left the Crown and Anchor with an annoying and unnecessary headache.

As she walked back via the beach to get some air, Jude reflected that she couldn't have asked for a more indiscreet witness. Anything that Sheena knew about the case – however confidential – she would have been happy to blurt out. The trouble was that she didn't know very much.

Still, the thought she had inadvertently planted about Theo having an interest in Nathan . . . that would be worth following up.

Chapter Fifteen

'Hello. Is that Carole Seddon?' The voice was male and unfamiliar. It had a light, almost joshing quality, but with an undercurrent of tension.

She confirmed her identity. It was about ten o'clock on the Monday morning. She had just had a very relieved call from Stephen. Gaby had spent a restful night. There had been no more bleeding and the baby was still moving as it should be. The only small cloud on his sunny horizon was that there were some worries about her blood pressure. The consultant wanted to keep her in for another twenty-four hours.

The news had come as a relief to Carole too, but after she had put the phone down, she felt restless. The day stretched ahead of her without enough to fill it. A bit of housework, a light lunch with the *Times* crossword, another walk with Gulliver. She was a woman who needed things to fill her time. Even after all these years, she missed the imperative of setting off every morning to her job at the Home Office. She didn't dare hope that the arrival of her grandchild would give her much more to do. In spite of their oft-stated intentions to move to West Sussex, Stephen and Gaby still lived in

London. Carole couldn't see herself being used by them for childcare on a frequent basis. When Gaby went back to work at her theatrical agency, they'd get a nanny or a childminder. Which would of course be a blessing. Carole didn't reckon her grandmaternal skills would turn out to be much more instinctive than her maternal skills had been. So her life would remain empty.

Her sleuthing with Jude had helped to fill the void from time to time, but on their current case they didn't seem to be getting anywhere. Once again she wished she was privy to what the police were doing, what was going on at the Major Crime Unit in Littlehampton, how far their enquiries had progressed. She felt isolated in the austere and sensible comfort of High Tor.

'My name,' said the voice on the phone, 'is Martin Rutherford.'

'Ah.' That he should be calling was so unexpected that the monosyllable came out almost as a gasp. Still, she could no longer complain that nothing was happening on the case.

'I'm the ex-husband of—'

'I know who you are.'

'I'm sorry to ring you out of the blue, but I hear that you saw me yesterday morning coming out of the back of Connie's Clip Joint.'

'Yes.' So Connie had done her stuff. The police had already been in touch with him.

'Listen, I'm calling from the salon and it's rather difficult to talk.'

'Maybe we could meet?' Carole wasn't going to let slip any opportunity to pursue the investigation.

'I'd like that.' He sounded relieved. He must have been anticipating resistance. Little did he know how welcome his call had been.

She suggested meeting in the Crown and Anchor, but he didn't have time that day to come so far. If she wouldn't mind coming to see him . . . There was a Caffè Nero just along the road from Martin & Martina.

Carole readily assented and, pausing only to tell her neighbour of this new development, set off for Worthing in her neat little Renault.

Martin Rutherford was again wearing a charcoal linen suit – maybe it was a kind of Martin & Martina livery – but today's shirt was very pale blue. He carried himself with a certain poise, though Carole could tell he was nervous. The fact that he'd arrived early for their eleven o'clock rendezvous was an indication of that, as well as the slight shake of his hand as he brought her cappuccino across to their table.

He got straight down to business. 'I gather you had the misfortune to be there when the poor kid's body was discovered, Mrs Seddon.'

'Yes, I did. And please call me Carole.'

'Thank you.' That seemed to relax him a little. He'd been expecting a more adversarial attitude. 'It must have been terrible for you. And for Connie too, of course,' he added, concern for his ex-wife apparently an afterthought.

Carole didn't say anything. As he was the one who

had made contact, he must have some kind of agenda. She waited to hear what it was.

'And you saw me yesterday morning.'

'Yes. I had been taking my dog for a walk.'

He smiled wryly. 'Early risers in Fethering.' He paused before asking, 'Did you inform the police?'

'No. My friend Jude told Connie about it, and Connie said she would tell the police. Mind you, it could have been me who passed on the information. The detectives did ask me to keep them informed of anything I discovered that might have relevance to the murder case.'

He gave a rueful nod. 'Yes, of course. And you would have been absolutely right to do so. Though, as it happens, what I was doing at Connie's Clip Joint had nothing to do with the murder case.'

'I'm sorry. I could only react to what I saw, and I'm afraid to me it seemed suspicious. I know the state of affairs between you and Connie since the divorce.'

'Do you?' He looked surprised.

'Yes, she talked to me while she was doing my hair. She talked to my friend Jude as well. It sounded as though you are still very much in conflict . . .'

'Well . . .'

'. . . so I couldn't imagine that you'd been at the salon to meet her . . . even assuming that she'd have been there on a Sunday morning.'

'No. All right. I take your point.' He looked relieved, as though he'd been expecting her to say something worse.

'So if you weren't there with Connie's knowledge,

and since I assume you don't still have any legal rights in the property . . . well, I came to the conclusion that you couldn't have been there for any legitimate reason.'

'You're a very logical woman, Carole.'

'I like to think so.'

'All right. I'll tell you why I was there.' And he did. He confirmed exactly the conjecture that Jude had spelled out to his ex-wife the day before. Kyra Bartos's departure from the Worthing Martin & Martina salon had followed her resistance to his advances. He tried to make light of what had happened. 'It was only in fun. Just jokey chatting-up, the kind of thing that goes on in the salon all the time, you know between the men and the girls.'

Carole sat stone-faced during his attempt to laugh it off and, embarrassed, he continued his explanation. Kyra, he said, did not have much of a sense of humour and she took his playfulness more seriously than he had intended. So yes, there had been a bit of awkwardness about her leaving. And though, on one of the rare occasions when he'd spoken to Connie, she'd said something about the girl contemplating legal action, he'd never taken it seriously . . . until he'd heard what Jude had to say to him in Martin & Martina on the Saturday morning.

'That made me think there was a real threat, and so I thought it was just possible that, if Kyra had actually got any information together or approached a solicitor or something, there might be a record of it left at Connie's Clip Joint. I knew she had a fairly tense relationship with her father, so she was more likely to have kept that kind of documentation at the salon than at home.'

He looked pleadingly up at Carole, offering himself to her judgement. 'So that's why I was there yesterday morning. I wasn't thinking very rationally. I just got it into my head that it was worth trying. If the police had found anything which suggested Kyra was contemplating legal action against me . . . well, suddenly that would put me in the frame with a motive to do away with the girl.'

'Yes,' Carole agreed implacably.

'Which, for anyone who knows me, is an absolutely daft idea. If there's any criticism ever made of me, it's that I'm a bit soft. I haven't got it in me to hurt anyone. It would just go against all my instincts.'

'Hmm. Did your wife not think it was odd, you going off early yesterday morning?'

'She would have done, I'm sure. I always give her exact details of where I'm going at any time. It's necessary when you're running a business together. But she's away this weekend. Her mother lives in Prague and she's not well . . . dying in fact, so Martina flies over there roughly once a month. She got a flight on Saturday afternoon and she's coming back tomorrow.'

'I see. So there was nothing to stop you making your illegal entry to Connie's Clip Joint?'

'No.' He sighed. 'In retrospect, it would have been better if Martina had been at home. Then I wouldn't have gone on such an insane wild goose chase. I didn't find anything in the salon, needless to say. But I was in a very manic state, and I thought there was a chance, and I was desperate to do anything that would stop the police wanting to question me any further.'

'Whereas in fact what you did has had exactly the opposite effect. The police now do want to question you about what you were doing at the salon yesterday morning.'

'Yes. I thought at that time of the day I'd be safe. I didn't reckon on you and your dog.'

'Lucky I wasn't taking my dog for a walk when the person who killed Kyra Bartos came out.'

It had been a risk to make the connection so openly, but Martin Rutherford was smart enough to pick up her implication. 'Look, I didn't kill her. I don't know whether any of the local gossip is suggesting that, but it's absolutely untrue.'

'As I'm sure you'll be able to prove to the police.'

'The police?' He sounded bewildered.

'When they question you about your movements.'

'Oh yes, yes, of course. Sorry. Bit slow there. No, it'll be fine when I talk to the police.'

'You mean you have an alibi?'

'Not for when you saw me yesterday morning. But you know that. You saw me. There's no way I can wriggle out of that and say I was somewhere else.'

Carole pressed him. 'But for the night of the murder? Do you have an alibi for then?'

'Of course I do,' he replied confidently. But then he seemed to lose his nerve. 'That is . . .'

'What?'

'Well, I . . . Look, I'm sorry, Carole, but I don't have

to tell you. When the police ask me, then of course I'll tell them where I was that night.'

'Fine,' she said, and then dared to add, 'If the answer's embarrassing . . .'

'No, it's not embarrassing.' He made a decision. 'All right, I was at a conference that night. There's a big annual one, the Brighton Hair and Nail Conference. I haven't been there before, but this year I decided I should.'

'Was Martina with you?'

'No, it started on the Wednesday evening. Someone had to be around the salon, in case anything came up in any of the branches. So she stayed and I went to Brighton. Just stayed the one night.'

It was an alibi that could be checked. On the other hand, it was not a totally watertight one. Brighton was not that far from Fethering. A determined murderer could easily slip away from the conference hotel for a couple of hours to do what he had to do. Unless he could produce someone who could vouch for his attendance at the conference all night, the alibi was pretty worthless.

But Carole didn't say any of that. Indeed, she didn't get the chance to. Martin Rutherford had finally got on to the real purpose of their meeting. 'Listen, this whole situation's very unfortunate. I've been stupid and, as a result, I'm going to have what I think could be quite a nasty grilling from the police.'

If he was fishing for sympathy, Carole didn't feel inclined to grant him any. She was surprised by how negative she felt towards Martin Rutherford. Connie was far from being a bosom pal, but Carole still had a lot of fellow feeling for her. The way Martin had behaved in their marriage – and indeed the way he continued to behave with girls like Kyra – was appalling. Carole felt empathy for Connie, the solidarity of divorcees who had been badly treated by men.

'Anyway,' Martin went on, 'that will be my punishment – and it serves me right.'

'It's possible,' said Carole waspishly, 'that that won't be all your punishment.'

'What do you mean?'

'I'd have thought, even if you used your keys to get into Connie's Clip Joint yesterday . . .'

'Which I did. Still got a set to the back door.'

'Even if you did, you could be charged with breaking and entering.'

The idea didn't seem to worry him. 'No, surely that'd only happen if Connie pressed charges. And she'd never do that.'

'Don't underestimate her.' And don't underestimate how much you have hurt her and how vengeful she might be towards you, Carole thought.

Martin still dismissed the idea of a criminal charge. 'Well, that is not currently among my many worries. But look, Carole . . . now this business about my going to Connie's Clip Joint yesterday is known to the police . . . and they'll probably soon know about the reasons for Kyra's dismissal too . . . could you please – you and your friend Jude – not say anything? I mean, don't spread the news to anyone else.'

'I had no intention of doing so,' said Carole sniffily.

'Good. I'm sorry, but I do have a business reputation round here. It's not going to be improved if anyone finds out the police are questioning me again. And I don't want to risk any further damage. So please, will you and Jude keep quiet about it?'

'Yes, of course we will.'

What does he take us for – a couple of local gossips? Carole couldn't help thinking.

'And look . . .' He produced a card from his top pocket. 'That's got my mobile number on it. If you hear anything that you feel's relevant, don't hesitate to ring me.'

'What kind of thing were you thinking of?'

'Anything that points to who might have killed Kyra . . . or . . .'

Or anything that gets me off the hook. Mentally Carole provided the end of the sentence for him.

Chapter Sixteen

There was one thing at least that she could check right away. As soon as she got back to High Tor, Carole got out the Yellow Pages and made a list of the main conference centres and hotels in Brighton. She started to ring round, asking if they had recently hosted a Hair and Nail Conference. On the third call she got lucky. Yes, they'd had some four hundred delegates there just over two weeks ago. The dates tallied with what Martin Rutherford had said. So the conference certainly existed; whether he'd been at it, of course, was another matter.

Carole asked for the name of the organizer of the Brighton Hair and Nail Conference. The girl on Reception couldn't tell her, but put her through to someone in the relevant department who very efficiently provided her with the name and contact numbers of the events company who had staged the conference. Another call confirmed that a Martin Rutherford had indeed been booked in as a delegate. And he had booked in for the dinner on the Wednesday night. What's more, he had been there. By chance, the girl at the end of the line had sat next to him during the dinner. He had been very charming and amusing. No, she didn't know where he'd gone after the meal. Now she really must be getting on with some work.

Carole was digesting this information when her phone rang. It was Stephen. He sounded tense again.

'What's up?' she asked.

'Gaby. They want to keep her in a few more days.'

'Any reason? Has there been more bleeding?'

'No. They just want . . . Something to do with blood pressure. They think she'll be safer there.'

'Then I'm sure they're right.'

'Yes . . .' He didn't sound convinced.

'Listen, Stephen, it's only about a month till she's due. If the baby was born tomorrow, it'd be absolutely fine.'

'Mmm.'

'And the baby's still moving around all right, is it?'

'Yes, yes. It's not the baby they're worried about. It seems to be Gaby.'

'Stephen, lots of women have problems with blood pressure when they're pregnant. The hospital is just observing sensible precautions, that's all. You should be grateful that they're doing so.'

'Yes. Yes, I am.' But he still didn't sound at ease.

'What is it?'

'Mum . . .' She was warmed by the word. 'I'm worried.'

'You wouldn't be human if you weren't. But I'm sure there's no need. Gaby and the baby will both be fine.'

'Yes, but what worries me . . . I'm so concerned

about Gaby that I don't really care what happens to the baby . . .'

The admission cost him a lot. For a moment Carole lost her nerve. She couldn't find the right response to what he had just said. Jude would have done it instinctively, immediately come up with the right formula of words. Carole didn't have those skills. But somehow she managed to swallow her anxiety and found herself saying, 'That's a natural thing to think, Stephen. You shouldn't feel guilty about it. You know Gaby, you love Gaby. If there's any threat to her, you don't care about anything else, so long as she's all right. But you will get to know and love the baby just as much.'

'Will I?' He still sounded uncertain, pleading.

'Yes. You will.'

After the phone call ended, Carole was assailed with doubt. She had had to sound more positive than she really felt. And a tremor of guilt ran through her too. Easy enough for her to tell Stephen about the love he would feel for his child when it was born, but had she ever had that instinctive reaction to him?

There were a lot of things Jude cared about which came under Carole's definition of 'fads'. Her work as a healer headed the list. To Carole's mind that was a fad, or at least the people who indulged in it were faddish. Healing was just a craze, there'd be another one along in a minute. It was Carole's view that if you were so unfortunate as to have something wrong with you, then you should make an appointment at Fethering Surgery and go and see a proper doctor.

She also thought a lot of the decor at Woodside Cottage was faddish. Nobody really needed wind chimes or aromatic candles. And certainly no one needed crystals lying about the place. But Carole couldn't deny the warmth and comfort that her neighbour's home exuded, particularly when contrasted with the almost antiseptic austerity of High Tor.

When it came to food, though, Jude was really faddy. Not faddy in the sense of being picky about what she ate when she was out; she didn't have a portfolio of personal allergies like a lot of the denizens of Fethering. But she was faddy about what she bought. Everything had to be organic. Carole thought such discrimination was an expensive luxury. The food she'd grown up with had kept her pretty healthy, and she couldn't be bothered with checking the source of everything. She didn't like shopping and the less time spent on her weekly trip to Sainsbury's, the better. Besides, the organic stuff was always considerably more expensive than the normal food and, although Carole was economically secure with her Home Office pension, she didn't believe in waste. As for all that nonsense about organic food tasting better . . . well, she could never tell the difference.

For Jude, however, it mattered. At home she liked to know the provenance of everything she ate. But she didn't go for the overpriced supermarket organic option. Instead, she had built up a network of local nurseries, farm shops and farmers' markets to source her supplies and either walked or travelled by train or bus to track down what she wanted.

That Monday afternoon a grudging Carole had agreed to drive her to a nursery outside Littlehampton which specialized in organic vegetables. Carole was not grudging because she resented doing the driving, only because of her innate suspicion of all things organic. In fact, she was still at a loose end and the trip had been her suggestion. At the nursery she was even prevailed upon to buy a bag of potatoes, saying stuffily that she'd 'see if they tasted any different'. Mind you, she couldn't fault the price. They were cheaper than the supermarket's cheapest non-organic offerings.

Their route back to High Tor and Woodside Cottage took them along the High Street and, as they were approaching Connie's Clip Joint, Jude said urgently, 'Slow down.'

'What?'

'Look.'

Carole watched as Theo emerged from the salon. He was dressed in his uniform black shirt and trousers and had his black leather jacket hooked on a finger over his shoulder. His tinted glasses with the gold stars at the corners were in place. He didn't exactly mince, but he sashayed along the High Street away from them, unafraid of looking camp.

'Follow him,' hissed Jude.

'Why? He's just going home, I assume. Must've done his last appointment of the day. So why on earth should I follow him?'

'Do you have other major plans for this afternoon?

Are you going to try out some new organic potato recipes?'

'No,' Carole replied testily. Then, with an 'Oh, very well', she put the car in gear and moved slowly along behind the stylist. 'Though I still don't know why I'm doing this.'

'So that we can see what he does.'

What he did was to click his key remote to unlock a dark green Skoda Fabia, into which he climbed and drove off.

'See, I told you. He's just going home.'

'Follow him,' said Jude mischievously.

Carole sighed at the pointlessness of the exercise, but in the tradition of endless Hollywood movies, followed the car in front. It wasn't very difficult. The prevalence of road bumps and assiduous traffic police, combined with the overwhelming sedateness of Fethering, meant that nobody ever drove fast there. And, unlike a character from a Hollywood film, Theo appeared to have no suspicion that the women in the Renault pootling along behind him had any ulterior motive. He wasn't about to break into a routine of sudden reversing and screeching tyres.

'I don't know why we're doing this,' Carole repeated grumpily.

'Just a hunch. But if you'd rather be making an organic potato salad . . .'

'Huh.'

The route Theo's Fabia was taking led out of Fethering in the direction of Bognor Regis, which was a mild surprise. Because of his gayness, Carole and Jude had expected him to gravitate towards Brighton. But, fair enough, there are gay men in Bognor Regis too.

That wasn't where he was going, though. He suddenly indicated and turned right off the A259 towards Yapton. No reason why he shouldn't. Maybe that was where he lived. There were almost certainly gays in Yapton too.

But his destination was not a private house. The Fabia turned into the impressive drive of Yeomansdyke, a luxury hotel and health spa which Jude had visited when she was investigating the murder of Walter Fleet, owner of a nearby livery stables.

'What shall I do?'

'Drive in. Keep following him.'

With bad grace, Carole did as instructed. By the time they reached the hotel car park, the Fabia was parked and Theo was walking towards the spa entrance. The Renault was neatly guided into a parking bay, but Carole didn't turn off the engine. 'What're we supposed to do now?'

'I don't know.' Jude was almost girlishly irresponsible, knowing that her attitude was irritating her neighbour, but blithely incapable of changing it. 'Odd place for him to come, though, isn't it?'

'It's a free country. People can go where they want to go.'

'Yes, but he's just walked into the spa like he's a regular. The membership for this place is seriously expensive. I can't think he pays for that on what he makes as a hairdresser.'

'He may not be a member. He could just have come here to meet someone.'

'Yes, but you'd have thought, if he was going to do that, he'd go in the main hotel entrance. That's where the bars and places are. Not so likely to meet someone in the leisure centre. I don't think the Yeomansdyke spa is like a New York bathhouse.'

Carole didn't get the reference. 'Well, I don't know,' she said huffily. 'All I do know is that I feel a complete idiot sitting here in the car, like I was some police detective on a stake-out.'

'Well, if you imagine that's what you are . . . does that make it any easier?'

'No.' Carole switched off the ignition. 'Ten minutes we're going to wait here. If he doesn't come out within ten minutes, we're going.'

'But look, if he's come here for a swim, or a work-out in the gym . . . well, that's going to take him more than ten minutes.'

'Ten minutes,' Carole reiterated firmly, and folded her arms behind the steering wheel. She wished she had brought the *Times* crossword with her on this wild goose chase. There were three clues in the top left-hand corner she hadn't managed to complete yet.

They didn't have to wait ten minutes. In just over five Theo emerged from the Yeomansdyke spa entrance, and moved briskly across towards his Fabia.

He was unrecognizable. Gone were the tinted glasses and the black gear. Now he was dressed in beige chinos and a light tweed sports jacket. His whole body language had changed too. There was no longer any feyness, but a firm resolution in his stride.

'What on earth . . . ?' breathed Carole.

'Wait till he gets back into the car, then follow him,' said Jude.

They watched the Fabia parked in front of them for what seemed an inordinately long time. Then their attention was drawn by the gunning of a powerful engine. They turned as one to see a silver BMW sports car speeding past them out of the car park. At the wheel, unaware of their presence, was the new Theo.

By the time they reached the road at the end of the Yeomansdyke drive, the car had disappeared, whether to the right or left they had no idea.

Chapter Seventeen

As the Renault nosed its way back along Fethering High Street, Jude suddenly shouted, 'Park!'

'What?' demanded Carole, obeying nonetheless. She brought the car to a halt behind a muddy Land Rover. The back was sticking out and she began to manoeuvre so that the wheels should be exactly parallel to the kerb.

'Don't bother with that.'

'But I must. I hate messy parking. What is this, Jude?'

'When we went past the salon, I noticed Connie was in there on her own.'

'So?'

'Well, we can go in and ask her about Theo.'

'Just ask her? Just like that?'

'Yes, of course. Why not?'

'It's a bit obvious, isn't it?'

Jude sighed with exasperation. 'And what's wrong with the obvious? We ask Connie about Theo. There's probably nothing sinister in what he's doing. There'll be a perfectly simple explanation. We ask her and she tells us.'

'But we can't just walk in. She'll think it's odd.'

'No, she won't. She owns a hairdressing salon. People walk in and out all the time.'

'But not without an appointment.'

'Carole, are you coming?'

'I should really be getting back to Gulliver . . .'

'Fine. You do that.' There were times, thought Jude as she opened the car door, when being friends with Carole could be quite difficult. 'Do you mind taking my vegetables? I'll drop by and pick them up later.' She was tempted to say she'd drop by 'without an appointment', but restrained herself. Carole agreed she'd take the vegetables.

Jude looked back just before she reached the salon. Carole had straightened up the Renault first, made sure it was exactly parallel to the kerb, before driving it out of the space on the way back to High Tor. Her neighbour shook her head in bewilderment.

As Jude entered Connie's Clip Joint, Barbra Streisand was trembling from the CD, doing one of those misleadingly quiet bits which always presages a full-volume screech. Connie herself was sitting with a cappuccino and a *Hello!* magazine, looking as though she hadn't a care in the world.

'Hi. Good to see you. Like a coffee?'

'Please.' So much for Carole's worries about not having an appointment. Jude wasn't even sure that she needed a cover story, but just to be on the safe side, she produced the one she'd quickly prepared. 'Actually, I wanted to ask you about Theo . . .'

'Yes?' Connie called from the back room by the

coffee machine where she was preparing Jude's cappuccino.

'I was talking to someone who was asking about hairdressers who might come and visit . . . you know, cut their hair at home. I know you told me you don't do that. I was wondering if Theo ever "makes house calls".'

'Don't think he does. He's never mentioned it.'

'I suppose it'd depend a bit where it was . . . you know, if it was near his home . .'

'Maybe.' Connie came back into the salon and closed the back room door. 'There's your coffee.'

'Thanks.' Jude took a sip and wiped off the moustache of froth before asking, 'Where does he live, actually?'

Connie looked surprised by her own reply. 'Do you know, I don't actually know.'

'Really? But if he's a member of your staff . .'

'No, I thought I told you.'

'Oh, that's right. He rents the chair.'

'That's right. And he pays me in cash, which is very good news. I've always believed there are some areas of one's life that should be kept a secret from the taxman.'

'I agree,' said Jude. 'So you really don't have an address for Theo?'

'No. I always contact him on his mobile. I mean, I just had a call from one of his clients this afternoon. Wants a cut and highlights tomorrow afternoon. Two o'clock. So I'll put it in the book and call Theo on the mobile so he knows to come in.'

'Is that the only booking he's got tomorrow?'

'Yes. Neither of us doing particularly well at the moment.' But it didn't seem to worry her. 'I haven't got a landline for Theo, so I've no idea whereabouts he lives. But then why should I? I mean, I get on with him fine, but it's purely a business relationship. We don't socialize together outside work.' Connie Rutherford pulled a lugubrious face. 'I may be looking for a man, you know, but Theo wouldn't be highest on my list of possibles.'

'No.'

'He'd be very good for my ego, keep telling me how wonderful I looked, but in other departments . . .' she giggled ruefully, '. . . I think I might be disappointed.'

'I think you might.' Jude took a sip of cappuccino. 'So you don't know whether he's in a relationship?'

'I don't know anything about his private life. Theo's a great one for gossip, he loves earwigging on everything all the women who come into the salon talk about, he really encourages them, they open up to him . . . but, now I come to think of it, he never gives away anything about himself.'

'Good trick if you can do it,' said Jude, who could do it and recognized the technique. She asked a few more questions about Theo, but got similar answers. Connie had no idea about his private life. He didn't volunteer any information, and few of his clients wanted to probe. Many Fethering women got quite a charge out of having their hair cut by a gay man, but they didn't want too much detail. And Connie seemed equally incurious.

One thing Jude felt pretty sure of after she'd finished her questioning was that Connie had no idea about the change of persona that Theo had effected at Yeomansdyke.

'If you like,' the hairdresser concluded, 'I'll ask him in the morning.'

'Ask him what?' asked Jude.

'Whether he does visit people's houses to cut their hair.'

'Oh, yes.' She'd completely forgotten her cover story. 'Don't worry, it's not important. I think my friend has a lead to someone else, anyway.' She looked around the salon. 'So did neither of you have any bookings this afternoon?'

'I had a two o'clock shampoo. One of the old dears who's never washed her own hair in her life. There are still a few of them around.'

'And that was it?'

'Yes. Might get someone else wandering in later . . . After school finishes, quite often get girls in with their mums . . . which is usually quite entertaining.'

'Why?'

'The mums want them to look like innocent little cherubs. The girls want shocking pink colouring and razor cuts.'

'Ah yes, of course. Don't you get frustrated when you're just sitting around?'

Connie shrugged. 'You get used to it. Part of the business.'

'But not a very lucrative part of the business.'

'No. You get used to that too. Business comes and goes. That's just part of being a freelance.'

'I suppose so.' But Jude was surprised how laid-back

Connie seemed about the salon's lack of success. Fethering gossip said that the business was in a dire state, and bets were almost being taken on how long it could survive. But the proprietor seemed unbothered. Indeed, she was as relaxed as Jude had ever seen her. The habitual restlessness that accompanied her every movement was no longer in evidence. Her make-up was perfectly in place, and her hair hung neatly, its red highlights recently done, a fine advertisement for her skills. Around her glowed an aura of fulfilment.

Which made Jude think of a time when Connie had not looked quite so soignée. Gently she moved the conversation back to the morning that Kyra Bartos's body had been discovered in the back room.

'It seems a long time ago,' said Connie.

'You haven't got around to getting another junior yet?'

'No.' She gave the impression that she hadn't thought about the subject for some time. 'No. I must do something about it, but . . .' She shrugged a gesture that took in the empty salon '. . . no great need when business is like this. Saves me a bit of money too.' But she didn't make it sound as though saving money was that important.

'And have you had any more contact with the police?'

'Nothing. Presumably they're still trying to track down that boy Nathan.'

'Maybe. They didn't give you any indication of how far they'd got with the investigation, when you spoke to them yesterday?'

Connie Rutherford looked puzzled. 'Sorry?'

'When you spoke to them yesterday? About Carole having seen Martin skulking round the back of this place?'

'Ah yes, of course.' It all came back to her. 'Sorry, I'd forgotten, because it was all over so quickly. I rang through to the number the detective chief inspector had given me, told him my piece, and that was it. Hardly even a thank you, let alone any useful information about how the murder case was proceeding.'

'And you don't know whether they've been in touch with Martin yet?'

'Jude, Martin and I are divorced. We contact each other as little as is humanly possible.'

'Yes, I'm sorry, I wasn't thinking.'

'So unless they suddenly arrest him for Kyra's murder . . . which is very unlikely . . . I can't really think it likely that I'll hear anything about his encounter with the police.'

'No.' Jude felt duly chastened. 'Thinking back to that time, though, Connie . . .'

'Mmm?'

'You know, the morning when Kyra didn't open up the salon as she should have done . . .'

'Yes?' The hairdresser looked wary. She had recovered a degree of equanimity since the tragedy, and apparently didn't want to have the memory brought back.

'Carole Seddon gave me a blow-by-blow account of what happened . . .'

'I'm not surprised,' said Connie with some edge.

'Probably the most exciting thing that had happened in her life for some time. But she at least was quite restrained while it was all happening. Unlike that woman Sheena . . .'

'Yes, I heard.' Not necessary to mention her recent encounter with the drama queen. But it did remind her of something Sheena had suggested. 'Sorry, Connie, going off at a tangent . . . back to Theo . . .'

'Mmm?' The hairdresser sounded more enthusiastic. She hadn't liked reviving the images of discovering Kyra's body. Discussing her fellow stylist was much more appealing.

'I mean, presumably he is gay . . . ?'

'Oh, come on, Jude! Is the Pope Catholic?'

'Yes. OK. Well, you never saw any sign of Theo . . . coming on to anyone, did you?'

'No. As I said, we don't mix socially. What he gets up to in his spare time . . . well, that's not my business, is it?'

'Of course not. I only mentioned it, because . . .' What the hell, time for another indiscretion. 'Someone suggested that Theo might have made a play for Nathan Locke.'

This was a real surprise for Connie. 'I don't know that he even met Nathan. I never saw them together.'

'But could there have been an evening when, say . . . you'd left early and Theo was still here, and Nathan came round to pick up Kyra . . . ?'

'Well, yes, there could have been. Quite possible, but I'm not aware of that ever having happened. And, even if they had met, I really can't see Theo having "made a play", as you put it, for Nathan. He's a very professional stylist. I've met a lot of gay men in this business – it goes with the territory – and they're all very camp with the clients, but I've never met one who came on to anyone in the salon.'

'No.' Jude was being tarred with the brush of homophobia, but it wasn't the moment to correct Connie's misapprehension. 'Sorry, it was just something someone said.'

'Everyone in Fethering's got something to say about Kyra's death, and I wish they'd stop it. Nobody really knows anything . . . except perhaps the police.'

'And they're keeping anything they know very firmly to themselves.'

'Yes.' Their recent conversation had spoiled the serenity of Connie's mood. 'Look, there are some things I've got to sort out, Jude.'

'Yes, of course, I must be on my way.'

'Just a minute.'

Jude stopped on her way to the door. 'What?'

Connie was looking curiously at her hair. 'You haven't had it cut again since I did it, have you?'

'No, of course not,' came the guilty reply.

But Connie was not deceived. Looking closely at the hair, she echoed exactly the words of Kelly-Jane at Martin & Martina, 'Dear, oh dear. Now do tell me where this was done.'

'No, look, I can't. Sorry, I must be on my way.' It took a lot to fluster Jude, but this had achieved the feat. She realized she had overstepped a diplomatic boundary. Having another haircut by another stylist at another salon within a week is probably about the most offensive insult you can give a hairdresser. And Connie's face reflected the affront she had just received.

Jude opened the door, but before she went out, turned back and said, 'There was one other thing I wanted to ask you . . .'

'Oh?' Connie wasn't a natural at being frosty, but the welcome had definitely gone from her voice.

'Something Carole told me. The morning Kyra's body was discovered . . .'

'Yes?' The hairdresser had already had quite enough of that subject.

'Well, I'm sure she must have got it wrong, because you always take such care of your appearance, but Carole said that morning you weren't wearing any make-up, and you hadn't done your hair.'

'No, I hadn't. I sometimes do all that after I've arrived here. Go through to—' She corrected herself. 'Do it in the mirror here.'

The image did not match the picture of the woman that had formed in Jude's mind. Connie had her standards as the owner of the salon; she wouldn't do her make-up in the mirror when she had a client present. She didn't say anything, but Connie seemed to feel she needed further self-justification. 'I just got delayed that morning, that's all.'

'Do you remember what delayed you?'

'The fact that my alarm clock didn't ring. With the result that I overslept.' Jude's welcome was in danger of being outstayed. 'Now, I really do have things to do . . .'

'Of course. Thanks for the coffee. See you.'

As she walked back to Woodside Cottage, Jude felt certain that, whatever had delayed the owner from reaching Connie's Clip Joint on the morning after Kyra Bartos's murder, it wasn't just that she'd overslept.

Chapter Eighteen

'But would you do that, Carole?'

'I'm not sure that I'm the best person to ask. I'm not one of those women who cakes herself in make-up every time I leave the house.'

'I know you're not. But you always look smart when you go out, don't you?'

Carole wasn't sure whether or not what Jude had just said was a compliment. She hadn't had much practice with compliments and did not receive them naturally. 'I don't know,' she conceded. 'I certainly don't like to look a mess.'

'No, none of us do. It's a feminine instinct. You check you look OK before you leave the house.'

Surely *you* don't, Carole was tempted to ask. Jude always looked as though her hair and her clothes had just been thrown together on a whim. But maybe she had to work at that look just as carefully as Carole had to check that the belt of her Burberry wasn't twisted. Anyway, it certainly did the business for Jude. Wherever she went, men drooled.

'Well,' she went on, 'imagine how much stronger that instinct must be for someone in what in the broadest sense can be called the "beauty industry". Connie Rutherford has to be a walking advertisement for what she's selling. If she looks a mess, she's going to discourage customers to Connie's Clip Joint. So we come back to the same point: what made her late that Thursday morning?'

'She didn't give you any answer?'

'Not a detailed one. Just that she'd overslept. I'm afraid once she noticed that I'd had my hair cut somewhere else, I ceased to be a welcome guest. I don't think I'm going to get a lot more information out of her now.'

'Perhaps it's as well that I didn't come in with you then. At least she doesn't have anything against me.'

'Except that you're a friend of mine.'

'Maybe.'

'And a fellow lover of organic vegetables.'

'I only bought these as an experiment. To see if they taste any different.' This was said very sniffily. Carole had low expectations for the results of her taste test.

'I was only teasing.'

'Oh.' From schooldays onwards, Carole had never been very good at recognizing when she was being teased.

'There's another thing, though, Carole . . .'

'What?'

'Well, OK, let's say Connie does sometimes leave the house in a hurry in the morning . . . for whatever reason . . . one of her car crash encounters with a man perhaps . . . and so she gets to the salon and she hasn't done her hair or make-up . . .'

'Like on that Thursday?'

'Yes.

'Well, she couldn't do her make-up then, because I was waiting to have my hair washed and cut.'

'But I'm sure if all had gone to plan . . . if Kyra opened the salon at eight forty-five as she was meant to and had already been washing your hair when her boss arrived straight from bed . . . there's no way Connie would have done her make-up in the mirror where you could see her.'

'No, I'm sure she wouldn't.'

'So she would have put on her war paint in the back room. She virtually said that to me. She said she'd "go through" – and then she stopped herself and said she'd do it in the mirror at the front.'

'Except that morning she couldn't do what she'd normally do, because I was already there waiting for my appointment.'

'Exactly.' Jude had a hand up in the bird's nest of hair and was tapping her skull reflectively. 'Every time I've gone into that salon, the first thing Connie's done is to offer me a cup of coffee. Did she offer you coffee that morning?'

'No, she didn't. I wouldn't have accepted it, because she was already late and it would have just taken more time and—'

'Are you sure she didn't offer you any coffee?'

'Yes. I remember thinking it was quite odd. Because it sounded as though she was about to offer me something . . . and then she stopped . . .'

'Hmm. You know what the reason for that could be?'

'No.'

'The coffee machine's in the back room. It's possible that Connie didn't offer you coffee because she didn't want to go into the back room . . . because she knew there was something she didn't want you to see back there.'

The following morning, the Tuesday, Jude was on the way down the High Street for a walk on the beach when she saw someone she recognized. Sitting in a parked car, looking patiently out towards the sea, was Wally Grenston. The day was warm and his window was down, so she greeted him as she passed.

After the customary pleasantries, she said, 'So Mim's let you out on your own, has she?'

The grizzled head turned nervously at the suggestion and nodded towards the building outside which he was parked. 'She's in at the chiropodist. A martyr to her feet, Mim. I tell her it's down to all those ridiculous stiletto things she wore when she was a singer. If God had intended women to walk like that He'd have put prongs on their heels. You don't go for shoes like that, do you?'

Jude laughed and lifted up one brown sandaled foot.

'Very sensible. If Mim'd worn shoes like that all her life, she wouldn't have her current trouble.'

'I haven't worn shoes like this all my life, Wally. I've had my time in stilettos.'

'Well, clearly not as much time as Mim.' Again he looked with some anxiety at the chiropodist's door, but he was all right. She hadn't come out yet. 'And are you still doing the amateur sleuthing, Jude?'

'Still trying to work out how Kyra Bartos died, yes.'

He nodded, mulling over an idea, then said, 'I had a call from her father yesterday.'

'Joe?'

'Jiri, yes. There is a meeting of the Czech Club in Brighton tomorrow night. He asked me if I was going.'

'You mean he is?'

He caught the eagerness in her voice. 'Yes, he is going. And no, Jude, there is no chance that you could go there too to meet him. The club is Members Only.'

'Ah,' she said, disappointed. 'And what do you do when you're there?'

'We sit and drink.' He smiled fondly. 'Some drink beer, some slivovitz. I drink Becherovka. And we talk about times . . .' There was a catch in his voice. '. . . about times that will never come back.'

'Does the club have its own premises?'

'No, no. We meet sometimes in a hotel room, a pub, sometimes at the house of one of the members. Two times a year we have big dinners, socials . . . with food from Czechoslovakia. Mmm, carp . . .' He smacked his lips nostalgically. 'Guests come then, to those dinners. They are good evenings.'

'Maybe you'd invite me to one, one day . . . ?' Jude joked.

Wally Grenston chuckled. 'Nothing that I would like more. Nothing, though, that Mim would like less.'

'Ah.'

He smiled and lightly whistled a couple of bars of a lilting but melancholy tune, almost definitely one of his own. Then he announced, 'I think it is good that Jiri rang me . . .'

'In what way?'

'It means perhaps he is coming out of his grief a little. Since Krystina died, so far as I can tell, he has hardly left the house.'

'Bereavement is a terrible thing.' Suddenly Jude had an idea for another approach to the old man. 'I have actually done work with the bereaved.'

'Work? How do you mean?'

'I do healing . . . you know, like counselling. It has proved very effective. Maybe Joe Bartos would—'

But her suggestion was cut short by a wry laugh. 'You couldn't have chosen a worse idea for Jiri. He does not believe in asking help from anyone, and certainly not help of the kind that might be called "psychological". Joe is very much of the old "suffer in silence" school. He has never talked about his emotions to me – or, I'm sure, anyone else. No, he will sort himself out. And, in fact, that he is talking of going to the Czech Club, this I think is good news. He is, as you say, "coming out of himself".'

'Do you think that means he's more likely to talk to me?'

The old man shrugged. 'Who knows? It's quite possible that he doesn't want to talk to anyone about

Krystina, that the reason he wants to go to the club is to talk about other things. I will only know when I see him.'

'Well, if he does want to talk . . .'

'Yes, yes. I have your number. I will tell him.' But Wally Grenston didn't sound optimistic.

'I don't want to put pressure on him to—'

But Wally was frantically shaking his head and gesturing for her to leave. He had seen something through the chiropodist's window. Jude moved off just as she heard the door opening. By the time Mim had emerged on to the pavement, Jude was twenty yards away. Once again Wally Grenston had lived danger-ously and survived.

The landline was ringing when she returned to Woodside Cottage after her walk. 'Hello?'

'Is your name Jude?' A woman's voice, cultured, confident.

'Yes.'

'My name's Bridget Locke.'

'Ah.' A coincidence? Except Jude didn't really believe in coincidences. There was an intention and synchronicity to everything that happened. Nor had she any doubt that the Bridget Locke on the phone was the one married to Rowley Locke.

'I was given your name by a friend called Sonia Dalrymple.' A horse-owning client with whom Jude had had some recent dealings. 'She said you do healing and stuff . . .'

'Yes.'

'I've suddenly done something to my back. I don't know if you do backs. Maybe I should be talking to an osteopath?'

'I do backs.'

'Well, mine's suddenly gone and—'

'Gone in what way?'

'Sort of seized up down in the small of my back, but the pain comes all over the place, if I try to turn my head round or lift my legs in a certain way.'

'Mmm. Lower back pain. So you'd like to make an appointment?'

'Please.'

'Well, I live in Fethering, just on the High Street. I'm fairly free at the moment, so if you name a time when—'

'Ah. The trouble is, I can't drive. I mean, I can drive normally, but at the moment I can hardly move off my bed, and even just lying there's terribly painful. I certainly can't bend my body to get into the car. It's agony. Look, I'm sorry, but would it be possible for you to come and see me?'

Jude needed no second invitation. She had heard enough from Carole about the Lockes' set-up to want to see it at first hand. If she could cure Bridget Locke's back pain – and she had a high success rate in such cases – then good. And if she could find out any more about Kyra Bartos's murder and the disappearance of Nathan Locke, then even better.

'Yes, of course I could come to you. Where do you live?' she asked, knowing the answer full well.

Chapter Nineteen

Jude fixed to go to Chichester that afternoon. After four, when the younger girls were back from school and could let her in. She could do the journey by rail. The coastal trains on the Brighton to Portsmouth Harbour line were slow and kept stopping in the middle of the bungaloid sprawl at numerous stations with 'wick' in their names, but they'd get her there eventually. Then a taxi from Chichester Station to Summersdale.

She knew Carole would have driven her, but Jude didn't want that, for a couple of reasons. First, the Lockes were presumably unaware of the connection between the two women. The sight of Carole's Renault outside their house could ruin that. Then again, when she was going to do a healing session, Jude needed some quiet time to build up her concentration and focus her energies. That would be difficult to achieve in a car full of Carole's scepticism.

Anyway, as it turned out, she couldn't have got a lift from her neighbour. The immaculate Renault and its owner were elsewhere.

*

Carole wasn't at home because she was on a mission of her own. An only child of borderline paranoid tendencies, she had never been good at sharing. Her relationship with Jude was one of the easiest and least judgemental of her life, but Carole still sometimes felt the necessity for secrets. Particularly in connection with their murder investigations. She could never quite suppress the pleasing fantasy of her doing something very successful on her own; of her finding the link of logic that brought together two apparently unrelated elements in a case. And the fantasy always concluded with the image of her casually presenting the vital new development as a rich gift to Jude.

For nearly twenty-four hours an idea had been simmering in Carole's mind. A piece of the investigation that she could do completely on her own. Indeed, it made sense that she should do it on her own. She was, after all, the one with the car.

The germ of the idea had come to her on the previous day when she had driven out of the Yeomansdyke car park, only to discover that Theo in his shiny BMW had vanished. When Jude had told her about his two o'clock appointment for the Tuesday afternoon, she knew exactly what she should do.

Carole Seddon's experience of stake-out work was limited. Though there were undoubtedly people connected with the Home Office who had honed such skills by long practice, it was not something that had ever come up in her own professional duties. She had spent most of her time writing and reading interminable reports. So her knowledge of surveillance techniques was based only on what she had seen at the cinema and on television.

The first important prerequisite, she knew, was an unobtrusive vehicle, and here she already scored highly. In Fethering a Renault like hers automatically became part of the landscape. The streets were full of such elderly but beautifully nurtured old cars. Nobody would ever give it a second glance.

The second essential was that the driver should also be unobtrusive, and in this respect she was not so well placed. Though she had few friends in Fethering, everybody in the village knew exactly who she was (just as she knew a great deal about all of the people she never spoke to). Anonymity is only granted to people who live in cities; in the country it is impossible to attain.

Balancing this in her favour was the fact that her quarry didn't know either her or her car well. Theo's behaviour the previous day suggested that he'd been completely unaware of the Renault tailing him.

Fortunately, at the end of Fethering High Street there was a small car park for people using the beach. Carole settled the Renault into a bay from which she had a perfect view of Theo's Fabia, parked more or less exactly where it had been the previous day. Having never undergone the procedure, she didn't know exactly how long a cut and highlights would take, but she reckoned it had to be at least an hour. Theo's appointment, she knew, was for two o'clock. Being, however, a person paranoid about being late, she was in her surveillance position by half-past two.

She hoped she didn't look too obtrusive. It was quite common for people – particularly old people – to sit in their vehicles in that particular car park, but the favoured way was facing the sea. To have one's back to the view was unusual but, to Carole's relief, did not attract any curious looks from passers-by. And she did have the *Times* crossword there as a smokescreen.

It was a particularly recalcitrant puzzle that day. Tuesdays, Carole knew from long experience, could be tricky. Mondays and Fridays were always easy. She felt sure that this was a deliberate policy on behalf of the newspaper. The pains of returning to work after the weekend, like end-of-the-week exhaustion, could be eased by an unchallenging crossword. Completing it quickly could give a disproportionate lift to the spirits of the weary commuter. But midweek was a different matter altogether; then the clues could be much more arduous. And Carole had a feeling *The Times* had taken on a new setter. Over the years she had become skilled at reading the minds of the people devising the crosswords, but some of the clues that had been cropping up recently seemed to express a whole new attitude to the English language. Carole found the newcomer's work both satisfying and frustrating – satisfying when she could get an answer right, frustrating when she couldn't. It would take time to find out precisely how the new mind worked.

That Tuesday's crossword was definitely one of his. Very unusually for her, Carole had to look at the clues for nearly ten minutes before she could get her first solution. Normally, even on a difficult day, she could get a couple straight away and then slowly grind through the others. And there were some magical occasions when the whole crossword opened up like a book and the answers came as quickly as she could write them down. Then, by simply narrowing her eyes, she could instantly pick out the anagram from a jumble of words. At such gilded moments she felt omniscient, there was nothing in the world she could not cope with. Such gilded moments, however, were rare.

Doing the crossword was meant to stave off the advance of Alzheimer's, but that afternoon she could feel it encroaching at a rate of knots. Even as she had the thought, though, she knew what was really to blame was her concentration. Constantly flicking her eyes away from the page towards the immobile green Fabia was not conducive to effective clue-solving.

She had a long wait and filled in very few more answers. A cut and highlights clearly took a lot longer than her estimate. She was beginning to think that Theo must've had some other customers booked in, when finally she saw a woman with newly highlighted hair emerge from Connie's Clip Joint. Only moments later Theo came out, and swanned along the High Street towards his car. It was just after four o'clock.

Once again Theo was dressed in his black livery. Once again his movements were light and mildly effeminate. Once again he got into the Fabia and drove out of Fethering in a westerly direction.

And once again Carole Seddon's Renault tailed him.

The previous day's history repeated itself. The Fabia stopped in the Yeomansdyke car park, and the hairdresser, looking neither left nor right, again went into the hotel's spa entrance.

No swim or workout on the Tuesday either. Within five minutes Theo was out again in his other persona. The day's clothes for this character were jeans and an oatmeal-coloured linen jacket. Without even a look at the Fabia, he got into the BMW and drove off.

This time Carole was ready for him. The Renault's engine was on before he was out of the car park, and she was in time to see him turn right out of the entrance. She followed. He was going north, through Yapton and past Fontwell Racecourse towards the A27, the major road that runs parallel to the South Coast. The BMW turned right, rejecting the delights of Chichester, Portsmouth and Southampton in favour of Arundel, Worthing and Brighton.

On the minor roads, there had been little traffic and Carole had had no difficulty keeping within sight of Theo's car. Indeed, her only worry had been that her trailing him was too obvious. On the A27 the problem was different. There were many more vehicles and an open stretch of road would give a car like the BMW opportunities to let rip and lose the more sedate Renault (not to mention the even more sedate Renault's owner).

But Theo proved to be a very law-abiding driver. He rarely took the car above fifty and Carole had little difficulty in keeping no more than one or two cars away from him. Where the traffic slowed to a crawl through the outskirts of Worthing, she found she was directly behind. Rather belatedly, she put on a pair of dark glasses from the Renault's neat glove compartment. It was unlikely that Theo would show any interest in the driver of the car behind – he was probably lost in a radio programme or music CD – but Carole still thought putting the glasses on was a prudent move. The action also gave her a *frisson*; she was behaving like a real private investigator.

Worthing left behind, the BMW showed no signs of stopping. It didn't take long before Carole started to feel less like a real private investigator and more like the middle-aged owner of a dog who would soon be needing a meal and a walk. She had no idea how far Theo was going. His destination could be anywhere – London, Canterbury, Folkestone. Yes, he might even be going through the Channel Tunnel. Paris? Lille? He could be going to any place in Europe or beyond.

With difficulty, she curbed her imagination and made a decision. Brighton would be the extent of her surveillance. If he went beyond Brighton, then that was it. End of adventure. She'd go back and feed Gulliver.

The possibility of a destination in Brighton or nearer was boosted by the fact that, after leaving the magnificence of Lancing College to his left and climbing the steep incline above Shoreham-on-Sea, Theo left the A27 in favour of the A2770. While the major road led up through a tunnel to all kinds of distant places, the one he had selected led through a variety of overlapping small towns until it reached Brighton.

The traffic was still heavy and slower on the minor road, so keeping the BMW in sight was again no problem. The two cars stopped and started through the

suburban sprawl, then took a right turn down towards
Hove. Where the road met the sea, Theo turned left,
along the magnificent frontage towards Brighton.
Carole knew it didn't really make sense, but she
seemed to feel a relaxation in his driving now, as if
he were on the home straight.

And so it proved. Taking his tail by surprise, Theo's
BMW suddenly swung left up into a magnificent
Regency square of fine houses frosted like wedding
cakes. Carole almost overshot the junction, but, to a
chorus of annoyed hooting from behind her, managed
to manoeuvre the Renault up the same way.

At the top, on the side facing the sea, Theo bedded
the car neatly into a reserved space. The lack of other
parking left Carole with no choice but to drive past
him. She juddered to a halt on yellow lines beyond
the row of residents' cars and looked ahead, trying to
find that rarest of phenomena – a parking space in
Brighton.

She was so preoccupied with her search that she
didn't look behind her. The tap on her window took her
completely by surprise. She turned in the seat to see
Theo looking down at her. Sheepishly, she lowered the
window.

'So, Carole . . .' he asked, 'why have you been following me?'

Chapter Twenty

Jude was let into the Summersdale house by one of the little Locke girls, dressed in a green school jumper and skirt. Whether it was Chloë or Sylvia – or indeed Zebba or Tarnil – she had no means of knowing, and the information wasn't volunteered. All the child did, when the visitor had identified herself, was to say lispingly, 'Oh yes, Mummy's expecting you. She's upstairs.' Then, turning on her heel and announcing, 'I'm playing,' she went back into the sitting room.

As Jude climbed the stairs, she tried to tune in to the atmosphere of the place. Beneath the surface chaos of lovable family life she could feel strong undercurrents of tension and anxiety. Those might be natural, given the Lockes' current situation, but the impression she got was that they pre-dated the disappearance of Nathan from Marine Villas.

At the top of the stairs she paused, and a weak voice said, 'I'm through here.'

Bridget Locke was wearing a plain white nightdress, and was propped up high on pillows in a single bed. But before Jude had a chance to process this information, she was told that this was the spare room. 'I'm so uncomfortable in the night that I can't share a bed with anyone. Rowley wouldn't get any sleep if I was in our own room.'

Jude, as usual with a new client (she preferred that word to 'patient'), began by asking a few general questions about Bridget's medical history. Apparently, back pain was not a recurrent problem for her. This was the first time it had happened, or at least had happened so badly that she needed treatment.

'Why did you come to me? Most people's first port of call would have been their GP.'

'Yes.' The woman seemed slightly confused by the question. 'The fact is, I've always favoured alternative therapy over conventional medicine. My experience of doctors has been that, whatever your complaint is, they reckon a drug prescription will sort it out. I'm rather reluctant to cram my body full of chemicals.'

While Jude entirely agreed with the sentiment, she wasn't convinced that Bridget Locke was telling the truth about her reasons for approaching her. 'You said it was Sonia Dalrymple who suggested you call me . . . ?'

'That's right.'

'How is she?' A bit of general conversation might relax the woman – even, Jude found herself thinking for some reason, put her off her guard.

'She's fine. Well, I say that . . . I think the marriage has broken up. Difficult man, Nicky.'

Jude, whose investigations with Carole into a murder at Long Bamber Stables had found out some interesting secrets about Nicky Dalrymple, might have put it more strongly. But she wasn't about to say more about that. 'So, if this is the first time your back's gone, Bridget, what do you think's caused it?'

'I don't know. Lifting something out of the car perhaps? Standing at a funny angle?'

'Was there any moment when you suddenly felt it go?'

'No, it sort of happened gradually.'

'Hmm. You know, a lot of back pain isn't primarily physical.'

'Are you saying it's psychosomatic?' The reaction was a common one. No one wanted to have their suffering diminished by being told it was 'all in the mind'.

'That's a word you can use, if you want to,' Jude replied soothingly. 'The mind and the body are very deeply interrelated. And whether the cause is something mental or something physical, it doesn't make any difference to how much your back hurts.'

'No.' Bridget Locke sounded mollified.

'What are your normal stress reactions?'

'Sorry?'

'Most of us have some kind of physical response to stress. With some people it's headaches . . . stomach upsets . . . insomnia . . .'

Bridget Locke seized on the last word. 'I don't sleep that well. I suppose that is my normal stress reaction, yes.'

'And presumably, with your back like this, you're sleeping even less?'

The woman nodded. She did look exhausted. Under the neatly cut hair, the skin of her face was tight with tiredness and there were dark hollows beneath her eyes.

'You're worried about Nathan?'

'Oh, you've heard about that?' Again something didn't ring true with Jude. Bridget knew she lived in Fethering, she must have known the level of village gossip that an event like Kyra Bartos's murder would generate in a place like that. Surely she would have assumed that Jude knew about it.

But this was not the moment for a challenge. 'Yes, dreadful business. It must be hard on you . . .'

'Quite tough.'

'. . . and of course the rest of the family.' Though from what Carole had said, Bridget was the only one who seemed worried about the boy.

'Yes.'

'Hmm. I gather, Bridget, you're not Rowland's first wife?'

'No. How did you know that?'

No point in lying. 'A friend of mine told me. Someone you've met. Her name's Carole Seddon.'

'Ah, yes.' Was Jude wrong to detect a note of satisfaction in the response?

'Can I ask you . . . I'm sorry, you may think it's being nosy, but it's a question anyone from Fethering would ask you . . .'

'Because everyone from Fethering has now become an amateur detective?'

'If you like.'

'Including you and your friend Carole?'

'Maybe. We can't help being interested.'

'No, only natural. So what was this question that everyone in Fethering would ask me? Do I know who killed Kyra Bartos?'

'No, not that one. They might be intrigued, but the question they'd ask is one that you might be more likely to have an answer to.'

'Which is?'

Jude looked the woman firmly in the eyes. 'Do you have any idea what has happened to Nathan?'

This time she had no problem in believing the response. A weary shake of the head and, 'No, I wish I did. I feel very close to him.'

'Oh?' As ever the gentle manner promised to elicit confidences. And it did.

'The fact is, this family . . . I mean, when I met Rowley, it was him I fell in love with. I didn't realize to quite what an extent by taking him on, I'd be taking on the rest of the Locke clan too . . .' Jude stayed silent. She knew more would come. 'They are very all-enveloping. They see themselves as a kind of coalition against the world. I think it all started when Rowley and Arnold were boys. They were brought up in Corn-wall . . .'

'At Treboddick?'

'Yes. And, you know, they were always playing these fantasy games. There's one in particular called the Wheel Quest.'

'Oh?' Jude responded as if she'd never heard of it. She'd admitted knowing Carole, but didn't want to suggest that they'd discussed the Lockes together.

'It's something Rowley devised. Started off as a

role-playing thing the boys acted out, then he turned it into a kind of board game. And a family obsession. I expect Chloë and Sylvia are playing it downstairs right now. Anyway, that stuff was all instigated by Rowley. He was the imaginative one, he invented everything, and Arnold was happy to be his acolyte, to go along with whatever Rowley said. Then, when they got married, the wives became part of the . . . well, it may be overstating it, but you could almost call it "the alternative Locke universe". Eithne was fine about the whole thing, still is, and of course the children love being part of it. Joan – that was Rowley's first wife – well, the impression I get is that she went along with it quite enthusiastically at first. She'd been an only child and suddenly being part of this huge, hermetically sealed comfort zone . . . she loved everything about it. But, as the years went on, I think she got a bit disillusioned with the whole set-up. It can be difficult for an outsider.'

Ignoring the implication about Bridget Locke's own position, Jude asked, 'And was Nathan something of an outsider too?'

She'd got it right. 'Yes. I suppose that's why I bonded with him. Neither of us swallowed the whole Treboddick and Wheel Quest business quite as much as we should have done. We liked it, we loved the individual members of the family, but both of us I guess had a kind of independence in us . . . something that meant occasionally we didn't want to do everything as a pack. At times it could all feel a bit claustrophobic. We both liked some level of solitude, which is very difficult to achieve in this family.'

'And that's the bond between you and Nathan?' Jude was rewarded by a nod. 'So is it worry about him that has got you in this state . . . and probably brought on the back trouble?'

'Maybe. Yes, probably.'

'Hmm.' Here was a slight dilemma. By asking what she wanted to ask next, Jude would be admitting that Carole had reported back every detail of her visit to the Summersdale house, and there were some people who would find that an invasion of privacy. Still, it was worth the risk. 'Another thing my friend said, Bridget . . . was that, having met you and your husband, and Arnold and Eithne . . .'

'Yes?'

'. . . you seemed to be the only one genuinely worried by what might have happened to Nathan.'

There was a silence, and Jude feared she might have made a misjudgement. But Bridget proved to be more concerned about the boy than about having her affairs discussed by total strangers. 'I know what you mean, but that's very much a Locke way of doing things. With their solidarity there also comes a huge confidence, so they really can't imagine that anything dreadful's happened to Nathan. He's a Locke – he'll be all right.'

'I don't suppose you think it's possible . . .' Again Jude was treading on potentially dangerous ground, '. . . that they're confident because they actually know where he is . . . they know he's all right?'

'No. Absolutely not.' But then came a concession. 'I did actually suspect that at first. Not very loyal of me, was it? But straight after the murder was discovered, my immediate thought was that Nathan had taken himself off to Treboddick and was lying low down there. That would have been a very Locke solution to the problem. Whatever goes wrong with anyone in the family, a few days at Treboddick is always reckoned to be what's required. That's the universal panacea. So I was suspicious.

'But the police were also suspicious and they went down to Treboddick . . . searched all the cottages and found nothing.'

'You've got a lot of cottages down there?'

'A sort of terrace of four. Old miners' cottages. Rowley's parents used to own all of them. Now one of them's permanently for the family, the other three are let.'

'During the summer holidays?'

'And any other time of year anyone'll take them. Mopsa lives down there and she's supposedly in charge of organizing the lets.' She didn't sound over-confident of her stepdaughter's organizational skills. 'Anyway, once I knew that the police had searched Treboddick, I stopped being suspicious of the rest of the family. They don't know where Nathan is. They've just convinced themselves that, because he's a Locke, nothing bad can happen to him.'

'It must be rather wonderful to have that kind of confidence.'

Bridget Locke grinned wryly. 'Well, it is . . . and it

isn't. Rowley and Arnold feel more secure in the family circle, being judged by family standards, than they do in the real world. So, if something goes wrong, like say when Rowley lost his teaching job, rather than going out into the competitive marketplace trying to get another one, he shrinks into himself. The world of Treboddick and the Wheel Quest is more benign than the real one.'

'Hmm.' Time, Jude decided, to get back to the purported reason for her visit. 'Well, let's have a look at this back, shall we?'

Obediently, Bridget Locke rolled back the duvet and lay on her front. Jude removed the pillows and began very gently to pass her hands up the line of the woman's vertebrae. Not actually touching the skin, she waited to feel the angry energy of pain rising from the body. After the scan, she asked Bridget to perform various movements and tell her which ones hurt. Then, rolling up the nightdress and anointing the shapely back with some aromatic oil she had brought with her, Jude started to do a deep hands-on massage.

The effect was almost immediate. Bridget Locke's body relaxed, and her breathing settled into a slow, regular rhythm. Her limbs twitched and, within minutes, she was fast asleep. She really had been exhausted.

As Jude tiptoed out onto the landing, her mind was full. She'd dealt with a lot of lower back pain, and this was the first sufferer she'd seen who was more comfortable propped up on pillows than lying flat. Nor had she seen many who could shake their heads and throw off duvets with quite such abandon.

Whatever Bridget Locke's reason had been for calling Jude to the house, there certainly was nothing wrong with her back.

Chapter Twenty-one

To leave while a client was asleep would not be the proper professional procedure, and yet to wake her seemed unnecessarily cruel. Bridget Locke's main problem was exhaustion, and the best remedy for that was a large dose of rest. Besides, Jude could hear the excited sounds of the two girls playing in the sitting room. She had been granted more information than she had ever anticipated from their stepmother. Maybe there was more to come from Chloë and Sylvia.

'Your mother's asleep. I'll just wait here until she wakes up.'

The girls hardly reacted to Jude's words as she settled herself into an armchair. They seemed to share the Locke lack of interest in people outside the charmed circle of their own family. And, as their step-mother had predicted, they were deeply absorbed in their game. Jude sat back to watch and listen to the two little, uniformed Pre-Raphaelites. From their conversation she deduced that the one who had let her in was Chloë (aka Zebba) and the smaller one Sylvia (aka Tarnil).

Carole's description left her in no doubt that they

were once again playing the Wheel Quest, and she found the mechanics of the game quite as puzzling as her neighbour had. The action still took place between the Kingdom of Verendia and the Forest of Black Fangdar, but, with more time to look at the board, Jude could now see that the main port of Verendia appeared to be Karmenka, over which loomed an extensive castle called 'Biddet Rock'.

Though she could not possibly understand the detail of what was happening, she did after a while work out that the game concerned a battle between Verendia and Black Fangdar and that the two powers represented – surprise, surprise – Good and Evil. Chloë was playing for Verendia and Sylvia for Black Fangdar. They moved their cardboard figurines around the map with great speed and no discernible logic. And they talked in the incomprehensible language Carole had described. 'The Ordeal of Furminal' was again referred to, as were 'the Vales of Aspinglad' and 'the blood of Merkerin'. And there was a lot more where that came from.

So far as the confused spectator could piece together the action, the forces of Good, in the person of Prince Fimbador, were being pursued by the evil hordes of Gadrath Pezzekan, who of course represented Evil. Prince Fimbador had suffered a heavy defeat at the Battle of Edras Helford, and was now being hounded by the enemy army of gedros, jarks, monitewks and various other monsters. He, cut off from his comrades, had retreated to the stronghold of Biddet Rock. His ghastly opponents were at the gates of the castle and about to break them down.

'Yield, Prince Fimbador!' lisped Sylvia. 'You cannot resist Gadrath Pezzekan and the power of Black Fangdar! Hand over the Grail and your life will be spared!'

'My life is worthless,' Chloë lisped back, 'if the Grail ends up in the evil hands of the Merkerin! I defy you and your false accusations! You have not yet defeated me, Gadrath Pezzekan!'

'Oh no? You are alone. Your army is vanquished. You are outnumbered by thousands to one. And now you are cornered in the Castle of Biddet Rock like a rat in a trap. There is no possible escape for you, Prince Fimbador. Yield the Grail to me!'

'Never! Biddet Rock still has its secrets. Pursue me if you will, but you will never find me in the labyrinth of the Wheel Path. No one has ever found anyone in the Wheel Path. No one has even found the Key of Clove's Halo nor used it to open Face-Peril Gate, which is the secret entrance to the Wheel Chamber. There I will go, carrying the Grail with me for safe-keeping. And from there I will escape, and come back to vanquish you another day, Gadrath Pezzekan!'

'You're bluffing, Prince Fimbador. Already my jarks have broken through the flimsy gates of—'

Quite how that particular Grail-quest might have ended Jude never found out, because at that moment Bridget Locke, yawning and with a towelling robe wrapped around her, entered the sitting room. As if a switch had been flicked, Chloë and Sylvia were instantly silent.

'Sorry, Jude,' said their stepmother. 'I do hope the girls have been keeping you amused.'

'You could say that.'

'I'm so sorry, though. I just passed out.'

'The best thing that could have happened to you. Lots of sleep, that's what you need, Bridget. How does the back feel?'

'Amazing. I don't know what you did to it, but it feels completely back to normal.' Hardly surprising, since there was never anything wrong with it. 'Now tell me – what do I owe you?'

Jude's charges for her healing services were very flexible. Some people she treated free; those who she thought could afford it, she billed for whatever figure came into her head. Even though the Lockes were not well-heeled, she charged Bridget at something near her highest rate. Jude was very sympathetic to psychosomatic sufferings, but not to non-existent ones.

She called on her mobile for a taxi, and exchanged conversation of little consequence with Bridget until it arrived. The two girls sat silently on the floor, in suspended animation until they could resume their game. A stranger's presence hadn't inhibited them at all; but their stepmother's did. Jude wondered how they'd react had it been Rowley who came into the room. She got the feeling the Wheel Quest would have continued uninterrupted.

When the cab arrived, Bridget Locke escorted her to the door. Her farewell words were: 'Do give my good wishes to Carole.' This possibly answered the question that had been building in Jude's mind since she arrived at the house: why had Bridget summoned her there? Could it be that all the Lockes had wanted to do was confirm that there was a connection between Carole and Jude? Were they aware of the two neighbours' interest in the circumstances of Kyra Bartos's death?

Jude couldn't be sure, but in the taxi back to Chichester Station, she certainly felt more that, rather than investigating at the Summersdale house, she herself had been being investigated.

Chapter Twenty-two

'This is where I live. Since you've come all the way from Fethering, can I invite you in?'

Carole had never felt so foolish in her life. To have failed so dismally at surveillance was bad enough, but to be patronized by the person she was supposedly tailing added insult to injury. Her first instinct was to drive off immediately, to slog shamefacedly back to High Tor and give Gulliver his supper and a nice walk.

But another part of her demanded that, having come so far, she had to see the thing through. She hadn't worked out precisely what she was going to do when Theo reached his destination, but she had prepared herself for the possibility that, if he did see her, he would tell her to get lost. Instead, she was being invited inside his home. Surely, for someone who occasionally dared to think of herself as an investigator, that was too good an invitation to turn down.

On the other hand, what she was investigating was a murder and Theo's odd behaviour suggested that at the very least he had something to hide. He was quite possibly in the frame as a suspect. To go into the house or flat of such a person could be risky to the point of recklessness.

Theo himself interrupted her indecision. 'Make your mind up. I'm going in. You can come with me or not. But I'm not likely to ask you again.'

'I'll come in,' she said with a boldness she didn't feel.

'Fine.' He showed his beautifully veneered teeth in a smile that looked just sardonic, but could easily have been evil.

The BMW turned out to be parked exactly in front of his home. He used a key to let himself in through the heavy black door with fine brass trimmings, and summoned an old brass-gated lift – or, when inspected more closely, a reproduction of an old brass-gated lift. Inside, the control panel was all high-tec and comput-erized. Politely he gestured Carole to go in before him, and pressed the button for the third floor. Nothing was said as the lift moved smoothly upwards.

The silence continued as he led her out and moved straight ahead to open his flat. There were no other doors on the landing, indicating that Theo owned the whole of one floor. Carole just had time to register that hairdressers must make a lot more money than she had previously thought before he ushered her into the flat itself. There her impression was confirmed. Through the open hall door, she could see that the huge sitting room, its tall windows looking down over the square to the sea, was exquisitely and lavishly appointed. Sun-light glinted on the deep dark patina of fine furniture, and the paintings on the walls looked as if they were the work of artists Carole had heard of. If all of this came from hairdressing, Theo's prices must be absolutely astronomical.

'I hope you don't mind if I close the door,' said Theo. 'I'm not sure what it is you suspect me of, but I don't in fact have any intention of either raping or murdering you.'

His words so closely matched the anxieties running through her head that Carole found herself blushing. Theo indicated an armchair for her and sat down opposite, his bright brown eyes fixed on her pale blue ones. She looked away. She got the unpleasant sensation that he was enjoying her discomfiture.

'So . . . what's this all about? You following me two days running? With your chubby friend yesterday . . . when I managed to give you the slip . . . and today on your own? As they say in the worst kind of thrillers – what's your game?'

Carole decided to brazen it out. 'I've been following you because I think you have a guilty secret.'

His hands flew up to his mouth in a theatrical gesture of shock. For the first time that afternoon, she saw some of the high campness he had demonstrated in Connie's Clip Joint. 'I heard you used to be a civil servant. Don't tell me you're from the Inland Revenue.'

'No, I'm not.'

He did an equally elaborate impression of relief. 'Thank God for that. If you had been, then I might have had to admit to the odd guilty secret, but then I regard it as a point of honour to deceive the taxman in any way possible. If it's not tax, though . . .' he spread his

hands wide in a display of innocence, '. . . my con-
science is clear.'

'It's nothing to do with tax.' Having started on a
course of confrontation, she had to continue. 'It's to do
with the murder of Kyra Bartos.'

'Ah.' The small brown eyes narrowed. 'I might
have guessed. In a hotbed of gossip like Fethering,
I'm sure there are quite a lot of busybodies who have
their crackpot theories about that. Yes, I suppose every
second pensioner over there sees herself as the reincar-
nation of Miss Marple.'

Carole's first instinct was to be affronted, until she
realized that 'pensioner' was in fact an entirely accurate definition of her status. She tried being a little
less combative. 'All right. Everyone is gossiping about
the case, I agree. And everyone is making wild conjectures about all the people involved with Connie's Clip
Joint . . .'

'Thank you for the "wild conjectures". The use of
the expression displays remarkable self-knowledge.'

'So,' she persevered, 'it therefore does become of
interest when one of those people turns out to have a
guilty secret.'

Theo looked puzzled. 'But I thought we'd established that, apart from a little finessing on my tax
returns . . .' Light dawned. 'Ah. You are referring to my
habit of changing cars at Yeomansdyke . . .'

'Not just cars. Changing personalities too, I'd say.'

She didn't know how he was going to react to
this, and was surprised to see him laugh. 'Well, I can
assure you it's quite legitimate. My membership at

Yeomansdyke is fully up to date. And I have special permission to park a car there overnight. I drive to the hotel in the morning, do a work-out in the gym, and then drive on to be a stylist at Connie's Clip Joint. Anything wrong with that?'

'You change clothes.'

'And when you were employed as a civil servant, Carole, didn't you quite frequently change out of your work clothes at the end of the day?'

'Maybe. But I didn't change cars. Changing clothes and cars suggests very definitely to me that you have something to hide.'

'Perhaps.' But the accusation still seemed to amuse rather than annoy him. 'Before we go into that . . . in your Miss Marple role . . .' Carole found herself blushing again. 'In that role, where do you see me fitting into . . . "The Case of Kyra Bartos"?'

She didn't enjoy being sent up and came back with some vigour, 'I see you as a murder suspect.'

'Do you?' This amused him even more.

'Yes, I do. And quite a strong suspect too.'

'I see. And would you be generous enough to tell me why?'

'Very well. First, you work at Connie's Clip Joint, which was the scene of the crime . . .'

He slapped the back of his hand on his forehead in a 'Foiled again!' gesture. 'How on earth did you work that out?'

Carole wasn't to be deterred. 'What's more you presumably have keys to the place, so you could get in and out at any time of the day and night . . .'

'That too I can't deny. God, where did you learn to be so devilishly clever?'

'What is more,' Carole pressed on, 'you had a very strong feeling of dislike for Kyra Bartos.'

'Did I? And where did that come from?'

'It arose, because she was the one who had got Nathan Locke to fall in love with her, and you loved him.'

Her previous statements had tickled his sense of humour, but this one reduced him to uncontrollable hysterics. Carole sat rigidly still and deeply embarrassed until the paroxysms died down.

'Oh, that is wonderful!' said Theo, wiping the tears from his eyes. 'That is so brilliant! Thank you, Carole. We all need a good laugh, and that is the funniest thing anyone has said to me for years and years. "I killed Kyra because she had stolen the affections of the man I love . . ." Too wonderful.' Relishing the idea brought on another spasm of laughter.

When the last ripples had died down, Carole said, 'I don't know that it's such a ridiculous idea. I've seen photographs of Nathan – he's a very attractive young man. Just the sort who would appeal to a . . .' she couldn't bring herself to say 'gay man' '. . . to a homosexual.'

'A homosexual like me, you mean? How many gays – how many *homosexuals* do you actually know, Carole?'

'Erm . . .' Her knowledge wasn't that extensive. There were one or two men in Fethering who everyone said *were*, but she didn't actually know any of them to speak to. 'There were quite a few in the Home Office,' she concluded lamely.

'I'm sure there were. And were they homosexuals just like me?'

'Well . . .'

Her answer was interrupted by the sound of a key in the front door. As soon as it opened, a tornado of two small children and a large Old English Sheepdog thundered into the sitting room and wrapped itself around Theo. Behind them, closing the door, stood a tall slender woman with long black hair. She moved forward and, picking her way between children and dog, planted a large kiss on Theo's lips.

'You haven't lost your sense of timing, Zara.' He grinned across at his guest. 'Carole – my wife Zara. Our children Joey and Mabel. And our dog, Boofle.'

'Ah.'

'I'm actually tied up for a little while, love.'

'Don't worry,' said Zara. 'The horde needs feeding. Come on, kids. Come on, Boofle. Teatime.' And she led them out into the hall, discreetly closing the door behind her.

Carole was lost for words. All she could come up with was, 'That's an Old English Sheepdog. You said you had a little Westie called Priscilla.'

'Ah – discovered! Mea culpa! Yes, I knew I could not keep my guilty secret from you forever. I do not have a little Westie called Priscilla.'

'Look, what is all this, Theo? Am I to gather that you're not . . . homosexual?'

'Once again nothing escapes the eagle eye of Miss Marple. It's uncanny. How does she do it?'

'But you . . . I mean, the way you behave at Connie's Clip Joint . . . Even when I was there, when you were talking to Sheena, you said things that definitely implied you were . . . homosexual.'

'I did. I admit it. So far as Connie's Clip Joint is concerned, I'm as gay as a pair of Elton John's glasses.'

'But I don't understand.'

He dropped into his arch hairdresser's drawl. 'Give the customers what they want, darling. Someone like Sheena positively loves having her hair cut by a gay man. She'd be disappointed if she didn't have a gay man doing it. So, if that's what she wants . . .' He gave a helpless, camp shrug.

'There must be more to it than that.'

'Ooh, there is, yes. It's also self-protection. Let's take Sheena as an example yet again. Imagine what'd happen with someone like her if she thought I was *available*. She'd be flirting, she'd be all over me. I tell you, behaving the way I do saves me a lot of aggravation. I'm much safer appealing to the fag hag in a harpie like Sheena than I would be if she thought I was hetero.'

Having met the woman in question, and having heard Jude's account of a lunch with her, Carole could see Theo's point.

'So did you invent the business for her about fancying Nathan and being jealous of Kyra?'

'I remember hinting at it to Sheena, just as a joke.

But maybe it got embroidered in her rather over-active imagination.'

'All right, that's possible. But it still doesn't explain everything. The changing clothes, the changing cars.'

'In Fethering everyone thinks I'm gay. In Brighton everyone thinks I'm heterosexual. Yeomansdyke is where I change identities, that's all.'

'That's not enough. There's more to it.'

'Oh? Tell me what there is more to it, Miss Marple.'

'Well, it's an incomplete disguise, for a start. Fethering and Brighton aren't that far apart. Maybe you don't see many of your Brighton friends in Fethering, but it must sometimes happen that you meet one of your clients here.'

'Less often than you'd think. And on the few occasions when it does, they see me out of context, with Zara, with the children and they do a sort of take. I can see their minds working. And usually I can see them concluding: I've just seen someone who looks extraordinarily like my hairdresser. I promise you, it's never been a problem.'

'Is that all the explanation I'm getting?'

Still with a glint of mischief in the dark brown eyes, he spread his hands generously wide. 'Why? Isn't that enough?'

'No, Theo. It isn't.'

'Ah, I see.' He gestured round the lovely sitting room. 'You're telling me that *all this* is a bluff. A cleverly constructed front. The Theo of Connie's Clip Joint is the real me. I am a closet gay, who fancied Nathan

Locke so much that I killed his girlfriend in a fit of jealous homosexual pique.'

Again Carole felt herself blushing under his sardonic gaze.

Theo chuckled. 'I'll tell you the truth, if you like.'

'Would you?' she asked pathetically. 'I mean, for a start, is Theo your real name?'

'Theo is my real name. I started off as an actor. And at one point I got involved in a production with one of those self-obsessed, power-crazed directors who builds up a show from months of improvisation.'

'Oh?' Carole didn't know a lot about the theatre. She hadn't heard of such a technique.

'Well, I was supposed to be playing a hairdresser in this show and so the director, true to his principles, sent me off to research my part by working in a real hairdresser's. I did three months. It could have been worse. I was lucky – one of the other actors had been cast as a cess-pool emptier's mate. Anyway, the usual thing – three months in the salon, three months of self-indulgent improvisation in the rehearsal room, and you end up with a show that would have been a lot better if the director had got a writer in in the first place.

'But after the run finished – and maybe because of what the show had been like – I go through a very bad patch work-wise. You couldn't give me away with soap. And after a long time sitting at home waiting for the phone to ring, I think: well, I'm going to have to get an income from somewhere . . . and I quite enjoyed that three months I spent in the hairdressing salon . . . so . . .'

'You became a hairdresser?'

'Exactly. I joined another salon, trained properly, and suddenly I was a stylist. Money's not great, but compared to being an out-of-work actor, anything's better.'

'And did you develop the, er . . . homosexual mask from the start?'

'Yes. As a joke at first. But then I saw the advantages. As I said, the customers like it, and it keeps them from prying into my private life. And there's a third big benefit – *they confide in me*. Things they'd certainly never tell their husbands or lovers, and a lot that they wouldn't even tell their girlfriends. You wouldn't believe the things a gay hairdresser hears about female behaviour.'

'Hmm.' Carole found she was beginning to relax, recognizing that Theo's sending her up was teasing rather than malicious. She gestured round the room. 'That still doesn't explain all this. I'm sure there are hairdressers who make a huge amount of money, but I'd have thought they're the ones with chains of salons and their own ranges of hair-care products. I can't think you make that much renting a chair at Connie's Clip Joint in Fethering.'

Theo grinned. 'Zara might have a lot of money.'

'Yes, I suppose she might.'

'But in fact she hasn't. Or she hadn't when I married her.' He stood up. 'Do you want to know the last part of my secret, Carole?'

'Please.'

'I'll tell you, but I really do want you to keep this to yourself. You're not to pass it on to anyone else.'

Not even Jude, was her first thought. Then she decided she'd wait to see what the last part of the secret was. If it involved illegality, then she might have to break the promise of confidentiality she gave to Theo.

He led her to a door on the left-hand side of the sitting room. With his family in the house, Carole now had no anxiety in following Theo anywhere. He ushered her into a beautifully designed office. On a desk in a window overlooking the sea stood a lone state-of-the-art laptop. Other purpose-built surfaces held the armoury of more electronic equipment without which no business can now flourish. On specially designed shelves on the back wall stood rows of new-looking books – hardbacks, paperbacks, many in foreign editions.

'Come on, has your brilliant sleuthing mind worked it out yet?'

The reluctant Miss Marple was forced to admit that it hadn't.

Theo took a hardback book from the shelf and held it across to her. On the jacket a determined-looking girl in a red dress stood on an outcrop of rock looking out at a departing steamship. The title was *The Sorrowful Sea*.

'Are you familiar with the *oeuvre* of Tamsin Elderfield?'

'No, I'm afraid I'm not.'

'Well, fortunately . . .' Theo gestured to the rows of shelves, '. . . lots of other people are.'

'You mean . . . you . . . ?'

'Yes.' He grinned. 'A third identity to confuse you, Carole. Theo the hairdresser in Fethering, Theo the family man in Brighton, and now – Tamsin Elderfield in virtually every bookshop in the world.'

'But . . . But . . . it's romantic fiction, isn't it?'

'It certainly is.'

'And you're a man.'

'Spot on. Can't pull the wool over your eyes, Miss Marple.'

'But, if you're such a successful writer, why on earth do you still bother with a day job as a hair-dresser?'

'Because, Carole, that is *why* I am a successful writer. A lot of authors have difficulty answering the inevitable question: where do you get your ideas from? I don't,' he said smugly.

'You get them from Connie's Clip Joint.'

'Of course I do. I actually quite enjoy hairdressing, but that's not why I keep on doing it. No, Connie's Clip Joint is the rich seam of experience which furnishes me with my plots. I don't want to boast, but I think there are few men who have the depth of understand-ing of women's romantic aspirations and frustrations that I do . . . or indeed that any other gay hairdresser does.

'So, Carole, now you know everything – as do the police, incidentally. I've been quite open with them about my different identities and apparently I'm not breaking any laws. So I'm sorry – none of what I've done is even vaguely immoral. Well, except possibly for my lying to you about owning a little Westie called Priscilla.'

There was a long silence, as Carole tried to balance her feelings of surprise and embarrassment. Finally, rather feebly, she asked, 'So there's nothing you can tell me that'll help me find out who killed Kyra Bartos?'

'Sorry.' He too was silent for a moment, before saying, 'Well, there is just one thing . . . I don't know whether Nathan Locke killed the girl or not, but I would think finding the boy alive and talking to him might be the best way of getting to the truth.'

'Do you know where he is?'

'No. But I did overhear him once saying something to Kyra when he came to pick her up . . . something that might be relevant . . .'

'What was it?'

'I also told the police this, so it's no great secret. Whether they acted on what I said, I've no idea. It's just . . . I was in the back room at the salon one evening tidying up, and Nathan came in to fetch Kyra, and she was getting her stuff together and he was talking, rather romantically, of how he'd like to take her away some time, spend a few days with just the two of them. And he said he knew a lovely place, a secret place he'd been longing to show her ever since they met.'

'Where was it?' breathed Carole.

'In Cornwall.'

She still felt sheepish when she got back to the Renault. Theo had compounded the impression that he was patronizing her by giving her a copy of one of Tamsin Elderfield's paperbacks: *The Roundabout of Love*. With some force Carole threw it onto the back seat, before starting on the rush-hour crawl back to Fethering.

Chapter Twenty-three

Jude was round at the front door as soon as she saw the Renault slide neatly into the High Tor garage. Unaware of how Carole had spent the afternoon, she had her own news to impart.

So while her neighbour dropped her *Times* on the table and tried to regain favour with an aggrieved Gulliver by feeding him, Jude opened a bottle of wine and supplied edited highlights of her visit to the house in Summersdale. 'But,' she concluded, 'I still don't know why I was summoned there. Bridget Locke had nothing wrong with her, but she was very determined that I should go over. I wonder what she wanted . . . ?'

'I should think it was more a matter of what her husband wanted. Even though Bridget seems to be a strong woman, I get the impression Rowley dictates what happens in that household – and in the whole family, come to that. He's used to getting his own way and he'll use any means – even throwing tantrums – to ensure that that state of affairs continues.'

'All right, say she was only following orders . . . what was Bridget trying to find out? I imagine she must have got what she wanted before she fell asleep, because she didn't ask me any supplementary questions afterwards.'

Carole was practical as ever. 'Just go through everything she said to you again. There must've been something that had a special meaning for her.'

Screwing up her face with the effort of recollection, Jude reassembled the conversation that had taken place in Bridget Locke's spare bedroom. At one point Carole interrupted her. 'Well, that's it!'

'What's it?'

'She effectively asked you whether you and I were investigating the case.'

'I suppose she did.'

'I think that's all she wanted – or all Rowley wanted. Confirmation that you and I were working together trying to find out who killed Kyra. And it would also tie in with the way Rowley's kept insisting that I should tell him any new developments I've found out about.'

'You reckon he's monitoring the progress of our investigation into the murder?'

'I would say that's exactly what he's doing, Jude. Which could mean quite a lot of things . . .'

'The most obvious being that he knows the truth of what happened and doesn't want us to get too close to it.'

They were both silent as the implications of this sank in.

'I also,' said Jude eventually, 'witnessed the two little Pre-Raphaelite models playing that ridiculous game.'

'Oh, God. The Wheel Quest.'

'Yes. What on earth is all that about? I couldn't make head nor tail of it.'

'I agree. Tolkien's got a lot to answer for,' said Carole darkly.

'You can say that again. But the girls were so caught up in the whole thing. I'm afraid I've never seen the attraction of all that Dungeons and Dragons nonsense or any of those fantasy computer games.'

'Be careful, Jude. Never compare the Wheel Quest to a computer game when Dorcas Locke is present. She'll bite your head off. She did mine.'

'Well, I thought it was all nonsense. Honestly, the way those two girls went on, all about Gadrath Pezzekan and Biddet Rock and the Vales of Aspinglad . . . just a load of meaningless words.'

'Like today's *Times* crossword.'

'Sorry?'

'I've got almost nowhere with it. Couldn't even do the anagrams, and I can normally spot those a mile off. Today the clues were like a jumble of nonsense words.'

'Well, maybe the answers are too, Carole. Try putting in some of that stuff from the Wheel Quest: "Ordeal of Furminal" . . . "Prince Fimbador" or—'

'Fimbador?'

'Yes, that was the name of one of the characters. The hero, so far as I could gather. Why?' Jude looked curiously at her friend's puzzled face.

'It's just something . . . Prince Fimbador . . . Fimbador . . . There's something at the back of my mind that . . .' She suddenly clapped her hands together. 'Fimby! The family nickname for Nathan is Fimby!'

'And you think that's short for Fimbador?'

'Yes.'

Jude was less than convinced. 'Well, it could be I suppose, but—'

'Come on, come on. Was there anything else the girls said that could have applied to Nathan?'

'Well, only . . . Let me think . . . Oh, they did say – that is, Chloë, in the character of Prince Fimbador, said: "I defy you and your false accusations!"'

'Did she?' Carole's pale eyes were sparkling with excitement. 'And just a minute – what did you say the name of the castle was? The castle where Prince Fimbador was going to escape by the Wheel Path?'

'Biddet Rock.'

'How many Ds? Quick, write it down, write it down!'

Jude found a pen and scribbled the letters down in a space next to the crossword. (It was a measure of her neighbour's excitement that she made no comment – normally she hated anyone touching her copy of *The Times*.) Carole narrowed her eyes and focused on the letters of Biddet Rock.

'Treboddick!' she shouted. 'Treboddick! "Biddet Rock" is an anagram of "Treboddick".'

'You know,' said Jude, 'I've a feeling we could be on our way to Cornwall.'

Jude had inherited a laptop from a former lover, Lawrence Hawker, who had died of cancer a few years back at Woodside Cottage. It was connected to the internet, though she had never mentioned this fact to Carole. Partly this was because the subject had not come up in conversation and also her neighbour was of the view that, having managed this far through her life without the new technology, there was no need to embrace it in her fifties. Another reason for Jude's reticence was the fact that she used email a lot to keep in touch with a wide variety of friends and lovers from her varied past. Knowing Carole's exclusive and jealous nature, Jude did not want to complicate matters by bringing to her friend's attention the life she had outside Fethering.

But for the task they faced that Tuesday evening the internet was the perfect tool, so they adjourned next door, where Jude immediately led her neighbour upstairs to the nest of a bedroom which spread across the whole frontage of Woodside Cottage. Carole had rarely been in this inner sanctum, and she could not help thinking of the lovers who had shared that broad bed – Lawrence Hawker for certain, but also many others (most of whom, it has to be said, existed only in Carole's fevered imagination).

'I don't know what you think this is going to achieve,' she said stuffily. 'It's not as if we even have an address for this place the Lockes have in Cornwall.'

'We have a name, though. That'll be enough.'

'How do you mean?'

'Ssh. Let Google work its magic.'

Carole watched in silence, as Jude summoned up a screen and typed into a dialogue box the single word

'Treboddick'. Within seconds a list of references appeared.

'Well, that wasn't so hard,' said Jude. 'Got the right one first time.'

'Just like that?' Carole looked curiously at the screen.

'Yes, well, I don't think "Treboddick" is that common a word. Quite possibly the one in Cornwall is the only one there is.' She scanned down the listings. 'Ah, here we are.'

Leaning over her friend's shoulder, Carole read: '"Treboddick Holiday Cottages – Perfect tranquillity in exquisitely renovated miners' homes in one of the most beautiful seaside settings in the British Isles."' There was a colour photograph of a terrace of stone buildings capped with slate roofs. Nearby were picturesque ruins of chimneys and outhouses, presumably vestiges of the mine workings. The position certainly was stunningly beautiful. Beneath the illustration were contact numbers. 'So what do we do – ring up the unfortunately named Mopsa and see if we can book in?'

'Let's make email contact first. Don't want to risk the phone being answered by Rowley Locke and him recognizing our voices.'

'But he's not down in Cornwall, is he?'

'Who knows? He wasn't at the house this afternoon when I went to see Bridget. I think it'll be safer if we remain anonymous at first.'

'Well, you can't remain anonymous on email, can you? Surely, if you want to get a reply, you're going to have to give your name?'

'You're going to have to give *a* name. I've got a "Jude" account, but I've also got others in the name of "Nichol" and "Metarius".'

Carole was excited by the direction the conversation was taking. Since she'd moved into Woodside Cottage, Jude had always been vague about the precise details of her past, particularly of her marital history. Now Carole was being given the perfect opportunity to get a little concrete information on the subject. She had heard the names from Jude before, but never had their provenance defined. 'Now one of those is your married name, isn't it?' she asked.

'They're both married names,' said Jude, muddying the waters even further.

'So you mean you have a third name too – the one you were born with?'

'That's right.' But before any supplementary questions could be asked, Jude had, as ever, moved on. Scribbling down the Treboddick email address, she announced, 'I think this is a job for Mrs Metarius.' As she made her way into the relevant account, she continued, 'Just a general enquiry first. Came across your details on the net . . . hear that the cottages are in a lovely part of the country . . . wonder if you have any availability . . .'

'When?'

'As soon as possible. We could leave tomorrow, couldn't we?'

'What?' This went against Carole's every instinct. Granted, they were going in the cause of investigation, but a trip to Cornwall sounded very much like a holiday to her, and you couldn't just shoot off on holiday without preparation. She remembered organizing family trips when Stephen was little. They had to be planned months and months ahead, with all the attention to detail of a major military offensive. First, dates had to be agreed with David, who always needed a lot of warning and thinking time before he got close to making a decision about anything. And then there had to be long discussions about the venue and the optimum form of transport to be used, and then . . . and then . . . You couldn't just shoot off to Cornwall overnight.

'Do you have a problem with that? Have you got something booked?'

Trying not to sound pathetic, Carole was forced to admit that no, she didn't have anything booked for the next day. Or for a good many days after that. But she kept that information to herself.

Jude was busy at the keyboard, typing in her enquiry. Signing off with 'J. Metarius', she sent the email off.

'How soon will you get a reply?'

'Depends how often Mopsa – or whoever happens to be there – checks her email. From the impression the Lockes have given of their financial situation, it should be quite often.'

'So what do we do now?'

'We go downstairs, Carole, and we have another glass of wine.'

*

Their other glass of wine led to further conversation about the case. Carole had missed the opportunity to get back on to Jude's marriage – or marriages – but she did somewhat shamefacedly describe her encounter with Theo. (She couldn't see any reason to abide by the confidentiality he had demanded.) When she heard what had happened, Jude was very good and just managed to stop herself from laughing. After the update, they went upstairs to find that there had already been a response from Treboddick Cottages. Mopsa was being appropriately vigilant.

Yes, there was current availability. Maybe J. Metarius would like to email back a more specific enquiry? Or telephone?

'Telephone,' said Jude firmly. 'I'll use the mobile. A Fethering dialling code might be a bit of a give-away.' She got through to the number on the screen. 'Good evening. My name's Metarius. I've just received your email.'

'Hello, so glad you've got in touch,' lisped the voice from the other end of the line. Had Jude met Dorcas, she would have recognized that Mopsa's voice was identical.

'Can I ask who I'm speaking to?'

'Yes, of course. My name's Mopsa Locke. I'm in charge of the lettings of Treboddick Cottages.'

'Oh, good. I'm glad I've got the right person. Now the fact is that a friend and I suddenly have some free time and we were wondering how soon we could book in to one of the cottages.'

'As soon as you like. They're all empty.' Mopsa

decided that this last comment made her business sound too needy, and went on, 'That is to say, they're all *currently* empty. You know, between bookings. But we could fit you and your friend in. When would you like to come?'

'Tomorrow would be ideal.'

'And how long would you be wanting to stay?'

'Well, till after the weekend at least.'

I can't suddenly go off and leave Fethering for nearly a week, was Carole's instinctive reaction. But when she thought about it, she realized that there was nothing at all to stop her. She couldn't even pretend to be restricted by Gulliver. The dog could come with them. There's nothing he'd like better. Gambolling on Cornish cliffs would be his idea of heaven. On the other hand, she wouldn't tell Jude that yet. She'd keep the potential problem of Gulliver up her sleeve in case she needed a get-out.

'Normally our minimum booking is for a week,' said Mopsa.

'Well, that's fine,' Jude responded airily. 'We'll book it for a week.'

What, thought Carole, and where's the money coming from? Although her Home Office pension and prudent savings habits meant she could easily have booked a round-the-world cruise at that very moment, a week in a cottage in Cornwall still sounded like an unwarranted extravagance.

'I'm not sure,' Jude went on, 'exactly what time we'll arrive tomorrow evening. Is there some arrangement we should make about picking up the key . . . ?'

'It's fine. I'm here all the time. I'll be able to let you in.'

'Good.'

'And there will be a Welcome Pack of basics in the fridge when you arrive. You know, bread, milk, butter.'

'That sounds fine. Oh, one thing . . . Is it all right if we have a dog with us?' The question showed that Jude was ahead of Carole. Gulliver wasn't going to be allowed as an excuse to get out of the trip.

'Yes, that's fine. Lots of our guests bring dogs. There are some lovely walks along the cliffs.'

'Great. Now which of the cottages is free, Mopsa? Which one would you recommend?'

'As I say, they're all free . . . just briefly. I live in Number One. Two and Four are really one big double room and one small single. Since there are two of you, Three would be best. That's got two large single bedrooms.' There was a slight hesitation at the other end. 'That is, if you don't want the double . . . ?'

Well, these days you had to ask. Jude suppressed a giggle and decided she wouldn't pass on that part of the conversation to Carole. Her neighbour was clearly already having difficulty accommodating the idea of the two of them swanning off to Cornwall for a week. The suggestion that they might be mistaken for a lesbian couple was probably more than she could cope with.

'No. Number Three sounds the right one for us. Now are you going to need my address?'

'If you can just give me a credit card number, that'll be fine. You can fill in the forms when you arrive. We take a non-refundable hundred pound deposit, and that'll come straight off your card. I'm sorry, but we have had unfortunate experiences in the past.'

'I'm sure you have. Can't trust anyone these days, can you? Just a sec. I'll get the card.' Jude reached into a capacious handbag and took out a battered wallet, from which she extracted one from a choice of credit cards.

Carole saw the name: 'J. Metarius.' 'Do you have another in the name of "Nichol"?' she whispered.

'Yes.'

'And in your birth name?'

'Yes.' But Jude wasn't about to elaborate. 'Hello, Mopsa. It's a MasterCard, and I'll give you the number . . .'

When the call finished, Carole was about to go into a long diatribe about how rash and extravagant they were being, but she was prevented by Jude immediately keying in another number.

'Who?'

'The Lockes. In Chichester. Ssh.'

Carole watched in frustrated silence while her friend spoke. 'Hello, who is that? Mr Locke, my name's Jude. Yes, I came to see Bridget this afternoon about her back . . . That's right. Just ringing . . . a sort of after-service call, to see if she's still feeling better. Oh, good, that's excellent news. No, don't bother her. If it's still fine, I don't need to talk to her. And if she gets any more trouble . . . well, she's got my number. Thank you so much. Goodbye.' She switched off the phone.

'Do you give "after-service" calls to all your patients?' asked Carole sourly.

Jude didn't bother to argue with the choice of word. Her neighbour knew she preferred to call them 'clients' and was only being annoying. 'Not all of them, no.'

'Then what was the purpose of that?'

'The purpose of that was to find out from Bridget whether her husband was around. But he saved me the trouble by actually answering the phone himself.'

'Ah.' Carole understood. 'Because if Rowley is currently in Chichester . . . then we know he's not at Treboddick.'

'Exactly,' said Jude. 'Now, one more glass of wine, and then I guess we should do some packing.'

Chapter Twenty-four

There was one call Carole had to make when she got back to High Tor. Her affront about the idea of suddenly swanning off to Cornwall (as she still thought of it) had now been replaced by a sensation that came quite close to excitement. Since the break-up of her marriage, she hadn't really done holidays. Partly this was due to the instinctive frugality of her nature, but she also had to admit to herself that she didn't like the idea of setting off somewhere to have a good time on her own. The prospect of booking into a cruise ship and being thrown in with all kinds of people she had never seen before was her worst nightmare. And there were no friends with whom she felt relaxed enough to risk exposing her personality to them over a sustained period. Jude was probably the person to whom she was closest, but the parameters of their relationship would not, to Carole's mind at least, encompass the suggestion of their holidaying together. So the forthcoming trip to the West Country, although in the cause of their murder investigation, had suddenly become rather an attractive proposition. As soon as she heard they wouldn't be sharing a room, Carole had become quite keen on the idea.

To her surprise, Stephen answered the phone. She hadn't expected him to be in his Fulham home, and had anticipated having to call his mobile number. Carole still felt a little old-fashioned about mobiles, as if they were new and experimental technology. She was never confident that a message left on a mobile didn't immediately vanish into the ether. Jude kept saying she ought to get one, but Carole didn't feel the need. She didn't get many calls on the landline at High Tor. What was the point of having two phones that didn't ring?

'I just rang to ask about Gaby.'

'She's still in hospital.' Stephen sounded weary. 'They say there's nothing to worry about, but they still want to keep her in, probably until the baby's born. Which is something I can't exactly understand, if there's "nothing to worry about".'

'I'm sure it's just precautionary. The blood pressure.'

'That's what they say.'

'She'll be fine.'

'I hope so.' Carole had never heard so much strain in her son's voice. The responsibility of approaching fatherhood, maybe even the masculine guilt about having put his wife into her current hazardous condition, was weighing him down.

'In a month you'll have a lovely little baby and you won't remember any of the anxieties you went through.' Stephen didn't reply to this. Perhaps he didn't think it was worthy of reply. 'Look, I'm ringing because I'm going to be away for a few days.'

'Oh? How long?'

'Well, it could be as much as a week.' Though somehow she didn't think it would be. That had been another reason for her shock at Jude's extravagance. Her neighbour seemed unthinkingly to write off a week's rent for an investigation that might only last a couple of days. And, come to think of it, what were they investigating? Because of some extremely iffy clues, they were hoping to find Nathan Locke at Treboddick. But, given the fact that the police had already searched the place, how small were their chances of success?

'Where are you going, Mother?'

Oh dear, he was back to formality. 'Cornwall,' she replied.

'Good.'

'Why do you say "good"?'

'Because you could do with a break.' A break from what, was Carole's instinctive reaction. Since the Home Office had decided to dispense with her services, she had never quite lost the sensation that she was totally unproductive. The work ethic remained strong within her, and she still felt people without work were, at some level, worthless.

'Are you going on your own?'

'With Jude.'

'Excellent.'

'As I say, it may not be a full week, but . . . Anyway,

if there are any problems with Gaby, you'll let me know, won't you?'

'Of course. Though I'm not sure how. You haven't got round to buying a mobile yet, have you?'

'No,' came the shamefaced reply.

'You really should. It's so convenient.'

'Yes,' she agreed humbly. 'But I'll call you when I get down there. There's probably a phone in the cottage.'

'Or you could just give me Jude's mobile number.'

But that somehow didn't seem right. Carole wasn't sure of the etiquette of mobile ownership, but she thought it must be bad form to give out someone else's mobile number as a personal contact – even though she knew that Jude would be the last person in the world to worry about something like that.

'I'll phone you when we get down there.'

'All right,' he said in the voice a cotton mill owner might have used to a potential Luddite. 'Oh, incidentally, Mum . . .' Thank God, he was relaxed enough to stop calling her 'Mother'. But Carole's joy was short-lived, as he went on, 'I was talking to Dad today.' He never seemed to have any problem using the word 'Dad'. 'He was saying he'd love to see you.'

'Why?' came the icy response.

'Well, look, you are both about to be grandparents.'

'That doesn't mean we cease to be divorced.'

'No, but I was thinking . . . you know, for the baby, it'd be nice if he or she was born into a family where everyone got on.'

'You and Gaby get on. That'll be the most important

thing for your child. And I'm sorry, Stephen, I wish that your father and I had "got on" like a perfect fairy tale couple, but we didn't, and at least we had the honesty to admit the fact.'

'I don't know. I think Dad would quite like you to get back together . . .'

This was more than Carole could cope with. Though aware of her son's fragile state of anxiety about Gaby, she couldn't stop herself from snapping, 'Well, I can assure you I do not share his opinion.'

After the phone call, she felt guilty about what she'd said. But by the time she went to bed – soon after ten, she and Jude were planning an early start – the reaction had receded. She'd have felt even more guilty if she'd lied about her feelings for David.

There was a feeling of holiday about their journey down to Cornwall. The Wednesday had opened to a cloudless sky, late September maintaining the illusion that winter wasn't just around the corner. And even as they drove along the M27 past Portsmouth and South-ampton, they got a feeling of life opening up. Jude had always been part of a wider world, but since her retire-ment Carole had felt her horizons narrowing down to Fethering and only Fethering. She felt exhilarated to be seeing somewhere new.

It was also interesting to have a different person in the navigator's seat. During her marriage Carole had done most of the driving, David beside her. Although he had a bad sense of direction and kept losing his place on the map, he was always convinced that he was right. As a result, the tension in the car quickly became palpable. So for Carole the mere fact of having someone else in the car was a stress trigger, even when the other person was Jude.

Though she had ferried her neighbour around on many short trips, they had never spent a whole day in the car together and, as ever in a new situation, Carole was anxious about giving away too much of herself. She had always eschewed intimacy. The idea that someone might know everything about her was appalling. The certainty that nobody did know quite everything was what kept her going.

But after about an hour of driving she relaxed. Jude was a very undemanding and unjudgemental companion. What was more, she had no interest at all in their route. She assumed that Carole knew the way she wanted to go and that was fine by her. Jude seemed more laid-back than ever. She didn't say much, but there were few uneasy silences. Indeed, Carole found herself talking quite a lot, even confessing the fears that she could never voice to Stephen about the health of his wife and their unborn child. Jude was predictably reassuring. She even volunteered the use of her mobile phone to check on the family, which made Carole feel very embarrassed. She knew she would only have had to ask.

They hadn't left quite as early as they'd intended. Eight-thirty had been the proposed departure time, and at eight-fifteen Carole had the Renault, packed with Gulliver and the luggage, parked outside Woodside

Cottage. But Jude hadn't been ready. She still had a couple of emails to do. Carole fumed quietly. It was all too reminiscent of travelling with David. Her husband had been the unusual and infuriating combination of a nit-picker and a bad time-keeper.

At about ten to nine Carole, unable to stand the wait any longer, had gone into Woodside Cottage to find out what was happening. Jude said she wouldn't be more than a quarter of an hour. Why didn't Carole have a cup of coffee? But Carole didn't want a cup of coffee. Apart from anything else, if she took on too much fluid, she might have to stop the car for an early toilet break, and that would be embarrassing. All she wanted to do was to leave at the time they had agreed to leave. So she just stumped around between the car and the two front doors.

Jude would normally have found the situation amusing, but she was preoccupied. She was sending an emotionally complicated email to a client who had just had breast cancer diagnosed. But she didn't tell Carole that. Eventually, they left at nine-thirty, 'exactly an hour after we intended to go, Jude'.

Only a couple of hours into their journey, however, there was already talk of stopping for lunch – from Jude, inevitably. This too went against everything Carole had grown up with. She was used to journeys during which you pressed grimly on until you reached your destination. If nourishment was required, you took sandwiches in Tupperware boxes. And yet Jude was proposing stopping at a pub for lunch, as if they were still in Fethering and wandering down to the

Crown and Anchor, rather than in the middle of a journey. The way Jude talked, it was as if travel could be an enjoyable experience in its own right.

Still, Carole wasn't about to sound like a wet blanket, so she didn't take issue with the pub idea . . . until Jude suggested that they should look for the pub in Lyme Regis.

'Lyme Regis? But that's not on the way.'

'It's not directly on the way, but it's not far off. Just a minor detour.'

'But if we start taking minor detours, goodness knows what time we'll get to Treboddick. Not till after dark, at this rate.'

'So? Did we say a specific time that we'd arrive?'

'Well, no. But it's a strange place. If we arrive after dark, we may not be able to find things.'

Jude couldn't suppress a grin. 'Carole, I think we'll find that the Treboddick Cottages do have electric light.'

'Yes. Yes, but . . . Well . . .'

By the time she actually turned the Renault off the A35 down the steep road that led to Lyme Regis, Carole had almost become used to the novel idea of what they were doing. 'But will there be somewhere I can take Gulliver for a walk?'

'Perfect place. You can walk him round the Cobb.'

'Cobb?'

'*French Lieutenant's Woman*. Meryl Streep in black with seawash all over her. Surely you remember that?'

'Well, I did see it, yes, but I wasn't really aware that it was in Lyme Regis.'

'It very definitely was. Anyway, Gulliver will love

the Cobb. Lots of lovely smells of bits left by the fishing boats.'

Jude was right. Though at first annoyed at being kept on his lead, the Labrador soon responded to his environment. As they walked around the great stone harbour wall, his nostrils twitched with pleasure. This was better than being cooped up on the back seat of the Renault.

When they got back to where the Cobb began, Carole announced that she'd better put Gulliver back in the car. 'Nonsense,' said Jude. 'There'll be pubs we can sit outside. He'd much prefer that, wouldn't he?'

'Yes, he would,' conceded Carole, not convinced that dogs – or indeed anyone else – should be allowed to have what they preferred.

The pub they found was perfect, with lots of wooden tables at the front, commanding a view over the wide sweep of Lyme Bay. 'I'll get the first drinks,' said Jude and went into the bar.

First drinks, thought Carole. We're meant to be going on a journey, not a pub crawl.

Jude came out with a menu. Carole had, as ever, had in mind a small lunch, but was persuaded that not to take advantage of the local seafood would be sacrilege. So they both forced themselves – not that there was much force required for Jude – to order the Three Fish Feast.

'I won't eat this evening,' said Carole, but with diminishing conviction. She had a feeling that abstinence was never going to be a major feature of travels with Jude.

Her friend looked out over the summery blue of the bay and sighed. 'Lyme Regis always does something for me.'

'Have you spent a lot of time here?'

'Nearby.'

'On your own?'

'No, with someone.' A deeper sigh. 'It didn't work out.'

'Ah.' Carole dared to ask a personal question. 'Was that with Mr Metarius or Mr Nichol?'

'No.' And once again the moment was lost. 'Incidentally, if you're worried about Gaby, do give Stephen a call.' Jude looked at her mobile. 'The signal here's quite good.'

Carole thought what she'd said about her daughter-in-law had been sufficiently casual, but Jude had read the depth of her underlying anxiety. Resisting her first instinct to say no, she gratefully accepted the offer. Stephen was at work, doing whatever it was he did, but unusually he didn't have his phone switched to voice-mail. No doubt leaving lines of communication from the hospital open. And the news about Gaby was better. Her blood pressure was down, but they still wanted to keep her in for observation. And Carole's grandchild was moving around in a very vigorous and healthy manner.

'Thanks for that.' She handed the mobile back.

'No problem. I'd be worried sick, if it was happening to one of my children.'

Was this a hint of yet another secret from Jude's

past? Carole seized the opportunity. 'Do you mean that you've actually had children?'

Her friend roared with laughter. 'I can assure you that I would've told you by now if I had.'

'Yes.' Carole was about to say it was difficult to be sure, because Jude was always so secretive, but that didn't seem entirely accurate. So she went on, 'Have you ever regretted it?'

Jude screwed up her face wryly. 'Not really. There have been a couple of times, with certain men, when I thought having a child would have put a seal on the relationship, but the timing was never right. And in each case I'm very glad it didn't happen. A child would have made the break-up even harder. No . . .' She grinned. 'I can't say I feel *unfulfilled as a woman*.' She dropped into a New Age Californian accent for the words.

Then she laughed and, before Carole could pursue the subject, said, 'Daft, aren't we?'

'What do you mean?'

'Two middle-aged women wasting our money on a wild-goose chase to Cornwall.'

'Actually, Jude, so far we haven't talked about the money. You did the booking on your credit card – well J. Metarius's credit card.'

'You don't have to worry. It is legitimate. It's not identity theft when the identity you're stealing is one of your own.'

'I wasn't suggesting that. I just thought we ought to work out how we're going to split the costs.'

'You're providing the transport. You've paid for the petrol.' Jude shrugged. 'Don't worry. It'll sort itself out.'

Carole was not of the opinion that money matters ever sorted themselves out, but she didn't say anything. 'Anyway, why do you say we're on a wild-goose chase?'

'Well, what are we hoping to get out of our little trip? Based on the flimsiest of clues, we're setting off to try and discover the Lockes' lost Narnia. We must be out of our skulls.'

'You say the flimsiest of clues, but we have got the anagram of Biddet Rock from Treboddick.'

'Yes, but that could be a coincidence.'

'Unlikely.'

'All right, Carole, it probably is an anagram, but there's no reason why it should have anything to do with the disappearance of Nathan Locke.'

'Do you think the girls knew it was an anagram? Chloë and Sylvia – or whatever their wretched nicknames are?'

'I wouldn't think so. They've grown up with that Wheel Quest game. I doubt if they ever think about where the names come from.'

'So you don't think they'd know where Nathan is?'

'I'd doubt it.'

'And do you reckon,' asked Carole, 'that the person who made up the anagram was Rowley Locke?'

'It'd make sense, wouldn't it, given what we know of his character?'

'Mmm.'

'So we've just got the one anagram,' said Jude,

uncharacteristically negative. 'I wish we had another clue to confirm that one. No, when I come to think about it, "wild-goose chase" is a pretty accurate description.'

Carole was worried. She'd just relaxed into their journey. Her anxiety about Gaby had been relieved by the call to Stephen. And now her fragile equanimity was being threatened by Jude apparently being an unwilling partner in the enterprise. 'Oh dear,' she said. 'Do you wish we hadn't come? You say it's daft. Do you think it's a bad idea?'

'No,' replied Jude, her brown eyes sparkling. 'I think it's a *brilliant* idea.'

Chapter Twenty-five

It was evening by the time they got to their destination. Treboddick was almost the furthest point of the British mainland, on the Atlantic Coast some miles north of Land's End. Carole was not a speedy driver, and their journey had got slower as they progressed through Cornwall. She hadn't been there since childhood holidays and the change that struck her most was the development of the tourist industry. Almost every house seemed to offer Bed and Breakfast, with such extra inducements as 'En Suite Rooms' and 'Sky Television'. Every side turning was festooned with signs to hotels, pubs and other attractions. So many facilities were advertised that there seemed an air of desperation about their pleading. And the drabness of some of the towns their route skirted reinforced the suggestion that all was not well with the local economy.

Mopsa Locke had emailed directions to Jude, and they had a very clear map for the last part of their journey. After Penzance they had to turn north towards Newbridge, then take the road to Pendeen. From there on the route was on very minor roads and they certainly wouldn't have found their way without the instructions. Carole drove cautiously along the high-banked lanes ('narrow, with passing places'), the Renault seeming to fit snugly between the sides as if on a green bobsleigh run. She sounded her horn frequently. What would have happened if she had met some demented local speeding in the other direction she did not dare to conjecture.

Finally they actually saw a sign to Treboddick, a mere three-quarters of a mile away. The road climbed upwards. They had glimpsed the sea many times on their journey and now, though it was invisible, they could sense its closeness. As the Renault breasted the hill, they suddenly saw the Atlantic in all its glory. The sun had just dropped behind the horizon, but its glow still flushed the sky. And outlined the jagged remnants of old mine workings on the clifftop, glowing through a twisted tower of rusty metal, the glass-free windows of a roofless pump house and the scattered rubble of other collapsed structures.

In strong contrast to this scene of dilapidation was the terrace of cottages a mere hundred yards away. Probably decayed too after the Cornish tin mining industry failed in the late nineteenth century, at some point they had been refurbished to a very high standard. The roofs were neatly slated and each of the four cottages had a white-fenced front garden with well-tended gravel path and beds of hardy shrubs and grasses. The cottage nearest the mine – presumably the one that the Locke family kept for their own use – had an extension built to the side that probably doubled its size.

The setting on that September evening was magically serene, but the landscape also carried hints of great harshness. The few trees leaned away from the sea, cowering as if in fear of its cruel potential. In a winter storm, when the rain and spray lashed against them, the little cluster of buildings would be a bleak – even frightening – place to be.

The situation was certainly dramatic, a ready inspiration for any over-imaginative child who wanted to create an alternative universe. Carole wondered whether the old pump house had been the building which the young Rowley Locke had creatively turned into the Castle of Biddet Rock.

Adjacent to the furthest cottage there was a clearly marked hard standing area for cars, its only occupant a beat-up green Nissan so old that when bought it was called a Datsun. As Carole brought the Renault to a neat halt, a tall red-haired girl emerged from the largest cottage. If she hadn't known who to expect, Carole would still have recognized her. Mopsa and Dorcas were absolutely identical twins. Though dressed in saggy jeans and a faded blue T-shirt, the girl still carried something of her sister's Pre-Raphaelite elegance. She came towards them, beaming a professional welcome and lisped, 'Mrs Metarius?'

'Yes,' replied Jude without hesitation. 'And this is my friend Cindy Shepherd.'

'Very pleased to meet you,' said Mopsa, fortunately not seeing the thunderstruck expression on the face of the thin grey-haired woman. Carole was looking away, busy putting a lead on Gulliver. His long period of incarceration in the back of the Renault, compounded by the amazing new cocktail of smells that greeted him when he got out, had brought the dog to a peak of panting Labrador excitement.

'If you come with me,' said Mopsa, 'I'll give you the keys to Number Three and you can fill out the paperwork for me.'

She led them back to the door of Number One and said it was fine to bring Gulliver in. But given his ebullient state and the possibility of there being breakables inside, Carole instead tied the protesting dog by his lead to a ring attached to the stone frontage.

The interior of the cottage did not maintain the promise of its exterior. The hallway was untidy with hanging waterproofs and abandoned gumboots. And the sitting room into which Mopsa led them was also a mess. The table was covered with newspapers, magazines and congealed coffee cups; the grey plastic of the outdated computer on the work surface was smeared with many fingerprints. About the cottage hung the same air of neglect and lack of investment as in the family's home in Chichester.

Mopsa herself also looked grubby. Her T-shirt wasn't that clean and there was a mark of what looked like soot across the back of one of her hands. Despite all this, she made no apology for the chaos in the cottage and she seemed to share the general Locke view that people should take them as they found them – and be grateful for the privilege. The girl riffled through papers in an overfilled drawer, saying that she'd got some forms somewhere. Carole disapproved. Mopsa had had twenty-four hours to prepare for the arrival of her guests and appeared to have done nothing about it. And if the same standards of cleanliness were going to be maintained in Cottage Number Three, Carole felt the beginning of a complaint coming on.

'I'm sorry,' said Jude suddenly, 'but could I use your loo? Been sitting in the car for ages, and dying to go since before Penzance.'

'Yes, of course.' Mopsa pointed down a passage. 'There's a little bathroom down there, through the kitchen.'

'Thanks. Maybe Cindy can sign the forms.' Unseen by Mopsa, Jude grinned at her friend and was rewarded by a furious glare.

'No, I'm afraid, Mrs Metarius—'

'Please call me Jenny.'

'Right, Jenny. I'm going to need your name on the forms, because the booking's been made on your card.'

'Oh, fine. Won't be a minute.'

And Jude disappeared. Carole was also feeling pressure on her bladder after the long drive, but her willpower would force her to wait until they got into their cottage. Anyway, it hadn't been that long since they'd stopped at the service station near Exeter. What was Jude up to?

Mopsa didn't seem about to initiate conversation, so Carole observed that it was very beautiful at Treboddick and asked whether the girl had lived there long.

'Not full-time, no. But the place has been in the family since before I was born, so I've been coming here all my life. You know, for holidays and weekends.'

'Very nice too.' Carole wondered what she could ask next. She must be careful. Carole Seddon might know quite a lot about the Locke family, but Cindy Shepherd certainly didn't. And why on earth had Jude chosen such a ridiculous name? Cindy was far too young for her, apart from anything else. And it was also common.

She decided that even a complete stranger might ask Mopsa if she lived there on her own, and did.

'Yes, at the moment. Some of my family'll probably be down soon.'

'So do you work round here?'

The girl looked affronted. 'This is my job. I run the lettings of the cottages.'

'Oh yes, of course, I'm so sorry. You told Ju – J – Jenny.' It didn't seem to be much of a job. Taking the odd phone call, checking the website. When business was as slack as it appeared to be, the duties could hardly be described as onerous. And when she had got something to do, like getting the forms ready for new visitors, Mopsa didn't appear to have done it.

Carole looked round the room for some other prompt to conversation. Fixed on two pegs over the fireplace was an old-fashioned single-barrelled shotgun. Gesturing to it, she asked, 'Is that a trophy or something? An antique?'

'Antique it may be,' Mopsa replied, 'but it still works. I use it when the rabbits get too close to the gardens.'

There was another silence, which the girl appeared quite happy to have maintained until Jude returned, but Carole thought she ought to say something more. 'I suppose you're very busy here during high summer?'

Mopsa jutted forward her lower lip. 'Not as busy as we should be. People don't seem to be coming in the numbers they used to. And there's lots of competition in self-catering accommodation.'

'Yes, I'm sure there is. We saw all those signs on the way down, offering "En Suite Bathrooms" and "Sky Television".'

'We don't have that kind of stuff here,' said the girl with an edge of contempt. 'Why, do you want an "En Suite Bathroom" and "Sky Television", Cindy?'

Carole winced. She didn't know whether she was more offended by the name or the suggestion. 'No, I certainly do not,' she replied icily.

Further awkwardness was prevented by Jude's return from the bathroom. As ever, her presence lightened the atmosphere. She signed the necessary form, listened to Mopsa outlining the small amount of housekeeping information new tenants required, and gratefully took the handful of crumpled flyers and brochures for local attractions.

'I'll show you Number Three now. Is there anything else you want to know?'

'Ooh yes. Is there by any chance a pub relatively nearby, where we could get something to eat?'

Carole's instinctive reaction was: again? But we had a pub meal at lunchtime in Lyme Regis. And we haven't even looked at the Welcome Pack in the fridge.

*

The pub Mopsa had recommended was the Tinner's Lamp in the village of Penvant, about three miles distant. Since she reckoned they stopped serving food at eight-thirty, Carole and Jude had only the briefest of visits to their cottage before hurrying off for supper. They did just have time to register, with some relief, that the standards of housekeeping in the rental properties were higher than in the Lockes' own cottage. (Probably there was a local woman who sorted them out, while Mopsa was responsible for her Number One.) Then Gulliver, tantalized by his brief taste of aromatic freedom, was once again consigned gloomily to the back of the car.

Very little was said on their way to the Tinner's Lamp, and Jude was pretty certain she knew the reason for her neighbour's frostiness. As soon as they had delivered their order at the bar, she was proved right. The pub was another stone-built building of considerable antiquity, but again skilfully and sympathetically modernized. There weren't many customers, but those present seemed definitely to be locals – not rustic fishermen with Cornish accents, but retired solicitors of the last generation to enjoy nice index-linked pensions.

At the solid wooden bar Carole had asked for white wine and been a little surprised to be offered a choice of five, including a Chilean Chardonnay, for which they inevitably plumped. Why did she imagine that, being so far from the metropolis, the Tinner's Lamp would not rise to the sophistication of a wine list? Pure Home Counties prejudice. Jude had then ordered a pasty –

'Well, after all, we are in Cornwall' – and Carole, feeling suddenly very hungry, had surprised herself by doing the same. Then, when they were ensconced at a small table between the bar and the open fire, Carole voiced the resentment she had been bottling up.

'Why on earth did you have to call me Cindy?'

'It was something I came up with on the spur of the moment,' replied Jude in a tone of well-feigned apology. 'I should have worked out names for us before, but I didn't think. It just came to me.'

'Well, I wish something else had "just come to you". Cindy! I mean: do I look like a Cindy?'

'We none of us have any control over the names our parents gave us.'

But Carole wasn't mollified by that. 'We might, however, hope to have some control over the names our neighbours give us.'

'I was thinking on my feet, and all I knew was that it was important to come up with a name that had the same initials as your real one.'

'Why's that?'

'Oh, really, Carole. Haven't you read any Golden Age whodunnits? The bounder who's masquerading under a false identity is always given away by the fact that the name he's chosen doesn't match the initials on his monogrammed luggage.'

'But I haven't got any monogrammed luggage.'

'Ah.' Jude suppressed a giggle. 'I knew there was a fault in my logic somewhere.'

'Cindy . . .' Carole muttered again despairingly.

'Putting that on one side,' said Jude, 'I do have a

result to report from my carefully engineered loo-break at Mopsa's cottage.'

'What? You didn't really want to go?'

'Not that much. But I thought . . . there we were actually in the place. Maybe it was a good opportunity for a little snoop.'

'And what did your little snoop reveal?' asked Carole, slightly miffed that she hadn't thought of the idea. 'Did you see Nathan Locke sitting in his hide-away, planning further murders?'

'No, not quite that. But I did see two steaks.'

'I beg your pardon?'

'You know I had to go through the kitchen to get to the loo . . .'

'Yes.'

'Well, on the work surface there was a meal being prepared. And there was a chopping board which had two slabs of steak on it.'

'Suggesting that Mopsa wasn't just cooking for her-self?'

'Suggesting exactly that, yes. Now, all right, maybe she's got a local boyfriend . . . some rough-hewn Cornish lad who is even now enjoying his hearty steak prior to enjoying the delights of Mopsa's wispy body . . . but if she hasn't . . . well, it might suggest that Nathan is on the premises somewhere.'

'If he is, he must be pretty well hidden. Don't forget that the police searched the place.'

'Yes, but if Mopsa was warned they were coming, there'd have been plenty of time to get Nathan out for the duration. There must be lots of places to hide along the coast round here.'

'Maybe . . .' Carole didn't sound convinced.

'Oh, come on, at lunchtime you were getting at me for talking about a wild-goose chase. Now you're the one who's going all wet blanket. I think those two steaks are going to be very significant. They're the closest we've got so far to confirmation that Nathan Locke is down here.'

'Hardly confirmation. There could be a lot of other explanations. Mopsa might just have an exceptionally healthy appetite.'

'She's very thin.'

'But very tall. Must need a lot of fuel for all that length.'

Jude's conviction was not to be shifted. 'No, I'm sure she was cooking for two.'

'We shouldn't really have come here then. Should be at Treboddick, watching out to see if a boyfriend has arrived.'

'Too late now. And, looking at what's just coming out of the kitchen, I think by being here we made the right choice.'

Carole also looked up to see the chubby landlord's wife bearing two plates, each swamped by a huge Cornish pasty. 'This right, is it? Some people want them with veg, but you didn't ask for that, did you?'

'No,' said Jude. 'A proper Cornish pasty's got lots of veg inside, hasn't it?'

'You're right, my lover.' The woman set the two plates down on the table. The smell that rose from them was wonderful. The pastry was solid – not the nasty flaky kind that features in so many mass-produced pasties – and there was a neat finger-pinched seam along the top of the plump oval. 'And the pasties at the Tinner's Lamp are certainly proper ones. Now do you want any sauce?'

'Again, a proper Cornish pasty shouldn't need any sauce.'

'You're right again, my lover. But we get so many emmets down here who want to smother them with ketchup and brown sauce you wouldn't believe it.'

'Have you had a busy summer?' Carole yet again envied her neighbour's ability to slip effortlessly into conversation with total strangers.

The landlord's wife pulled a glum face. 'Not that good. Weather's been fine, but the tourists've stayed away. Nope, lot of people round here have felt the pinch. All the B&Bs and what-have-you been half-empty. So where are you two staying?'

'Treboddick.'

'Ah.' There was a wealth of nuance in the monosyllable. The landlord's wife knew exactly where they meant, and exactly who ran the place. And she had some reservations about the owners. 'Don't think they've had a great summer either. Worse than most people round here, I reckon.'

'We've only just arrived, but it looks to be a beautiful spot,' Carole contributed.

'Oh yes, no question about that. But everywhere in Cornwall's beautiful. You've got to provide more than beauty if you're going to get the punters in.'

'"En Suite Bathrooms" and "Sky Television"?'

'All that certainly. But you got to do a bit more. Make your guests welcome, not treat them like you're doing them a favour by letting them stay in your place.'

The implicit criticism struck a chord. Mopsa's lack of interest in them and lack of preparation for their arrival was characteristic of the Lockes. Rowley welcoming guests to his precious Treboddick would no doubt be even more condescending.

'How long're you staying down here?'

'Oh, probably just till the weekend.'

'Well, it's a lovely area for walking. And if you want to go out for a day's fishing, just let me know. My brother can organize all that for you.'

They thanked her, but thought it unlikely that they would want to go out fishing.

'He does just pleasure trips too. There's some bits of the old mine workings and that you can only get a good view of from the sea.'

'Well, thank you. We'll bear it in mind,' said Carole politely.

'Looks like there was a mine at Treboddick,' Jude suggested.

'Oh, certainly, that's Loveday. There are mines all along the coast here. Hence the name of this pub. Tin mining was very big in the mid-nineteenth century. That and smuggling, of course. There've been attempts to revive it since – the tin mining I'm talking about now – but not very successful. If you want to see how it works, though, they've got this kind of working museum just down the coast at Geevor. That's worth a look. Most of the places, though, it's just ruins. Particularly of the pump house. A lot of the mine workings was under the sea, so they had to be constantly pumping the water out.'

'It looks like the remains of one of those at Treboddick.'

'You're right. About all there is left of Wheal Loveday.'

Carole and Jude exchanged looks. Of course! Now they really had got something. They'd both known that the Cornish word for a mine was 'wheal', but neither of them had made the connection. They'd never seen it written down, but now they both felt sure that what they'd observed the young Lockes playing was 'The Wheal Quest' with an 'a'; and that its inspiration definitely came from Treboddick.

Chapter Twenty-six

Whether because of the long drive or the Tinner's Lamp's excellent pasties and Chardonnay, both Carole and Jude slept exceptionally well that night. By her standards, Carole in fact overslept, waking at seven-thirty in a panic about getting Gulliver out before he soiled the cottage floor. Neither of the women were big breakfasters – except on those days when Jude suddenly felt like an All-Day Special – and they made do with the rather meagre Welcome Pack which Mopsa had left in their fridge.

It was warm enough for them to sit in the little back garden and look out over the sea as they finished their morning drinks – herbal tea for Jude, black instant coffee for Carole. Gulliver panted restlessly at their feet, the loop of his lead round the leg of a chair. His nose was giving him lots of impressions, the most dominant being that they were in excellent walking country. If the smells around the cottage were good, how much better might they be along the coastal path.

'So we're here,' said Carole. 'What do we do now?'

Jude looked out across the Atlantic, apparently not ready to commit herself.

'I mean, Gulliver's definitely going to need a long walk.'

'Yes, and in these wonderful surroundings it would be madness for us not to go for a long walk.'

'On the other hand . . .' Carole lowered her voice histrionically, '. . . what are we going to do about . . . *the case*?'

'Well, anything we are going to do about *the case* . . .' Jude echoed the drama of Carole's diction, '. . . is going to involve getting inside Cottage Number One. And we can either do that when Mopsa is there, which is going to set every alarm bell in the world ringing, or . . . we wait till she's gone out and see if we can get in then.'

'So that means we have to watch her front door all day until she goes out.'

'It might not be all day.'

'How do you mean?'

'Well, she might go out early.'

'Really, Jude, I don't think you're taking this seriously.'

'No. Sorry. I am really. Promise.'

'Huh.'

'Of course, there is another way of discovering when Mopsa's going out.'

'Which is?'

'We could ask her.'

'What!'

Jude was only away a few minutes. Carole was washing up their breakfast things when she returned, humming. 'Mopsa's going out to the shops at about eleven.'

'How do you know?'

'Like I said I was going to, I asked her.'

'But didn't she think it was odd?'

'No, of course she didn't. She has no suspicion of us. She just thinks we're a pair of punters who are – thank God – paying some rental money at the end of what's been a very bad season.'

'So what did you say?'

'I said: "Are you by any chance going to the shops because if you are would you mind getting a few things for us?"'

'What things?'

'Oh, I thought of some stuff. Muesli, yoghurt.'

I might have known it wouldn't have been anything useful like bacon and eggs, thought Carole.

'And Mopsa said that was fine. And I gave her some cash, and she's going to give me some change. It wasn't very difficult.'

'And did she say where she was going shopping? Because that'll give us an idea of how long she's likely to be away.'

'Yes. Like the man with seven wives, she's actually going to St Ives.'

'Must be half an hour each way.'

'At least.'

'Give her half an hour for shopping . . . we've got at least an hour and a half to investigate the cottage . . . assuming, that is, that we can get in.' Carole looked at her watch. 'So what do we do in the meantime?'

'We do exactly what two mature ladies with a dog would do if they were staying in a rented cottage in

Cornwall. We go for a walk along the cliffs. But before we do that . . !' Jude held out her mobile, '. . . you ring Stephen. Then you can relax properly into a day's sleuthing.'

Carole did as she was told. Anxiety about what was happening in a London hospital was a constant background to all her other feelings. Her son sounded less tired and stressed than he had on their previous call. Gaby was getting very bored lying on her back all day. She just wanted the bloody baby to arrive, so that she could get on with her life. Stephen thought this bolshieness was a good sign.

Carole was deeply sceptical about Gaby's idea that the baby's arrival would allow her to get on with her life, but she didn't say anything. Every woman had to come to terms in her own way with the inevitable disruptions that motherhood would bring.

Still, she felt cheered by the call, and did give Stephen Jude's mobile number to use if there were any further developments.

The clifftop walk brought Gulliver to an eighth heaven, beyond all his previous doggy imaginings.

And they timed their return to perfection. Just as Treboddick came into view round a curve of the cliff path, they saw the ancient Datsun leave the parking space and set off inland. Soon it was out of sight over the brow of the hill. Mopsa had gone on her shopping errand.

'Oh dear,' said Carole. 'I should have asked her to get something for me too.'

'What?'

'A *Times*. Somehow I never feel complete if I haven't got a crossword to do.'

'Don't worry. Maybe there'll be other clues for you to solve right here. After all, you were the one who worked out that "Biddet Rock" was an anagram of "Treboddick".'

'That's true,' said Carole. And she felt a warm glow.

When they got back to their cottage, Gulliver was locked in. He let out one feeble bark of protest, and then settled down comfortably to dream of all the exotic sights he had seen and smells he had smelled. Fethering Beach may have been seaside, but it wasn't seaside on the scale that Cornwall was.

'How're we going to get in?' whispered Carole out of the side of her mouth as they walked across to Cottage Number One. Although there was no one in sight, she felt as though an entire battery of surveillance cameras was focused on her every move.

'Well, first we'll see whether Mopsa locked up or not.'

'Oh, come on. She must have done.'

'I don't know. Everything down here seems pretty laid back. There's nobody about, and Mopsa doesn't seem to be the most diligent of guardians. It's quite possible she's left the cottage open.'

'I'd doubt it. But, anyway, Jude, I'm not sure that we should be looking at the cottage.'

'Why not?'

'Well, you said when Chloë was playing the role of Prince Fimbador, she talked about the Wheel Path . . . and we thought that was something to do with wheels that go round, but now we know that it was a "wheal" as in Cornish tin mine. So shouldn't we look at what's left of Wheal Loveday first.'

'Good idea.'

Their search didn't take long. In the bottom of the ruined pump house and round about there were a few old shafts, but all of them had been blocked up to the surface with stones and rubble. Grass had grown over some, so that they were little more than indentations in the hillside. The fact that there were no protective railings around them meant that they must be safely sealed. They offered no possible access to the tunnels below.

'That was worth trying, but I've a feeling what we're looking for has to be in the cottage.'

Carole nodded, still feeling the scrutiny of a thousand unseen cameras as they moved towards the door. Jude's fantasy that Mopsa might have left it unlocked turned out to be exactly that, a fantasy. But the girl's burglar-deterrent system proved not to be very sophisticated. They didn't have to lift many of the potted plants around the front door before they found what they were looking for.

'I wonder,' mused Jude as she lifted it up, 'whether this is the Key of Clove's Halo . . . ?'

'Looks more like a Yale to me,' said Carole sniffily. She was feeling a prickling at the back of her neck at the illegality of what she was doing, and this intensified as they went inside the cottage.

'Quick tour, looking for obvious hiding places,' said Jude. 'You do downstairs, I'll do up.'

But they both looked crestfallen when they met again at the foot of the stairs. Every available door and cupboard had been opened. Not only had they not found anyone, they hadn't even found a space big enough for anyone to hide in.

Carole looked nervously at her watch. 'Nearly forty minutes gone, from the time Mopsa drove off. What do we do now?'

'Well, if there is a secret entrance . . . the Face-Peril Gate . . . we haven't found it. Come on, you're more logical than I am. Tell me what I should be thinking.'

Carole was touched by the compliment – though she thought it no more than an accurate assessment of her character – and concentrated hard to come up with something that would justify it. 'Presumably what we're looking for is a hiding place that has some-thing to do with the mine workings. The Wheal Path . . . that's where Prince Fimbador was going to hide . . .'

'Right.'

'So logically we should be concentrating on the side of the cottage that is nearest to the ruins of the mine buildings.'

'I like it. This is good.'

'Maybe there's some secret entrance in the new extension . . . though I think that's unlikely . . . It looks like it was built in the last twenty years, and I'm not sure how many modern builders are up for making secret passages.'

'Something in the older part would also make more sense, because it might have some connection with smuggling. Most of the secret passages and hidey-holes around here would have been built for hiding contra-band goods.'

'Good point. So if it's not in the extension . . .' Carole moved through as she spoke, '. . . the place which is closest to the mine workings is the kitchen . . .' Jude followed her in, '. . . and this one must be the closest wall.'

They both looked at it. There was a door to a larder, but Carole had already checked that. Otherwise, it was just a stone wall that could have done with another coat of whitewash, about a third of whose width was taken up by a deeply recessed fireplace. The floor was stone-flagged, and the individual slabs looked too heavy to hide any cunning trapdoors.

'There's something here, there's something here . . . I can feel it.'

'Oh, Jude, you're not about to tell me the place has an *aura*, are you?'

'No, I know you too well to bother saying that. Mind you, it does have an aura.'

'Huh.' Carole sat defeatedly on a kitchen chair and fiddled with a pencil and piece of paper that lay on the table. 'If only . . . if only . . .' A thought came to her. 'Just a minute . . .'

'What?'

274

'Well, look, I got the "Biddet Rock" anagram because the words looked funny. That's how you usually spot anagrams in crosswords. The words don't look quite right – or their juxtaposition doesn't, so you start playing with them. Yes, I think whoever invented "The Wheal Game" likes anagrams. "Biddet Rock" sounds and looks funny . . . Good God, so does "Face-Peril Gate"!'

Carole scribbled out the letters in a circle, the first two opposite and the others next, going round clockwise in turn. It was the way her father had done anagrams for his crosswords and one of the very few things that he had passed on to his daughter. She looked at the ring of letters and narrowed her eyes, hoping that the solution would leap out at her.

'No, it won't come. I can get "place" out of it.'

'Well, that's good, isn't it? We're looking for a place, aren't we?'

'Yes, but then the rest of the letters . . . it doesn't leap out at me.'

'Well, maybe there are too many letters? Maybe you shouldn't be using all of them?'

'That's not how anagrams work, Jude. You've got to use all the letters, otherwise . . . Oh, my God . . .' Carole's jaw dropped as she moved forward to the paper. 'You're right. Forget the "Gate". Just concentrate on "Face-Peril" . . . which is an anagram of . . . "fireplace"!'

They both turned to look at the shadowed space, blackened by centuries of cooking and heating. Jude moved excitedly forward, saying, 'And Mopsa had a streak of soot on her hand! There must be something here!'

Close to, there were definitely vertical lines either side to the grate, lines that could be the outline of a door. And the soot had been worn thin along the lines, as though the edge had been moved quite recently.

'It's here! It's here! This is the Face-Peril Gate. But how on earth do we open it?'

'Is there a keyhole?'

Jude, oblivious to the soot that was smearing her hands and clothes, scrabbled away at the back of the fireplace. Her fingers found a narrow slot. 'Yes, yes, there is! But what do we use to open it?'

'Presumably,' said Carole, 'we use the Key of Clove's Halo.'

'And what the hell is that?'

This one came easily. 'Forget the "Key". And the "of". Is there a "Coal Shovel" anywhere, Jude?'

There was. An ancient implement, rather too narrow to be practical for lifting much coal. The scoop was curved and thin, more like a garden tool for cutting plant-holes than a coal shovel. It was black, except where, abraded by familiar grooves, the dull original metal shone through.

'I'll see if it fits,' said Jude. 'I'm so filthy already, a little more soot's not going to make any difference.'

The end of the coal shovel slipped into its predestined slot with the ease of long practice. Tentatively, anticipating resistance, Jude turned the handle to the right. But no resistance came. The smugglers of the nineteenth century had known their craft. The key turned.

Cunningly counterweighted so as to move as lightly as a cupboard door in a designer kitchen, the great plate of soot-covered steel gave way, moving almost soundlessly on rollers, to reveal a set of stone steps leading down into the void.

Chapter Twenty-seven

Both knew they should have made some kind of plan, but they hadn't. After all, if their surmise was correct, they were about to confront a young man who might well be a murderer. Having guarded his privacy so fiercely for three weeks, how was he likely to react to the discovery of his hideaway? If he had already killed Kyra Bartos, would he be worried about the killing of two inquisitive middle-aged women, so long as it kept him safe from the attentions of the police?

The opening of the door at the back of the fireplace, though quiet, had not been entirely silent. It was a sound their quarry would know well. Mopsa had quite possibly told him that she was going out, so he would know they were intruders. The welcome he was preparing for them could be ugly.

And yet still neither of them said anything. Instinctively, Jude drew back and let Carole lead the way. They didn't even look around for a torch. From whatever was at the bottom of the steps a thin light flowed.

They had not defined in their minds what they were expecting to see, but neither had anticipated the

bright airy space they stepped into. The light was natural, sunlight streaming in individual, focused beams
through narrow fissures in the natural rock of the walls.
These openings, created by the erosion of the exterior
cliff face, were too high up the walls to offer any hope
of escape. But the chamber their light illuminated was
not the primitive cave Carole and Jude's imaginations
had suggested. It appeared to be a section of a circular
vertical mineshaft, some twenty feet across, which
would have reached the surface right next door to the
Lockes' cottage. But, many years before, the space had
been separated off by a wooden floor and ceiling to
form the hidden room. The carpentry had not been
professional, there was a rough-hewn quality to everything. But it looked sturdy and secure. The smugglers
of Treboddick had known what they were doing when
they constructed the Wheal Chamber.

These were the peripheral impressions of a
nanosecond, because what arrested the attention of
both women was the figure sitting at a table facing the
sea. They had seen the family photographs and had no
doubt that it was Nathan Locke.

The shock they both felt, though, arose from their
assumption that he had hidden away of his own accord.
They hadn't expected the chain from an iron ring on
the wall which was attached to the boy's ankle.

Chapter Twenty-eight

Whoever Nathan Locke had expected to come down the stairs into his lair, it wasn't a pair of middle-aged women. He looked at them in frank amazement. But rather than reacting with violence, he remained seated and asked politely, 'I'm sorry, but who are you . . . ?'

No time for aliases now. 'My name's Carole Seddon. This is my friend Jude.'

The blankness on the boy's face told that he had never heard of either of them.

'And what are you doing here? Are you from the police?' His natural good manners couldn't completely exclude a note of disbelief from the question. He looked scruffy, a wispy three-week growth of beard around his chin, but not as though he had been mal-treated.

'No, we're nothing to do with the police. You don't need to be frightened. You're quite safe with us.'

He let out a bitter laugh. 'I think I might be safer with the police than I am here.' He gestured to the chain on his ankle. It gave them a moment to take in the space in which he was incarcerated. There were loaded bookshelves, a cassette player, even an ancient-looking television. Jutting out from one wall was a shed-like structure with two doors, possibly leading to a kitchen and bathroom. The area had more qualities of a furnished flat than a prison.

Jude moved forward alongside Carole. 'Listen, Nathan, we know who you are and we know why you're here.'

'Oh, do you? I sometimes wish I did.'

'It's in connection with the death of Kyra Bartos.'

The name hit him like a slap. His lip trembled and tears glinted in his eyes. At that moment he looked less than his sixteen years. 'Kyra? What do you know about Kyra?'

'That she's dead.'

'And that I killed her? Do you know that? Just like everyone else who seems to be so sure of it?'

'We don't know that. But we'd like to talk to you about it.'

'Would you? Well, there's a novelty.' The bitterness was back in his voice. He still wasn't being overtly rude to them, but there was in his voice a deep weary negativity, an acceptance that he had entered a world in which normal logic did not operate.

'A novelty, why? Because nobody else wants to talk to you?'

'Nobody else wants to talk except to give me orders. No one wants to listen to what I have to say.'

'We'd very much like to hear what you have to say.'

He was tempted by the sincerity in Jude's voice, but his scepticism remained. 'Oh yes?'

Carole decided it was her turn. Jude had been

trying the good cop approach, without marked success. Maybe something harder might be more effective.

'Listen, Nathan, you know you're in a lot of trouble. Circumstances dictate that you're the major suspect for Kyra Bartos's murder. And the fact that you've run away only exacerbates the problem.'

'Excuse me.' The boy looked affronted. 'What's all this "running away" business?' He indicated the chain round his ankle. 'Does it really look as though I'm stuck down here voluntarily?'

'Are you saying you were kidnapped?'

'Not exactly. No, I came down to Cornwall of my own accord. In all the confusion of what happened – and the kind of mental state I was in – yes, lying low for a few days did seem a good idea. In retrospect I'm not so sure it was, but I wasn't thinking very straight after I heard about . . . what happened at the salon.'

'Who did you hear about it from?' asked Carole.

'My uncle.'

'Rowley Locke.'

He looked at them curiously. 'Are you sure you're not police?'

Jude promised that they weren't.

'Because you do seem to know rather a lot about me.'

'Everyone in the West Sussex area knows a lot about you. There's been blanket coverage in the papers and on television.'

'Yes, I suppose there would be.' He sighed and gestured to the ancient set. 'That doesn't work. Not that I'd get Sussex local news down here anyway.'

'No.'

Carole picked up his narrative. 'So you were saying . . . you came down here of your own free will . . . ?'

'Yes. More or less. Uncle Rowley can be very persuasive.' Both women shared the thought that they were sure he could be. 'But when they got me here . . . suddenly he says I've got to be chained up.'

'Does it hurt?' asked Jude.

'Not really. It's quite slack. Only hurts if I try to get out of it, and I gave up on that idea after the first couple of hours. And the chain's long enough so's I can get to the bathroom.' He grinned wryly. 'No, as prisons go, I suppose this is a very humane one.'

'But don't you get bored out of your skull?'

'Well . . .' He gestured to the bookshelves. 'I've got plenty to read. And I keep comforting myself with the thought that it's not for ever.'

'For how long, though?' asked Carole. 'Did your uncle give any indication of that?'

Nathan shrugged. 'Not precisely. Presumably he's just keeping me here until the police find out who actually did kill . . .' Again emotion threatened. Something in his throat rendered him unable to speak his late girlfriend's name.

'Hmm.' Neither Carole nor Jude was persuaded by the explanation.

'Uncle Rowley did say I was being kept here for my own good. He said if the cops got their hands on me, I'd never escape. They'd stitch me up good and proper.' That sounded in character from what Carole had heard of Rowley Locke's estimation of the British police force.

'I have to listen to what Uncle Rowley says,' Nathan continued lamely. 'He does know what he's talking about.'

This was a tenet of Locke received wisdom to which neither Carole nor Jude subscribed. They both had strong suspicions about Rowley Locke's agenda.

'Well,' Carole announced practically, 'the first thing we should do is get you free from that chain.'

The suggestion brought a light of paranoia into the boy's eye. 'Oh, you'd better not do that. There's a girl – my cousin Mopsa who—'

'We know all about Mopsa. She's gone off shopping.' Carole consulted her watch. 'She won't be back for at least another twenty minutes.'

'So,' asked Jude, 'should we find some tools upstairs to cut through the chain?'

'You don't have to bother with that.' He gestured towards the foot of the stairs. 'There's a key to the padlock hanging over there. Just about six feet beyond my reach. Don't imagine I haven't tried to grab it.'

'Right,' said Carole. 'Then the first thing we do is get that key.'

'I don't think so.'

They all looked up at the sound of the lisping voice. Mopsa stood halfway down the stairs, back-lit from the kitchen above. In her hands was the shotgun that had been hanging on the sitting-room wall.

Chapter Twenty-nine

Carole was unfazed. 'Put that down.'

'No, you back off. Get away from that key, or I'll shoot.'

'Don't be ridiculous.'

'Move back,' hissed Nathan's anguished voice. 'She means it. She will shoot.'

Something in the girl's eye told Carole that her cousin was speaking the truth. She retraced her steps until she and Jude stood together, an inadequate defence in front of the chained boy. The chamber suddenly felt very small.

Mopsa moved on down the stairs. 'I should have been on my guard. A sudden booking out of the blue this time of year. I should have known you were up to something.'

'All we were up to,' said Jude reasonably, 'was trying to find Nathan. The police are looking for him. He can't be hidden away here for ever.'

'Oh no? Prince Fimbador spent seven years night and day in the Wheal Chamber.' There was a gleam of fanaticism in the girl's eye as she said the words.

'Yes, maybe. But that's not real. That's just a story.'

'A story?' Mopsa was deeply offended. 'The Chronicles of Biddet Rock tell how Prince Fimbador resisted the evil hordes of Gadrath Pezzekan. The tale of the ultimate battle of Good against Evil is not just a story.'

Carole and Jude caught each other's eye, as into each mind sank the sickening truth. Mopsa was not sane. This was why she had not followed the course of her sister Dorcas to university. Her unhinged mind had swallowed the nonsense of the Wheal Game whole. For her the incarceration of Nathan as Prince Fimbador was completely logical. She was just fulfilling her role in the legend. And if the fulfilment of that role involved bloodshed, she would not shirk her duty.

She waved the shotgun dangerously in their direction. 'You have broken through the Face-Peril Gate. Already you have invoked the Great Curse of the Leomon! The fate of all who sully the purity of Karmenka is death.'

'Mopsa,' said Carole firmly, 'you are talking absolute balderdash.'

'Contempt has always been the fate of the Prophetesses of Biddet Rock.' 'Prophetesses' was really quite a mouthful for someone with a lisp. The situation would have been laughable but for the fact that the girl so clearly believed all the nonsense she was spouting.

'We rise above it,' she persisted. 'We know the Right Course and we still pursue it till the last drop of the blood of the Leomon is shed.'

'Yes, well, fine. Let the blood of Leomon be shed, but don't let's shed anyone else's. How about that?'

But Jude's jokey approach was not the right one either. The girl pointed the shotgun very definitely in the women's direction and gestured them to move away from Nathan's table, till their backs were to the sea-facing wall. Not quite believing the situation they were in, but all too aware of its gravity, they did as they were instructed.

'When you sacrifice your pathetic lives, acolytes of Black Fangdar,' said Mopsa, 'there must be no risk of harm to Prince Fimbador.'

Under normal circumstances Carole and Jude would have giggled, but there was nothing funny about the way Mopsa was sighting them down the barrel of the shotgun. Through both their minds went the thought that she could only get one of them with her first shot. Then, since it was a single-barrelled gun, she would have to reload. But neither felt very cheered by the increased odds on survival. And neither was about to volunteer to go first.

Mopsa cocked the rifle. The way she did it suggested a discouraging familiarity with the weapon. Her talk of shooting rabbits had not been mere bravado.

She shifted her stance, so that the sight was trained on Carole's chest.

'Mopsa, this is daft,' said Jude, the calmness in her voice masking the desperation in her mind. 'You can't just shoot us in cold blood. You don't even know who we are.'

'I know all I need to know,' the girl responded

implacably. 'You are intruders who have broken through the Peril-Face Gate into the Wheal Chamber. You are probably Grail-seekers, sent from Black Fangdar. You are certainly a threat to Prince Fimbador, which means that you must be in the pay of Gadrath Pezzekan.'

'We are not a threat to Prince Fimbador,' said Jude.

'No, we certainly aren't,' Carole agreed.

'We're here to help Prince Fimbador . . .' God, how easy it was to slip into this nonsense talk. 'Nathan. We are here to help Nathan.'

'And how do you propose to help him, you who betrayed Prince Fimbador at the Battle of Edras Helford?'

'For a start we'll get him away from here.'

'And then?'

Neither woman answered. Neither could, on the spur of the moment, come up with a reply that they could be sure would not enrage the girl further.

'How do I know that you will not hand him over to the police?'

Still they couldn't reply. Handing him over to the police was the solution uppermost in both their minds. The shotgun was still pointed firmly at Carole's chest.

It was Nathan's voice that broke the impasse. 'It would be good if I could talk to the police, Flops.' Oh, God, another of the Locke family nicknames. 'Clear up a few details about what actually happened that night . . . You know, the night when . . . when . . .'

Again he was unable to speak his dead girlfriend's name.

'No!' Mopsa's voice rang against the stone walls of the Wheal Chamber. 'My orders are to guard you. My orders are to keep you safe from the police. And to kill anyone who challenges your safety.'

'Your father didn't really mean that, Flops. He was just going over the top, as usual. You weren't meant to take it literally.'

'The Prophetesses of Biddet Rock pride themselves on obeying all of their orders *to the letter*.'

'Well, not that one about killing people. Look, Uncle Rowley wrote me a note . . .'

His scrabbling in the table drawer distracted her for a moment, long enough for Carole to step forward with her hands locked and knock the rifle barrel upwards. As it jerked in her hands, Mopsa pulled the trigger. In the enclosed space the report was shockingly loud. It prompted an enraged cacophony of complaint from seabirds on the cliffs outside.

Nathan's chain was long enough for him to leap across and snatch the gun from his cousin's hands. Unarmed, Mopsa lost all resistance and sank to her knees, overtaken by hysterical weeping. Carole crossed to the bottom of the stairs and finished what she'd been about to do when the girl disturbed them. She removed the key from the hook where it had tantalized Nathan for nearly three weeks, crossed to him and undid the padlock on his ankle.

'Thank God for that,' he said, flexing the constricted muscles of his foot.

Carole, aware of the danger in which she had been, and slightly shocked by her action in hitting away the shotgun, felt suddenly rather feeble. 'What do we do now?' she asked.

'We get the hell out of this place as soon as possible,' said Jude.

'But . . .' Even in these circumstances Carole could not repress the instinctive words 'we booked for a week.'

Her neighbour didn't bother to reply. Instead, she looked at the boy and asked, 'Are you going to come with us, Nathan?'

He looked at Jude for a long moment, and then slowly nodded. 'Yes. I've got to find out the truth . . . you know, about what happened to . . . to . . .' He still couldn't do it. A tear glinted in his eye.

'Right, let's assemble our things, and get out of here as soon as possible.'

As Jude moved towards the steps, Carole looked down at Mopsa, still limp as a rag doll on the wooden floor and crying in long shuddering sighs. 'What do we do about her?'

'Lock her in,' suggested Nathan. 'Give her a taste of the medicine she's been dishing out to me.'

'I don't think we need do that,' said Jude. 'We don't want to sink to her father's level.'

'If we take away the gun, are there any other weapons in the cottage that she could use?' asked Carole.

He shook his head. 'I'm pretty sure there aren't.'

'I don't think violence from Mopsa is going to be a

problem.' Jude looked down at the weeping girl. 'She's not a threat to us any more.'

Responding to the compassion in Jude's voice, Nathan knelt down beside his cousin. 'It's all right, Flops . . . Fimby's not cross with you. Fimby forgives you. And everyone else will forgive you.'

'No, they won't,' the girl wailed. 'I have failed in my appointed task. I have not defended Prince Fimbador of the Blood of Merkerin.'

'You will be forgiven.' Nathan Locke stood to his full height and held a hand over the girl in a majestic gesture. 'You have the word of the Grail-Holder Prince Fimbador that you will be forgiven!'

Mopsa apparently drew comfort from this mumbo-jumbo. The weeping eased. Nathan looked across embarrassedly to Carole and Jude and shrugged a shrug which seemed to say, 'Don't knock it. It worked.'

'Right. Let's get ready,' said Carole, very much the teacher in charge of a school trip. 'It'll only take us a couple of minutes to get our bags. Have you got much stuff, Nathan?'

'Very little. I was rather whisked away from Fethering the morning after—'

Jude interceded before the memory of Kyra could upset him again. 'Don't worry. You can tell us everything in the car.'

They left Mopsa in the Wheal Chamber, but did not close the Face-Peril Gate. For safety they put the shotgun in the Renault's boot, along with their luggage and Nathan's rather pathetic plastic carrier bag.

As Carole drove off, with the boy and Gulliver

SIMON BRETT

sharing the back seat, they all looked back. Mopsa was
standing outside Cottage Number One, talking into a
phone. Though none of them voiced it, they would all
have put money on the fact that the person the other
end of the line was Rowley Locke.

Chapter Thirty

Maybe it was delayed shock that kept them quiet for the first half-hour of their journey back. The only one making any noise was Gulliver, who started off by panting excitedly. For him getting in the car gave the signal that he was about to be taken for a walk. But as the journey continued with no signs of stopping, he got less excited. Honestly, humans were so unreliable. The memory of the excessively long journey of the day before came back to him and he subsided into an aggrieved lump on the back seat, not even responding to friendly stroking from Nathan.

They had passed Penzance before the silence was broken. And, surprisingly, it was the boy who broke it. 'I'm sorry about Flops – Mopsa. She's . . . well, she's always had problems.'

'Mental problems?'

'Yes. She's got a twin sister called Dorcas.'

'I've met her,' said Carole.

'Well, Mopsa's . . . Incidentally, I don't understand how you know everything about my family.'

'Don't worry about that for the moment,' said Jude. 'Tell us about Mopsa.'

'Well, as I say, she's a twin. Dorcas has always been the bright one . . . school, university, she's done well all the way. And Mopsa could never quite hack it. In another family I think doctors or psychologists would have been consulted, but the Lockes always think they can sort everything out for themselves, so they've kind of protected her from the outside world.'

'As they were trying to protect you from the outside world?'

He let out a mirthless laugh. 'I suppose you could say that. Anyway, there's been a long history of Mopsa sort of dropping out of things, having breakdowns I reckon, but she's always been at her calmest and most sane down at Treboddick.'

'That was her most sane?' Carole couldn't help asking.

'No, obviously she lost it when she found you'd broken into the Wheal Chamber. She's . . . she's potentially quite dangerous.'

'That was the impression I got.'

'But do she and Dorcas get on?' asked Jude.

'Yes, very well. Distressingly well. Dorcas is a strong character. I think in a way with Mopsa – and indeed with the two younger sisters – Dorcas has made them what Shakespeare would have called her "creatures". She kind of controls them.'

'So how long has Mopsa been down at Treboddick?'

'She's spent an increasing amount of time down there, you know, since she dropped out of school, or since she dropped out of the last of a series of schools.

And then when Uncle Rowley remarried . . . well, Mopsa and Bridget were never going to see eye to eye.'

Carole agreed. 'No, Bridget seems quite a sensible woman.'

'Yes, she is.' He spoke with warmth.

'I gather you and she get on well.'

'Very well.'

'You both approach the whole Locke family bonding process with a degree of scepticism.'

'You could say that. As soon as I got into my teens I got rather bored with all that Wheal Quest business . . . little realizing that I would end up playing it for real during the last three weeks.'

'There's something that struck me about Bridget,' said Carole. 'I've met your father and mother, and Rowley, and Dorcas, and the younger girls and, of all of them, Bridget is the only one who seemed worried about what had happened to you, where you'd gone to.'

'Well, she would be. All of the rest of them knew exactly where I was.'

'But Rowley didn't tell his wife?'

'Of course not. As you said, Bridget is a sensible woman. The minute she knew that I was locked up at Treboddick – particularly being guarded by Mopsa – she would have contacted the police.'

There was a silence. Then Carole said, 'I think we'll have to get in touch with the police, Nathan.'

He made no objection. Though he didn't welcome what lay ahead, he recognized its inevitability.

'If only to clear your name.'

'Yes.'

Jude joined in. 'Did Rowley – your uncle – did he say precisely why he was locking you up at Treboddick?'

'He said he'd got my best interests at heart. He was afraid of what might happen to me under police interrogation.'

'Yes, he doesn't have a very high opinion of what he insists on calling "our fine boys in blue",' Carole recalled. 'So he thought they'd force a confession out of you?'

'Something along those lines, yes. Uncle Rowley said the police always liked to get a conviction, and weren't too bothered whether or not it was the right one.'

'That sounds like one of his lines. And do you think he thought you were guilty?'

'What?' Nathan Locke's surprise was so unfeigned that clearly the idea had never occurred to him.

'Well, if your uncle did think you'd strangled Kyra, then there'd be an even stronger reason for him to lock you away at Treboddick. To stop you from being arrested . . . until the family had worked out a more permanent way of keeping you from justice.'

'What kind of way?'

'I don't know.' Carole shrugged. 'Sending you abroad? Changing your identity? Maybe even plastic surgery . . . ?'

'Oh, come on, they wouldn't do that.'

After what they'd witnessed at Treboddick, Carole and Jude's estimation of what the Lockes might do had expanded considerably.

'I think Uncle Rowley really was doing the best for me.' But Nathan's insistence was wavering. 'At least what he thought was the best for me.'

'Hmm.'

'Presumably . . .' Jude posed the question very gently '. . . you didn't kill Kyra?'

'No, of course I didn't! I loved her! You don't kill someone you love.'

Many authorities, including Oscar Wilde, would have questioned that assertion, but Jude didn't take issue as Nathan continued, 'I can't imagine what happened. I mean – who would do that to her? She was a sweet girl . . . wouldn't hurt anyone. I can't even think of anyone she didn't get on with . . . well, except her father . . .'

And possibly Martin Rutherford, thought Carole as Jude asked, 'Yes, we've heard about some difficulties between Kyra and her father. What was the problem there?'

'I think basically he's just old-fashioned.'

'Did you meet him?'

'Just the once. K – Kyra . . .' He did actually manage to get the word out that time, '. . . she took me home to meet him, thought it'd be all right.' He sighed wearily. 'It wasn't. He virtually showed me the door.'

'What was it about you that he disapproved of?'

'In a way, I don't think it was anything about me. Kyra said I shouldn't take it personally and I tried not to. It was just that I was interested in his daughter. He would have been equally down on any other person of the male gender who was interested in his daughter. He thought she was too young to have a boyfriend.'

'But, she was . . . what?'

'Seventeen.' He gulped down the emotion that the thought prompted. 'Yes, well old enough to . . . do anything she wanted. But that wasn't the way old man Bartos saw things. He got furious when she had her ears pierced and . . . It was . . . I don't know . . . something to do with the way he was brought up . . . in Czechoslovakia.'

I really would like to talk to 'old man Bartos', thought Jude. I've somehow got a feeling that he holds the key to this whole case. I wonder if Wally Grenston could set up a meeting . . . ?

'Nathan,' said Carole, her voice only just the right side of sternness, 'you did go to Connie's Clip Joint that evening with Kyra, didn't you?'

There was no attempt at evasion. 'Yes, I did. Perhaps it was a silly thing to do, but . . . well, it was very difficult for us to be alone together. Her father's attitude ruled out the possibility of meeting at her place and then my parents . . .'

'They wouldn't have objected to you taking a girl back to the house. They told me as much.'

'Yes, but it would have been hideously unrelaxing – particularly for Kyra. My parents can sometimes be so "right-on" that it hurts.'

'Constantly saying how broad-minded they are . . . how delighted that you feel sufficiently relaxed to bring your girlfriends into the house . . . ?'

He grinned without amusement. 'You've clearly met them, Carole.'

'Yes. Yes, I have.'

'So what happened that evening?' Jude prompted gently.

'Well, as I say, Kyra and I found it very difficult to be alone together . . . you know, unless we were in one of the shelters on the sea front at Fethering . . . or on the golf course . . . neither of which were particularly romantic . . . or relaxing . . . And then that day she rang me on the mobile and said that Connie had given her the keys to the salon because she wanted her to open up the next morning and . . . it would be our opportunity to . . . you know, to do what we hadn't had a chance to do before . . .'

'You mean make love to each other?'

He nodded agreement to Jude's question. His speech slowed as he clawed back the painful recollection. 'Yes, it was going to be our big night. I felt bad about sort of being in Connie's salon without her knowing, but I did want to . . . you know . . . And Kyra said if I joined her there at about ten, there'd be nobody about, and it'd all be fine. So I bought some beer and vodka and . . . you know, some cigarettes . . . because I wanted us to be relaxed about it all and . . . I was dead nervous. I think Kyra was too.'

'So what happened when you got there?'

'Well . . . I don't know whether I should tell you this . . .'

'You're going to have to tell the police,' said Carole, 'so you might as well have a dry run.'

Nathan saw the logic of that. 'All right. Well, it's embarrassing, but . . .' He took a deep breath. 'Basically, it didn't work. Nothing worked.'

Jude's voice was mesmerizingly soft as she asked, 'You mean the sex?'

He nodded, now looking very young and confused. 'Maybe I was too nervous. There'd been such a long build-up and . . . I don't know . . . I wanted it to be a really romantic moment.'

Hence the dozen red roses, thought Carole.

'But when I actually got there . . . you know, in the back room of the salon . . . I just lost it. In a strange place, afraid we'd be interrupted at any moment . . . I mean, at one stage it seemed to be going all right, but then I thought I heard someone coming in . . .'

'You mean coming into the salon?'

'Well, I thought I heard the back gate bang, and then like footsteps . . .'

'Are you sure?'

'No, I'm not sure. As I say, I was terribly nervous . . . and also I'd got through most of the vodka . . . and I was worried about what Kyra would think of me. Anyway, it didn't work . . . you know, the sex,' he concluded lamely.

There was a silence before Jude asked if he and Kyra had quarrelled.

'No, not exactly. It was . . . just awkward. I felt kind of humiliated . . . She said it didn't matter, but . . . I just had to get away. I feel dreadful about it now . . . after what happened, but I left her on her own.'

'What time was that?'

'I don't know exactly. Half-past twelve . . . one o'clock . . . ?'

'You didn't see anyone outside?'

'What?'

'You said you'd heard the gate bang.'

'That was a lot earlier. And I could have imagined it. I don't know.' He let out a little gasp. 'I suppose, if there really was someone there, it could have been the murderer.'

Jude agreed that this was quite possible, then Carole asked, 'Why didn't Kyra go home?'

'Because she'd set up this big alibi with her dad. You know, she was supposed to be with some school friend for the night, so she couldn't suddenly say she wasn't. Also she'd been drinking, and if her old man had smelt that on her breath . . .' He didn't need to complete the sentence.

'And what about you?' asked Carole. 'Did you go straight home?'

Nathan shook his head, still traumatized by the images he had brought back to life. 'No. I don't know what I did really. I was pretty wasted, for a start. I'd drunk most of the bottle of vodka. And I felt terrible about, you know, what'd happened.' He let out a bark of pained laughter. 'Or rather what hadn't happened.'

'So where did you go?'

'I wandered along the beach. I don't know how long I did that. Just walking back and forth, back and forth, thinking terrible thoughts. You know, I loved Kyra . . .' there was a naked appeal in his voice, '. . . but I couldn't, you know . . . When it mattered, I couldn't . . .'

'So when did you go home?'

'Not till the morning. I don't remember exactly what happened, but at some point I fell asleep in the dunes . . . you know, about as far along Fethering Beach as you can go. I felt dreadful, but I'd slept through till after half-past ten. So I started back home.'

'I'm surprised no one saw you at that time of day,' Carole observed.

'I kept off the roads. I didn't want to be seen. So I was on the beach and then up by the side of the Fether. There's a way into our back garden from the tow-path. Anyway, by the time I got back to Marine Villas, Uncle Rowley was already there. Mummy had some-how heard about Kyra's body being found . . .' Another triumph for the Fethering bush telegraph, thought Carole. 'And Mummy had called Uncle Rowley and—'

'What did your father do?'

'He did what he always did – waited for Uncle Rowley to come and make the decisions.' He said the words with resignation rather than contempt.

'Anyway, as soon as I saw him, Uncle Rowley said I was bound to be the police's prime suspect because I'd been going out with Kyra and he soon got me to tell him that I had actually been to the salon to see her . . .'

'Did he ask you what had happened when you were there?'

'No, he'd already made his plans that I should lie low at Treboddick. As soon as I'd got my stuff together, we drove off.'

Carole and Jude exchanged looks. As alibis went, Nathan Locke's was not of the greatest. Poor boy, he wasn't going to have an easy time when they handed him over to the police. Neither of them believed that he had strangled Kyra Bartos, but the circumstantial evidence was against him. It had become even more imperative that they should find out who had really committed the murder.

Carole and Jude knew it would be late when they got back to West Sussex, but no one suggested breaking the journey, except for a brief stop and a taste-free Little Chef meal. Though none of the Lockes had any power to identify or stop the Renault on its way, the two women still wanted to get home as soon as possible. In both of their minds suspicions of Rowley were developing apace, though they knew they should not share such ideas with his nephew.

They outlined what they proposed to do, and Nathan was docile in his agreement to their plan. They would take him to the police station in Littlehampton, from which the investigation into Kyra Bartos's murder was being co-ordinated.

Jude said he could use her mobile if he wanted to call his parents to tell them he was all right, but he declined the offer. Arnold and Eithne Locke had presumably heard by now from Mopsa about their son's escape from the Wheal Chamber at Treboddick, and if he didn't want to talk to them, then that was his decision. The only person who'd seemed genuinely worried about the boy was Bridget Locke, and Jude decided she'd give the woman a call first thing in the morning. For the rest of his family, the longer they stewed in their own juice the better.

Before he got out of the car in Littlehampton, they wished Nathan luck. He looked very young as they deposited him outside the police station. They watched him go inside and then drove on the few miles to Fethering. No need for them to get involved at this point. There was plenty for the detectives to ask Nathan Locke about without Carole or Jude's names being mentioned. They thought he might need the luck they had wished him.

Chapter Thirty-one

When she got back to High Tor, Carole found a message on her answering machine. It was, predictably enough, from Rowley Locke.

Although by now the small hours of the morning, she immediately phoned Jude and they ended up opening a bottle of wine in the sitting room of Woodside Cottage.

'So what did Rowley say?' asked Jude as she poured Chardonnay into two glasses. 'Is he furious?'

'I'm pretty sure he is, but the message is a bit tentative. You see, he's only got Mopsa's description to go by, so he's not absolutely certain that we were Jenny and . . .' The name wouldn't come.

'Cindy.'

'Yes,' said Carole with distaste. 'So he's not accusing me of anything. All he's saying is that he's had some news on the whereabouts of Nathan, and he'd like to tell me about it.'

'Did he sound relieved?'

'Yes, he did quite a good impression of the concerned uncle. He said that Arnold and Eithne were ecstatic to have news of the boy.'

'So he wants you to ring him?'

'Yes, "ring and fix to meet up" was how he put it.'

Jude pursed her full lips. 'Could be risky. I mean, I'm sure Rowley Locke has worked out that we were the two women who went to Treboddick . . . and if he is actually the murderer . . .'

'But do you think he is?'

'I'm not sure. It would explain why he wanted Nathan kept out of the way. So that the boy remained the number one suspect.'

'A more charitable view would be that he was just trying to protect his nephew . . . if he wasn't the murderer himself, but he thought that Nathan was.'

Jude had the nerve to say, 'Unlike you to take the charitable view,' and Carole had the grace to smile. 'I've got to see Rowley,' she said. 'Got to find out what on earth he's up to.'

'Mmm.' Jude took a thoughtful sip from her wine. 'Incidentally, I did believe everything Nathan told us. Did you?'

'Oh yes. A boy of that age isn't going to make up that business about the sex . . .' Carole looked embarrassed, '. . . you know, not working.'

'No. Poor kid. Poor kid on many counts.'

'So . . . I'll ring Rowley in the morning.'

'I think if you do fix to meet him . . .'

'Yes?'

'. . . you should insist that I come too.'

'Safety in numbers?'

'That's it.' Jude suddenly raised her glass. 'To us. I think we've had a really good day today.'

'Found Nathan and freed him. Yes, not bad.'

'Now he's back in circulation, it's going to open the whole case up.'

'For the police certainly.'

'And for us too, Carole. We'll soon have a solution. I can feel the tumblers in the lock slotting into position.'

'Oh yes?'

'Yes. Definitely.'

This optimistic feeling was reinforced for Jude the next morning when she had a call from Wally Grenston. After greetings and a few lavish compliments (Mim was clearly not in the room), he said, 'Told you old Joe Bartos was thinking of going to the Czech Club on Wednesday . . . ?'

'Yes.'

'Well, I saw him there.'

'Did you tell him I wanted to talk to him?'

'I did, yes.'

'Did he agree?'

'No, he didn't.' Jude was suitably cast down, but Wally, playing his narration at his own pace, continued, 'I've just had a call from him this morning, though . . .'

'And?'

'And maybe he's changed his mind.'

'Oh?'

'Thing is, he's heard from the police that the boy – you know, Krystina's boyfriend, the one who'd disappeared – well, he's turned up.' Jude restricted herself to a non-committal response, waiting to hear what came next. 'The police won't tell Joe anything and he was thinking, you're interested in the case . . . maybe you know something. Maybe he should talk to you . . . ?'

That was her cue. 'Maybe he should. I actually spent most of yesterday with Nathan Locke.'

'Did you? How's that?'

'I'll tell you when you introduce me to Joe Bartos.'

The old man chuckled. 'Playing hard to get, are you?'

'No, not at all. Always available for you, Wally . . . assuming, that is, that Mim's not there.'

He chuckled more. She'd hit the right tone. They fixed that the meeting would take place at teatime. 'Four o'clock. On the dot. That's when Mim and I always have tea. Because I'm so English,' he added with a wheezy laugh. 'Oh, and one thing, Jude . . .'

'Yes?'

'Mim'll be there, so try not to make it too obvious that you fancy the socks off me.'

'I'll do my best.'

'But that's exactly the time I've arranged to meet Rowley Locke,' Carole complained.

'Well, I can't really change what Wally's set up. I get the impression Joe Bartos's goodwill towards me may be short-lived. I don't want to mess him around. Where have you fixed to meet Rowley? At Marine Villas?'

'No, I thought somewhere public was better. Safer.'

'Sure.'

'So it's the Seaview Café at four.'

'Oh, you should be all right there. There'll be lots of people around.'

'And I'm going to take Gulliver.'

'As a guard dog?'

'You must be joking. Gulliver hasn't got a suspicious bone in his body. He'd lick the hand of Jack the Ripper. But if I've got the dog with me, Rowley's not going to be able to abscond with me quite so easily.'

'Is absconding with you Rowley's style?'

'I don't think so. But who knows? It'll be very interesting to hear what he's got to say.'

'Certainly will. Is he coming on his own?'

'He didn't say. I'd doubt it, though. Those Lockes seem to go everywhere mob-handed.'

'Yes, Rowley can't function without his admiring audience. Tell you what, after you've talked to Rowley and I've talked to Joe Bartos, let's meet up in the Crown and Anchor to debrief.'

Carole bit back her instinctive reaction to say it'd be rather early to start drinking, and agreed that that was a very good idea.

Jude was just about to leave for her tea party on the Shorelands Estate, when she had a call on her mobile. She recognized the voice immediately, Martina Rutherford's distinctive accent. Strange how many Czechs seemed to be involved in the case. Could there be some undiscovered link between Martina and Joe Bartos? Or between her and Wally Grenston . . . ? Another idea to stir into the soup of conjectures that was swilling around in her mind.

'The reason I am ringing,' said Martina, 'is that I gather the boy Nathan Locke has been found.'

'Yes, he has.'

'And I hear a rumour that you were one of the people who found him?'

'There are always lots of rumours around down here.' Jude wasn't going to confirm that particular one until she had a clearer idea of what Martina was after.

'All I am asking,' said the Czech woman, 'is for you to confirm that the boy is in police custody.'

'I can do that. Though "custody" may be too strong a word. The police are certainly asking him some questions.'

'They will charge him soon,' Martina announced confidently. 'This will be a great relief to Martin.'

'Oh?'

'So long as the boy has been missing, Martin has been afraid he himself is a suspect.'

'You can see why the police would be interested in his movements.'

'I'm sorry?' Martina sounded puzzled.

'Well, Martin having been seen at Connie's Clip Joint?'

'You mean the night the girl died?'

'I don't know that there's any proof he was there then, but he was certainly seen coming out of the salon last Sunday.'

'Really?' The woman tried to maintain her professional cool, but was clearly shaken by the information.

'I had not heard this. I was away in Prague at the week-end.'

'So Martin didn't tell you? The police must have talked to him about it.'

'Oh yes, he said he had to see the police. I hadn't connected it with him being in Fethering on Sunday. Of course, now it makes sense.' The confidence was back in her voice, but Jude reckoned the cover-up was too slick to be true. Martina Rutherford hadn't known that her husband had been seen by Carole coming out of Connie's Clip Joint.

'Still, all I wanted, Jude, was for you to confirm that Nathan Locke is with the police. When I tell that to Martin, he will be very relieved. Thank you so much for talking to me.'

After the phone call Jude tried to define the emotions she had heard in the woman's voice. Shock certainly . . . but there had been something else as well. Suspicion. A new and sudden suspicion. For the first time Martina Rutherford had contemplated the possibility that her husband might have had something to do with the death of Kyra Bartos.

Chapter Thirty-two

During the summer season (which was coming to an end) tables and chairs spilled out of the Seaview Café onto Fethering Beach. Carole, arriving with Gulliver early as ever, took one of the seats furthest away from the self-service counter. She didn't go up there to order anything. She'd wait till Rowley Locke came and see how their meeting panned out. Her position, she reckoned, was well chosen. In sight of a lot of people, but good for a quick getaway. And also far enough away from the curious ears of Fethering for their conversation to be confidential.

Rowley Locke arrived on the dot of four. This time he wasn't heading a large family contingent. Only his brother Arnold, who was immediately despatched to fetch tea. Just tea. Carole had declined the offer of sandwiches and sticky cakes.

Rowley turned his innocent blue eyes on her. 'I assume it was you.'

'What was me?'

'Yesterday two women, matching descriptions of you and your friend Jude, abducted Nathan from our holiday cottage in Cornwall.'

'I'm afraid I take issue with the word "abducted". It might be used more accurately to describe the means by which he was taken to Treboddick in the first place.'

'Carole, you don't know the background to what you're talking about. This is a family thing.'

'I'll tell you what I do know – and that is that Nathan was being held down there against his will.'

Rowley Locke was unworried by the accusation. He shrugged and said, 'Sometimes young people don't know what's best for them. Then someone else has to take decisions on their behalf.'

'And if it's anything to do with the Locke family, then you're the person who takes those decisions.'

'Someone has to be a leader,' he said almost smugly.

'A leader like Prince Fimbador is a leader?'

She had managed to embarrass him. He looked away as he said, 'The Wheal Quest is a family game. You wouldn't understand it.'

At this moment Arnold arrived with the tea. After it had been poured, Carole turned her pale blue eyes on the weaker brother. 'You and Eithne must be very glad to hear that your son has been found.' He didn't respond. 'Or perhaps not, since you both connived at his imprisonment.'

'I think "imprisonment" is rather a strong word,' said Arnold feebly.

'Strong maybe, but it's accurate.' She turned back to Rowley. 'What on earth did you think hiding the boy away was going to achieve?'

'I hoped it would keep him safe until the police found out who really killed the girl.'

'Wouldn't it have helped the police more if they could have talked to Nathan? So that he could tell them what he saw that night, and help them to sort out a timetable of events?'

'I didn't want him to get into the hands of the police. Our fine boys in blue don't have a great track record when it comes to—'

And he was off again on his hobby horse. Carole couldn't stand any more of this tired old leftie agenda. 'Oh, for heaven's sake! You were deliberately perverting the course of justice. And I would imagine you'll be looking at a hefty prison sentence for what you've done.'

From his expression of dismay, this was clearly a possibility Rowley Locke had not considered. Like most control freaks, he was quickly vulnerable when threatened.

'I assume you've heard from the police in Littlehampton?' She addressed this question to the boy's father.

'Yes, they told me they were holding Nathan. He's "helping them with their enquiries". Eithne and I are going to visit him this evening.'

That would be an interesting encounter to witness. What do parents say to a son who knows that they've connived in having him imprisoned for three weeks? But that wasn't Carole's business. She moved on. 'Presumably you both know that Nathan didn't commit the murder?'

The look Arnold referred to his brother suggested

314

that at least one of them wasn't entirely convinced on the subject.

'Well, he didn't,' Carole continued. 'As I'm sure the police will find out in the course of their enquiries.'

'I wouldn't be so sure. The British police only want to get a conviction and they—'

'Oh, shut up, Rowley!' Carole was surprised by her own vehemence. So was its recipient. But she went on in similarly forceful vein. 'Listen, your ill-considered actions have wasted a lot of time. They've wasted police time, and they've certainly wasted time for me and my friend Jude.' In the magnificence of her flow neither man thought to question exactly what right she and Jude had to be involved in the investigation. 'What I suggest you do now, to make some kind of amends, is to tell me anything you know that might have a bearing on the case. Anything that you may have been holding back.'

Rowley Locke looked genuinely at a loss. 'I haven't been holding anything back. When I heard about Kyra Bartos's death, my only thought was that Nathan would immediately become a suspect. And that I had to get him to a place of safety.' Again he avoided Carole's eyes. 'I don't know anything else about the murder.'

'When I first came to see you, you told me that Eithne had met Kyra Bartos briefly in the street, but neither of you had. Is that still true?'

Rowley looked perplexed. 'Well, of course it's still true. The girl was already dead when we met you.'

'Yes. What I'm asking, though, is this. *At the time*

you said you hadn't met Kyra. Has your recollection maybe changed since then?'

'Are you accusing us of lying?'

'After what you said about Nathan's whereabouts over the past three weeks, don't you think I might have some justification?'

'Actually,' said Arnold quietly, 'I was lying.'

The announcement came as much of a shock to his brother as it did to Carole. They both looked at him in amazement as he went on, 'I did meet Kyra one evening a few weeks before she died. Eithne and I had gone out to a concert in Brighton. The Monteverdi *Vespers*, as it happened. Anyway, I had a bit of a stomach upset. My stomach has always been my Achilles heel . . .' He confided this mixed metaphor to Carole as though it would be of vital interest to her. 'So I went back to Marine Villas and found Kyra there with Nathan. Of course, I didn't mind his being there with the girl – Eithne and I have always made it clear that we have no old-fashioned moral scruples about that kind of thing – but I was a little upset that he'd done it without asking us. You know, choosing an evening when he thought we'd be out . . . it was all a bit underhand and hole-in-the-corner, if you know what I mean . . .'

Yes, I know exactly what you mean, and will you please get on with it, Carole thought.

'Anyway, when I found Nathan and the girl together that evening . . .' Arnold's pale features reddened, '. . . I must confess I was rather upset by what they were doing.'

'Do you mean they were having sex?'

316

'Oh, good heavens, no!' He dismissed the suggestion almost contemptuously. 'That would have been fine. Eithne and I wouldn't have had any problems about that. We've always brought up Diggo and Fimby to believe that sex is a perfectly natural and healthy act between two consenting—'

'Then what were they doing that you objected to?' demanded Carole, who had had quite enough of this spelling-out of right-on liberal credentials.

'Oh. Oh, well . . . they'd . . .' Arnold looked across at his elder brother, as though afraid of his reaction to the forthcoming revelation. 'They'd got out our box of the Wheal Quest.' He turned back to Carole. 'The Wheal Quest is a kind of family—'

'I know exactly what the Wheal Quest is, thank you.'

'What were they doing with it?' asked Rowley, suddenly alert.

'They'd got the game spread out on the floor, and I think Nathan must have been explaining to Kyra how it worked, and . . . and she was laughing at it.'

An expression of pale fury crossed his brother's face. 'Laughing at it?'

'Yes. And I think they must have been drinking, because the girl went on, saying how silly it was, and she even got Nathan to agree with her.'

Rowley snorted with anger at this betrayal.

'And I remember thinking . . .' Arnold went on quietly, 'this girl is not good for Nathan. She's a disruptive influence. She's trying to drive a wedge between him and his family. This relationship must be stopped.'

Carole had heard that cold intensity in a voice only the previous day. And when she looked at Arnold, she could see burning in his eyes the same demented logic that had driven Mopsa.

Chapter Thirty-three

Though in his eighties, Jiri Bartos was still an impressive man. Well over six foot and hardly stooping at all, he towered over Jude as he rose to shake her hand. There was still a full head of hair, white and cut to about an inch's length all over. His face was the shape of a shield, concave beneath high cheekbones, and his eyes were still piercingly blue. In the Grenstons' sitting room he seemed too large an exhibit, amidst the array of awards and the tables littered with tiny *objets d'art*.

While Wally made the introductions, Mim fluttered around over her tea tray, on which lay an unbelievable array of Victoria sponge, fairy cakes, tiny éclairs, coconut kisses and other fancies that Jude remembered from her childhood. There were even some slices of chequered Battenberg, which her father had always called 'stained-glass window cake'.

But Jiri Bartos did not appear interested in the spread of goodies. As soon as he sat down, he took a packet of cigarettes and a lighter out of his pocket.

'I'm sorry, Joe,' said Mim, 'but we don't smoke in the house.'

'I do,' he replied, lighting up. His voice was deep, like the creaking of old timber, and heavily accented.

'It isn't nice when we are eating food,' Mim protested.

'I will not eat food.'

'But I've prepared all this—'

'Walter . . .' He spoke it in the German way. 'We will have drink. Where is drink? Where is slivovitz? Where do you hide Becherovka?'

Mim tried again. 'Um, Wally doesn't drink in the afternoon.'

'Yes, he does. When with me he drink and smoke in afternoon.'

Mim turned to her husband, who studiously looked out of the window towards the sea. Then she turned back to Jiri Bartos. 'Listen, Joe, this is our house and—'

'Go. Leave us to talk. This is not wife's subject we talk of.'

She tried one more appeal to Wally, whose eyes still managed to evade hers, and then, with as much dignity as she could muster, left the room. As soon as her back was to him, her husband watched her go with a kind of wistfulness. Maybe he should have tried the Jiri Bartos approach a lot earlier in his marriage.

To Jude the exchange between Jiri and Mim had sounded unusual. Although his words were rude, he had not come across as ill-mannered. It had been a clash of wills rather than of words, and there had been no doubt whose will was the stronger.

Silently, Wally Grenston rose from his chair and went to a glass corner cupboard, from which he extracted a tall green bottle. He looked at Jude. 'You join us?'

'Please. I love Becherovka.'

Wally picked up three small glasses with a whirly design of red and gold on them. He put them on the table, unscrewed the Becherovka and after pouring about an inch into the bottom of each glass, handed them round.

He and his old friend looked into each other's eyes as they raised their glasses and in unison said, 'Na Zdravi!'

Jiri made no attempt to include Jude in the toast, but again for some strange reason this did not feel offensive. She took a sip of her drink, anyway, remembering and relishing the stickiness on her lips and the herbal, almost medicinal, glow that filled her mouth.

'I am very sorry about what happened to your daughter,' she said.

'Thank you.' Jiri Bartos left it at that. Jude did not imagine there were many circumstances in which he would let his emotions show. 'You find boy who police think killed her?'

'Yes. Yes, a friend and I went down to Cornwall and . . . we found him.'

Jude didn't particularly want to go into the details, but the old man insisted. Though hardened against showing any emotion about his daughter's death, he wanted to find out everything that might have some connection to it.

So Jude told him how Carole and she had tracked down the boy to Treboddick. She did not spell out the

321

fact that he had not been hiding there voluntarily. At the end of her narrative, there was a silence. Then Jiri Bartos asked, 'You think he kill her?'

'No.'

'Why not?'

'For a start, I don't think it's in his nature to kill anyone.'

The old man let out a guttural hawk of dissent. 'It's in all men's nature to kill when they have to. We know that – yes, Walter?'

Wally nodded uncomfortably. Jude wondered what secrets the two men shared, and reckoned it was pretty unlikely that they'd ever share them with her.

'So, if not boy, who you think kill Krystina?'

Jude was forced to admit she didn't have an answer. 'But there are quite a few suspects.'

Jiri Bartos shrugged at the inadequacy of her reply. 'Boy was there. Boy have motive.'

'What motive?'

'He want make love Krystina. She good girl, no want to. He lose control. He kill her.'

Jude would have liked to reveal the true nature of Nathan and Kyra's sexual encounter, if only to exonerate the boy, but she realized she would be betraying a confidence. So instead she said, 'You didn't approve of Kyra – Krystina seeing Nathan, did you?'

'Girl too young. One day she meet right boy. Now she too busy with job, look after house. Both too young.'

She decided to take a risk. 'You had another family once, didn't you? Another wife and children, in Czechoslovakia?'

Wally didn't like the direction of the conversation. 'Jude, I don't think—'

'No. She ask me. I answer. Yes, I have other family. Not in Czechoslovakia. Well, first in Czechoslovakia. Then the name changed. Then it called "Protectorate of Bohemia/Moravia".'

'That was when the Nazis took over?'

'Of course.'

'What happened to your other family?'

The old man shook his head. 'They do not exist.' That was all she was going to get out of him on the subject. 'I come to England.'

'Do you think it was because of what happened to your other family that you were so protective of Krystina?'

The blue eyes looked at her bleakly. That question wasn't going to get any kind of answer. Someone like Jiri Bartos did not have time for psychology; his only imperative was survival. Jude tried another tack. 'Do you know Connie Rutherford . . . the one who runs the salon?'

'I meet. Pick up Krystina from work one day. Also she live near.'

'Near your house?'

'Yes. Two gardens meet at back, only fence between.'

Distantly this rang a bell with something she had heard from Carole. 'And did Krystina like Connie?'

'I think. Krystina happy in job.'

'But she wasn't happy in her previous job?'

Puzzlement etched new lines in his craggy brow. 'Not happy? This I not know.'

'She worked at Martin & Martina in Worthing. But not for long. Then she went to Connie's Clip Joint. Why?'

'Better job, she tell me.'

'No other reason?'

He shook his massive head.

'Did she say whether she got on with her boss at the Worthing salon? His name was Martin.'

'I know who you mean, yes. I've seen him around. Krystina say she like him very much.'

It made sense. If her father was so protective, Kyra wouldn't have told him about Martin Rutherford coming on to her. It could have made for rather an ugly confrontation.

Jude sighed and went back to the most basic of questions. 'Can you think of any reason why someone would want to kill your daughter?'

'If not boy, no.'

'I'm absolutely certain it wasn't Nathan.'

He shrugged. Tell me why, he seemed to be saying, you still haven't convinced me.

'Look, you disapproved of their relationship, Nathan and K— Krystina.'

'Yes, I disapprove. That not mean I kill my own daughter.'

'I wasn't suggesting that. But can you think of anyone else who might have disapproved of their relationship?'

'I don't know. I don't know boy at all. Maybe he have other girlfriend not happy.'

'From what I can find out, Krystina was his first girl-friend.'

'Then I not know. Unless his parents disapprove of my daughter.'

'Did you ever meet his parents?'

'Of course, no. I only meet boy once. But his parents . . . maybe rich. Maybe think they important family. Maybe not think daughter of Czech electrician good enough for boy.' He looked at her, challenging, almost amused through his pain. 'Maybe they kill her . . . ?'

It's a possibility, thought Jude, that I certainly haven't ruled out.

Chapter Thirty-four

Rowley Locke had been just as shocked as Carole by the sudden change in his brother's manner. 'Arnold, what are you saying?'

'I am saying that that girl Kyra was not worthy of Nathan. We can't allow anyone into the Locke family who thinks that the Wheal Quest is funny. That girl would only have been a disruptive influence.'

Rowley now looked positively worried. 'I agree, it's a family thing, and it should be kept within the family.' And then he said something so out of keeping with his usual attitude that it showed the extent of his anxiety. 'But we shouldn't take it too seriously. The Wheal Quest is only a game.'

'No, it's more than that! It's a philosophy, it's a life system!' The sudden vehemence with which Arnold spoke drew disturbed glances from people at adjacent tables. The serenity of Fethering Beach on a September afternoon was rarely broken by shouting.

But if the geriatric onlookers had been shocked by Arnold's outburst, they were about to get more free entertainment. Before he could say more, the group at

Carole's table was joined by a fast-striding Bridget Locke, with an embarrassed Eithne in her wake.

'Rowley! What the hell have you been doing?'

He quailed visibly under his wife's onslaught and asked feebly, 'What are you talking about?'

'You know bloody well what I'm talking about! What you did to Nathan.'

'I did it for his own good. I was trying to protect him.'

'Rowley, that is so much crap! I can't believe that you didn't tell me what you'd done. I've spent the past three weeks worried sick about the boy, when you could have put my mind at rest at any moment by telling me where Nathan was.'

'But I thought if you knew, you'd have told the police.'

'Too bloody right I would.'

'Bridget, if the police had got hold of him, God knows what would have happened. Our fine boys in blue are not—'

'Oh, shut up, Rowley! You sound like a record whose needle's stuck. I've had enough of your right-on *Guardian*-reading claptrap to last me a lifetime!' (Carole was rather enjoying this conversation. What a very sensible woman Bridget Locke was. She thought exactly like Carole did.) 'You weren't thinking about Nathan at all! I wonder if you've ever thought about anyone else apart from yourself, except to see if you can make an anagram out of their name. As ever, with Nathan in trouble, your first thought was about you. A Locke family crisis? Someone's got to take control here. And,

because the rest of the family are so bloody pusillani-
mous, it had to be you, didn't it? He's only your
nephew, not your son, but it's still got to be you who
comes to the rescue. Don't worry, Rowley can sort
everything out! Here comes the hero, galloping up on
his white charger.

'And then what did you do? What was your solution
to the crisis? You made it all part of a game. Yes, the
bloody Wheal Quest. And you took advantage of your
vulnerable daughter Mopsa and made her play along
with your stupid, sub-Tolkien fantasy. And you never
for one moment thought of what you might be doing to
Nathan!'

Bridget Locke paused for breath. Her geriatric audience settled in their seats, and took another sip of tea
in anticipation of Act Two.

'How do you know all this?' Rowley managed to
ask.

'I know because the police rang the house to tell
me that they were questioning Nathan. Because he's
a juvenile, they wanted a family member there.' She
turned the beam of her displeasure on the shrinking
Eithne. 'And apparently I was the one who he wanted
to be there with him.'

'But surely you should be at work?'

'Yes, Rowley, it's a Friday. I should be at work. But
some things are more important than work. Listen, that
call I had from the police was the first I knew that the
poor boy was still alive. So, since I couldn't get hold of
you anywhere, after I'd been to the police station to see

Nathan, I went straight round to Eithne's, and made her tell me what the hell had been going on.'

Arnold's wife appealed apologetically to the two brothers. 'I'm sorry. You know what she's like when she gets forceful.' She still looked to Carole like Mrs Bun the Baker's Wife, but the game was no longer Happy Families.

'Anyway,' Bridget steamed on, 'the police are extremely interested in talking to you, Rowley. I'm sure they won't have any problem finding you, but you might make things easier by turning yourself in.'

'What do you mean, "turning myself in"?' he asked petulantly. 'I haven't committed any crime.'

'No? I think the police could probably think of a few. "Perverting the Course of Justice" . . . ? I don't know the proper terms, but I'm sure there's one called "Abduction of a Juvenile". And there's certainly "Unlawful Imprisonment".'

'For heaven's sake, Bridget! These weren't crimes. They were all in the family.'

'God, Rowley, that sums you up, doesn't it? "All in the family." Everything's all right so long as it's kept within the magic circle of the Lockes. That's always been your escape. When you fail publicly, when you lose a job . . . never mind, because you're still a little god within the family. And everyone in the family does as you say. I've even done it myself. Pretended to have a bad back, so that you can find out if some woman's snooping on you. But that's always been your approach. Never mind your inadequacies in the real world – in the Wheal Quest you are still a hero. Rowley, if you only knew how bloody pathetic you are!'

He rose from his chair with an attempt at dignity. 'I'm not going to stay here to be insulted.'

'Fine. Go to the police. Let them start insulting you instead.'

'That kind of remark is not worth responding to. Come on, we're going.'

Arnold rose obediently to his feet and crossed to his wife, who had yet to sit down. Rowley joined them, then looked back at Bridget. 'Are you coming?'

'No. Certainly not now. And I'll have to think about whether I ever come back.'

He did not respond to that, but led his acolytes back across the sand towards the front. The animated language of his back-view showed that he was telling Eithne off for her betrayal of Locke confidentiality. And Arnold was joining in the castigation.

Exhausted, Bridget dropped into a seat next to Carole. 'Sorry about all that. I was just bloody furious. Letting off the steam of a good few years, I'm afraid.'

Realizing the climax of the play had passed, Fethering's elderly matinee-goers returned once more to their tea and cakes.

'Yes.' Now the others had gone, Carole felt awkward. The dissection of the Lockes' family life – and indeed marriage – had been rather public. She didn't quite know where the conversation should move next. Jude, she knew, would instinctively have found the right direction.

Still, there was always one safe English fallback. 'Would you like me to get you a cup of tea?'

The drained woman looked pathetically grateful for the offer and accepted.

By the time she returned with a fresh pot for both of them, Carole had decided which tack to take. 'How did Nathan seem when you saw him?'

'Oh, fine. No physical harm, anyway. Though what effect it's going to have on him emotionally, I hate to think.'

'What's he doing now?'

'Asleep. He didn't get much sleep last night. The detectives are being quite gentle with him.'

'Rowley would never believe that.'

'No.' She sighed. 'I just feel so sorry for Nathan. I mean he's still in deep shock about that poor girl's death. He did love her, you know, with that intense adolescent passion of a first love. He must be so cut up. And I can't think that being shut away for three weeks and ministered to by his loony cousin has made the grieving process any easier.'

'I'm surprised to hear you use the word "loony".'

'Yes, very remiss of me, isn't it? If I wasn't in such an emotional state, I wouldn't have been so politically incorrect. Mopsa is, after all, my stepdaughter. But it's true. I've never managed to get through to her. I mean, she loathed me, because I replaced her beloved mother, but . . . there was always a problem there with Mopsa. Poor concentration, no grasp of reality. I'm sure there's a name for it . . . Somebody-or-Other's Syndrome, no doubt. But, of course, the Lockes never had her properly diagnosed. No, as ever, they reckoned they could sort everything out themselves.'

'Do you know why Rowley's first wife left?'

Bridget Locke smiled grimly. 'After the scene you've just witnessed, do you need to ask?'

'Maybe not.' There was a silence, broken only by the gulls and the soft swooshing of the sea, before Carole asked what was, for her, a daringly personal question. 'Do you think you will go back to him?'

'I don't know.' There was a weary shake of the head. 'At the moment I'm so seething with fury that . . . I won't make a quick decision. There is still something there, you know. There's a side of Rowley that very few people ever see. He can be quite enchanting.'

I'll have to take your word for that, thought Carole. And again she asked herself the perennial question: why do bright, intelligent women stay with such unsatisfactory men? But then she thought of the alternative, the divorce she and David had shared. And wondered whether that was actually a much better solution.

'I was wondering . . .' Bridget went on, 'you spent most of yesterday driving Nathan back from Treboddick . . .'

'Yes.'

'Did he say anything to you . . . you know, anything that made you think differently about who might have killed Kyra Bartos?'

'Not really. I mean, he told me and Jude what he'd done that night . . . which sounded pretty convincing to us . . . though whether it'll convince the police . . .'

'As I say, the police are being much more sensitive

than I'd ever have expected. They very definitely want to question Nathan, but I didn't get the impression that they regard him as a major suspect.'

'Good. Well, the one thing he did mention was that that night, while he was in the salon with Kyra . . . he thought he heard someone trying to get in through the back gate.'

'The murderer?'

'Possibly. Whoever it was couldn't have got in then . . . but maybe came back later.'

'Hmm . . !' Bridget Locke swept her hands slowly through her long blonde hair and looked thoughtful. 'There was one thing that Nathan said to me, just now, at the police station . . . which I thought was interesting . . !'

'What was that?'

'He said that there were a dozen red roses in the back room at the salon the night Kyra Bartos died.'

'Yes, I saw them. Part of Nathan's romantic set dressing, I imagine. Which, given the circumstances, is pretty sad.'

'No.'

'What?' Carole looked curiously at the woman.

'Nathan said the red roses had nothing to do with him. They were there when he arrived.'

'Didn't he ask Kyra if they were hers?'

'Apparently not. He assumed they were something to do with the salon's owner . . . Connie, is it?'

'Yes. Did he say whether he had told the police about seeing the red roses?'

'I asked him and he said he hadn't. I got the

impression they'd been asking more about where he'd been for the past three weeks, and in the next session they're going to get on to the night Kyra Bartos died. But I thought the red roses were interesting.'

'Certainly. And one assumes that the police took them away from the salon as evidence?'

'I would think so, Carole. What were they then – a love token for somebody?'

'Perhaps.'

'So,' said Bridget Locke, 'the two obvious questions are: who brought them to the salon? And who for?'

So far as Carole was concerned, the answers to those questions were very straightforward. As soon as she got back to High Tor, she fed Gulliver, hardly noticing what she was doing. Her mind was racing.

She could only think of one candidate as the bearer of red roses for Kyra. Apart from Nathan, there was another man who had fancied her. Or at least come on to her. Maybe the girl hadn't been so immune to his attractions as she pretended.

Carole found the card and dialled his mobile number. Martin Rutherford answered immediately. She identified herself, and reminded him that he'd asked her to get in touch if she found out anything more about the murder.

'Well, I have found out something.' She told him about the red roses, and the fact that they hadn't been brought to the salon by Nathan Locke.

'Ah. Maybe we should talk . . . ?'

'Just what I was going to suggest.'

She looked at her watch. Just before five. Jude would surely be back soon. Maybe they'd have to delay their debriefing meeting at the Crown and Anchor. If she made an appointment to meet Martin somewhere at seven, they could both confront him. But that wasn't going to be possible. Martin wanted to meet earlier. 'The salon closes at six, and I have, er, other commitments for the evening.'

'So you're there now?'

'Yes.'

'I'll be right over.'

'Very well.' He sounded resigned to whatever the interview might bring.

After she'd put the phone down, Carole contemplated ringing Jude's mobile. But no, she didn't want to interrupt her neighbour's meeting with the elusive Joe Bartos.

Besides, once again Carole felt that charge of doing something on her own. She'd find the truth and present it to Jude, neatly gift-wrapped. She'd show she was no slouch in this investigation business.

Chapter Thirty-five

'Did boy say anything?' asked Jiri Bartos. 'Yesterday you drive long time with him. Did he say anything about Krystina?'

'He said that he loved her.'

The old man snorted dismissively. 'What boys of that age know about love?'

'I think they probably know quite a lot. They find it all very confusing, but they do know the strength of their own feelings.'

'Love often dangerous. Many murders committed for love.'

Wally Grenston, who had been silently topping up Jiri Bartos's glass throughout their conversation, moved forward again with the Becherovka bottle poised. The old man waved it away. 'No. Slivovitz.'

Wally nodded, returned to the drinks cupboard and produced a bottle of the famous Jelinek Plum Brandy. He poured some into a new glass, and handed it across.

'Not cold?'

'I'm sorry. It very rarely gets drunk.'

'Huh. Wife not like?'

Wally didn't argue. He had long since reconciled

himself to his henpecked image. With a nervous look around the room, he was no doubt anticipating trouble ahead, from his wife. It was surprising how much of a fug one man's chain-smoking could produce. And Mim's obsessively produced tea lay untouched. Wally Grenston might be in for a difficult evening.

And yet there was something about him that was relaxed, as if sitting drinking in a haze of smoke felt natural to him. It probably echoed previous evenings that Wally had sat with Joseph and other compatriots. Jude had the feeling that, if she wasn't there, the two men would be speaking Czech.

Jiri Bartos once again focused his bright blue eyes on her. 'Tell me more about boy. What he say he do night Krystina died?'

Jude replied accurately, but not completely. She recounted the timing of Nathan's arrival at and departure from the salon, but she didn't detail his unsuccessful love-making with Kyra.

'Huh. And boy not see anyone else around salon?'

'No. He thought he heard someone coming through the back gate at one point, but he didn't see anyone.'

'Who could that be?'

'Well, putting on one side the explanation that it could just have been a burglar who was trying to break in . . . there might be an argument for thinking that the visitor was someone who could get into the salon by the back door . . . in other words someone who had keys.' Jiri Bartos did not challenge her logic. 'So that would mean Connie Rutherford herself or the other stylist Theo or—'

'Not Connie. She not go out that evening.'

'How do you know?'

'I tell you, my garden back on to hers. When hot in evening, I sit on balcony with drink, can see her house. Summer no curtains drawn. That evening I see her all evening.'

'What was she doing?'

He shrugged. 'She move round house from room to room. Like she nervous. I don't know. But she not go out.'

'Are you sure she didn't? Even later? Midnight? One o'clock? Hadn't you gone to bed by then?'

'No. I go to bed much later. Sometimes not at all. No point in going to bed if you do not sleep. I did not see Connie leave all night.'

'Well, that's good, thank you. I'm glad she's off the hook. I'd hate to think of her being in any way involved in what happened to your daughter. But the one other person who we now know did have keys to the back door of the salon is her ex-husband, Martin Rutherford. Do you know who I mean?'

'I know him, I tell you. I live in house long time. I saw him back when they two still married.'

'Well, Martin's got an alibi for the night Kyra died. He was at a conference in Brighton and—'

'He not at conference in Brighton.'

'What?' asked Jude, thunderstruck. 'How do you know?'

'I see him.'

'You saw him that night? At the salon?'

338

'No, not at salon. I in my house all night. Eleven o'clock maybe I see him in Connie's house.'

'Really?'

'He come through back garden. Way into house people not see. Only I see. He go to back door. Connie let him in.'

'And then what happened?'

'I not know. They close curtains.'

Jude took a triumphant sip of her sticky Becherovka, and felt the cough medicine taste burn in her throat. This was a result. The night Kyra Bartos died, Martin Rutherford had actually been in Fethering.

Chapter Thirty-six

The Worthing branch of Martin & Martina was still busy when Carole arrived. All the stylists seemed to be occupied, and it looked unlikely that they could all be finished by the six o'clock closing time. There was no sign of either of the proprietors, but the girl at the desk said she was expected and directed her to the staircase that led up to Martin's office.

The two-room suite had been designed by the same person who had done the salon downstairs. The Martin & Martina logo was very much in evidence, and all the furniture featured black glass and brushed aluminium.

Martin, who must have been alerted to Carole's arrival by the receptionist, was standing in the outer office, waiting for her. He shook her hand, the model of urbanity, but she could feel the tension in his body. 'Please come through.'

She did as she was told, leaving the door between the two offices open. Although the presence of all the stylists and customers downstairs gave her some security, she still wanted to have an escape route.

Martin Rutherford gestured her to a chair and sat down behind the black glass top of his desk. As ever, he looked what he was, the successful entrepreneur, hair subtly darkened, teeth expensively straightened.

'So, what can I do for you, Carole? I'm sorry I can't be long. As I say, I have somewhere to go this evening.'

'With your wife?'

'No, Martina is going to Prague to see her mother, who's very sick. She gets the 21:05 flight from Heathrow. I have to be away by six.'

'What I have to say won't take very long.'

'Good. Now, something about red roses, wasn't it . . . ? How romantic.' The laid-back flippancy of his tone was contradicted by the unease in his darting brown eyes.

'Yes. As I say, I was told this by the missing boy Nathan Locke. When he arrived in the back room of the salon that night, the red roses were already there.'

'Perhaps Kyra had another admirer . . . ?'

'That's rather what I was thinking, Martin.'

He looked genuinely puzzled for a moment before he caught on to what she was saying. 'Oh, me? Are you suggesting that I had the hots for Kyra?'

'She used to work for you, right here in this salon.'

'A lot of young women work for me, in this salon and in many others. That doesn't mean I fancy any of them.'

'No, but Kyra Bartos left the job here, because you were sexually harassing her.'

'Oh, we're back to that again, are we? Incidentally, where did you hear about it?'

'Your ex-wife Connie told my friend Jude.'

'Ah. Yes.' The explanation seemed in some way to

relax him. 'Of course, your friend Jude. The other half of Fethering's very own Marple Twins.'

Carole didn't react to the gibe. 'So there might be a logical connection between your "coming on" to Kyra when she worked for you and your giving her red roses when she no longer worked for you.'

'There might be, but I wouldn't say it was that logical. Nor would I say it's the kind of thing that would be possible to prove.'

'Did the police ask you about the red roses?'

'Sorry? No, not at all. Remember, I only talked to them right at the beginning of the case. Then all they wanted to establish was the set-up at Connie's Clip Joint . . . you know, the fact that Connie was my ex-wife, what our financial arrangements had been since the divorce. They didn't ask me anything connected with the actual murder case.'

'I wasn't referring to the first time, Martin.'

'What?' He looked puzzled.

'Not the first time the police talked to you, immediately after the murder. I'm talking about when they questioned you about having been in Connie's Clip Joint last Sunday morning.' Now it made sense to him. 'Because Connie told them about that break-in. And you're not going to tell me they didn't follow up on it with you.'

'No. No.' Martin Rutherford looked thoughtful. Then he said, 'You know, Carole, I think you and your friend Jude are very stupid to get involved in situations like this.'

'Oh? Why?'

'Because they're potentially dangerous.' There was no twinkle in the brown eyes he fixed on hers. 'It's very common that someone who is about to be exposed for committing one murder doesn't have much compunction about committing another.'

Jude was full of her news. When she got back, she went straight round to High Tor to share it with Carole. But there was no reply, just a disgruntled barking from Gulliver.

She returned to Woodside Cottage, the information about Martin Rutherford still bubbling inside her. Then she rang through to the Crown and Anchor, to see whether Carole had gone there, according to their earlier arrangement. But Ted Crisp said she hadn't been in. Jude moved round the house, unable to settle to anything, and kept looking out of her front window to see whether the Renault had reappeared.

Martin stood up from his chair and moved round to the front of his desk. He sat on the edge, in what should have been a casual posture. But his body was tense, in the grip of some strong emotion. He was only a few feet from Carole, and she could feel the energy sparking off him.

'There's a lot you don't understand,' he said at length. 'A lot of secrets that should stay secrets.'

'If keeping things secret leads to people being murdered, then I would have thought perhaps they ought to be made public.' The sentence was a lot more articulate and confident than Carole felt.

'Huh.' Martin Rutherford rubbed the back of his hand wearily across his brow. 'It's terrible how easily things go wrong, how easily they get out of hand.'

'Are you talking about what you did to Kyra?'

'I did nothing to Kyra.'

'No? Do you deny that you went round to Connie's Clip Joint the night the girl died?'

He slowly blew out a long breath, then said, 'No, I don't deny it.'

'When did you go there?'

'About seven, before the girl arrived.'

'But you didn't stay?'

'No, I had to get back to Brighton.'

'For your Hair and Nail Conference?'

'Yes.'

'To establish your alibi.'

'If you like.' He now sounded very weary. 'Yes, I sat through a dinner there and talked to a lot of people.'

'But then you went back to Fethering.' He nodded. 'What time did you get back?'

'Ten, half past.'

'And you went back to Connie's Clip Joint?'

'Yes, but I didn't go inside.'

'Really? You expect me to believe that, Martin?'

'I don't know whether I expect you to believe that or not, but it's the truth.'

'So why didn't you go in?'

'Because the boy was there, with Kyra. I saw them through the window.'

'So you went in through the back gate . . .' That would explain the noise Nathan Locke had heard, '. . . you saw the young couple were there, and then you left?'

'That's exactly what I did, yes.'

'But surely you must have been furious to see Kyra with another man?'

'For heaven's sake, I had no interest in Kyra! I never had!'

'Never even when you came on to her downstairs in this very salon?'

'No. No. No . . .' The monosyllable got weaker with repetition. Martin Rutherford let out a deep sigh, then seeming to reach some conclusion, went on, 'Look, I'm going to tell you what actually happened. Not because I particularly want to, but because you seem to have got some dangerous ideas fixed in your mind, and if you start passing them on to the police . . . well, it could be very inconvenient.'

'And what if I pass on to the police what you're about to tell me?'

'It's possible that when you've heard it, you won't want to. And if you do, that may not be such a bad thing. I'm sick to death of lying.' His head sank into his hands. 'Maybe telling the truth will *take some of this bloody pressure off me!*' The outburst was so sudden and uncharacteristic that it was a measure of the stress he was under.

Carole waited while he composed himself. Then he started. 'Most of my life I must have heard the expression "living a lie", but only when it happens to you do you understand what it means. I've been living a lie for the past few years, and it's been destroying me.' Again Carole let him take his own time. 'Obviously you know that I divorced Connie and married Martina.' He gestured round the room. 'That had a very good effect on all this. Martina is a wonderfully talented businesswoman. I could never have built up Martin & Martina to this level without her.

'On the emotional side, though . . .' he was having difficulty framing the words, '. . . things didn't work out so well. Some people have said Martina only married me because she had her eyes on the business. I don't know whether that's true or not, but certainly after the first few months . . . the emotional side of the marriage . . .' You mean the sexual side, thought Carole. 'Well, it virtually ended, and I realized I had made a horrible mistake . . .'

'And was that when you started coming on to the young girls in the salon . . . like Kyra?'

He shook his head in exasperation. 'No! I've never come on to any girl in my salon. For a start, younger women have never appealed to me that much and, then again . . . well, it's one of the first things you learn. If you're going to run a successful business, keep your hands off the staff.'

'Oh, come on, Martin, that won't wash. Connie told Jude there was a great history of you touching up the juniors, going right back to when you were married to her.'

'Oh, God,' he groaned. 'How complicated things become. You invent one little untruth to get you out of a hole, and suddenly you find you're having to fabricate more and more of them, and the hole is getting bigger and bigger.'

'I think you'd better tell me about those little untruths,' said Carole in her most magisterial Home Office committee-chairing voice.

'All right. I said I'd made a mistake in marrying Martina, but I did it because I was infatuated with her. When the infatuation faded, I looked around and realized what I'd done. And I also realized that there was only one woman I had ever loved and that was Connie.'

'Did she feel the same?'

'Yes. I had to summon up a lot of nerve to ask her, but yes, she did.'

'So all that business about what a bastard you'd been to her . . . ?'

'That bit was true.' A wry chuckle. 'I had been a bastard to her.'

'But you touching up the juniors in your salons . . . ?'

'Was a complete fabrication. A smokescreen. Connie and I would do anything to hide the fact that we still loved each other.'

'But why? Surely if you'd divorced once, you could do it again?'

His lips tightened as he said, 'Not from Martina. Martina is a Czech Catholic. She doesn't believe in divorce. Or at least she didn't object to marrying a divorcee, but there's no way she'd let me divorce her.'

'But these days a lot of people don't bother with divorce. They just move out.'

'I don't think I could just move out from Martina.'

The chill with which he spoke made it abundantly clear that Martin Rutherford was actually terrified of his second wife. 'She is a very powerful woman.'

'So, going back to where we started this evening, were the red roses for Connie?'

He nodded. 'It was very hard for us to meet. I had to fabricate alibis. Martina did not trust me being out of her sight. So the Hair and Nail Conference seemed perfect. I set up to meet Connie that evening.'

'In the salon?'

'Yes. I couldn't risk our being recognized in a hotel. Then where Connie lives – the house we used to share when we were married – well, there's a snoopy neighbour, old boy at the back who watches everyone's comings and goings, so that wasn't safe. But in the salon . . . I could park out of sight, go in the back way. It had worked well for us in the past.'

'But when you went back there that particular night, you found out that someone else had set up their own romantic encounter?'

'Kyra, yes. As I say, I went in early to set up the flowers, did the dinner in Brighton, and came back to find our little love nest occupied.'

'So you told Connie?'

'Our arrangement was that I'd get there and give her a call on my mobile, to say that the coast was clear, then she'd come and join me. But of course the coast wasn't clear.'

'What did you do?'

'I was stupid. I should have gone straight back to the conference hotel in Brighton. But I thought: I've actually managed to get a night off from Martina. I've got my alibi. Who knows when I'll next get a chance to be with Connie? So I went to her place.'

'And stayed all night?'

'Much longer than I should have done. We were just so happy to be together. The time was so precious. We talked and talked all night and well into the morning.'

'Was that why Connie was late into the salon? And why she hadn't done her hair or make-up?'

Martin Rutherford nodded ruefully. 'We talked about everything. About what we were going to do. About how I was finally going to face up to Martina and tell her it was all over. But then, when I heard about Kyra's death, everything had to be put on hold. Connie and I couldn't risk letting the police find out what we'd been up to. If they found out I'd been at the salon that night . . .' He shuddered, then concluded glumly, 'Everything still is on hold.'

'But you are planning to see Connie tonight, aren't you? Because Martina's going to Prague? Is that why you couldn't fix to see me later?'

His nod had something of bravado in it, the action of a cheeky schoolboy doing something he shouldn't. 'Sad, isn't it, a man having to set up elaborate deceptions so that he can go and see his ex-wife?' He looked at his watch. 'Connie's waiting for me in the back room of the salon even as we speak.'

They were interrupted by the sound of the outer office door closing. Carole looked up in alarm, but Martin said, 'Don't worry. Girls locking up. I must go down in a sec to check everything's all right.'

'Yes, well, I don't think I need to detain you much longer.' Carole looked at him sternly through her rimless glasses. 'You realize you are going to have to tell all this to the police?'

He sighed, then dropped his head. 'Yes, you're right. We probably are.'

'It could be material to their investigations. Now they're talking to Nathan Locke, they'll need all the information they can find on what actually happened that evening.'

'All right. I'll do it. But not tonight. Tonight's just for me and Connie. Tomorrow we'll face the consequences.'

'And stand up to Martina too?'

'Yes. I think facing the police is going to be easier than facing Martina.' He rose from his perch on the desk and picked up a briefcase. 'I'd better be off.'

'Just one thing before you go . . .'

'Yes?'

'We've established that you never came on to any of your juniors . . .'

'I hope we have, because I can assure you—'

'No, no, that's fine, but what I want to ask is: if Kyra Bartos didn't leave this salon because you'd been molesting her, why did she leave? She hadn't been here very long.'

'Ah.' Martin Rutherford looked embarrassed. 'Yes, there was a bit of a problem.'

'What was it? Come on, you've told me all the rest.'

'Well, all right,' he said wretchedly. 'The fact is, as I said, I've never touched any of the juniors. But the pretty ones . . . well, occasionally I might say some-thing. Nothing offensive, just a compliment. And Kyra was very pretty, so . . . well, I never think it hurts to tell a woman she's pretty. It was completely innocent.'

'Then why did it become a problem?' asked Carole implacably.

'Because of Martina. Martina did not like me mak-ing these compliments to Kyra. She got the wrong end of the stick. She thought that I fancied the girl.'

'So that's why Kyra had to go? Because Martina was jealous of her?'

'Yes. Well, I suppose that's right.'

'How jealous is she?'

'What do you mean by that?'

'Well, if Martina had got it into her head that the rela-tionship she imagined you to be having with Kyra was still continuing, then she might have a motive to—'

'No, no, you're talking nonsense. Dangerous non-sense. Come on, I must go. Just check Kelly-Jane's got everything tidied up.'

Down in the salon all was neat and swept clean. The manic activity of half an hour before might never have happened. A tall girl who must have been Kelly-Jane stood with a bundle of keys, clearly waiting for the all-clear to go home.

'Thanks, Kelly-Jane, looks great. Not sure whether I'll be in in the morning or not.'

'Will Martina?'

'No, of course not. She's off to Prague.'

'Oh, I thought she might have changed her plans.'

'No, she'll be on her way to Heathrow now. Friday night traffic, she'll have left about five.'

'No, she was here.'

'Here? When?'

'Came in within the last half-hour. Went upstairs. I assumed she was talking to you in the office.'

'I didn't see her.'

Kelly-Jane shrugged. This wasn't her business. 'Well, I don't know what she was doing up there then.'

'Is she still here?'

'No, she rushed out about ten minutes ago.'

'Did she say where she was going?'

'She didn't say anything. She just swept out, looking absolutely furious.'

The realization came to Martin and Carole at the same moment. Martina must have been in the outer office. It had been she who had closed the door. She had heard all of their conversation.

'Oh, my God!' shrieked Martin. 'Connie!'

The speed with which he rushed out of the salon left Carole in no doubt as to who he thought was responsible for the murder of Kyra Bartos.

Chapter Thirty-seven

Jude had been expecting to hear from Carole, but not from such a panicked Carole as the one who rang from the Martin & Martina in Worthing. It took a moment for Jude to take in the information that her friend was on her way, but that Connie Rutherford was at her salon and in immediate danger. Carole was going to call the police, but could Jude get down there as soon as possible?

She rushed to Connie's Clip Joint as fast as her chubby legs could carry her. There was nobody around; the moment the shops shut, Fethering High Street became deserted.

A sleek green Jaguar was parked outside. No lights showed in the salon, but to her surprise when she tried the front door, it gave. Moving very slowly to avoid creaks, Jude advanced into the body of the shop.

The door to the back room was slightly ajar, and a pencil of light spread out across the salon floor. As Jude advanced towards it, she became aware of a passionate, heavily accented voice coming from the back room.

'. . . and I know he is coming here, because I follow him. I see him bring in red roses and I think it is for that girl who work here. Martin always fancied her, I could see from the way he looked at her. I didn't then know it was you he was visiting. I thought he had enough of you when you were married. I didn't expect Martin to be coming back . . . like, how do you say it . . . a dog to his own vomit?'

The lack of response to Martina's speech suggested that her victim had been gagged or otherwise incapacitated and, as Jude got close enough to peer through the slit of the door, this was confirmed. Connie was cowering in an old chair, a thin white towel tied tightly around her mouth. Her jaws moved as if she was trying to speak, but no sound came out. Ominously, the dome of a hair dryer loomed over her head.

'So there's a good cause of guilt for you, Connie. You start an affair with a married man and what effect does it have? An innocent girl gets killed. The blood of Kyra Bartos is on your hands, and for that reason I'll not feel so much guilt about having your blood on my hands.'

Even through the towel, the whimper that Connie let out at that could be clearly heard. Jude knew she had to move quickly. Martina was still invisible to her, probably with her back to the door. She certainly wasn't near the lead to the dryer, so if she was planning to replicate her previous murder method . . .

Jude decided quickly. She had to. If she burst in through the door, there was a good chance of knocking Martina off-balance, certainly of keeping her away from the electric flex. Jude put her shoulder down and barged forward.

She hadn't thought of a gun. Nor, when the automatic was pointed at her, did she think of arguing with it. Instead, she sat obediently on the seat next to Connie's.

'You, Jude. Of course, nosy Jude. Jude who so conveniently told me about my husband being seen here last Sunday. So now it will be three deaths you have caused, Connie. That's what you get for stealing someone's husband. And I'm afraid it will have to be your nosy fat friend who goes first.'

The gun was still pointing at Jude, but now Martina Rutherford brought up her other hand to steady it. Not one to mess about, thought Jude. Oh well, at least she'll save me from rheumatoid arthritis.

What happened next was so quick that only later could Jude piece together the sequence of events.

The back door crashed open and Martin Rutherford burst into the room.

For a moment his wife's aim wavered. Then she laughed and said, 'Don't worry, Martin. I'm not going to shoot you. You're mine.'

Just as she steadied the automatic to target Jude's chest, Martin leapt forward. In the small space the gunshot was hideously loud. He let out a gasp of pain and dropped to the floor. But in his hand he held the captured gun.

Martina let out some curse in her own language and rushed out of the front of the salon. As Connie and Jude crouched down with towels, trying to staunch the blood pumping from Martin's shoulder, they heard the Jaguar screeching off into the night.

Carole and the police arrived almost simultaneously.

Chapter Thirty-eight

'The trouble is these days,' said Mim, 'children don't even learn the rudiments of politeness. Not even the rudiments. I mean, there was someone in our road the other day . . . not just visiting, he actually lives in the Shorelands Estate, where you'd have thought at the very least you'd get someone who was well brought-up . . .'

'You'd hope you would,' Theo agreed.

'. . . and this man said to me . . . Ooh, not so much off the top there, Connie. We don't want you going round Fethering like a skinhead, do we, Wally?'

'No, Mim, we don't.'

'Anyway, this man, he had the nerve to say to me . . . to me, mind, and you would have thought he could see I was someone who had been brought up with standards . . . and he said to me . . .'

Jude grinned across at her neighbour, as if to say, 'See, I told you it was worth seeing.' Carole had not been keen on the idea of their having their hair cut at the same time, but the promised attraction of the Wally and Mim double act had won her round.

It was nearly three weeks after Martina

Rutherford's arrest, a Tuesday, five weeks to the day after the Grenstons' last joint appointment. Fethering had settled down after its recent excitements, and, though well into October, the weather had remained so tranquil that there were dark mutterings about the melting of the polar ice-cap.

Apart from the fact that Nathan had been allowed to return to his family after only twenty-four hours of questioning, Jude had heard nothing of the Lockes. She would like to know for sure whether Bridget had returned to Rowley, but felt gloomily certain she had. She would also like to have heard that Rowley Locke's recent experiences had made him less of a control freak, but didn't feel much optimism about that either. All she really hoped was that Nathan got good A-levels and went to a university as far away from Fethering as possible. Then he would be able to develop his own personality.

The Grenstons' haircuts were finally finished. At Mim's insistence Connie had snipped a little more off above her husband's ears – 'don't want him walking through Fethering looking like the Abdominal Snow-man.' Theo waved a mirror around behind Mim's head for her to check her flame-red Louise Brooks look. 'There, you'll have all the men flocking round, Mim.'

'Just like you do, Theo,' she said rather daringly.

He giggled prettily at the idea, then caught Carole's eye and grinned.

Mim paid for the haircuts and carefully distributed the tips. While Theo was helping her into her coat,

Wally sidled up to Jude and winked at her. 'Our secret, eh?' he whispered.

'Our secret,' she confirmed. 'Oh, and I was sorry to hear about Joe Bartos.'

'Yes, well, probably best. Not one for showing his feelings, but losing Krystina . . . that destroyed him. You know, there had been his previous family . . . then his second wife . . . I saw Jiri the night before he died. He said he was tired, very tired. He suffered a lot through his life. He never talked about such things, but I knew. And the next morning he just did not wake up. Joe had had enough of suffering. No, very sad, but he went quickly. How we all want to go, eh?'

'What's he talking about then?' asked Mim, mentally scolding herself for letting her husband escape her surveillance even for a moment.

'I was talking about death,' he replied with some dignity.

'Oh, death,' she said dismissively. 'We won't have to worry about that for some time yet. Now, come on, Wally, are you coming or not? We can't be wasting these good people's time with all your idle chit-chat. Come along.'

'Usual appointments?' asked Connie. 'Five weeks today for the two of you?'

'Please. 'Bye, Theo. Lovely to see you, Connie.'

'And you, Mim. Goodbye, Wally.'

'Goodbye, Connie. And good luck with Marnie!'

'Who's Marnie?' asked Jude, as she was settled into her chair.

'Oh.' Connie blushed prettily. 'Just an idea Martin

and I had. Still some way off yet, but, well . . . the Martin & Martina branding has got to go . . . given the circumstances . . . so I thought of calling the chain "Marnie". It's Martin and Connie put together.'

'As you are.'

'Exactly.'

'How is he?'

'On the mend. But he will be permanently disabled. Won't be able to cut hair again.'

'I'm sorry.'

'Never mind. I'll cut the hair. He can run the business. Now . . .' She unpinned the shapeless topknot and ran her fingers through Jude's long blonde hair, '. . . how would you like to have it today, Madame?'

'Today,' replied Jude, with a huge beam, 'I would like to have it short.'

'Hooray! Did you hear that, Theo?'

'I did indeed. Well, well, well. Today's clearly a day for taking a plunge.' He looked in the mirror at his client. 'And what about yours, Madame? Are you going to take the plunge too? How would you like yours today?'

'Same shape, but shorter,' said Carole Seddon stolidly.

After Connie's Clip Joint, they went to the Crown and Anchor for lunch. Ted Crisp recommended the Chilli con Carne with Rice. It was surprisingly delicious.

While they ate, they watched the landlord holding up his fingers and gleefully demonstrating something to a customer. 'No, everyone gets that wrong, you know. The fingers that all hairdressers use are . . . yes, the thumb, like you said. But the other one isn't the middle finger. It's the one between the middle finger and the little finger. And do you know, that's the only one that moves. The thumb stays completely still.'

The customer was appropriately frustrated by getting it wrong. 'So, deal was if I beat you, you buy a pint for Les here. All right?'

Les Constantine grinned in anticipation. The old shipwright had recently given up his regular booth for a seat at the bar. Now Ted had made him the recipient of his winnings on the hairdresser bet, there was a plentiful supply of free pints.

'Hey,' the landlord went on to his customer as he pulled the pint, 'I must tell you . . . there's this joke I heard. Polar Bear walks into a bar . . .'

Jude looked across at her friend, and grinned.

When Carole got back to High Tor, she went through the automatic processes of emptying the contents of the tumble dryer, folding her clothes and putting them away. She was interrupted by the phone. Picking up the receiver at her bedside, she heard Stephen's voice.

'Hello, Granny,' he said.

BLOOD AT THE BOOKIES

*The bets are on whodunnit when a body is found
at the bookies . . .*

Jude has never been averse to a bit of a flutter; her friend
Carole, on the other hand, thinks that the local betting
shop is a den of iniquity. But when Jude stumbles upon
the body of Polish immigrant Tadeusz Jankowski the race
is on to find his killer.

As they question the local residents, Carole finds an
unexpected friend in an inveterate gambler and Jude
finds herself in potentially more trouble than she can
handle with a lecherous and charming drama professor.

In this race there can only be one winner, but with no
leads and several suspects in the running will our lady
detectives be pipped at the post by a cold and calculating
killer?

Blood at the Bookies, the delightful new novel by
Simon Brett, is out now in Macmillan hardback.

The opening scenes follow here.

Chapter One

'Come on, everyone likes a bet,' said Jude.

'Well, I don't,' sniffed Carole.

The response was so characteristic and instinctive that her friend couldn't help smiling. In a world where everyone was encouraged to be 'hands-on' and 'touchy-feely', Carole Seddon's approach to life was always going to be 'hands-off' and 'keep-your-distance'. But those idiosyncrasies didn't diminish Jude's affection for her. And that February morning the affection was increased by the diminished state her neighbour was in. The response to the idea of betting would always have been sniffy, but on this occasion it had been accompanied by a genuine sniff. Carole was drowned by a virulent winter flu bug, and Jude felt the last emotion her neighbour would ever wish to inspire in anyone – pity.

'Anyway, I've promised Harold I'll go to the betting shop and put his bets on, so I can't not do it.'

'Huh,' was Carole's predictable response. Her pinched face looked even thinner behind her rimless glasses. The pale blue eyes were bleary and the short grey hair hung lank.

'Come on, it's one of the few pleasures Harold Peskett has at his age. And he's got this wretched flu just like you. It's the least I can do for him. I can't see that there's anything wrong with it.'

'It's encouraging bad habits,' came the prissy reply.

'Carole, Harold is ninety-two, for God's sake! I don't think I'm going to make his habits any worse at this stage of his life. And it's no hardship – I've got to go to the shops anyway, to get my stuff . . . and yours.'

'What do you mean – mine?'

'You're in no state to go out shopping.'

'Oh, I'm sure I will be later. I've got a touch of flu, that's all.'

'You look ghastly. You should go straight back to bed. I don't know why you bothered to get dressed this morning.'

Carole looked shocked. 'What, are you suggesting I should be lolling round the house in my dressing-gown?'

'No. As I say, I'm suggesting you should go back to bed and give yourself a chance of getting rid of this bug. Have you got an electric blanket?'

'Of course not!' Carole was appalled by the idea of such self-indulgence.

'Hot water-bottle?'

With some shame, Carole admitted that she did possess one of those luxury items. Jude picked the kettle up off the Aga and moved to fill it at the sink. 'Tell me where the hot water-bottle is and I'll—'

'Jude!' The name was spoken with considerable

asperity. 'This is my house, and I'll thank you to let me manage it in my own way.'

'I'm not stopping you from doing that. But you're ill, and there are some things you can't do at the minute.'

'I am not ill!' Carole Seddon rose assertively from her chair. But she was taken aback by the wave of giddiness that assailed her. She tottered, reached for the support of the kitchen table and slowly subsided back down.

A grin spread across Jude's plump face. Her brown eyes sparkled and the stacked-up blonde hair swayed as she shook her head in the most benign of I-told-you-so gestures. 'See. You can't even stand up. There's no way you could make it down Fethering High Street even as far as Allinstore. I will do your shopping for you, and you will go to bed.'

'There's nothing I want,' Carole mumbled with bad grace. 'I'm well stocked up with everything.'

'Not the kind of things you need. You need nice warming soups and things like that. Lucozade, whisky . . . When you're ill, you need to feel pampered.'

'What nonsense you do talk, Jude.' But the resistance was already diminishing. Carole felt so rotten that even her opposition to the idea of pampering, built up over more than fifty years, was beginning to erode.

What defeated her residual contrariness was the issue of her dog. Gulliver, slumped by the Aga in his usual state of Labrador passivity, was going to need walking very soon or there might be a nasty accident on the kitchen floor. What was more, the house was completely out of dog food. And Carole was just not strong enough to complete either of these tasks. Much as it went against her every instinct, she was going to need help. And getting that help from Jude, who had already witnessed her parlous state, was preferable to involving anyone else, letting a stranger into her life. Grudgingly, Carole Seddon bit the bullet and agreed that her neighbour should add to her own errands the task of walking Gulliver out to buy some of his favourite Pedigree Chum.

She still showed token resistance to the idea of pampering. She certainly wouldn't contemplate the idea of Jude helping her undress and get back to bed. But she did let slip where the hot water-bottle was to be found.

Jude was discreet enough to tap on the bedroom door before she entered with the filled bottle and a steaming drink. She looked at the drained face peering miserably over the edge of the duvet. 'There. At least you look a bit more comfortable.'

'I'll be all right,' said Carole, who hated the notion of being ill.

'Don't worry. We'll soon get you better.'

'What do you mean – "we"?' A spark of disgust came into the pale blue eyes. 'You're not going to try and *heal* me, are you?'

Again Jude had difficulty suppressing a grin. Nothing would ever shift her neighbour's antipathy to the idea of healing . . . or indeed any other alternative therapy.

'I promise I am not going to try and heal you. It

wouldn't work, anyway. Bugs like this just sort themselves out in their own time.'

'Then who's this "we"?' Carole persisted suspi-
ciously.

'For heaven's sake, it's just a figure of speech. "*We*'ll
get you better" – it doesn't mean anything more than
the fact that I'll keep an eye on you, see you've got
everything you need.'

'Oh, but I don't want you to . . .' The words trickled
away as Carole realized just how ghastly she did actually feel. She had no more resistance left.

'Anyway,' said Jude cheerily, 'we – or "I" if you
prefer – have got to see you're all right by Sunday.'

'Why?'

'I thought you said that's when Stephen and Gaby
are bringing Lily down to see you.'

But this reminder of her status as a grandmother
didn't bring any warmth of Carole's manner. 'No,' she
said, 'I've put them off.'

'What?'

'I don't want to breathe germs over the baby, do I?'
replied Carole piously.

It was in a way the correct answer, but it stimulated
an anxiety within Jude about how Carole was adjusting
to her new role as a grandmother. Still, this was not the
appropriate moment to follow up on that. She handed
the hot drink across to her patient.

Carole sniffed. 'It's got whisky in it,' she said accus-
ingly.

'Of course it has,' said Jude.

*

Jude was unused to walking a dog, but Gulliver's equable temper did not make the task difficult. His benevolence was more or less universal. When he barked it was from excitement, and his encounters with other dogs were playful rather than combative. Most important, he was never aware that Carole, not a natural dog person, had only bought one so that she wouldn't be thought to be lonely as she was seen walking with him around Fethering.

After her divorce and what she still thought of as her premature retirement from the Home Office, Carole Seddon had planned her life in Fethering so that she would be completely self-sufficient. She didn't want other people in her life, and Gulliver had been just one of the defence mechanisms she had carefully constructed to prevent such intrusions.

But then Jude had moved into Woodside Cottage next door, and even Carole found her resistance weakened by the charm of her new neighbour's personality. Jude rarely spoke about her past, but the details she did let slip led Carole to deduce that it had been a varied – not to say chequered – one. There was something of the former hippy about Jude. She was a healer and had introduced into the bourgeois fastness of Woodside Cottage such exotic items as crystals and wind-chimes. It would have been hard to imagine a more unlikely friend for Carole Seddon, but, though Carole would never have admitted it out loud, she valued the friendship more than almost anything else in her life.

Jude took Gulliver on to the beach and let him scamper around off the lead, playing elaborate war games with weed-fringed plastic bottles and lumps of polystyrene. She allowed him twenty minutes of this, while she scrunched to and fro on the shingle. Then she let out a hopeful whistle, and was gratified that Gulliver came obediently to heel and let her reattach the lead.

It was a typical early February day. Though the people of West Sussex bemoaned the lack of winter snow and spoke ominously of global warming, the weather proved itself able still to come up with good old-fashioned coldness. Jude's face, the only part of her not wrapped in a swathe of coats and scarves, was stung by the air, and underfoot the pebbles were joined by links of ice.

She did her shopping at Allinstore, the town's only supermarket (though many Fethering residents reckoned the prefix 'super' in that context was an offence under the Trades Descriptions Act). Jude bought organically when it came to meat and fresh vegetables, but she was not proscriptive about it. There were also baked beans on her shelves and hamburgers in her fridge. She knew her own body and, though she generally ate healthily, she would occasionally indulge in a massive fry-up or a fish supper in one of the local cafés. Jude believed that in all things well-being came from variety.

As well as the Pedigree Chum and a couple of other items her neighbour had asked for, Jude bought some of the things she thought Carole *needed*. As she had said, warming soups, Lucozade and whisky. Jude was very definite about the style in which one should be ill.

Illness made you feel miserable, so there was no point in making yourself feel even more miserable. Pampering was the answer. Oh yes, and of course, magazines. *Country Life* and *Marie-Claire*. She bought them, already relishing Carole's reaction to such frivolous extravagance.

As she emerged from Allinstore the heavens opened, vindictively spitting down a fusillade of hailstones. The parade was suddenly evacuated, as the denizens of Fethering rushed for shelter. So fierce was the blizzard that Jude, scuttling to her destination, could hardly see a foot in front of her face. Fortunately, the betting shop had a projecting canopy over its frontage, and she was able to tie Gulliver's lead to a metal ring which would keep him out of the weather.

Fethering High Street still had an old-fashioned parade of shops. Although this meant there weren't many of them, it did ensure that they were all close together. But the choice was limited. You could still get your hair styled at what used to be Connie's Cuts but had now been made-over and rebranded as 'Marnie'. You could still investigate house purchase at Urquhart & Pease or one of the other estate agents. But in the previous ten years the independent butcher and greengrocer had both closed and been replaced by charity shops.

And Sonny Frank's, the former independent bookmaker's, had been taken over by one of the major national chains. This Jude knew from no less an authority than Sonny Frank himself, who had been unable to cut his links with the business completely and was still a fixture on the premises. Sonny, who in his days as a bookie had been known as 'Perfectly' Frank, always sat on a tall stool near the betting shop's central pillar, from where he could command a good view of the wall of television screens, as well as the enclosed counter where bets were taken and winnings paid.

And, sure enough, there he was at one-thirty that Thursday afternoon, when Jude hurried in from the sleet to put on Harold Peskett's bets. Sonny Frank was a small man, whose arms and legs seemed almost irrelevant appendages to the round ball of his body. On top of this was another ball, his head, across which dyed black hair had been combed over so tight that it looked as though it had been painted on. He wore a frayed suit in subdued colours but large checks, and he greeted Jude cheerfully. Sonny Frank greeted every-one who went into the shop cheerfully, as though he were still its owner, but he held back an extra ration of cheerfulness for attractive women.

Though Jude had popped in sporadically since she'd been a Fethering resident, during the fortnight of Harold Peskett's flu she had become a regular, so Sonny knew her name. 'Hello, Jude darling. You look like you just come out of the fridge.'

Sure enough, in the short dash from Allinstore to the betting shop, her head and shoulders had taken on an encrustation of ice.

'Yes, look at it out there. It's quite revolting.'

'I would look at it, but I can't see a thing.' It was

true. The opposite side of the road was invisible through the icy downpour.

'So we're all much snugger in here, Jude. So . . . got a hot tip for me today, have you . . . as the actress said to the bishop?'

'You're much more likely to know something than I am, Sonny,' Jude replied, as she brushed the ice off her shoulders. 'You're the one with the inside knowledge.'

'Don't you believe it, darling. What you've got and I haven't is women's intuition.'

'A fat lot of good that's ever done me.'

'What, with the men or the horses?'

'Either. Both totally unreliable.'

'What's old Harold up for today then?'

'Heaven knows.' She reached into her pocket and flourished a sheaf of closely written betting slips. 'All his usual trebles and Yankees and goodness knows what. I don't understand what he does – I just put the bets on.'

It was true. Harold Peskett's betting system was arcane and deeply personal. Every morning he spent two hours religiously scouring the *Racing Post* and checking the tips given in the *Sun*, *Daily Express* and *Daily Mirror* before coming up with his recipe for 'the big win'. This involved a complex combination of horses at meetings across the country in formulations which, to the untrained eye, made Fermat's Last Theorem look straightforward. The total sum invested never exceeded two pounds, so it didn't make too many inroads into his pension. And at least his betting habit kept the ninety-two-year-old off the streets.

Jude handed over the betting slips to the vacuously beautiful blonde behind the counter, whose name badge proclaimed her to be 'Nikki'. She got an automatic 'Thank you', but not the automatic smile she would have received had she been a man. Behind the girl, the shop's manager, Ryan, fiddled on the keyboard of a computer. He was an edgy and uncommunicative man in his mid-thirties, thin with nervous dark eyes and with spiky black hair that could never quite be flattened by comb or brush. He always seemed to be sucking a peppermint. Both he and Nikki were dressed in the blue and black livery of their employers. Supported by other part-time staff, Ryan and Nikki provided the continuity of the betting shop. Though there was a lot of banter flying about the place, they never really joined in. They produced the manufactured smiles they had been taught during their training, but neither gave much impression of enjoying the job.

'So . . .' asked Sonny Frank, as Jude passed him on the way to the door, 'know anything?'

It was another of his regular lines. And anyone incautious enough to ask what he meant – as Jude had been when he first said it to her – would be treated to the full explanation. As a young man Sonny had actually met Edgar Wallace, who, as well as being a prolific writing phenomenon, was also an obsessive gambler. And Wallace's opening gambit to betting friends had always been the punter's eternal search for the life-changing tip: 'Know anything?'

'You've already asked me, Sonny, and I've already said you're the one with the inside knowledge.'

The ex-bookie looked elaborately furtive, then leaned forward on his stool till his cracked lips were very close to Jude's ear and his purple cheek brushed against the hanging tendrils of her hair. 'Well, as it happens . . . I do know a good thing.'

'Oh?'

'1.40 at Wincanton. Hasn't raced for over two hundred days. Gonna romp home.'

Jude looked out of the window. Still the sleet fell relentlessly. But Gulliver, under his sheltering roof, had lain down with his front paws forward and looked perfectly content. Maybe she could leave him out there a little longer. 'Which horse are you talking about?' she whispered, knowing that Sonny wouldn't broadcast his tip to the entire room.

He pointed up to the screen displaying the odds for the Wincanton race. 'Seven down,' he murmured. 'Number Four.'

The horse's name was Nature's Vacuum.

'If you're going to bet, do it quickly. That twenty to one won't last.'

Jude looked at the central screen, where the horses were ambling their way towards the start. Down in Wincanton the weather looked almost springlike. She wished she were there rather than Fethering.

'Go on, are you going to have a punt?'

She took one more dutiful look out of the window. In spite of the ice bouncing off the pavement only feet away from him, Gulliver's tail was actually wagging. He really did have a very nice nature.

'Why not?' replied Jude.